JUST LI

Just Living is a good tale well told. It's filled with mystery, intrigue, life, spirit, and, best of all, healing.

Brent Bill, Author of
"Life Lessons from a Bad Quaker" and other books

There is so much more to this fine novel than meets the eye, and its rich exploration of the human experience touches the soul deeply on many levels. With Meredith Egan's keen and compassionate understanding of correctional services and community, her respect for Aboriginal and other spiritual teachings, and led by her finely drawn and authentic characters, we are helped to stand in many places, and come to yearn for justice in new ways. Absorbing! Compelling! Genuine! Heartwarming!

Jane Miller-Ashton, Criminology Instructor, Kwantlen Polytechnic University Senior Manager, Correctional Service of Canada (retired)

Meredith Egan brings the reader to the sacred circle in Just Living. We are invited to hold space for Beth as she navigates the tender space that connects humanity on all sides of harm. Egan deftly walks us carefully full circle around the complexities of trauma and its aftermath, letting us feel the hurt, the fear, the shame and the wretched losses that ripple from the broken-heart center of it all.

Along the way she weaves a container to hold the pain, its threads made from life's simple, joyous pleasures: the breaking of bread, the turning of soil, and the caring of animals. Just Living teaches us by example what it means to live restoratively and offers hope for the way we can do justice

Katy Hutchison, Author of "Walking After Midnight: One Woman's Journey Through Murder, Justice & Forgiveness"

Just Living grabs your interest from the start...the pace is maintained by flashbacks and forward (I realize that these are Tim's words but I don't understand the use of the word forward. I would remove the words "and forward") reflecting the complexity of life for people who have had horrific experiences in their lives, and have caused serious harm to others. This is a good read for those who hope for a better future in justice with its wide rippling consequences. It's also a good read for those that seek a love story in exceptional settings.

       Tim Newell, past Prison Governor (UK)
       and founder of Escaping Victimhood

Just Living is a wonderful book, filled with characters that moved me. Each of their stories was so unique, and yet they were all connected to one another. I felt I knew all of them.

Beth is an awesome character, all of her doubts and faults, and emotions and goodness, she is a model for those of us who want to change the world.

At one point she shares, "What is the point of blame when there's so much healing to be done?" This sums up all of our lives, whether we are victims, prisoners or people who work and volunteer in Corrections. We all have things that need to be healed and need places like Just Living to be able to do so.

Thank you for bringing this story alive.

       Marlyn Ferguson, Valley View Funeral Home
       Homicide Support Group

Just Living is emotional honesty. Meredith Egan's compelling characters catapult readers into the world of brutal injustice whereby intergenerational trauma wreaks havoc. In the terrain of both the literal and the figurative of 'doing time' we come to better understand the power of compassion, of healing, of reconciliation, of resilience.

      -Margot Van Sluytman, Victim/Survivor,
      Founder of The Sawbonna Project for Living Justice.

A compassionate and challenging read. Meredith Egan has taken up the complex challenges of addressing the many issues experienced by marginalized peoples in our Canadian society, and has succeeded in creating believable, sympathetic characters whose human strengths and foibles carry us along in this fascinating narrative.

Far reaching, Just Living takes us to a remote BC halfway house of that same name where convicted criminals are given a kinder life after having served time in prison, and prior to being released from the system. Beth, the primary narrator, is a 'preacher's kid' serving a practicum toward the completion of her own seminary studies - in which she is seeking a genuine connection with Spirit, and a meaningful life purpose. Other narrative voices are those of inmates, many of them Aboriginal; of others in this caring network; and of an addict who is on the run after having murdered a priest.

Compassionate justice; alternatives to violence; the risk-taking engendered by honesty; empathy, growth and healing; and the depth of spiritual journeying: all are addressed in Just Living, and will affect readers in a real and memorable way.

Alison Lohans, Award-winning author of
26 books for young people

Just Living is an adventure, an open-hearted search for ways to recover from harm. What happens when people respond to harm by listening to the deep reasons for it, and focusing on bringing healing out of the consequences? It's life, it's exciting, and it takes courage. The other thing I like about Just Living is that the author very seldom gives a physical description of the characters. Who they are comes through their responses to each other, and the reader gets to know them well. Now that I've finished the book, I miss them!"

Gianne Broughton, Author of *"Four Elements of Peacebuilding"*

To Ben+Liisa, thank you for the support! Meredith

Just LIVING
a novel

MEREDITH EGAN

Copyright © 2016 by Meredith Egan
Amity Publishers edition published 2016

All rights reserved. The use of any part of this publication, reproduced, transmitted in any form or by any means electronic, mechanical, photocopying, recording or otherwise, or stored in a retrieval system without the prior written consent of the publisher – or, in the case of photocopying or other reprographic copying, a license from the Canadian Copyright Licensing Agency – is an infringement of the copyright law. Amity Publishers and colophon are trademarks.

National Library of Canada Cataloguing in Publication
Egan, Meredith
Just Living / Meredith Egan
ISBN 978-0-9731557-7-8.

I dedicate this book to all the who have been hurt by crime, especially those who relentlessly labour to dance when stuck.

CONTENTS

Chapter 1: The Unlikely Rev. Hill	1
Chapter 2: The Addict	13
Chapter 3: An Unhappy Christmas Story	19
Chapter 4: A Tentative "Send"	23
Chapter 5: Sister Paulette	31
Chapter 6: The Prodigal Son	35
Chapter 7: A Good Man	43
Chapter 8: Midnight Mass	49
Chapter 9: The Twelve Visits of Christmas	59
Chapter 10: Happy New Year?	67
Chapter 11: An Intriguing Tour Guide	71
Chapter 12: Welcome to Just Living	79
Chapter 13: The Anniversary	89
Chapter 14: A Calling?	95
Chapter 15: In Service	105
Chapter 16: Visitor Access Granted	111
Chapter 17: Expect the Best	121
Chapter 18: Support and Accountability	131
Chapter 19: The Rabbit Hole	139
Chapter 20: Make New Friends…	149
Chapter 21: Family Matters	159
Chapter 22: The Other, Gold	163
Chapter 23: Facing the Music	173
Chapter 24: Flashbacks	183
Chapter 25: Natural Consequences	189
Chapter 26: Ora et Labora	199
Chapter 27: Blessed Solitude	209

Chapter 28: Something's In the Air	219
Chapter 29: Waterfalls and Heartbeats	229
Chapter 30: The Picnic	239
Chapter 31: A Failed Reprise	249
Chapter 32: Getting to Easter	257
Chapter 33: Easter Miracles	267
Chapter 34: Playground Mischief	275
Chapter 35: The Accident	279
Chapter 36: Stepping Up and Owning it	289
Chapter 37: Four Days Later	295
Chapter 38: Learning and Transformation	305
Chapter 39: Napping with Contentment	315
Chapter 40: Walking the Path	321
Chapter 41: Endings and Beginnings	333
Chapter 42: Unpacking Love	343
Chapter 43: Hen Party	349
Chapter 44: Goodbyes	357
Chapter 45: Hearing a Call	365
Chapter 46: Big Brother is Watching	379
Chapter 47: Lamentations	383
Chapter 48: Rituals	393
Chapter 49: Acknowledgements	399
Chapter 50: The Quest	405
Chapter 51: Promises	415
Chapter 52: Possibilities	423
Chapter 53: Superheroes	429
Chapter 54: Segregation Kent Institution, BC	437
Afterward: Christmas-time	443
Acknowledgements	447
Resources for readers of Just Living	449

CHAPTER 1
THE UNLIKELY REV. HILL

I jumped, then tried to look unfazed when the heavy steel bars clanged shut behind me.

Holy Mother of God, if I get away with this, I WILL do anything. Honest. Forever. My heart was pounding, my head was pleading -- praying, really --which led to two compelling realisations.

I don't believe in prayer. At least not prayer that whines. Who wants to believe in a God who gives in to whining? That's what Nana Beth said, and she was the wisest woman I know. And then, another prayer.

But if this works, I'll re-visit that whole "don't believe in prayer" thing. Promise. Hmmm. How certain I am. Until it doesn't suit me.

I followed the uniformed officer down the dim hallway, and trusted he wasn't taking me somewhere sinister, because no one but Glenn knew I was here. The smell of institutional cleaners stabbed at my brain, and I wondered if it was supposed to help me believe the grey tiles, grey bars, grey walls, and grey furniture were clean. It didn't.

Cries and shouts echoed off the concrete and steel. I tried not to peer into each cell, but people called out, and damned if I didn't look. Disturbing, really. Them. Me. When I glanced over, small slots framed their freaky faces.

From time to time the din was punctuated with the banging of a heavy steel door, the clanging of sliding bars, the jangle of keys.

"Sister! Look over here!" Good God, did they think I was a nun? (Not a prayer.)

"Chaplain! Help me! I need a Bible," followed by laughter.

"Please. Help me," came a weirdly plaintive wail. That one disturbed me enough that I shot a second look and was startled by the hollow eyes of a young woman with greasy hair. Reminiscent of too many on the Psych Ward when I was a nurse.

"Don't let her bother you, she's fine," the guard reassured me. Only it didn't.

What the hell? We passed a guard walking towards us, clean and polished, just out of the locker room. He was carrying a huge bag, a riot shield strapped on top.

"Thanks for your help today, Fred," my escort said as we passed. "See you later."

"Not likely, unless you're transferring to Kent or Mission," he replied. So, prison guards had been a part of the riot squad? I'd never even thought about jails before this morning, and now I was trying to piece together random facts. Get over yourself, Beth.

Stunned that I'd been able to get this far with my weak ruse, I reminded myself for about the hundredth time not to tug at the stiff clerical collar around my neck. And I asked myself for the millionth time, "Do I really want to wear one of these for the rest of my life?" Focus, Beth. The costume I'd "borrowed" from my father's cupboard for Hallowe'en had come in handy. Now I had to pull off the act.

I'd used a few stitches down my back to hide the volumes of grey cloth that usually covered Dad's ample girth. Then, a simple mid-calf A-line skirt with "sensible footwear" and a heavy grey cardigan. I was stunned how much I looked the part.

I couldn't believe that this getup, with my hair in a bun, had gotten me into the local cells. Knowing the lingo from living with Dad, and two years in seminary, well, just a few more minutes and I'd find out why Julie was so upset. Was that her wailing up ahead? As I realized where I was, what I was doing, I hoped I'd still avoid arrest. A record might crimp my future plans, whatever they are; I'd heard that can happen. I'm quick that way.

It had all started when Glenn and I had shown up to volunteer at the students' protest. We were to field calls and texts from students, provide them with "reassurance" and information, out of the reach of the law. So much for that.

Bored, Glenn and I had started to watch the live TV coverage of the large, peaceful protest on the big screen in the Students' Union Building. Tens of thousands of people had gathered in Robson Square (it was surprisingly nice for November) and soon folks were stuffing sweaters in their backpacks. There were colourful banners, and loud bullhorns, people drumming and chanting. News teams reported while crowds sang *We shall overcome* in the background, and I wondered if this was what life was like on college campuses in the seventies. In Vancouver, birthplace of Greenpeace.

Then, as we watched from our safe vantage point, it all went horribly wrong. Throngs of riot police moved in and surrounded the group, cutting off the streets and sidewalks, containing them. It looked like the detours set up by police to "assist with crowd traffic" were actually helping isolate the protestors. Soon no one could get in or out, and the few journalists who were "on the ground" were escorted away or had their cameras seized. There was screaming, people being hit by shields and batons, rounded up. This was Canada, and I couldn't believe what I was seeing.

The phone videos quickly streamed onto the Internet. Staff and students around us began shouting in outrage; this action was planned by the cops. The tweets that crossed our phones were at first jubilant, almost excited.

"I can't believe I'm here. I feel lucky? #PipeOff"

"Well, this just got interesting! #PoliceBrutality"

"What do they think we are doing? Smoking dope? #NoLawsBroken #PipeOff"

"Can't believe they are stupid enough to take us on! #ProtestorsFTW #PipeOff"

"Never been arrested before. Is it wrong that I'm kinda looking forward to it? #GoingToJailMom"

Then the sky grew dark and it started pelting rain. The outrage amped up both around us on campus and on the TV. Tear gas, marching cops in riot gear, defied the peaceful intent of the day. Soon the media was drawing a parallel to the Stanley Cup Riots except this time no one had been looting or starting fires. The police were holding the protesters in the rain for no reason, and I was a bit of a mess, worrying about my friends. New tweets, now different.

"This is just a little terrifying. Riot police en mass marching, containing us. Reminds me of Germany c. 1944. #NowI'mScared #PipeOff" Me too, I thought.

"Okay, I'm cold and wet and I have to go to the bathroom. ENOUGH. #LetUsGo"

"When are they going to release us? I don't even know what's happening. Anyone? #PipeOff"

Then, things went silent, and my stomach churned. Who knew silence was worse? Cell phones must have been confiscated, because there were no more calls, videos or tweets. From the TV we saw there were arrests happening, the imposing paddy wagons backing up to the barricades. People were being forced into them through a "riot police gauntlet." Outrage seethed around me. I ducked out when my phone rang.

"Beth! Beth! You've got to save him!" It was my friend Julie, and she was hysterical. No one could do hysterical like Julie; she was young, and dramatic. But this felt different, real. She was at the Remand Centre downtown, and begged me to come. In that moment I stopped thinking, and decided to help. At least I dragged Glenn into my half-assed plan; someone had to stitch the back of Dad's shirt, after all.

I'd decided my best bet for getting in was to become a UBC chaplain, perhaps not my smartest idea, but the first one that popped into my brain. I presented myself at the front desk, showing my driver's licence. Then my plan quickly deteriorated. Or rather, I'd used it up. Sigh.

The guard behind the desk was speaking to one person at a time and there was quite a line-up. We perched on benches lining the small waiting area. It felt like a border check, and I remembered I always felt guilty at the border. This time, I had reason to.

A fellow jumped the line, and went straight to the desk, clearly known to the staff member.

"Hey Frank. Who're you here for again?" the guard asked.

"Paul Rafael. I think Hugh Ward called," the dark haired man said.

"Right. Picked up without a pass," the guard noted, glancing at a piece of paper in a binder.

"Noooo. He had a pass. He just lost it in the kerfuffle. I'm heading up the Valley so told Hugh I'd drive him back," Frank answered. His dark hair, slightly unkempt, and pullover sweater under Gore-Tex spoke of casual, but cultured. In no time the paperwork was done, and a sullen-looking fellow was led out in cuffs.

"I don't need those," Frank said, and the guard removed them.

"Sorry to be such a bother," mumbled the fellow. "Didn't mean to get you out in the rain," he added, glancing up at Frank from under his bangs. He worked hard to look small, shoulders pulled in, hands in his pockets.

"No problem, Paul. It can happen to any of us." Frank turned to go, and Paul snorted.

"At least us guys are under warrant," he chuckled, and Frank turned back and smiled. They headed out the front door, and I heard them talking about some guy named Al on the way out.

And finally I was next.

"Who'd you say you were again?" the guard barked at me.

"Reverend Hill from UBC Chaplaincy. I'm here to see Julie Kwan, who was picked up across the street. She called me in distress. I need to see her." I sounded way more determined than I felt. And sealed my fate.

"I'm sorry, if you ain't a lawyer, or someone we asked to come, you can't come in here. You ain't on the list," he said, pointing to a piece of paper on the counter.

"Then how do I get on the list? Is your manager here? Because I'm not leaving until I see Julie. What's your name again?" I didn't realize "knocking knees" was a literal description until that moment; I was trying hard not to bump mine against the front of the counter. The back and forth kept up for a few more minutes, and I surprised myself by being relentless.

"If something happens to her, I'm holding you responsible." I couldn't believe I said that. Then, magically, a sliding frosted-glass door opened behind him and someone with many stripes on his epaulets came through. WTF? Was someone listening to us? Then I noticed a camera in the corner.

"What's the problem, Tony?" the guy asked, and believe it or not, a few minutes later he decided it would be easier to let "Rev. Hill" in to see the UBC student who was "raising quite a ruckus down in the cells." So, after signing in and surrendering my driver's licence, I pinned a "V" badge on my shirt and was escorted down the hall.

I kept praying, making promises to God (weird, I know) as we turned a corner, and I understood that the guards weren't kidding. Julie was beside herself, not coherent anymore. The guard spoke to her in quiet, measured tones.

"Calm down, put your hands through the slot in the door so I can put the cuffs back on you. Calm down and you'll get to speak to Rev. Hill."

There was an older woman detained in the cell, arm around Julie, helping her focus. The guard only had to repeat himself twice more before Julie calmed down enough to do what he asked.

It was surreal watching Julie's wrists appear through the slot, and then the handcuffs tightened around them. She quickly pulled her hands back, raised both hands to her face and wiped her nose on her sweater. The guard opened the heavy door, and let Julie join us in the hallway. I reached out in what seemed to me like a priestly way.

"Thank you, Claire," she said to the woman left behind, and started to sob again.

"Julie, breathe. Focus on your breathing, and we can pray," I said to her as we made our way to a grey table in the hallway. There were chairs on either side of the metal table, and as I sat opposite Julie the chair legs scraped loudly on the concrete floor. At least the décor was consistent; everything, including me, was grey. The table clanged when Julie put her cuffed hands on it, and as I put my hands over hers and bowed my head, I was startled by a loud voice from down the hall.

"No touching!" the guard bellowed, and I scowled, wondering why Claire could touch her but I couldn't. I gave my head a shake and removed my hands. In case he was still in earshot, I started to pray. Moments later, I peeked and saw that he was gone.

"What's wrong? Stay calm and just tell me." I looked right into Julie's eyes.

"They took Chris," she said, and started sobbing again. "I think he's in trouble. He didn't take his insulin pump with him this morning because he thought we'd just be taking a walk and he never needs it when we're walking. And he has no snacks. He was already getting woozy when the police surrounded us. I think he might be in a coma by now. They won't listen to me!" Julie's leg was bouncing up and down, jiggling the table and making quite a racket. I tried distracting her with conversation. She told me how scary it was, being kettled by cops in riot gear, watching the anger rise. I heard about what it was like being strip-searched, and having her possessions seized.

"They didn't even offer to let us go home, even if we promised to never do it again," she said, and even I could hear how silly *that* sounded. Whatever I was doing seemed to help her, and she was calming down.

My focus started to shift to Chris. Somehow I had to get someone to listen to me.

"Okay, I'll look into things with Chris. Just keep breathing," I said as I heard the boots thumping down the hallway towards us. I lowered my head again.

"In Jesus name. Amen," I finished what hadn't really been started.

"Thank you, Officer," I said, turning to face the guard who had come up behind me. He locked Julie up again and retrieved his cuffs, and we walked back down the stark corridor towards the heavy door

I heard Julie say, "Where's Claire?" and someone said, "Claire Arsenault? She got out." That wasn't going to help Julie. We waited for the heavy door to unlock.

"How long will she be here?" I asked. "She's pretty upset."

He snorted. "You her lawyer now, too?" he asked without looking at me. "She's upset. Poor girl." Clearly he didn't think I had a right to inquire. Honestly, I had no idea what I could and couldn't ask.

At the front desk, as I was signing out, I asked to speak to the manager again. The guard on duty chuckled.

"What's wrong? We treating your friend wrong?" he asked.

"No, I have information about another student who is in medical distress. I want the manager to know, so he can get help," I answered. I collected my keys and cell phone from a locker, and turned in my visitor's badge.

"Give me his name, and I'll see," the guard said, and I couldn't believe it when I decided not to.

"No, I'd rather speak to whoever is in charge. He was down here before; how do I talk to him again?" I asked, looking straight at the camera. Again I asked for the officer's badge number, and thanked him for his prompt and courteous attention. It seemed to work, because soon enough an older woman with just as many stripes on her shoulders was walking towards me.

"You have some information, Reverend Hill?" she asked.

"Yes, I just met with a young woman being detained and she told me her boyfriend was here also. She's worried about him because he's diabetic and without his insulin pump or anything to eat. She said he was acting woozy even before they were detained and that was several hours ago." I kept going, not giving her a chance to interject.

"When I was a nurse working in Emergency, sometimes diabetics in ketoacidosis presented like drunks. In reality, they were in serious medical distress. I don't want your staff to be confused by Chris' presentation and smell, and decide he's just sleeping off a bender." I hoped the mix of medicalese and hard reality would prompt her to action. "I know things are crazy today for you, but it would be awful if there was a tragedy," I finished, smiling at her.

She looked at me again, and I started to tremble a little more. Again, where had those words come from?

"What's his name? I'll have an officer look into it," she finally said.

"Chris Alden. He was brought in from the same protest. I can wait if you want and take him to the hospital," I said, and realized right away that was a mistake. I had to trust them. Her eyebrow rose.

"We will call an ambulance if we need to," she said, clearly suspicious now. Damn!

"Thank you," I said, turning quickly. The officer sitting in front of the computer at the desk called out as I was leaving,

"Say hello to Father Anthony Parker for us, will you?" Double darn. I was sure Fr. Anthony was overseeing the operation on campus, and one phone call to him and my jig would be up. I wasn't sure impersonating a minister was against the law, but I really didn't want to find out.

I raced down the stairs, texting Glenn to let him know I'd wait around the corner. Before I knew it, I was climbing into my car, and wrapping my hands around a fresh Timmy's coffee. *Thank God for Glenn.* (A prayer.) A few seconds later we heard an ambulance siren approaching, and I started to breathe a little easier.

While I was changing, Glenn phoned St. Andrew's Hospital and pretended to be Chris' brother. Found out he had been admitted and was receiving IV support until his electrolytes and sugars stabilized. I breathed a sigh of relief.

Do ends justify means?

Luckily, we arrived back at the chaplaincy office before the students started to pour in, but only by moments. Fr. Anthony asked where we had been, and Glenn and I glanced at one another, making a silent pact.

"Just dashed out for a bit. I'll tell you about it later," I promised. "People are being released. Maybe we should get ready to help them?" I realized I'd "gotten away with it," and owed the Holy Mother a study of prayer. Sigh. Add that to my to do list.

"How can we help?" Glenn asked. Fr. Anthony had some ideas. We helped the students as they arrived, listening, connecting some of them with their friends, feeding and clothing others.

And then Julie arrived, rushing towards us, babbling about how glad she had been to see me. Fr. Anthony smiled, and I wondered if he knew what we'd done. I steered her away from him, towards hot coffee and blankets, and Glenn joined us. She'd visited Chris, and was jubilant.

"He's looking so much better! You saved his life, Beth. I mean it. We won't forget." My heart started to pound. What did the "Student Code of Conduct" say about impersonating a chaplain six months before your graduation?

"Claire got out when we were talking, but she left her number for me. You remember her, right? Well, I called her and we're going to meet for coffee next week. She was asking about Chris. She's really nice. I don't think she got charged." Julie was talking a mile a minute, but soon started to wind down.

"Glenn, why don't you drive Julie home?" Fr. Anthony inquired from over our shoulders.

"Sure, Glenn, take my car," I said, moving them towards the door and away from the Chaplain.

"We're in this together. I'm just as guilty," Glenn insisted.

"I'm not sure it's like bank robbery, Glenn." This was mine to own, and I intended to. Soon.

They left, and Fr. Anthony continued on his way, not ignoring me, but not giving me a chance to talk.

Ends and means. Why was I okay with it when it was MY ends and MY means, but not when war was used to work for peace? A prayer for clarity?

In the end, I didn't come clean with him, conveniently using his busyness as an excuse, breaking a promise I'd made to myself. And somehow I convinced myself it was okay because I'd saved Chris' life. Now who was into drama?

Instead I listened. Students talked about the people they had shared their cell with, the hookers and drunks, the crazies and homeless. The middle class privileged had come face to face with some unsettling truths about the community just down the road, where eyes wept from infection and addictions, and the scent of the unwashed masked the horror of disease and homelessness. It all reminded me of my nurse training, where I'd learned I didn't mind "the unwashed" like lots of my classmates. One Aboriginal student was especially unnerved by the numbers of his "Aunties and Uncles" who were in the cells. I didn't know what to say, so I kept listening.

People were disturbed by the stories of strip-searching and knew way too much about the effects of cavity searches. They were determined to change things, and I thought "fat chance." Someone was going to write about it for the student newspaper, and another was going to research how effective such measures were in creating safety in the cells. Good luck finding that study, I thought.

I couldn't help but think about the people we'd crossed paths with in the cells, whose lives were very different from ours. Would this help,

I wondered? Would this mean something in my life? *Could my life have meaning?* I had poetic thoughts about seeds being planted and questions stirred up, but I just wasn't sure how to water them, or if I should give them fertilizer. Or was it all bullshit?

The next day, I wasn't surprised when I was summoned by the practicum advisor, Dr. Aaron Neufeld. Sigh. Maybe I should have kept my promise to confess, or maybe I was just about to. Maybe he could help me with my promise to reconsider the usefulness of prayer. Great, I thought, rolling my eyes. Prayers. Penance. Lots of maybes. I was glad I'd ducked trouble. Or had I?

Dear God, what am I getting myself into?

CHAPTER 2
THE ADDICT

Eight months later...

The Addict glanced at the door handle and cursed. He thought he'd washed the blood from his hand, but clearly he'd failed at that, too. He dug his T-shirt from his hoodie pocket, and turned it over and over, looking for a piece that was still white. He finally found a bit, and wiped the handle. Squinting, he was aware of the sunshine, and the cloying sweet smell of iron. He had to get out of here. What the fuck? Why was it still bright?

He looked up and down the street, surprised. He could've sworn he'd been in the house for hours, that it should be the middle of the night, but fuck. Whatever. He couldn't hang around. Fuck June. He needed to get his ass away from here.

Turning from the door, he hurried down the three steps to the sidewalk, and flinched when the screen door slammed behind him. Fuck! Did anyone hear that? He scanned up and down the street, but no one seemed to notice. He forced himself to stash his bloodied T-shirt back in his pocket, pull up his hood, and head down the path. Slowly. His body wanted to run, flee, scream, but he knew better.

He decided to get himself into the bush just outside town and figure out what the fuck to do next. Or maybe figure out if there should be a next. Stealing glances left and right, he tried to focus, but he was struggling to concentrate. He wasn't sure what to do. Beyond not being noticed, that is.

He'd try to get to the river on the other side of town. Thank fucking God it was a small town. Not too far to go, and once in the water he knew he'd lose any trackers they sent. A half-mile in the river should do it, he figured.

Crossing the street in front of the gas station, he thought about going in to wash his hands, and discarded that idea. Too risky. Then he saw someone he thought he knew. He struggled not to break his stride and run.

"Head down. Keep walking. Head down. Keep walking," he said to himself over and over. Now there were just occasional houses; clearly he'd been travelling for a bit. Fuck! Why wasn't it dark yet?

A pickup truck drove by and the driver honked and waved. What the fuck? Who the hell knew him here? No one, he hoped, but he gestured with his hand, almost waving, not looking up. Disappear, he thought. I need to disappear. Now. He kept going.

He could feel his breath calming, and when he looked back towards the town, he noticed the street lights were starting to turn on, one at a time. Was the sky finally getting dusky?

Soon the Addict realized he'd left the houses behind and was on the dirt road heading to the hatchery. There was the water tower. What the fuck? He'd walked at least a couple of miles, but he couldn't remember passing the ranch, the auto-wreckers.

Looking around, he knew he was near the river -- he could still make it out in the dimming light. He pulled his hood down off his head -- he thought he might hear better -- and glanced once more up and down the road. No one.

In a flash, he jumped over the guardrail, and scrambled down the bank towards the few trees between him and the river. He heard a truck approaching, and froze. Was he far enough into the small trees that he wouldn't be seen? Was he low enough to avoid the headlights? Was it dark enough to hide in the shadows? Would they drive right by?

The driver gunned the engine and he breathed a little easier. It was just those young punks from town, out joyriding on a Friday night. Cops didn't gun their engines on a dirt road. That much he knew.

Seconds later he dropped into the water, not bothering to remove his shoes, focusing on moving upriver, finding his footing, ignoring the feel of his wet jeans clinging to his legs. He had to get far enough upriver that he wouldn't be seen from the road. And he had to resist the urge to cross right away. He was glad his brain was slowing down enough to plan.

They wouldn't expect him to get out on the same side, would they? If he stayed on this side, he could use the old train tracks to get himself away from town quickly, and into dense trees. Then he'd know his next step. Or figure out if there was one. In the corner of his consciousness he heard a "Skreeeka! Skreeka!" and saw a flash of black swoop in and settle on a low branch of a tree. It was hard to see the bird in the twilight, but he knew she was there.

"Fuck. Fuck off. Fuck," he chanted, willing the bird to leave, to stop tormenting him. Each step became easier, even though he was walking through water. And more surreal. He was glad he'd resisted the urge to stop at the gas station and wash up again – he'd felt the stickiness of the priest's blood between his fingers, but knew the quicker he got out of Dodge the better. He rinsed his hands in the fast-flowing river, cupped some water and rinsed his face again and again as he walked. He didn't care how wet he got, he didn't feel the cold. Except he was shivering.

Discipline! Fuck! He had to calm down, slow down, and blend in. Stop splashing, which is fucking impossible when your head keeps remembering that you'd just fucking stabbed the Devil to death, a priest, a goof, the worst kind of evil. Like he'd had a fucking choice. Fucking diddler. Fucking fuck. He focused on slowing down his breathing, remembering what his Uncle Joe had taught him when trapping decades ago. Slow down. Focus. Be silent.

And when he started to calm down, the hunger in his bones started to rise up. How long since his last fix? He bent over, leaning his hands on his knees, and started to heave. His hands were shaking, he was shivering, but what the fuck? It was June...warm, really. He turned so his puke -- bile, really -- was carried away downstream, and realized he hadn't eaten in days. His stomach tore at itself. He doubled over until the heaving slowed down, then tried to drink a little from his cupped hands, started to heave again. He found a rock on at the edge of the water, and sat and drank, and heaved, over and over again until his stomach settled.

Fuck. How did he get here? His mind tried to wrap itself around this reality he'd fallen into, hard because every fucking time he tried to figure out what to do, something flashed into his head.

That priest walking down the road with his hand on that kid's shoulders.

Then flashing back to what it felt like when the Devil had touched him. First the shoulder, then meddling with his innocence.

Back to the kid turning to look at the Priest, saying goodbye at the curb, and heading across the street. The Priest calling out "See you tomorrow," as he headed up his walk.

Then remembering all the times he wished he'd been big enough to shout "NO!" at the Devil. "NO! NO! NO!" And then a wish to drive a hunting knife into the solar plexus of the Devil, gutting him like the deer he hunted with his uncles.

The kid turned and waved at the Priest, and the Addict had snapped. What the fuck. You fucking won't. You won't get your fucking hands, ass, dick on that kid ever again, he'd promised as he followed that asshole priest inside the house.

The Addict breathed heavily as his puke was carried away in the current. He pulled his T-shirt out of the hoodie pocket and dipped it into the water, pulling up his sleeves to keep them dry. He let the force of the river twist and turn it, holding on as the cold water cleaned his shirt, his hands, his forearms, bringing his tats back to life. Fuck, he thought, looking at the Medicine Wheel inked carefully on his left arm to remind him of the Teachings. Fuck.

Again, he heaved, this time doubled over as the force of his awakening to what he'd done drove deep into him. His face burned, his strength depleted. What the fuck had he done? How many Teachings had he turned away from? What the fuck would he do now?

What would the Elders say?

Would they even talk to him?

His head clouded again, and he wrung out his T-shirt, wiped his mouth again and again, sucking the river water from it, trying to convince himself it was safe to move on. Then he stuffed it back in his pocket, and started to slowly pick his way upriver, wet jeans clinging cold to his legs. The spring surge made the going harder than he'd imagined, but the water would cover his presence, the evidence, and maybe he could focus on the cold to drive the flashbacks away for a bit longer.

Focus! He couldn't afford to let the river trip him up – either literally or in his planning. He couldn't fall over. He'd be cold enough tonight in the bush without being totally soaked, too. He kept walking, trying to figure out how long he'd been in the water as darkness embraced him. The forest beside him was dark, and he knew he'd be able to disappear into the trees with only a few strides. He started to look for a place to get out of the river without leaving a trace.

Thinking about climbing out, he wondered if it was even worth it. Maybe he should just put his face into the river and breathe it in. That would cool the burning of his skin. God knew, he didn't deserve to go on – and the life he'd face when caught would be almost unlivable. He'd be sent back to Kent, an almighty hellhole, and he'd be left to rot there for the rest of his days.

He knew he deserved nothing more. He would be caught, he was certain. If only he could get that fucking diddler's last words out of his brain.

In fact, the Addict could almost believe he'd heard wrong, that it was the smack talking. Or maybe the coke. What the fuck had he been thinking, speed-balling like that? Fuck. He could feel the darkness start to bring him down, and decided he couldn't wait any longer. He climbed out of the river, flinching when a twig broke as he pulled himself up.

He disappeared between the trees, and tried to decide if he could afford a fire tonight. No. He couldn't risk it.

Soon, the Addict was lying down in the underbrush, trying to cover himself with leaves and branches, as much for warmth as camouflage. He secretly wished that he could hear the dogs coming for him, that this nightmare would be over soon, that the inevitable would happen. Then the darkness descended and the smack took over when the crack wore out.

As blessed drowsiness overtook him, his last thought was of her, that angel who'd gotten under his skin and next to his heart, who'd promised to be there, whose childish innocence had been too sparkly to bear.

How the fuck did the priest know her name? Some fuckin' mumbo-jumbo dark magic, no doubt. Or maybe that wasn't who the priest was talking about, right? Then blessedly, he passed out, shivering, hoping the cold and the smack would take him away to his Dreamtime forever. But in his dreams, he saw the priest, over and over, bleeding on the carpet in front of those kids' toys.

"Tell her it's not her fault," he'd whispered, barely breathing, blood bubbling out of his mouth. The Addict heard it over and over again. The nightmares kept rolling, every time he closed his eyes, and in the torment he couldn't tell if he was awake or asleep.

CHAPTER 3
AN UNHAPPY CHRISTMAS STORY

Eight months earlier...

Glenn leaned down and kissed Adam's damp head, softly, almost not at all. Adam was curled up on his lap, smelling sweet and clean, sporting his fuzzy Vancouver Canucks pyjamas. Bruce was tucked under his arm wrapped in his Ironman bathrobe, and they were hoping for a calm Christmas story. The boys were excited, waiting anxiously for the holiday that seemed to take forever to arrive. Just ten more days, Glenn thought.

He was grateful the boys were settling down after a day that was amped up with Santa anticipation, and an early Christmas party filled with carols, stories and their church friends. Finally they'd said their prayers, and now were waiting for a story; the day had exhausted everyone, and tomorrow was a school day for Bruce.

And then Donna walked into the room, leaning her lithe body on the door frame, a glass of red wine held casually in her hand, her smile taking Glenn's breath away.

"Shall we tell them now?" she said, and in that moment Glenn knew she was serious. He noticed her words were just a little slurred; he cringed as she swayed towards them on the bed.

"Now? Is this a good time? Bedtime?" Even to him, his voice sounded strident, but he knew that this could all still be undone if it stopped right now, and he struggled to engage the brakes.

"I don't know about a good time, but it is time," she said emphatically. That afternoon, while wrapping presents, they had discussed how to tell the boys, Donna insisting they tell them that "Mommy and Daddy can't live together anymore," and Glenn insisting they tell them the truth …. Donna didn't want to be his wife anymore. Like with so much else, her decree had won out.

"I know if we are really committed we can work this out," he had insisted. Even as he'd said it, her square shoulders had told him she was done. This was the last Christmas they'd be together as a family. If they made it until then.

"The boys will hate me if you blame it all on me," she had said.

"They could never hate you, but I'll be the one leaving. I need them to know why," Glenn had insisted. "I don't think I'll ever want this. I really don't know how I'll do this." His sobs caught in his throat, which wasn't going to win points for his side, but he just couldn't help it. All his plans, all he'd expected was shifting like quicksand. How could he focus on what was above him, ahead of him, if he wasn't sure he would be able to keep his footing?

The Bishop had told him about an Anglican parish in the interior of BC, a wild, mountain area full of beauty and nature, clean and rugged. He had felt a sense of rightness when he'd heard, had imagined his boys learning to ride their bikes on the hills outside their home, swimming in freezing clear lakes in the summer, surrounded by the love of the community members he'd serve. He'd imagined Donna getting involved in the community, perhaps finding AA again. He had to remind himself now that he could still do those things with the boys when they visited, but he had to re-invent his future without Donna. Somehow that seemed inconceivable. He was due to go up there and check it out after Christmas, see if it was a good fit.

As Glenn breathed in the boys' scent, he wanted to scream "NO!" but instead watched as Donna sat at the end of the bed. He felt the tension in Bruce's body come alive, as it did every time his parents disagreed, every time Donna had been drinking. As if in sympathetic chord, Adam's body went tense. He watched his big brother.

"What is it, Mom?" Bruce asked.

"Well, we wanted to let you know that Daddy might have a new parish assignment," she began. "It's far away, a long car trip," she added.

"I don't want to go," Bruce whined, and Glenn knew that when the boys were tired and anticipating Christmas, this was not the right time to do this. The family had talked about what would happen when he got a parish, how they would pack up all the boys' stuff and find a small house together -- somewhere new.

"That's okay," Donna continued. "You don't have to." In that moment, Glenn knew he was going to be the bad guy however this played out, and he felt the betrayal in his core.

"Mommy doesn't want to come with me," he said lamely, knowing he wanted to hurt her as much as anything. "She doesn't want us to be together anymore." He felt Donna's blame fling towards him, across the boys' heads.

"What Daddy means is that we are going to keep living here, and he is going to see if he can help people up near Pemberton, and when he goes, he'll come back and visit you lots. Once he has a great place to live up there, and has beds and all kinds of other stuff for you, he can come and get you to go up there for visits, and everything. It will be fun!" Glenn doubted it sounded very fun to the boys; he knew he wasn't convinced. And the parish wasn't even assigned to him yet. When he heard what came out of Donna's mouth, Glenn thought he might throw up.

"What is most important is that you know that Mommy and Daddy both love you very much, and that this isn't happening because of anything you've done." She leaned over and ruffled Bruce's hair. Adam was lost, trying to reach out to Bruce for an anchor. Glenn wrapped his arms around his little boys, trying not to cry in front of them. He felt the fabric of their family tearing, the security the boys had always experienced, unquestioned, slipping away. Nausea and anger collided in his throat, and he lashed out, quietly, at Donna.

"Of course we will always love them! Why do you have to raise any doubts! They never would have even thought of that! Oh my God!" He knew it fell on deaf ears. How could this be happening to him, to them?

Somehow he got Donna out of the room and helped the boys settle. They read *T'was the Night before Christmas* (three times) and *The Polar Express* with the lump in his throat, in his chest...in his life. He tucked them in and curled up between them on their bed, wanting to stay there forever.

After a few minutes, Bruce whispered to him. "Daddy, I can't turn over. How long are you going to stay?" and he knew it was time to get up and face his life in the living room. Adam's even breathing told him his youngest had drifted off, and when Glenn lifted himself carefully over his son's body, Bruce reached for the warmth of his little brother. They curled up together, as they always had, and Glenn hesitated only a moment at the door to make sure all was well with them. His kids were the most amazing little beings, and he was astounded at their ability to bend with this, too.

"Daddy, I love you," Bruce said into the dark. "Do you think Santa will still come?" And Glenn couldn't tell if Bruce was worrying about next week, or the rest of his life.

"Of course, he will, son," Glenn reassured him. "Just like God, he'll always find you."

Dear God, help her be asleep, too. I just want to head to bed, and have Christmas with my family. Glenn didn't want to have to explain any more bruises to his buddies at the squash court, and he didn't have the heart to defend himself tonight if Donna started whaling out in frustration. He was just so darned tired.

CHAPTER 4
A TENTATIVE "SEND"

I tromped down the hallway outside the professors' offices, my rain boots smacking against the tile floors. I took off my wet backpack and Gore-Tex; I like living in a place where fabric describes our fashion. Denim. Fleece. Year-round Birkenstocks. A place where Mountain Equipment Co-op seems to do a brisker business than Elle or even Joe Fresh. I shook my jacket, and rolled it up, fluffed my hair, and once again scanned the list of practicum postings on the bulletin boards. I closed my eyes. I had been summoned.

Good God, I hope this takes me somewhere interesting. I cannot bear to think I've come this far to be bored to tears in my last four months. I knew this praying thing was becoming a habit. Or maybe I had always carried on like this, but now I was noticing. I suspect promises to Mother Mary can do that.

I opened my eyes and scanned the listings again. Oh great. Soggy jeans, frizzy hair, and now disappointment from the board, too. The postings hadn't changed: hospital, parish, parish, old folks' home, parish. The only one that piqued my interest was a soup kitchen in the Downtown East Side. But it's the Sally Ann, and the work they do is great and all. I just can't make people pray for their supper; it takes away my appetite.

I wondered if Dr. Neufeld would let me pound the pavement, door-knocking on agencies to see if any wanted the able help of an almost-Priest. The needle exchange clinic, or even the safe injection site. Maybe that nursing degree wasn't a total waste of time after all.

All of which is to say I was avoiding Dr. Neufeld's summons, and hoping he wasn't going to nail me for crimes against integrity. Not really a solid footing to start a conversation that was all "trust me – let me try something new!" Postponing the situation wasn't helping my anxiety so I knocked on his door. I didn't even have time to take a breath and he called me in.

I loved Dr. Neufeld's office. It felt like a sanctuary, rare on campus. Lots of weighty books on the shelves, some of them dog-eared. Important Books, I am sure. Stacks of papers waiting to be consulted, marked, filed, and beside his computer there was stuff – icons really: pictures, candles, small reminders of the earth, of Spirit. There was even a stuffed angel-bear, and a box of Kleenex beside a comfy chair reserved for guests. Today, though, I wasn't relaxing.

"Sit down, Beth. Really. Let's chat," he said. I imagined him pulling a wrinkled plaid shirt out of a laundry basket and buttoning it up unevenly, not noticing because he pulled his grey sweater vest on top, but wondering why he felt twisted all day. His dark blond curls more than touched his collar. I admired his Clarks shoes with just a hint of envy.

"You asked me to drop by?" I tilted my head, wanting to convey "innocuous;" I still wasn't sure if I was going to be busted for impersonating a chaplain.

"Have you made a decision about your practicum placement? You are the last student to choose, so opportunities are limited," he said. I sighed and looked down at my hands.

"I have some ideas, maybe?" And then I waited as Dr. Neufeld peered at me over steepled fingers. As a 27-year-old once-again-single woman, over-educated and under-defined, I thought I knew what I wanted, but I only seemed to have figured out what I didn't. I mean, I knew I wanted my life to matter, but "matter" mocks me. Even *I* wonder what the hell I mean by that.

How did I get here? I'd almost finished my coursework for a Masters in Divinity, on the heels of completing a life course on marriage and divorce. Doesn't that sound all hifalutin? Before that, five years of university to train to be something I decided I don't want to be – a nurse. Do I hate that I'm in a place of not wanting to be what I am thundering towards? Ummm…yeah…and I swore I didn't plan this. And I hoped I wasn't a flake. I really, really hoped I wasn't a flake. And I wished I knew what I wanted to be when I grow up.

I needed four months of practical experience to finish my degree. A gift, right? "A small space of time to figure out who you are, and where you are called," the brochure said (I hear it in Dr. Neufeld's voice). Yeah. Sort of. I was aware that my "enthusiasm" for the journey wasn't translating into, well, decisions or anything.

I come from a long line of Anglicans, and being raised a PK (a priest's kid, to the unfamiliar) meant church was just always there. I think I chose nursing first because it was "Acceptable." Autonomy, and a wage. Lots of women in the world don't get both, I know. I'd get to help people. That was important.

Too bad I didn't factor in that I don't like hospitals. At all. Or even sick people. Sigh. "Become a nurse," they said. "You'll get over it," they said. Not. I'd started early, and hobbled to the end-zone, finished my degree, but only barely. Shame kept me from quitting the training I knew I'd never use.

Sometimes it felt like my path in life was a maze, and I'd mastered hitting all the dead ends.

So, to get back to "Acceptable," I'd decided on a Masters of Divinity. Now I needed a practicum and quick. I wanted, as a priest-in-training (a PIT, perhaps?), to figure out my "meaningful life." The only thing I'd figured out so far was that the thought of hanging out with blue-haired ladies over tea in a parish hall made me want to gouge my eyes out. Or someone else's.

The eye gouging thing, and the added bonus of wanting to puke when I thought about working with "white people problems" in a city of abject privilege, made me think maybe this, too, wasn't the life for me. And so, here I was. Uncomfortable, but not yet busted for my adventures in maybe-crime. (I admit a quick Google search had told me it was a misdemeanor to impersonate a minister in Alabama, and that the Catholic Church in Canada frowns on this behaviour as evidenced by someone claiming to be a Catholic priest in Ontario, and the subsequent freak-out. I wondered if the Anglicans had ever caught anyone impersonating clergy before.)

Perched on my chair, I advised my Advisor that I didn't like any of the practicums posted, and asked if there was anything other than the Salvation Army in the DTES.

"At the Portland Hotel Society? Maybe?" I hoped I didn't sound too much like a dissatisfied, whiny student, because, well, in that moment that is exactly what I was.

"I hear you have an interest in prison chaplaincy," he said. *Damn! Cover blown.* I collapsed in the chair, and looked over at him, sheepishly.

"They told you?" was all I said. He looked at me but didn't blink.

"I just heard chatter that you have an interest in justice, and have been working with the folks who were detained last week," he said, waving his hand as if it was nothing. And I realized it was better if I STFU. Plausible deniability.

"I have an idea, if you are up to it. I sit on the Board of a men's halfway house in the Fraser Valley. It's a great place, uses restorative principles, which makes it very Spirit-centred. I think there may be some interest in having you, and I think you'd be a good fit. How about it?"

The hair on my arms prickled, and I had to remind myself to breathe. I tried to still myself – flakiness bursting everywhere. Why did this feel so right? Was I pushing against my church and my Dad's vision for me, or moving towards a calling? I guess my expression was enough.

"You *will* have to work hard, and probably quite independently because they tend to work 'to capacity.' They've never taken a theology student before, but I think they've had criminology students. I'd be willing to offer you spiritual and academic advice and support, because they don't have a resident chaplain. Or I could call my friend Ben in Corrections' Chaplaincy and ask him to help with support."

I think I continued to look deer-in-headlight-ish. Dr. Neufeld just kept going.

"Okay, so let me ask. You seem interested." I assured him I was. Very interested, in fact. He pulled a couple of things for me to read off of a stack of books on a shelf, and dug into his filing cabinet for some articles.

"These will introduce you to restorative justice concepts, and a little bit about the practice." He asked me to drop by soon, and I realized that, without actually speaking to him, I was being dismissed.

"Um, Dr. Neufeld?" I asked quickly before I was outside.

"Yes?"

"I think I'd like to focus some of my study on prayer during my practicum. Would that be okay?" I asked, thinking it couldn't hurt to have Saint Mary on my side.

"Sure, I suppose so. Ben could help you with that. Or he could connect you with other chaplains," he said. And then he was done with me, looking again at his computer. I tiptoed away.

As I closed his door, I glanced at the book list on the top of the stack in my hand. I *was* intrigued, and my step was lighter. On the bus heading home, I started *Touching Spirit Bear*, a novel he'd lent me. I finished it by supper and was hooked (okay, it *was* written for middle-schoolers). That Ben Mikaelsen knows how to spin a tale.

It was about a young troublemaker who beat up a fellow student bad enough he was seriously injured, and how the delinquent had to go off on his own with support from Elders until he figured out that he couldn't keep doing that. Then he had to try to make it up to the boy he put in a wheelchair. It all made so much sense to me; I think it's a concept my Nana Beth, the fearless suffragette, would have clutched to her housedress-shielded sagging bosom. Which got me thinking of her. She had loved me so thoroughly.

God, I loved that woman. And I miss her. Nana Beth --what do you think? Another prayer, BTW.

I was excited beyond anything I could remember (okay, my horse camp at age ten was close). Trepidation. Actually, I admit, gut-liquefying terror. This was what "calling," and "rightness" felt like, right? I jumped in with both feet. Euphemistically-speaking. Truthfully, I emailed Dr. Neufeld three days later and told him I really wanted to do this. Sometimes the beginning of an epic journey starts with a tentative "Send."

Later that week, a bunch of us met in the Student Union Building to talk about what had happened during the protest, the "riot," according to the cops and cameras. The meeting was to tell people about their "rights" when they are arrested or detained (different occasions, I learned), and what to expect from the legal system. A guy named Dan came from the John Howard Society, and joined some pretentious law students from the Legal Aid Clinic. Actually, it was interesting, and let's just say that as they talked, the feeling in the room went from exasperated to, well, really tight and red. Kinda like when the soundtrack lets you know something bad is coming in Hannibal.

Did you know, for example, that if the police stop you, even for no real reason (like you haven't been in a car accident, or weren't holding up the liquor store), and demand your ID, you don't actually have to give it to them? I bet that pisses them off. A truly great idea – then you have angry police "detaining" you. But just don't lie to them – that can get you charged with obstruction or something. Piss them off, but don't lie. These folks were filled with brilliant advice.

If you're driving, you have to give them your licence, registration and insurance if they ask for it. Like name, rank and serial number if you're captured by the enemy. And you have to tell them your name and address if you're on your bike and they catch you doing something wrong and they want to give you a ticket. If you lie to them, that's a different reason for an obstruction charge I think. Or maybe it's the same reason. It's complicated. BUT any time you can ask them if you are allowed to go, and usually they let you unless they are going to arrest you. Or if you're at a peaceful protest, for example.

What really seemed to crank people up were the search laws, though. Even if they just detain you, if they think "you are a risk to them or others" they can pat you down. And if they put you in a cell with other people, then they can *strip search* you. Really. Like, totally naked. Which is what happened to lots of people on Saturday. Not a cavity search, but a strip search. They're different. Think about it. Either has to be done by someone of the same sex, BTW.

The legal beagles are looking into whether there was *reasonable grounds* (whatever that means – why do I think maybe the police get to say what's reasonable?) and the students are OUTRAGED that they had to take their clothes off. Or maybe that their friends did. Not sure. Or maybe that they could've been strip searched. Again, not sure. Anyway, it's clear they are pissed. Which I understand, but then, really, if I'm being put in a cell, I want to know nobody else has a knife or anything, so I'm a bit confused.

And then I got thinking. I wonder where the outrage is when Aboriginal women who happen to work in the sex trade are disappearing? Or are being slaughtered on a pig farm a few miles up the road? Me thinks rich, educated white kids aren't used to what police are allowed to do to them. Me thinks this could get interesting. Their plan? Invite the police next. Oh that's a good idea. Let's hope they don't ask for ID. Snort.

And now I have more questions than answers, 'cause I remember a lot of haunted eyes in the cells. And I can't really talk about it with anyone but Glenn because, like, I wasn't there. Remember?

Hey God, not too sure about this. No idea. But how about a deal? I'll look for "a meaningful life," and you keep me safe. 'Kay? Mary helped me last time....

And now, I just have to get through Christmas. *God, I hope it goes okay.* At least my brother's coming home...that'll deflect the questions. And I miss him so much....

CHAPTER 5
SISTER PAULETTE

The rain fell softly, sizzling on the embers and rocks that had been burning for hours. Al stood to tend the fire, adding logs to keep heat on the stones, careful to keep them handy in case the Elder called for more Grandfathers for the sweat. The men inside the lodge had been there for some time, and it wasn't likely they'd need more, but being ready was Al's job. He was glad for this time of sweating, the second this month because of the winter solstice ceremony a few days ago.

He remembered the winters of his childhood, standing at attention or kneeling on the cold stone floor listening to the priests and their mumbo-jumbo language, when he was told they were celebrating the coming of Jesus. He didn't pretend to be anything but scared, and really didn't understand that way of "celebrating"; it was too sore on the knees and it didn't taste very good. Give me a feast with salmon and bannock any day, he thought with a chuckle.

The sound of his own laugh brought him back, reminded him to focus. Focusing wasn't easy, but he wouldn't let on; he took his job as Firekeeper seriously. He didn't trust anyone else to do it, and luckily

Elder Hugh didn't either. Al scanned the area, making sure all was well inside the Sacred Grounds, that nothing would be interfering with their space, the fire, the Sweat Lodge, the path between the two. And then he saw her.

High up on the pine tree just past the fence she was calling him. "Skreeka! Skreeka!" Insistent. Persistent. Loud! Al smiled. He went to the plate of food that they had placed as an offering to the Great Spirits, and unearthed some almonds, a slice of apple and a juicy piece of steak from last night's stew. He carried them back to his log, tucking them away and sat quietly. "Skreeka!" The Steller's Jay came closer, landed on the fencepost and tilted her iridescent head in that funny way that made Al chuckle. He held out his hand with the apple, and after another quick scan of the area, she came to him.

Al didn't flinch as she landed with her claws working as a brake on his sleeve. It had taken some time to teach her to land on the denim and the scabs on his wrist from those lessons were still healing. She climbed up onto his hand and her ebony eyes pierced him, demanding. His fingers opened and she took a couple of bites of the apple slice, savouring it, and then tossed it in the dirt.

"Come on, then. You find them," he whispered. She cocked her head at him again and climbed his arm, stopping a couple of times on the way up. On his shoulder, she reached into his chest pocket, pulling out the nuts she loved. She held one in her claw, and ate it, chattering at him the whole time.

"I swear, you either love me or hate me, and I can't tell which, Little Sister."

He was reminded of Sister Paulette from his early days at St. George's Residential School, and wondered if this was her, coming back to haunt him. Everything he did seemed to remind him of that damned time when he thought his parents and uncles and aunties had forgotten him, tossed him out. Spending time remembering didn't help, and he felt anger bubble up his throat. He threw the stew meat away, and stood abruptly, brushing the friendly Steller's Jay from his sleeve.

"That's enough, I've got work to do," he said gruffly, and the jay yelled as it headed into the trees. He poked at the fire, waiting for the tarp over the lodge to open and the men to emerge to bathe in the creek just behind the tipi he had helped raise last month.

As he swept the ashes into the fire, Al was thinking about being here, now. He tried to stop the memories, but he couldn't. This evening, his mind insisted, took him back to his days at school. He thought about his friend Joe, and how he'd "died mysteriously" one night after talking back to the Devil, fighting the Darkness that visited them at night in the dorms. Al had hidden in the cupboard in a room behind the chapel for hours, surrounded by robes and embroidered linens, afraid that the Devil knew that he knew the truth. By the light coming in through the crack in the door he quickly scribbled a note to his Mama, telling her what had happened and that it wasn't Joe's fault. Then, in the dark, he took off one shoe and his sock and hid the note between his toes, and got dressed again.

He knew if the Devil killed him too, his Mama would find the note when she washed his body to prepare him for his final journey. As he retied the uncomfortable leather shoe, he wondered why the white people dressed so funny. And uncomfortable. And he struggled to stay awake, hoping to sneak out once everyone else was sleeping. It wouldn't be the first time he'd escaped, but this time he was determined to make it all the way home. And then his little body fell asleep.

As the memories of that time overtook Al once more, the shame he felt was real, and big, and heavy. He shouldn't have fallen asleep in that cupboard, shouldn't have missed his chance to escape and find his way home, and then maybe it would have all ended differently. His face burned red, and he could feel his anger rise. And then, as he once more heard "Skreeka! Skreeka!" he remembered what Hugh had told him: he wasn't to blame. He was only a child.

He wasn't to blame. Maybe if he said it often enough he'd believe it. He scanned the treetops just to glimpse a sight of Little Sister, to bring himself back to this time, and he reminded himself that the little boy was gone. What had he been —maybe eight when Joe died? Of course he had dozed off. He sighed, and the tightness in his chest eased just a little bit. He wasn't to blame for that night, for all the other nights in that hellhole. There was enough other shit he had to take blame for, but leaving that stuff behind was hard.

He remembered the next morning in the cupboard, woken up by his Uncle's voice in the chapel where Joe was laid out. Uncle had come to take his boy home, and Al had burst in, running towards his Uncle, begging Uncle to let him come home with him and Joe. His Uncle scooped Al up, and hugged him, and all Al could remember was how good he smelled, of smoke and grease and hunting trips. Al didn't let go of his Uncle's neck, sobbing endlessly for Joe, for his family, for the community he so missed.

And in that moment, the Devil decided to give Joe's body to Uncle, but hold on ever-more-tightly to Al, refusing to even consider if Al should be allowed to travel to the community for the funeral. Uncle and the Devil fought briefly, but Uncle didn't have much fight left in him, and the Devil reminded Uncle that he had the robes and the law on his side (whatever that meant), and Uncle unwrapped Al's arms, and gave him into the hands of the Devil, and left, cradling his son's body and weeping.

That night, when the Devil had visited Al as he slept, Al vowed he would kill the Devil. For Uncle. For Joe, and all the other boys. And most especially, for himself.

And then, one day, he did.

He just wished killing that priest years ago had settled the score. He was glad that Hugh and the other Elders couldn't see into his head, into the darkness that overtook him again and again, threatened to overtake every moment. And a small part of him didn't believe in Hugh who believed in him, just because the Elder did.

CHAPTER 6
THE PRODIGAL SON

I caved somewhere between the stuffed turkey and minced tarts, just like I knew I would. Like I always did. I would go with Mom to the midnight Christmas Eve Service, even though the thought of sitting through another one of my father's sermons made my stomach hurt.

One might think I'd have grown up enough by now to say no. Apparently not. It was like my childhood all over again, mandatory attendance at church. At least from me; big brother Stephen always seemed able to duck out.

Oh, good God, make me an instrument of your peace. Or at least get the slaughter over with quickly. This family stuff is agonizing....

And once again, I see I'm praying, even though I don't believe in prayer. Sorry about that.

And if I did, let's be clear, God, I don't get prayer that begs. But it seems to be all I do. I am so far from nailing this "spiritual thing" my soul aches...sigh.

Mom seemed tired, relieved, and for that, it was worth going. I hoped Dad would squirm, though. I knew he'd told them all I was in theology school. But maybe tonight I'd rant against being ordained. There were so many ways I could embarrass him, it was hard to decide. What *would* I say? I wondered. Sometimes my outside voice even surprised me.

"Thank you, Beth," Mom said quietly.

"You won't be sorry, Beth," Dad said, avoiding my eye. And then I was. Sorry. "I've got a great sermon planned, and I think you'll like the message." I laughed under my breath.

"Oh God, Dad, I'm not the Prodigal Child or anything. Surely Stephen gets that title this year. I'm going to sit with Mom, keep her company. That's it."

"I know, I know. It will just be nice to see you there, that's all," he said, and I wondered if that was a dig. Maybe, but I decided not to rise to the bait. Peace, and all that. He walked behind Mom, putting his hands on her shoulders he leaned over to kiss her. I felt a little nauseated when she tilted her head and his lips connected with her temple. I might have even looked away. Do kids ever get over that? Jeesh.

"Thank you for the wonderful dinner, Helen. I'll catch up with you all after the last service. Nice to meet you, Sarita. Good to have you home, Stephen." I noticed that he hadn't included me in his goodbyes. Ouch. Tender, much?

He headed for the front door, for the first of the all-important five services he would conduct in the "Christmas Marathon." God, it was so predictable. So pedantic. So boring. This routine was why we ALWAYS did Christmas dinner on Christmas Eve, and why I was the ONLY child I knew who had had to wait to open my presents until the afternoon on Christmas Day. *But I am getting over it. Right, God?*

Mom pushed herself back from the table, and began to stack the mountain of "good china." I put my hand on her arm, maybe because it was expected, but maybe because I really wanted to.

"It's okay, Mom. Steve and I will do that. Your turn to rest; you've been cooking all day."

Mom smiled and wrapped her "for good" blue-grey cardigan a little tighter around her shoulders, then went to the door to see Dad off. I rolled my eyes at Steve and we got up to clear the table, slipping easily into the tradition. He came over and hugged me from behind as I stood in the kitchen doorway, watching my father leave.

"Get to work, brother-of-mine. It'll be a few hours yet before I get home to bed! I can't believe Mom and I made this colossal mess just for you." The mountains of leftovers had already been crammed into the fridge, but we had a good deal of scrubbing ahead.

Mom joined Sarita on the couch in front of the fire and soon they were both napping. As I ran a big sink of hot water, I started wiping the cement gravy spots off the stove and thought back on the day. Much had changed in the past six hours.

At noon, Dad had rushed to the airport to greet my wayward brother home, but now it seemed like Stephen had been back for weeks. And like he'd never left. AND as if he'd been gone forever. I'd arrived at the house early so I'd be there the minute Steve arrived.

When I'd gotten there, the turkey was in the oven, and minced tarts were on the sideboard. I'd hugged Mom in her apron that said "Mrs. Claus" and she'd set me to work on the carrots and potatoes. The smells of Christmas were in the air and made my mouth water. Mom finished setting the table for four, humming carols the whole time.

While I peeled the veggies, I noticed the mountain of food being cooked, ready for the freshly polished silver serving dishes from Nana Beth. I'd miss her place at the table again this year. She gave me love, and a passion for baking. And her name. But at least Steve would be here; it had been almost ten years since he'd had a holiday at home with us. I was SO excited I'd be seeing him soon.

When he'd left I'd been in nursing school, and I'd missed him more than I could have imagined. He'd always been there, him and his buddies, and they'd let me tag along -- street hockey, hide and seek, playing board games around the dining room table, later at the pubs on campus. I'd never expected to miss him, but then, I hadn't ever had to. And now, soon, he'd be back.

"Help me carry the food through, Bethy. They'll be here any time," Mom said as she started to spoon everything into the serving dishes. I took some of it through, came back for more.

"Are you expecting a crowd?" I asked, tossing Mom a grin. She was stirring the gravy on the stove, and tucking a wayward strand of hair behind her ear. I gave her a quick kiss, and "Love you, Mom" as I passed. I'd never heard "I love you" from Mom or Dad growing up, and I was trying to change that, to let her know that even though I caused some grief, I still loved her.

Our kitchen had always been filled with great smells, and lots of good home cooking. THAT was Mom's "love language." Those street hockey games, and my love of running in the woods had kept me from becoming too round. Years of baking with Nana Beth hadn't helped in my quest for fitness, so I'd needed the balance.

"No Beth, not a crowd. Just the three people who matter more to me than life itself. That's enough. I'm just happy." She was fussing, making sure everything was perfect, nothing forgotten.

"Your Dad can carve at the table," she said as the phone rang.

"No, dear, you don't need to pick up anything. We have quite enough," Mom said into the phone. She looked at me, her eyes dancing.

"She's here. She took the bus earlier." There was a pause. "See you in a few minutes!" She hung up the phone and looked over at me.

"He said to set another place at the table." Mom took off her apron and hung it in the kitchen, reaching for her good cardigan. I grabbed another plate, and found her checking her hair in the kitchen window. She straightened her dress.

"You look fine, Mom. Stop worrying," I tried to reassure her. "I'll get an extra wine glass from the cupboard and wash it up. You get the silverware. Steve is still bringing home strays? Some things never change." I smiled as I thought about the many Christmases when his friends had joined us around the table. As I folded another napkin and tucked it under the forks Mom had put out, I realized I liked the table with five place-settings. It was fuller, safer, somehow, and I missed Nana Beth just a little bit less. I turned to say something and saw Mom head towards the front door.

Dad and Steve were laughing as they came into the house, struggling with enormous suitcases. They were taking off their dripping coats as I rounded the top of the stairs, and Steve looked up and winked. At his side was a tiny, dark-eyed woman.

"Mom, Beth, this is Sarita. She joined the camp last year to help in the Women's Health Clinic. I asked her to come here to Vancouver, told her there were almost as many people from the Punjab here as there are in her home village." Sarita jabbed him in the ribs.

"Stephen! Enough!" She looked up at Mom. Her words danced with her accent, familiar and lilting. "My family still live in the Punjab where I grew up. He thinks he's funny. It is good to meet you," she said, reaching out to shake Mom's hand as she gave Steve his wet sweater from around her shoulders. At that moment I saw Sarita was pregnant, maybe six or seven months along.

"I hope you don't mind, Mom. I thought she could stay in your old room, Bethy." His leprechaun eyes were darting back and forth as Sarita poked him again.

"Steve! I'm so sorry Mrs. Hill– I wanted him to tell you I would be coming. He wanted to stage a "Great Christmas Surprise."

"He can be impossible!" Mom laughed, reaching again for Sarita's hand. "Welcome. Of course, you may stay as long as you wish. There is plenty of food and space here. And if your staying will keep Steve here longer, I'm even happier you joined us. And I already know he's impossible," Mom added, grinning. As we shuffled out of the crowded front hallway, Dad and Steve started dragging suitcases into our old bedrooms. Mom rushed into the dining room to light the candles, and I poured the wine.

"This smells delicious, Mom. I can't wait to eat!" Steve said, as we gathered around the table behind our chairs, bowing our heads for grace.

"Bethy, would you share the blessing tonight please?" Dad asked, and so, disgruntled, I did.

Thank you for this family, this home and safe journeys. Thank you for the food we are about to eat, and bless all of those who toiled that we may feast. Bless those who are hungry, lonely, or sick and who don't share our wealth. May they know dignity, and love, this Christmas. There was a long pause, and I heard Dad finish.

"In Jesus name. Amen." Authoritative. Clear. And so damned unnecessary. I glanced at Sarita apologetically, and she smiled back. Dad carved. We made small talk, and ate. And ate. And talked. And ate. It was good to be here. It was good to laugh and joke with Steve, to get to know Sarita, to see Mom smiling from ear to ear.

I even laughed when Dad told Sarita about our antics as children at Christmastime, trying to out-fox our parents and open presents early. Sarita told us about Steve's chance encounter with a wild water buffalo the previous Christmas, how he'd run crashing into the camp afraid for his life.

"They were a bit unusual around the camp in that part of the Philippines," Sarita continued, "but they really are very sedentary. Kind of like cows here. Stephen came running through the compound, and we were sure a stampede was hot on his heels. Turns out the water buffalo had barely raised its head when Stephen startled it. Let's just say we weren't really in any danger," Sarita chuckled, and soon we were all laughing, Stephen included.

And then, before I knew it, I caved and agreed to go to church. And Steve wheedled his way out of it, just like every other year. Even so, it was good to be here, now, up to my elbows in hot, soapy water.

Cleaning up was a surprisingly easy dance with my brother, like we'd never been apart. We had a chance to catch up with each other's lives, and while I didn't confess my need to figure out my future, it was wonderful just hanging out with my big brother and sharing the small stuff. I told him a little about my plans for after Christmas, and he told me about the sabbatical he had planned from Médècins sans Frontières.

"Remember Nana Beth used to say 'Not much wrong in the world that can't be made better by running a sink of hot, soapy water'?" I said as I drained the sink and started wiping counters. Steve was putting away the last of the silverware.

"Well, right now I think not much in the world could get better than a comfortable bed and clean sheets. I'm gonna get Sarita upstairs and head to bed. We'll see you tomorrow, 'kay? My body thinks it's already tomorrow afternoon. You sure you're all right with her sleeping in your bed? You weren't planning to stay here tonight were you Beth?" Steve paused at the door as he glanced back.

"Not for some time, Steve. Not for some time. No worries – I'll get home and I'll be back to visit tomorrow. No doubt there will be more dishes then, too." I smiled at him.

"You know you don't have to go to church, right Bethy?" Steve smiled tentatively.

"I know, Steve. I'm doing it for Mom. No worries." I dried my hands on Mom's apron and reached for him. We hugged hard and long, and I didn't let go until he did. My delightful, successful big brother was finally home. I almost didn't mind the shadow.

"You really okay, Beth?" He pulled away and looked at me. A tear pooled in my eyes, damn it.

"Yeah. Nothing that can't wait. I'm just confused, that's all. And you need to sleep. Mom and I need to get to church. Time to catch up tomorrow, right?" Another quick hug and we turned to find Mom in the doorway, her coat on, handing me mine.

"I showed Sarita to her room and got her fresh towels. She's already heading to bed, Steve. Beth, we need to get going. If you drive, you can take my car home tonight and bring it back in the morning. That'll save you from Christmas bus schedules." And, with that, we were off.

Kind. Good. Wise. Loving. I'm working on it. Honest?
Why is it so damned hard with family?
Were things like this with you and Jesus? Mary? The Apostles?
Was there angst over people changing and growing up?
I can't imagine they wouldn't write about it if there had been…other people's drama is so delicious.
When did this begin —the family drama, the conflict, the never-ending need for therapy?
But there's nothing in the world that can't be made better with a sink-full of hot, soapy water.
Thank you for the hot water, God. And the soap.
And for reminding me to think about those who don't have either.
Or a big brother to help with the cleanup.
I'm gonna try to do better. Provided I survive church. I promise?

CHAPTER 7
A GOOD MAN

Ben chose the fourth pew back from the altar, where he could look up at the blue and green colours of the rainbow of glass that embraced the Abbey. As the colours reflected darkly into this concrete sacredness, he felt a wash of calm roll over his spirit. In the summer, the light flowed in, but the winter months reminded him that this space was a cold, dark tomb. That felt right, being in this familiar space, listening to the familiar liturgy and watching the monks stand, kneel and sit in their stalls at exactly the familiar moments. He began his own liturgy: *What is it, Oh God, that you are calling me to?*

His hand wiped his forehead, stopping to knead his temple. He hoped he would lose himself in the organ music, the simple melodies and voices rising and falling. Attending Vespers the week after Christmas was both comforting (because of the familiar ritual) and distressing (because of the familiar ritual), but he had yet to figure out how to stay away, how to deny the lure of the space between the comfort and the distress.

Magnificat anima mea Dominum,
et exsultavit spiritus meus in Deo salvatore meo,

quia respexit humilitatem ancillae suae.
Ecce enim ex hoc beatam me dicent omnes generationes,
quia fecit mihi magna,
qui potens est,
et sanctum nomen eius,
et misericordia eius in progenies et progenies
timentibus eum.

He watched the monks in their dark robes and the young seminarians wishing for robes of their own during as their voices lifted in song; The Magnificat always stirred his soul, especially when beautifully sung in Latin, male voices invoking heartfelt adoration. He was taken back to his first, happy days at the monastery in Québec, where he had studied and taken vows that he thought would lead to a long and satisfying life of service in the Order. But here he was.

He remembered those days as succulent. Bells calling him to rise almost before the day began, another for prayer in the chapel. A simple shared breakfast in silence. More quiet during the physical work – the fences, the gardens, the animals all needed tending. His body came to recognize the repetitive movements, the fresh air and being in the outdoors ;it would settle into quiet communion with his surroundings moments after the work began. He delighted in the sound of the flies in the barn, the bees in the orchard, the smell of the fruit being harvested, the brilliance of a newly painted fence. He came to understand his relationship to God differently through those acts, at that time.

Then came all the rest. It began when he noticed that some of the youngsters at the boarding school were treating some of the monks badly. Acting out. Being withdrawn. Some didn't want to talk to him when they were helping him with chores. The boys hid when some of his fellow monks – his Brothers! – came around. He started to realize that sometimes he came upon the boys alone with one of them – something that was strictly forbidden. And he started to wonder if everything was as healthy and good and honest as he had wanted to believe.

At first he spoke to an older monk about his concerns, who dismissed what he was noticing.

"Young boys change, you know that. Peter is just growing up, that's all. Brother Frances would never do anything to harm the Order. You have to know that."

"Stop making waves. Let the Abbot know and trust him. Really. You have to stop being so high and mighty! Living in community is difficult work, and not judging others is a part of that," came next.

Over time, it got worse. The youngsters lost their laughter, their eyes haunted. They flinched when he put an arm around them, hid when he came into the barn until they were sure it was him. And still they didn't talk to him, didn't trust him enough to believe their pain. And he didn't blame them…everyone just pretended it wasn't happening, and he became "the good man who does nothing."

Then he began to speak out more clearly, first to his Abbot, then to a visiting abbot who assured him that "the situation is being handled." He never really knew the particulars of what was going on, but he suspected… and the inability to talk about it only made it worse. Worse. One boy committed suicide, but it was all just treated as a horrible tragedy, as if his sadness was separate from what was going on. Yes, it was a tragedy, but that wasn't the whole truth. Everyone knew it, yet no one was doing anything to change things. And he continued to be "the good man who does nothing."

Finally he couldn't take it anymore. Monks were moved from monastery to monastery, but there were no real consequences for the never-mentioned crimes that were going on. No one cared about those children – *children* - being hurt. He knew in his heart that young boys *were* being horribly hurt, young boys who already had a mountain of struggles ahead of them.

When he heard about the "situation" at Mt. Cashel, and the cover-up that had persisted into the 90s, he couldn't deny any longer that something horribly wrong was going on in his Order as well. What happened in Newfoundland sickened him; he couldn't live in a community that allowed such hurt to happen, and worked hard to pretend, to look the other way.

In that fourth pew, years later, he sang the closing psalms reflexively in the cold, dark tomb, vividly remembering the day he was done. He had gone to the Abbot, Bible in hand, given him an ultimatum, convinced his voice could change things. How naïve!

Ben had been startled when the conversation quickly turned to questions about *his* vocation, *his* obedience to the church and its leaders. He was told he didn't love the Church, that the Pope had been involved in many of the discussions "personally" and was "taking care" of the situation. He was told he just needed to trust. More. Again.

That day, through his rising nausea, he knew that he couldn't go back to his cell at the monastery. He left, stayed on a friend's couch, returned his robes, and tried to put his life back together. He had never walked away from anything, but now he understood those who did. It hadn't been an easy road; he still had nightmares about the boys, and what they endured. He knew his imaginings didn't come close to the horror of their experiences. While he stopped being "the good man who does nothing," he knew he hadn't done anything of consequence. He'd saved himself from more grief, but he sure hadn't helped the boys, who deserved so much more.

Yet, here in the Abbey in Mission, he still came and prayed to God, with God, listened to the music and delighted in this small window into the community of the Brothers. They, too, had had abuse in this place, struggled to make sense of it all. Had he really made a terrible mistake in leaving that day? Should he have stuck it out and trusted? Could he have lived with himself? His Brothers?

He found it easy to worship with the Quakers, and serve the prisoners and staff at Corrections as a chaplain, but he missed the intimacy of living with others day to day. Sharing meals, laundry, an evening of reading. Tending to chores, and dreams, and their calling, together. He wondered what kind of a freak he was that he wasn't able to connect with people outside the monastery in the same way.

His apartment was quiet and lonely, his meals often eaten at the counter, his computer an unsatisfying connection to the outside world. Thank goodness for those Alternatives to Violence Project workshops and the folks at *Just Living*, or he would have very little real connection with anyone. His prayers rose from his pew as he sat in the silence.

Will I, Oh God, know the kind of freedom that comes from being with someone I love and trust ever again?

And what is it, Oh God, that you are calling me to?

CHAPTER 8
MIDNIGHT MASS

Oh Dear God, I'm sorry.

Or am I?

Should I be?

I can't stop grinning.

    Is it ever okay to laugh in church? Like, a full-bodied, milk-out-your-nose, belly laugh? Or a "suppress it 'til you die" laugh as you dare a peek at your high school friend down the pew who is mocking Mrs. Thomas? Mrs. Thomas, the ancient soprano who treats this night as if she was soloing at Carnegie Hall? Does God think it's okay to laugh during the service on Christmas Eve?

    Because, let me tell you, Mom sure doesn't. And I suspect Dad thinks it is the worst possible behaviour from his seminarian daughter. At least, the worst tonight.

    I love the feeling I get when I first come into the church, especially in the evening. The calm beauty of the hushed darkness, the shadows of the stained glass hinting at their muted stories. Candles flickering, and the scent of the incense and the pine and cedar decorations underlie the scent of damp overcoats and umbrellas. The rain on the roof reminds me of summer camp, and the quiet organ music keeps us hushed as we prepare ourselves. Those few moments ground me like none other; perhaps it's the reminder of the hundreds of times I've gathered here, perhaps it's the invitation. It feels safe. It feels lovely. I hate that.

As soon as the damned voices intrude, demanding that we "please rise," I feel my blood pressure begin to rise too. So much of the language is old and tired and meaningless, so many of the "rituals" feel lifeless, removed from Spirit. People stand and sit and kneel on command, and recite-without-noticing the words that haven't changed in forever. *And then they go home and behave as if none of it matters.* Maybe it doesn't matter to them, but I really want it to. Ah, ritual. Does it help them? Does it speak to them? *Can it speak to me?*

I yearn for my soul to be stirred. Anywhere, really, but especially in church.

Tonight, the church is beautiful. The purple vestments of Advent have given way to the beauty and joy of white and gold for Christmastide. Barely-contained anticipation from the few children present mix with contentment from the adults; the parents are happy that for the next hour and a bit they can return to the familiar Eucharist, knowing that all of the possible preparations for the next day are as done as they are going to be.

I hadn't expected to run into Trish in the foyer (okay, narthex) of the church, and clearly we were gleeful. We hugged and laughed a bit, then had to take our seats. I headed up to sit beside Mom, and Trish commandeered the third pew on the other side of the aisle. A "regular" was displaced, no doubt, but she didn't care. She sat down with Mark, her new husband, and shot me a glance. There was devilment in her eyes.

Trish and I had grown up together at church, enduring Sunday School, complete with blue-eyed-Jesus attendance stickers. Then we sang together in the Junior Choir. And sometimes, if we were very, very lucky, Mrs. Thomas led the choir, and oh boy, we were in trouble those weeks. Dear Mrs. Thomas had this way of over-conducting with her hands that somehow emphasized and mocked the notes at the same time. Her wagging triceps escaping from her polyester, flowered dress didn't help.

Trish started mime-conducting behind the pew so that from the front she looked serene, a quiet smile of bliss on her lips. But her hands were moving so fast that I couldn't help but chortle. I was truly unacceptable. And enjoying it.

Then I felt Mom's hand on my knee, "reminding me" to behave while she gazed forward, listening to the choir. I calmly picked up her hand and put it back in her lap. Not much was keeping me in the pew and if I felt like giggling with Trish, giggle I would. How mature, I know.

At least I felt alive.

Soon, I got to hear Dad read the familiar gospel from Luke. "In those days a decree went out from Emperor Augustus that all in the world should be registered…," followed by Dad's trite homily. He got my blood boiling for a moment when he talked about how Mary must have felt trepidation, her baby destined for a path that was difficult and unsafe, and how hard it was to watch a child "embark on a foolish path."

"At least Mary knew Jesus wasn't choosing His path out of naïveté," he said, and I thought about hitting something really hard. Or someone. Well, him. I didn't bother with Communion (communion with what? Whom?), and just waited for it all to be over so I could drive Mom home, and head for my apartment, and my own Christmas Eve ritual of Baileys and coffee and Handel's *Messiah* on full volume. Yes, at 1:00 a.m. But with headphones.

I don't often feel Spirit at Church, and after those first few moments, tonight hadn't been any different.

Except for *The Magnificat*.

It's true, God. Some of "those prayers" stir my soul even now. Singing The Magnificat in a quiet church takes me out of myself, and ties me to the generations of Christians who have always sung the Song of Mary. Sigh. Sometimes I revel in rejecting the Anglicans, my Anglicans, but truthfully? The Magnificat will always draw me back. Especially when it's sung well....

My soul proclaims the greatness of the Lord,
my spirit rejoices in God my Saviour;
for he has looked with favour on his lowly servant.
From this day all generations will call me blessed:
the Almighty has done great things for me,
and holy is his name.
He has mercy on those who fear him
in every generation.
He has shown the strength of his arm,
he has scattered the proud in their conceit.
He has cast down the mighty from their thrones,
and has lifted up the lowly.
He has filled the hungry with good things,
and the rich he has sent away empty.
He has come to the help of his servant Israel,
for he has remembered his promise of mercy,
the promise he made to our fathers,
to Abraham and his children for ever.
Glory to the Father, and to the Son, and to the Holy Spirit:
as it was in the beginning, is now, and will be for ever.
Amen.

Sigh. I had to admit it. That one felt good.

Sometimes once the service is over, the candles are out and the robes and crosses have left, I settle down and hear God's voice. Tonight the organ played something haunting and beautiful.

I knew in my soul I wanted to experience God, to find struggle and joy and peace and be challenged in the church, but it didn't happen like I wanted. Glenn and I argued about it. He found it in church. I didn't. And that's why I'd decided to graduate and *not* be ordained, not promise myself to this church I didn't trust. The one that didn't touch me.

Trish ducked into my pew and simply said "Coffee next week?" and I grinned in assent, giving her the thumbs up. It would be good to spend time with her.

Soon I went and found Mom, hugged her and we found our way to the parking lot in the rain. A CD of Bach's choral works on the drive home, the streets quiet and calm. Everyone had left their Christmas lights on, and they reflected in the puddles on the street, and the raindrops on the windows. We drove in comfortable quiet, and when I pulled into the driveway, she turned and hugged me.

"Thank you Beth," she quietly said. "See you tomorrow. Come by before lunch and we can visit."

"Thanks Mom. I'd like that. Why don't I come around 10:00 or so and Steve and I can make you brunch?" I offered. She smiled.

"Bacon and egg quiche is already buried somewhere in the fridge, and I'll pop it in the oven in the morning. If you come at ten, you can make the coffee." She shut the door and headed up the walk, aware that neither of us had said the obvious. Dad left for church at 9:30, and wouldn't return until after noon; I'd have two whole hours with Steve and Sarita before he got there. Quiche and quiet with Mom and Steve on Christmas morning was another tradition I loved. I hummed along to a cantata as I drove myself home. Damn, I reflected, it was even feeling good to be part of our family again.

The next morning, I found Steve in his room unpacking. I snuck up behind him and wrapped my arms around his chest from behind. He leaned in, and for a moment I worried that he thought I was Sarita.

"God, Bethy, I have missed you so much. I think it was the hardest part about being away." He turned so he could look at me.

"I hear you and Dad have had a rough go of it. I'm sorry Mugwump, but maybe it's about time. Are you alright?" His concern cracked something in my chest, and my chin started to wobble. He folded me into his broad chest and warm sweater, and I tried not to sob. I loved that he never tried to console or hurry me, but just let me be where I am.

"You're EXACTLY what I need right now," I said to him as I pulled back a bit. He grabbed a dirty T-shirt from his suitcase and offered it to me to use as a hankie.

"Are you done? Wipe your face. Go ahead, blow, Bethy. You'll feel better. Don't worry about the shirt; Mom loves doing my laundry." I giggled, remembering my resentment. I had washed my own clothes, but Steve's were washed and pressed with Mom and Dad's every week. Really. T-shirts. Pressed. Who does that?

Steve took the defiled T-shirt to the laundry chute, and I sat down on his bed. He kept unpacking, and the banter continued, a familiarity that only growing up together brings.

"So, how is that 'Saving the World' project coming along?" I teased. Steve spent about fifty weeks a year in some remote location working to bring medical care to those who needed it desperately, and I stayed home and worked hard on Nothing Important. The other two weeks he went Somewhere Important, like India, and worked on healing himself. Maybe doing yoga, maybe doing a ten-day meditation retreat, maybe hiking up a mountain.

"Sounds like you miss me," Steve teased back, and I sighed.

"Yeah, I could've used some brotherly wisdom right about three months ago…."

"Ouch! I thought you didn't want to be smothered? You could have called me, you know."

And then there was silence, me wrestling to find the words without my sobbing taking over again, Steve wrestling to find room in his already-full drawers for the clothes he had brought with him. "Do you think Mom will ever get rid of these old clothes, Beth?" he asked.

"I think you'll have to; this is her shrine to you. And I know I could have called, but the phone isn't the same. I was scared you'd say 'I told you so,' and you did tell me so. About seminary. About living in Vancouver still. About everything. I'm just confused, that's all. It all seemed so sunshine and rainbows when I decided to go to seminary, and now it all seems so…middle-class. I really don't want to be a parish minister, but…." And he hugged me again. *Thank God*. That's a prayer.

"Well, as long as you remember I told you so, I don't have to say it, do I?" he teased. And then he dropped the bomb, whispering in my ear.

"I'm going to be a Daddy!"

My mouth gaped, and in that moment, I instantly felt better. Steve always knew how to do that. I felt my soul rise up. I couldn't believe it! I hadn't dared to assume Sarita's babe was Steve's – he would just as likely bring a pregnant friend home and care for her, and he hadn't said they were a couple. No PDAs. No sharing a room.

"Why didn't you say something last night? I can't believe it!" I realized my voice was rising even as I whispered.

"Shhh…I haven't said anything to Mom and Dad yet. Thought I'd tell them after lunch but we wanted to be sure you knew first." Sarita knocked on the door, and joined us.

"So I guess he let the cat out of the womb, so to speak," she said, grinning as Steve draped his arm over her shoulder.

"Oh my God! I'm so excited!" I quiet-squeaked, and they dragged me into a group hug. My legs started a happy dance. *"Oh my God. Oh my God. Oh my God! I can't believe it!"* Prayers, all of them.

"I know, eh? Auntie Beth. Who'd a thunk I'd trust you with that one?" He looked at Sarita. "She's going to be the aunt that borrows the child and spoils the child, and excites the child and then drops it back home and doesn't so much as feel sheepish. No sorries. No remorse." He was grinning.

Sarita and I looked at one another, and our eyes were dancing. "Oh my God. Tell me everything. He can unpack," I said, and patted the bed beside me. "How did this happen?"

Sarita looked at Steve, raising an eyebrow. "I thought you told me your sister was smart, Steve. Or is it just here in Canada that things are backwards and women and girls aren't taught how babies are made?"

I laughed, cringing. "No, I meant how did he trick you into making a baby with him? I can't imagine. And into coming to Vancouver to visit his family. We are weird, you know. Really weird. I want to know everything! I'm going to be an aunt! I can't believe it!"

"Shhhh...." Steve said again. "Mom's coming." We heard a knock on the door.

"Brunch is ready everyone," she said as Steve opened the door.

"Thought I heard you Beth. Come on down." We probably looked like we were up to no good, and Mom's cheerfulness was working hard. As we tumbled out of the room, she drew me off to one side.

"You know what I really want for Christmas, Beth? I want you to really forgive your Dad, more than anything." She turned and headed for the stairs, but I reached out to stop her. Steve glanced back, and stopped to listen.

I caught my breath and closed my eyes for a few seconds before I answered.

"You know that what he does affects me, Mom. Ever since I was a teenager, I haven't been able to stand up to him, and more and more I'm regretting what went on. Lots of that stuff is coming up for me now, and I have to find some backbone around him, or I'll never feel like I am living *my* life." I paused for a second. "Now let's go eat. Really. Don't worry, I won't bring it up today."

As we headed down the stairs, Steve grabbed me.

"What's up, Beth? What did Dad do?"

"Later Steve, really." We gathered around the table, now set with our everyday dishes.

It wasn't until after the four of us had eaten, laughing at stories from their trip, that Steve got me alone. (Again over a sink of dishes. I am noticing a pattern and not embracing it.)

"Mom and Sarita are lying down. What's up, Bethy?"

"Oh, I don't know, Steve. It's all hard. You know how I am with Dad. And I have some tough decisions to make. Or maybe I just have to tell him about them." And in that moment, thinking about Sarita and the baby, I knew I wasn't ready to tell my big brother all of it. How could I? What would he, Doctor Save the World, think of me, Sister Make All the Bad Decisions?

"I know, Mugwump. He can be hard. I'm so sorry. He told me some stuff was going on." Steve reached for me and drew me into his arms. I decided to try his tactic and change the subject.

"I'm so happy for you and Sarita, Steve. Really I am. I can't wait. Will you stay in Vancouver until the baby's born?"

"Of course," he whispered. And then I was curious, and my strategy flew out the window.

"What did Dad say is going on between us, Steve?"

"Oh, he said you were having 'Ordination jitters.' He didn't really get into it, but I got the impression he was mildly amused."

Pulling away, it was my turn to slam cupboards. "He still doesn't hear anything I say. I can't believe it. I am NOT going to be ordained. Why can't he get that?" He smiled at me.

"Shhhh...you'll wake Mom and Sarita. And don't worry. When you don't get ordained, he'll get it, even if he doesn't like it. Sounds like there's more for us to catch up on." He was grinning at me, and I squirmed. Not yet, Steve.

A little while later, I was heading home, cradling my new sweater in my arms, a sweater Sarita had knit for me from this lovely Indian wool. Or Nepalese. Or something.

I felt blessed. Happy. And grateful to be heading to my apartment for some time to just be, and figure some stuff out. I hoped.

Dear God,

Keep this promise safe, please? And Sarita too.

I know women around the world have done this forever, and that sometimes it goes horribly wrong. AND I know I don't deserve your grace after the mess I made of the last promise in our family.

But please, please...please? Not because we deserve it, with Steve and Sarita saving all those babies, or because of modern health care...but just because?

I am realizing that even when I intercede for others, at some level it's still all about me. And I don't know that I'm comfortable with that. I already have so much privilege and opportunity. Is this what you meant by life not being fair?

I'm here. I'm trying. Is that enough?

CHAPTER 9
THE TWELVE VISITS OF CHRISTMAS

So, I took full advantage of the Christmas Break to hang out with friends, visit with my brother, and think about my practicum. And to hang out with Glenn, my study buddy. Instead of worrying about later. Mostly.

Dear God, what the heck am I going to do? Could you give me a little hint to follow? A little guidance would help....

I met Glenn at our campus hangout. The place was quiet, most students were home for the holidays, so we enjoyed the calm.

"Good to see you!" I called out when I entered the café. "Do you want anything?" He held up a mug, and I ordered a steamed milk for myself.

"How are you?" I asked as he stood to hug me.

"I'm okay," he said, but I could tell he was feeling tender. He was sporting a bruise on his left eye that was an ugly yellow.

"More hockey?" I asked. I knew Glenn's bruises weren't from hockey, but it was my way of saying "I see them, and I care." Glenn smiled sheepishly at me.

"Yeah. We're not really playing on the same team right now. Not sure about our future." Hmm. That didn't sound good.

Or maybe it did.

"Well, happy to lend a hand, any time. But you know that." We got comfortable in the booth.

"What's your news?" I asked. We tried to keep in touch, but between families, Christmas and Glenn's work at the local parish, it had been a few weeks.

"So, Bishop Tom thinks he has a parish for me, if I want it. Up north. Near Pemberton." Glenn's eyes were dancing. I sighed.

"Will you explain to me again why you want a parish? I am so messed up. Still haven't finalized my practicum. Dr. Neufeld is bugging me. When I go to my Dad's church I want to puke." I was glad I didn't have to mince words with Glenn. He looked over my shoulder, and his eyes got all wistful.

"I love the thought of having a group of people I can work for. Offer worship. Try to make a difference in their lives. Really get to know them. It's about doing service, I guess." He smiled at me. "It's what I've always wanted. I guess I'm as confused at why you don't. Why you're in seminary." I sighed. Again.

"Me too. I am sick of not knowing. First, nursing school. Now this." I took another sip of my warm milk. And kept going. "God, I hope I'm not a flake. I really, really hope I'm not a flake."

"Down with flakedom," Glenn sympathized. A few more minutes of whining, and Glenn changed the subject.

"Fr. Parker wants us to do some follow-up with some of the students from the protest. He suggested you call Julie. Can you do that?" he asked, knowing I would.

A few minutes later, we parted ways, and I was gentle with my hug. That bruising looked painful.

"Take care, eh? And say hi to the boys from me. And Donna."

I didn't really like Glenn's wife, but I knew he loved her. Families were hard. I headed to the bus stop, with a light step. I was going for a walk with Steve, and then for a visit with Trish, a chance to share takeout just like the old days, and catch up. I smiled as I boarded the bus.

I got off at the entrance to Stanley Park, and found Steve on the seawall. It wasn't a perfect day, but that meant the crowds stayed home, so we had some space to walk for a few miles together. The wind was a bit brisk, so we kinda shouted at each other as we travelled.

"So, looking forward to fatherhood?" I asked, and we were off.

"Um...yeah. And terrified. It's weird. It never seemed like such a big deal when I was doctoring new parents, but now everything is...amplified."

I smiled, remembering how special I'd felt when I was pregnant. It was like everything was wondrous and shiny and new, and I had a secret. Stephen shared a little about all the things he was terrified of (none of them likely) and all the things he was excited about (all of them likely), and I guess I looked just a little too wistful.

"Hey, Mugwump, what's up?" he asked, stopping. I jumped when he reached out and put his hand on my shoulder, and I choked up even more.

"I don't know, just feeling a little blue," I said.

"About what? Being an aunt?" He was clearly mystified.

"No, I just wonder if I'll ever have a baby, I guess." I could tell he didn't really believe that that was what was bugging me, but we just walked in silence for a bit, listening to the waves hit the rocks. The seagulls were yelling at each other. Or maybe at us.

A moment later, Stephen poked me a little more.

"Hey, I see you. Are you sure you're okay?" and I burst into tears. It was, for some strange reason, all too much to admit to my big brother that I was feeling blue because of a baby that hadn't been born...but there it was. And before I really thought about it, the whole story was tumbling out.

"Do you remember me talking about Jesse?" He was nodding, steering me slowly towards a bench.

"Vaguely," he said. "Some guy you dated a million years ago, right?"

"Did I ever tell you about Chaos?"

He looked a bit mystified.

"Chaos was our baby...Jesse's and mine. I was seventeen; you'd just gone on your first trip oversees. Jesse was older, 23. He'd just finished his GED, and was hoping to do a mechanics apprenticeship with his brother. He was the gentlest, kindest guy, considering where he had come from. At least he was with me."

Steve stopped me, putting his hand on my knee.

"Wait. You were pregnant? Just after I left?" I knew he was struggling to figure out how I kept *this* secret.

"Dad was convinced that I would be 'throwing away my life.' He told me to have an abortion, and I didn't want to. He made the plans anyway." I took a breath. Steve turned right at me.

"You had an abortion?" I could hear his incredulity, and nodded.

"When Jesse heard what was happening he lost it. He came over to talk to me, and Dad pushed all his buttons. He made rude comments about Jesse's clothes, his old car, and his lack of education. They got into a shouting match, and Dad told him to stay away, that he didn't trust Jesse's temper."

Steve's fists were clenched and he turned his head away from me. I could see his pulse on his neck. Hoped his anger wasn't directed at me.

"I'm sorry, Steve. I know I shouldn't lay this on you right now. It's a part of why things are bad between me and Dad." He looked at me, a little too much fire in his eyes.

"I wish I didn't believe it, Mugwump. Why didn't you call me?"

"There wasn't any time, and I was kind of mad at you for leaving me alone. I felt like Dad and Jesse were in a pissing contest over me, and I was scared. I only saw Jesse once more after that fight. He met me after work one night and begged me not to go through with the abortion. I'd already had it, and when I told him he stormed off. I never saw him again."

I could see the anger in Steve's shoulders.

"It's too bad the nurses in the clinic weren't able to get you alone and ask you what you wanted," he raged. Ever my brother, taking my side. I hugged him, trying to reassure him I was fine now.

But his words had caught me up a little short. What? Had the nurses gotten me alone? Later.

"I still worry about Jesse, pray for him. Chaos, too. I ran into a friend of his a couple of years later, and he said Jesse started running with his old friends after we broke up, riding his bike and, well, I didn't ask what else. For all I know he's in prison now. And I'm not sure I ever really recovered, whatever that means." I pointed to my heart.

"I'm so sorry, Beth. That's horrible. I could wring Dad's self-righteous neck." He stood up and started pacing, back and forth. I chuckled.

"Sit down, Steve. You're going to get hit by a cyclist if you're not careful. And don't bother with Dad's neck. For what it's worth, that's why I married the first 'suitable' guy who came along, and married him instead of Jesse. I'm actually glad you couldn't make it home for that fiasco." I sighed again.

"Of course, it didn't stand a chance. I think a piece of ME died that day in the clinic, Steve, and I'm not talking about Chaos. The part of me that was idealistic, put others first. Dad said I grew up, but I think maybe it's more like I gave up. I just don't know.

"I guess with your upcoming excitement, it's all come back to me. And I'm trying not to stay mad with Dad because, well, ten years, right? And Mom. You know." My voice trailed off.

"I don't even know what to say, Mugwump. I can't believe Dad did that to you, it's not right." And again I thought maybe I needed to look hard at that story. Just not now. Then he had a confession.

"I don't think I can stay at the house any more, Bethy. Can Sarita and I camp out with you? I keep expecting a comment about "out of wedlock" and I'm afraid I'll lose my shit. I thought I could do the whole "separate bedrooms" thing, but I don't want to anymore. I miss my baby!"

"Of course! Do you need help packing?" I asked, and he reassured me he was fine.

"But can I borrow your car to move Sarita and our luggage? I know you hardly ever drive it," he asked, and I peeled my key off my keychain as we headed back towards the city.

"It's in the parkade, you'll find it. You've seen the pictures."

A few minutes later, I was getting back on a bus, and he was heading back to Mom's in a taxi; he offered to cook dinner at my place, but I told him I wouldn't be home. I let him know he owed me one, though. Not that I minded the couch. Much? I headed to Trish's. I had planned a light day of visits, but my body was limp.

Being loved by my brother can have that effect.

The door swung open as I lifted my finger to ring the bell.

"Beth! Come on in. Shhhh...." Trish greeted me. "I'm babysitting my niece and she just fell asleep." As I took off my shoes, I saw a little baby sleeping on the couch, cushions piled around her.

"She can't roll yet, but I'm not going to take a chance." Trish was grinning. I cooed appropriately, and soon we were sitting, sharing some hot chocolate I'd brought, reminiscing about high school, and catching up with our lives.

"So, what about you?" Trish asked. "I heard you were back at school!"

"Yeah, almost finished my Masters of Divinity. And I've got no idea why." I sighed.

"What do you mean? You were always into 'spirituality' (yes, she used finger quotes) even in high school when the rest of us left it. You actually liked going to different churches, trying out different ways of doing things, trying to figure out the meanings. I'm not surprised."

"I know. But I *really* can't see myself with a parish. The thought makes me crazy. And I've got to figure it out in the next couple of days. Really." I was glad Trish got me. That I didn't need to pretend everything was okay. But I wasn't ready to tell her about *Just Living*. I was afraid to jinx that opportunity, and I hadn't heard back yet.

"So, why *did* you go to theology school, then?"

I thought long and hard about that.

"I was curious about God? I love the conversations. And studying how people can really make a difference. I just don't see how working with the blue-haired ladies in Kerrisdale is helping. Not convinced." I took a sip of wine. "God, that sounds pretentious," I admitted.

"Oh Beth, you're hilarious. So much angst. You'll figure it out." Trish's niece started to fuss, and Trish picked her up, rocking, shushing her. She looked right at me, eyes piercing.

"I adore her. Really. I had no idea. I think *this* might be what I'm meant to do," Trish said, eyes misting. Um…duh. I reminded her that when we were kids and I tried to play school, or church, she turned our pupils into babies. She actually *sought out* babysitting opportunities when we were teens. I remember refusing to babysit any child under two unless she'd join me.

"Ya think?" I said, smiling. "You have always loved children. You didn't even resent your little sister tagging along all the time. Not that I did; she's cool." I remembered going to movies and having to pick Disney so she wouldn't be scared. And then she was scared. By Disney. Sigh.

"Can I share a secret?" Trish said, looking at me sideways as she changed her niece's diaper on the couch. And in that moment, she didn't have to tell me.

"Oh My God! You're having one!" I whispered.

"I never even said! I promised Mark I wouldn't say anything until we were safe. Miscarriages, and all that. I'm only ten weeks along," she added. "Don't tell anyone!"

I promised. And felt a little stunned – first Stephen and Sarita, and now Trish and Mark. Maybe I was just a certain age. It made my arms ache just a little for paths not taken. And then I was back at it.

"You look so happy! Glenn, this afternoon, sure of where he's going, now you. Stephen, too. I just wish I could have one tenth the certainty you guys have." Whine. Whine. Whine. How attractive.

"Really Beth, are you worried?"

I teared up just a little.

"Because really, I think you're going to make such a difference, whatever it is you do. And I know this sounds *so* trite, but you gotta have faith, girlfriend! There's a reason you felt called to seminary. Really. And I think you're right – it isn't just parish work. I can't help but sense that you're going to get another call – one that will feel so right." Now I was looking at my hands, which Trish put hers around. Her niece was lying on the floor on a blanket.

"Beth. Really. You always encouraged me to have faith when we were teenagers, angsting over boys or tests or schools. You told me I'd know. And I did, when I met Mark. I think you'll know. And just trust. Even if you have to plug your nose and pick something in the meantime. What about a hospital chaplaincy position?"

I glared at her. She was grinning.

"At least I know you're listening. Anyway, one day at a time. That's what Mark tells me when I worry about losing this baby. And what you'd tell me at camp when I couldn't wait to get home. In any event, you have to get ordained so you can baptize this baby of mine," she said, picking up her niece who was fussing.

Dear God, I promise I'll never give anyone the advice to just trust ever again. Have faith. One day at a time.

What a stupid idea. The world was run by those who showed up, I was sure.

I just wished I knew where that should be. Sigh.

A few minutes later, I was hugging her goodbye, and kissing her niece on the forehead. She was cute, I admit. We promised to keep in touch over the next few weeks, so I'd know when to start knitting publicly. She reassured me I'd be telling her where my life was headed.

Dear God,

I'm here.
A little being, doing a little life.
And I get that I'm insubstantial...but....
What next, God? If you could give me a little clue, one I understand, I'll move on it. Promise.

I couldn't wait to hear from Dr. Neufeld, to confirm my practicum placement.

CHAPTER 10
HAPPY NEW YEAR?

"I can't go back. There's nothing there good. Oma died, and there's no one there anymore," Ricky said, his strident voice rising.

"Let me see. Powell River. No one else there who could help you? Anyone there you'd want to connect with? A minister, or relative? An old teacher, maybe?"

Ricky's eyes started darting around the office again. "Nope. No one. Don't want to go back. I'll just stay here," he said, and Peter reached out with a brochure to distract him. Ricky glanced at it and tossed it on the desk.

"Rick, I've tried to explain, you can't stay here anymore. You are doing really well here, no fights for the past year. It's time to talk about where you do want to settle if you don't want to go to Powell River. How about Kamloops? There is a halfway house there that might take you."

"Because I'm loopy? Kam*loops*?" Ricky said, smiling, his voice rising on the last part of the word. Peter smiled.

"No, Rick, Kamloops because I don't think it's a good idea for you to move to Vancouver, and there aren't a whole lot of options. Up north, I suppose, but you don't know anyone there. Kamloops is nice. The guys are solid at the house there. Lots of them are in the program," Peter shared, searching for the puzzle piece that would help Ricky feel more comfortable.

"Nope. Not going. That other guy went there and he wasn't...he didn't... not going there."

"Something you want to share, Rick? Is there something I should know about?" Peter's voice was calm, quiet. He looked intently at Ricky, hoping for some information that would help him help Rick.

"Nope, I'm good. I'll just stay around here, thanks." Peter sighed, frustrated. What would help him figure out how to support this guy? No doubt someone had been taking advantage of Rick; maybe that guy had ended up in Kamloops. No point trying to investigate, because the only thing that seemed to have sunk in during Rick's stay was the first rule of the con code: don't rat to the Man. This wasn't worth pursuing, but neither was Kamloops.

Ricky was due to be out soon, and January was always a tough placement time. Peter figured Ricky would last on the street until the end of spring before he'd be back inside on a parole breach or new charge. No doubt he'd be using again within a few weeks of getting out, in debt to some scumbag within a month or two. From there it would be downhill.

A group home for adults who needed support was the best option, but those were provincially funded through the health ministry. Ricky was Correctional Services of Canada's (CSC's) financial burden until his warrant expired, so putting him in a provincial facility was darned near impossible. Easier to wait until his parole was completed, and Peter knew he wouldn't last that long without structured support, even with the help of a halfway house. But he started again at the beginning.

"Rick, what things do you really like to do?" He waited a moment between each question, looking for a sign, anything.

"What do you want to do when you get out?" Pause. Nothing.

"What are you really good at?" Pause. Nothing.

"Think about it. We'll find a good place for you." He noticed Ricky was starting to silently snap his fingers and rock back and forth in his chair. He figured he had about ten more minutes. Why did he let Jenny talk him into taking over this case?

"I like to walk. I'm good at cleaning up. Sweeping. I really like AVP. I can draw. I do my laundry."

"Wait. You did AVP? Really? When?" Peter turned and started scanning the file. There wasn't anything in it. AVP – the Alternatives to Violence Project. A series of workshops run by volunteers that sometimes did more than the CSC programs, if Peter was honest.

"Yup. Last year. I still have my certificate." Peter felt relief. Perhaps there was a spot for Rick after all.

"Can you get it for me? Bring it down to me? I have an idea," Peter said. "How'd you like to go live in a halfway house where there are lots of AVP folks? Where there are horses, and cats, and gardens, and books and everything. You can sweep and wash laundry and stuff for them, and they will work with you to figure out your next steps. It's in the woods, and there is a creek, what do you think?"

"I don't like horses." And that was that. Peter had seen one quick flash of terror cross Ricky's face, and then complete shutdown, more rocking. There would be no more conversation today, Peter grasped, but at least he had a plan.

Once more in his file cabinet, and Peter pulled out a piece of paper with some photocopied pictures of *Just Living* on it to give Rick. He was feeling better; he'd call Nora and see if there were any spots open and if she would take one more high-needs client. He knew they'd figure out how to get enough support to make it work. Ricky was a short stay; he only needed a place until the fall, and by then his community Parole Officer could find him a group home.

"Here, Rick. You don't have to go anywhere near the horses if you don't want. They have cats and small dogs that need help. And lots of AVPers are there. Just think about it. And bring me your certificate. Have a good New Years, okay?"

Ricky shuffled out the door with the paper in his hand, and headed back to his cell, keeping his head down and lurking along the walls. Three young punks were playing cards around a table nearby.

"Do you see the freak? I hear he screwed Bobby," one whispered loudly to another.

"Nah. I hear he did his mama," another answered.

"I think I'll visit him tonight, let him know we don't like rats," the third piped in.

Peter saw Ricky cringe, his shoulders rising in his big coat. He hugged the wall as he walked by the men.

Peter reacted, even though he knew it would only make a difference for a moment. Maybe even make it worse later.

"Enough," he called out, and the men looked up, startled. "Don't you have somewhere you guys need to be? Jeez, it's the holidays. Lighten up."

Some days, Peter felt like a Vice Principal in a giant cesspool of troubled teens-gone-bad. He headed back into his office, shaking his head.

He wondered if Rick had really done AVP, and whether he'd be able to find the proof anytime soon. Hell, Rick was so afraid of horses he might be flushing his certificate right now. Peter would make a few phone calls and see what he could find out before he started the paperwork outlining his recommendations. Nothing was ever simple in this game, but maybe he'd just found the clue to move this guy off his pile of cases.

CHAPTER 11
AN INTRIGUING TOUR GUIDE

The next Tuesday I got to the Skytrain station early, and then realized I didn't even know what kind of car to look for. I was both exhausted (little sleep) and excited (little sleep). I hadn't planned well. I wasn't sure exactly where Ben was picking me up.

Imagine my happiness when a few minutes later a guy stuck his head out of an older white Corolla and called me over.

Well, dear sweet Jesus, would you look at that. That man is definitely a gift from heaven. Be still, my beating heart. Prayer?

"Are you Beth?" Well, that works out...better than I imagined. The quintessentially practical car -- that fit with Dr. Neufeld's description of Ben. He hadn't mentioned that Ben was a ringer for a young Russell Crowe. If I tilted my head just right.

We were headed out to *Just Living*, where I was going to do my practicum. Dr. Neufeld wanted me to check it out before I completely committed, but I knew what I wanted; this felt right. I was excited that I was getting to see it; didn't know what to expect, and had a lot to learn. Ben had offered to be my tour guide, so I climbed into the car.

"You've got picture ID on you, right Beth?" he asked. "I hope Aaron mentioned that you need it today. And, you'll have to leave everything locked in the car. I brought a blank notebook for you."

I looked over at Ben, and thought, "Duh. Do you think I don't listen?" but this was quickly crowded out by, "Dang, he *is* cute." And then, "That's awkward. A priest." Luckily, and unusually, the thoughts stayed inside my head.

"Thank you, I've got it," I said. And even to me my tone sounded a little snide. Not that it seemed to register; Ben was still smiling at me.

I'm a total amateur about "inside," except what Dr. Neufeld told me. "Nothing in. Nothing out. It's that simple." Because the site is about 100km from Vancouver, I'm actually going to move into the dorm for a few months. Which does strike me as kinda mad – a woman in a dorm full of male ex-prisoners. So clearly I *do* have a lot to learn.

That's one reason I'm going out to see the place today. I suspect the other is so that they can see if I'm a total dud. The plan is that Nora, the Executive Director, will give me the list of contraband items to help me when I pack for next week. I've been moving slug-style for months, and now things are travelling at the speed of light. As Ben pulled away from the curb into traffic, I noticed the sweet aroma of coffee and chocolate in the car. *Thank God.* Prayer. God really does answer them. Grin.

"I bought us mocha for the road, kind of to celebrate our marvelous adventure. I didn't have a ring, so I brought coffee instead," Ben said, and I grinned at what I hoped was a LOTR epic metaphor. Otherwise things had just gotten really weird.

"I hope we get there in good time," he said. I smiled, and glanced at him sideways across the car. I reached into my bag in the back and brought out a few scones I had baked that morning, offering one. He put down his coffee in the console, changed lanes quickly, and then took the currant scone.

"I also brought something to mark the occasion," I said, hoping I didn't sound foolish. "I hope it satisfies as much as elevenses. I made them myself," I bragged. Ben took a big bite, and groaned. He looked over at me, and judging by his grin back, I had nailed the reference. Or the baking. Maybe both.

I was glad I'd thought to bring something. I wrapped my hands around my precious mocha, and blew gently on the foamy cream. It smelled delicious, and far more decadent than my student budget usually allowed. I think I thanked him again. Maybe twice.

While Ben drove in and out of traffic I took a moment to notice that he was younger than I had imagined. Dark hair curling over his denim shirt and green sweater; I realized he wasn't wearing a priest's collar. Maybe he wasn't a priest. Why did I think he was? Because he was a Catholic chaplain? Were they all priests?

It was confusing, knowing a little about someone, but not really knowing what you don't know. His jeans were newish, and clean, and his shoes looked like a cross between hiking boots and runners. Yes, I can take in the view quickly and covertly when needed. He looked over at me, and thought I might have been caught appreciating the view. Again, he didn't seem to notice. I smiled.

Before long, the miles were speeding underneath us and we were chatting about nothing in particular. Soon, our conversation devolved -- or maybe evolved – into an analysis of how a courtroom mimics a traditional church. "God the omnipotent judge," definitely an old man, sitting high on a throne in the clouds, definitely respect being paid, lots of judgment and fear...only priestly-experts, or maybe angels, allowed to talk to him, approach him...the priestly or apostolic authority. It was creepy.

"But that's everything I can't stand about the church!" Oversharing, Beth.

"I mean, those are the things that don't work for me," I edited.

"Yeah, some of the traditions are uncomfortable for contemporary students," Ben said. "It's why people are leaving the church in droves, I suppose. Finding what's meaningful in tradition can be challenging."

I couldn't tell if he agreed with me or not, so I decided to shut up. But I didn't stop thinking about it. What was I getting into? Frying pans and fires came to mind….

What the heck? Maybe I wasn't cut out for this work after all. I just wanted to hang out and be useful. Maybe, oh I don't know, seek the elusive Meaningful Life? He switched gears as we turned off the highway, heading into the thick forest. *Thank God.* Prayer.

"*Just Living's* on thirty acres of leased municipal land. They have a couple of operations they coordinate from here. See the signs for the animal shelter up there? This is Mission's shelter, for strays."

We passed a couple of buildings with large outdoor runs. There were six or eight dogs barking their brains out (clearly we were intruders), and some chillaxing under the trees. The runs were really big, fenced, in the forest. Ben explained that the other building housed the cats. We didn't even get out of the car. Ben pulled around the driveway and we headed out. I was to consider myself oriented, I guess.

"A Humane Society runs the facility for the District of Mission, and *Just Living* supports it with staff, land, whatever is needed. The men keep up the buildings, and look after the place after hours. They even bathe and walk the animals, and do night feedings for the really young ones. It's all intertwined," he said. I tried to picture a scary biker dude feeding a premature kitten, and realized my imagination didn't stretch quite that far.

We headed left, towards the bears. A little ways further along was a sign for "Phoenix Horse Rescue," and Ben pulled over.

"Is this is another project of *Just Living?*" I asked, wondering how to appear interested; I was way more curious about the halfway house, and wondered when we'd get there.

"Do you know what therapeutic riding is?" Ben asked.

"I think so. They teach riding to kids with disabilities, right?"

"Yup. There's one down the road a few miles that works with people with all kinds of disabilities, and the classes are integrated with local kids who want lessons who aren't 'disabled.' Shalom Riding Academy." I swear he used air quotes, and it was cute.

"Most of the horses there are rescued, or donated. A couple are on loan, for the cost of boarding. Anyhow, they came to *Just Living* a couple of years ago and asked for help with horses that need rehab before they can even be assessed for therapeutic work. *Just Living* built a barn – just seven stalls with paddocks – and they rehab the horses until they can move up the road with the others. Some of the horses that come in are a real mess, so Phoenix keeps one or two healthy horses to be with them. Do you want to check it out?" Ben parked beside the barn and got out, and I knew the question was rhetorical.

He grabbed a paper bag from the back seat, and we headed into the stable. I could hear nickering in a nearby stall, and a big ass beige and brown horse stuck his head over the door to his stall, enormous doe eyes staring at Ben. I didn't want to admit how far out of my comfort zone I was. It had been years since I'd been near horses, and all I could remember was that these beasts bite, right?

"Hey boy. How are you doing?" The beautiful beast bobbed his head, rubbing his chin on the door. Ben scratched him under his ear. "This is Thud, Beth. Come and say hi."

I reached out my hand for the requisite sniff, and wanted to scratch his forehead. I would have had to reach up, but thankfully he lowered his head. Clearly he was a softy. A brown horse in the next stall began to chuff, wanting some attention, too.

"Settle down, Tex. You're next. Jealous boy." Ben was crooning, and I felt like I was intruding. I did wonder what that crooning would be like directed at a woman, though. And not just any woman.

Thud nuzzled Ben's chest, and Ben pulled a bundle of carrots out of a paper sack. He extracted one for Thud, then meandered down the middle of the aisle, sharing carrots and scratches with all the horses. I know, because I appreciated the view from behind. Four horses leaned out for treats, and at the last stall there was some stomping but no nose.

"It's okay, girl. I won't hurt you," he said, his voice calm and soothing. He tossed a couple of carrots in her manger. "Boy, she is still really thin." I peered into the poorly lit stall, and saw a small, dull brown horse. She *was* thin, and her coat was broken by scars and sores.

"She was rescued about a week ago. Neglected, on her own too much, and she's pretty shy still. She's starting to warm to some of the horses. They can't leave her in the pasture because she gorges. She'll be okay with some loving, and she'll get plenty of that around here."

I wasn't sure if Ben was referring to loving from people or horses, but I guessed either would help.

The back doors of the stable opened and a couple of guys came in, stomping their boots. They seemed a bit startled that the lights were already on, but one of them smiled when they saw Ben.

"Hey, you're a bit early!" Ben introduced us; Tom wasn't tall, but he wasn't small either. Clearly throwing hay or shoving horses built some fine muscle. Paul, on the other hand, was tall, lanky, and hid in his big jacket. I don't think they smiled for anyone.

Tom shrugged off his dusty jacket, tossing it over a hook. Paul kept his on. For some reason, he seemed really familiar to me. I almost asked him if he worked at the University, but he didn't look like the student set, and he definitely wasn't an academic.

"Tom looks after the grounds here, and helps with the horses." Ben turned towards Tom. "Beth is thinking about doing a practicum here, starting next month," he explained. "Paul helps out around the grounds, a 'Paul of all trades.'" I bobbed my head, looking stupid, I'm sure. Paul's eyes were drilling into me. He grunted at me, but shook my hand. I still couldn't shake the idea that I'd met him.

"I'd better get everyone out to pasture or we'll be late," he said. As he turned away, I swear he snorted. He didn't seem very excited about my arrival.

"Do you want help, or should we just get out of your way?" Ben asked.

"Just let your boy out on the way by," Tom called. He glanced into the mare's stall. "She's eating the carrots," he added. We headed for the far door, and as Thud went past us, he gently rubbed against me.

"Don't let him lean into you. He'll end up knocking the kids over," Tom called out. Ben shoved Thud, and the gelding just kept on plodding towards the open door and the pasture beyond. He nickered at the mare as he passed by her stall, and she raised her head.

We shut the door tight behind us and headed back to the car. In a few minutes we had backtracked to the main road, and Ben turned right at the lake, heading further away from the highway. Before I knew it, we headed up a driveway and into the bush. It was unmarked, and unremarkable, really. "We're here," he announced. And we were.

Hey God, make sure those bears stay busy in the woods far away, okay? Feel free to move this human in a little closer, though....

CHAPTER 12
WELCOME TO JUST LIVING

Oh, Dear Clarity, where am I? This is nothing like I imagined when I thought I'd be working in the Downtown East Side. What am I doing here?

The sign was solid, wooden, and noticing it jerked my thoughts from Thud, and bears. It was grand – a carved scene, painted in black and red with some yellow. Ben and I started up the path and into the building, and he stopped, pointing to a larger building off to the left.

"That's the Lodge – the dorm where you'll be staying, They can house up to 30 folks here, but it's usually about 20, plus staff," he said. "Lots of them leave every morning for work and are kind of scarce - you won't see them much." I smiled.

The lodge had an upper balcony and a porch on the ground floor with a small dock that extended into a large pond. I saw a creek coming from behind the Lodge that fed the pond, which fed the creek under the bridge we'd driven over. So the pond was made of ditch water. We live in a weird place here on the West Coast. I noticed a small hand-painted sign by the pond. "The Puddle," it declared, and I laughed.

The setting was gorgeous, snowdrops poking out of the rich loam. January in Lotus Land. Behind the dorm, I could see tall cedar trees dripping with moss and the mountain rose behind. I could hear a waterfall from somewhere above, and hoped I'd get a chance to explore. I *would* be allowed to come and go, right?

"And the building joining the office to the Lodge is the kitchen," Ben continued. They fit together like Lincoln logs complete with green steel roofs, the ubiquitous wet-coast covered walkways connecting buildings. Ben turned and pointed to our right, to a building way off in the distance through the trees.

"That's the animal shelter we passed," he said, "and the stables are behind these." He held the door for me. Inside, the room was magnificent, and I was gobsmacked by the view; the rear wall was nearly two storeys of glass overlooking fields and gardens. In the background were the pastures, where the horses grazed, and a tipi. While this wasn't exactly Oz, it also wasn't my idea of prison, and I was trying to reconcile appropriate suffering with the amazing pastoral view. What did I expect? Not this, for sure.

"We made it, Nora," Ben called into the office. From above I heard a gravelly voice, and I recognized I was standing under a loft.

"Hey Ben! Good to see you. About time you got here – just in time to miss morning chores."

"Hey Sohan! Good to see you! Hope you got those morning chores done in good time! I bet I've been up longer than you, though." I was still taking in the leather couches, colourful quilts, and the kitchenette behind me.

"Come on down and meet Beth," Ben called up. Sohan came bouncing down the stairs, but my attention was drawn to Nora -- slight, with a long braid of salt and pepper hair. Her simple jumper fell to just below her knees, and a colourful sweater was draped over her shoulders. Her smile radiated, as she reached out to shake my hand.

"Slow down Sohan! Ben's going to be here all day!" she called out. Ben grabbed Sohan and enveloped him in a big hug, knocking him gently with his shoulder. Guy stuff. I shook Nora's hand and smiled.

"Beth Hill, meet Nora Edwards. Nora, Beth. And this is Sohan." Ben looked after the introductions, and then stepped back.

"I'm so glad you made it! In time to join our circle this morning!" Nora grabbed Ben in a big hug, and I felt a little out of touch both literally and figuratively. There was an awful lot of full body pressing going on, which was not what I expected in a halfway house. With just a little flash of envy, I realized I wouldn't avoid a man-hug from Ben.

"Please, come in and sit. I have a couple of minutes before circle; you guys must have either left at first light, or made good time," she added.

"A little of both," Ben answered. "I feel like we've already been up for half the day, but the company was good," he said, smiling at me. I kinda blushed. We sat down on the couches, and my real orientation began.

"Nora's the one who has the answer to questions you might have. I don't know how she does it," Ben said. Nora smiled, looking at her hands.

"We all work hard," she answered, and looked right at me. "I hope you're ready for that. Everyone here works, and I hope your experience here will be rich, but it won't be easy." Prophetic words, those. She smiled, while she was welcoming, but I knew I couldn't take too much of her time.

"You can come talk to me any time, but you might have to get in line. We try to keep work to work hours, but it's not really nine-to-five… living here has benefits, *and* can take it out of you," she explained. "Feel free to ask questions, especially at the beginning. Truth be told, almost anyone can answer almost anything," she said, smiling.

"Or she's not doing her job right," Sohan piped up from across the room. I was a bit stunned; I'd assumed he was a resident, but now I wasn't so sure. That seemed a little close to insubordination to me.

"You are welcome here, Beth. And Sohan's right."

I felt like I had to say something, so I smiled and said, "I hope that I can be of some help here, even with my little experience. I'm willing to do just about anything…." My voice tapered off. Damn. SO not confident.

"She bakes a mean scone," Ben followed, and I smiled at him.

"Oh, we'll find something useful for you to do…no worries. Everyone starts off in the kitchen, so let's go meet Cook." Out the window, I could see Tom approaching.

"The men are starting to come in for circle; we'll just have time to say hi to Cook and see the kitchen. We can head out to the Sanctuary from there."

She pointed at the round building nestled in the grass between the office and a white three-rail fence. There was an older Aboriginal fellow opening the doors and windows, setting out a small rug.

As we headed out, Ben told me about building the Sanctuary. "The men helped do everything, raise the roof, lay the hardwood floors – just wait until you see the amazing job they did. It's become like a healing centre for this place…all the circles are held there," he said.

"Not all," Nora corrected. "The Native Brotherhood often holds circle in the tipi, and sometimes we still meet in the field, or in the forest. It's wonderful to have that space, though. There are fewer soggy, uncomfortable circles, I can tell you!" I noticed Ben was beaming at her. Sigh.

We walked through the breezeway into a darkened dining room. The chairs hung on pegs in two rows along one wall, in the old Shaker style. It was like conservative clashing with liberal; hugs and hanging chairs. A narrow wooden table, large enough to seat 25 or 30 people, ran down the middle of the room, and built-in cabinets on one wall held dishes, a coffee pot and hot plates.

On one wall was a plaque that said:

> *Just Living* is a home, a community and a way of life.
> At *Just Living* we ask:
> Is it just?
> Is it safe?
> Is it compassionate?
> Is it honest?
> Is it responsible?
> We support people to make meaningful change,

be accountable as their best selves,
and live together with dignity in the aftermath of crime and tragedy.
We are *Just Living*.

Wow. That's profound. I thought about how comfortable Nana Beth would have been here. We headed through the far doorway into the cooking area.

"This is Cook's domain, Beth. And you'd better be afraid of him," Nora said, with a twinkle in her eye. "He rules us with an iron fist. Cook, meet Beth, our new practicum student. She's almost a Priest, so show her some respect."

A giant in white rose from behind the stove, putting a cookie sheet on the grill to cool. He took off his oven mitt, and extended his hand. My heart pounded as I faced one of the largest men I had ever seen. He wasn't tall, perhaps six feet, but he was thick and strong, and his hand consumed mine. Cook was bald, and from his non-neck down, every piece of visible skin was covered with blue tattoos. I was flummoxed. How do I get my hand back? Do I look? Not look? If I don't look at the ink, where do I look?

A quick scan of his meaty arms told me that not one of the pictures was recognizable; perhaps a banner over a heart, a few letters. Not exactly works of art, they made a statement. He looked to be between 50 and 60, and as he released my hand and ducked his head in a quick nod with a "pleased to meet you, Beth," I saw that this mountain of a man was shy. He nodded at Ben, cracking a full smile, and I wondered if anyone here would ever look that happy to see me.

The smells of gingerbread and something simmering on the stove were divine; this was a kitchen that fed people's bodies and souls, and it reminded me again of Nana's; the smells and the feelings were the same. The space was bright, and clean, the worn appliances shining. There were large pots on the stove, and tools were hanging on hooks on the walls, outlined in black felt marker. I noticed some large knives in a block, and felt a little dis-ease. I hoped there were no knife-wielding slashers in residence, and had a quick realization that I had never thought about how many dangerous things are around me every day.

I decided to break the ice.

"Mmm…ginger. Cinnamon. Just a hint of nutmeg. Freshly ground, I think," I guessed, glancing sideways at Cook. He smiled at me.

"Good nose," he said. "Just some snaps I baked up for after circle." He took a step back, and grabbed a spatula to loosen the freshly baked cookies. "You guys must have been up for hours to get here. Do you want to sneak one now?" he asked, and Ben extended his hand. I took a cookie too, and it melted in my mouth.

"MMMMmmm…this is fabulous. I hope I learn how to make these," I said, and Cook smiled.

"You'll be coming soon, right?" Nora asked as we left Cook and the kitchen. It wasn't really a question, and Cook laughed as we headed past a small table and chairs and out the French doors into the backyard.

"Oh yeah, just turnin' down the stove and pullin' out the snaps," he said. "I'll be there in a jiffy. May need help with the lunch prep later," he said, looking at me.

"No doubt! We can help," Ben offered. "No one around here dares miss Morning Circle, unless they are dying or in court," he explained to me. "Even I try to make it out on the days I volunteer."

"Well, that way we each only need to say things once, and everyone knows everything," Nora explained. "And, we can touch base with one another, find out how we are doing."

As we headed across the lawn towards the building, Nora slowed.

"Let me tell you a bit about this place," she began. "*Just Living* started about six years ago," Nora continued, "as a more holistic way of integrating federally-sentenced prisoners into community."

I could tell she was telling a story she had told many times, and I was surprisingly interested.

"A part of it was wanting to live in intentional community, governed by common principles. Over a couple of years, we built ideas. We discarded as many as we adopted, and finally, with a ton of hard work, some hurt feelings, and almost as many healed, we came up with a plan CSC approved of in principle, and the fundraising started.

"We partner with CSC and the Justice Department, Aboriginal Elders and some local reserves, some faith communities, the artists in Mission… others." Nora was ticking off partners on her fingers. "The Municipality, Social Services. We agreed to expand our residents to include men who are difficult to work with – the brain injured, sex offenders, some with physical disabilities, and we built our team."

Wonderful. I'd be staying with the clearly demented, and broken sex-offenders. I hope I only squirmed a little.

"We needed more than government funding, both to build, and to give us the autonomy we thought was important. We needed to know that we could continue to exist without government support if it was ever pulled.

"A log-home builder in town, together with a crew from the prison, helped us build as we had the money. The company has been loyal, and some of the guys who were trained by building these buildings still work with them, building log structures all over BC.

"They started by building that one," she said, pointing to the office building, "then that one," pointing to the Lodge. "We lived in those two buildings for a couple of years. Then the stables and kennels were built to give us with a secondary income, and then the kitchen came next. Believe it or not, until about a year and a half ago, Cook fed us all out of the small office kitchen," Nora said, shaking her head in disbelief. So the kitchenette wasn't a luxury.

"Then last spring the funds came to build this healing space." She pointed to the Sanctuary. "We didn't expect to be able to afford it for years, but some of the first facilitators in Canada gave us a gift. We've been enjoying the space for about six months. We even offer workshops to the community from there – I'm working on making this more of a community shared-space. Who knows what's next? Maybe a garage so we can repair vehicles and do some training for mechanics," Nora said.

"Or an arena so the men can ride," Ben chimed in. Nora visibly snorted.

"No money in horses, Ben; we have to get these men jobs," and I could tell this wasn't a new conversation.

"Well, that's the tour," Nora said to Ben. And she smiled at him again. Hmmm. "It's turned out to be more than we could have imagined." Now she sounded like a brochure. "If I had known how hard it would be, I don't know if I would have taken it on. But now I don't know anywhere I'd rather be." Her face was glowing, even under the grey skies. My skin prickled hearing Nora talk about living her dream. I recognized a "meaningful life," and was more than a little envious, at least of the clarity, if not the life. Nora headed off to talk to others, and Ben and I kept walking slowly towards the Sanctuary.

I looked around. Fruit trees, well pruned and sleeping for winter, dotted the grass around the buildings. A large vegetable garden was just beyond the picnic table, and beyond that the white, three-rail fence separated the lawn from the pasture. Behind us, near the Lodge, was a large tipi, the skeleton of a sweat lodge low to the ground, and a large stone fire ring.

Tom and another Aboriginal fellow were welcoming people into the building with burning sage. As we approached the doorway, Ben introduced us.

"Al, meet Beth. She'll be moving in in the next few weeks. Beth, meet Al. He's a Spiritual Advisor from the Native Brotherhood."

Al nodded without even looking at me. I was glad that I knew how to smudge, that my eyes didn't sting from the sage as I wafted it over my face, my ears, my eyes and heart, reminding me to stay focused and kind. I followed Ben into the building and sat beside him on a cushion on the floor. There were people on chairs, others on blankets or cushions. I sat listening to the birds, the waterfalls, the horses and dogs in the distance, and waited.

The colours danced into the round room through stained glass windows that circled the walls near the ceiling. The triangular skylights drew my eyes upwards towards the sky, and I imagined that even on a cloudy day the canvas of light and shadow would lure anyone. In the centre, on a cloth on the floor, were stones, a feather, and an abalone shell with more sage. A bowl of water and a candle were juxtaposed across from one another and I was reminded of the candles and holy water on the altar at Dad's church. I think I counted sixteen of us in the circle, mostly men, and many of them First Nations. My eyes skipped over them, not really seeing. I felt safe, like in Dr. Neufeld's office. And waited. Still waited.

"Speak! Dear God!" *I shouted. Beseeched? In an inside voice. Thank God.* Prayer.

And a few moments later, it was answered. And I thought of the study I was doing with Dr. Neufeld on prayer.

Adoration: noun.

1. The act of paying honour, as to a Divine Being; worship.

2. Reverent homage.

3. Fervent and devoted love.

That's what I feel in this place. This is the embodiment of the prayer of Adoration. Glory be, I thought as I entered into the Sacred.

As I sat in awe, I realized that for once I wasn't begging for something in my prayers.

CHAPTER 13
THE ANNIVERSARY

Kenny turned the outdoor tap until the cold water started to rinse the rich loam from his hands. He grabbed the brush from the shelf and scrubbed his nails, then cupped his hands and splashed water on his face, leaning over so his clothes avoided all but a few drops. He ran his clean, wet fingers through his unruly light brown curls, and smiled, thinking about the pile of rotting leaves he had moved as the sun rose.

Nora had given Kenny permission to trip the alarm, aware of what today meant for him. They'd known he wouldn't sleep last night, and he'd need his hands in dirt. He called today The Anniversary, although anyone who's done time knows there are many anniversaries, and all of them affect you, even when you pretend they don't. The anniversary of that event that brought you to prison. Of your trial. Your sentencing. Sometimes your arrest. The day your family stopped visiting. The first time no one remembered your birthday. Perhaps the day your Dad died, and you didn't get to go to the funeral. It was weird, though, when they "doubled up" like today. Today was the anniversary of Kenny's crime. And ten years later, the death of his lover.

Fifteen years ago today, Kenny got caught holding up a convenience store in the posh suburb of West Vancouver when a fellow he was with shot the clerk in the arm. That part definitely hadn't been planned, and Kenny had hesitated long enough during their escape to toss the clerk some clean cloths. His buddy had left in the car without him, and although Kenny could run fast, he couldn't outrun the dogs. They never found the gun, and assumed Kenny had ditched it. He gladly did the time for his buddy, rather than rat him out and get killed for it. Funny that. Since that day, Kenny had been clean and sober. Another anniversary.

Then, five years ago, Kenny's lover and best friend, Carl, had been killed inside Matsqui Prison...while he watched and did nothing. Not a shining moment, he thought, but at least he was still alive.

It had been risky, getting close to Carl. All the old timers warned against it; when you start to care, you're vulnerable. To the uniforms, to the system, to the other guys. The people who work for Corrections don't care about friendships, or lovers; they only care about security, keeping the prison calm, and controlling everything as much as possible.

Guys would share a table at breakfast, call "See you at lunch" as they headed to work, and then be whisked off to another institution before mid-morning count. Their stuff was tossed into boxes or garbage bags by staff (and sometimes borrowed stuff too, causing all kinds of troublesome debts), and shipped while they ate, unaware. Their security level might have changed (Your girlfriend dumped you? You might be at risk of hurting yourself, or someone else...Your father died? You might be flight risk if they think you want to exact revenge. Or get out to help your mom. Or go to his funeral. Someone coming into the institution you don't get along with? Best to move you along to another prison.) Or you might have pissed off your boss. It could take weeks to find out what had happened, to challenge the decision through grievance procedures, and maybe have it changed. By then, you usually didn't care, as long as your paper record didn't reflect badly and you weren't farther away from your outside supports.

Kenny knew his connection to Carl had been once-in-a-lifetime; Carl was someone he could love forever. Unfortunately, Carl had run up lots of debt because of a little habit he'd picked up inside. He had been getting better, using less since he and Kenny had hooked up, and had promised to stop chasing the dragon…but not soon enough. The debt accumulated, and lending stopped. Carl didn't have anything of value to sell, but he was working on a beautiful carved mirror for another guy, a gift for his daughter's sixteenth birthday. They hoped his payment would be enough, soon enough. Then his debts doubled through "compounded interest," and the lenders leaned on him to do favours.

Kenny wished he'd had the money to offer his gentle lover, but he didn't. Making less than $5.00 a day, buying personal items like shampoo and shaving gear, the odd snack from the canteen, sending a little out to his sister didn't leave any to share, and he didn't have any outside money to add to his earnings. His savings had been used up paying legal fees.

Carl, desperate, had asked his buddy for an advance on the mirror, for "materials," he said, but everyone knew he'd feed the burning instead of paying his debt or buying materials, and his lenders didn't like that. So Carl had done what he had to do, and sent a kite to let staff know he wasn't safe…but again, not soon enough. Five years ago today, they'd cornered Carl in a stairwell, maybe for debts, maybe for ratting, and Kenny'd had to act like it didn't matter. It wouldn't help to let those bastards know he gave a damn what they did.

The only people who knew about Carl were Nora and Frank; Frank because he cared, and Nora because Frank had to tell her, to keep an eye on him during The Anniversary. No one else could know, and really, when he thought about it, Kenny was glad. He didn't need anyone's pity, and Frank and Nora weren't likely to give him any.

Kenny glanced at the watch hanging from his belt loop, grateful for a few minutes. He took some time to talk to Carl, send up a prayer. Last week, he'd realized how glad he was that they'd had six months together, that they'd found each other. A bit of a miracle, all things considered.

Kenny had been gay forever...he'd known it and anyone who knew him knew it, too. His Mom still joked about having three children; a son, a daughter, and Kenny. He'd never cared whether his playmates were girls or boys, but he'd always been clear; he only dated boys. His family was supportive, his Mom grateful that he was born at a time when "gay" didn't mean "ostracized." Or worse. He'd never even considered a closet, until the day he was remanded to custody.

Then, no one knew his fantasies were of being touched by a hard body, kissed by rough cheeks. He figured out in remand how much he *did* know about hiding his sexuality from years of watching his friends. He and Carl used to joke about how if only they weren't in prison, they could really enjoy the uninterrupted daily view. The other prisoners assumed they were "institutionally adjusted," enjoying sex with each other because there were few other options. It was a secret Kenny had kept until he'd gone to that AVP workshop, and found a small group who accepted him, and helped him stay safe.

By and large, his sexuality was a non-issue, and he didn't want another relationship while he was doing time. It just hurt too much. That morning, he wandered over to the fence to watch the horses chasing each other around the pasture, and thought about how much Carl would have loved this place. Tom waved good morning, and he smiled, and waved back. Paul barely grunted on his way by.

Carl hadn't been around for the plants...the day Kenny'd started caring for plants was the day he'd started to thaw...it was healthy. You couldn't really get attached to something that was literally rooted in one place, and besides, he was good at it. They had saved him, and he was grateful...they sensed his devotion, and flourished.

And now his body was waking up in all kinds of unexpected ways. Maybe five years was long enough to mourn, and besides, he was on day parole now, with weekend passes and everything. In another year, he'd be on stat release, then warrant-expiry, and he'd be an almost-free man...as free as any ex-con. He'd think about it; maybe it was time. Kenny turned and headed for the Sanctuary, passing Nora, Ben, and a young woman on the way. It was good to start the day in circle…he hoped he'd always be able to.

Start the day in circle, end the day in circle, and know who to call if you get in trouble in between…that had been his mantra since he arrived at *Just Living*, and it was working. He wasn't stupid, though. He knew there weren't too many places like this out there…he'd never heard of another one. A little voice in his head wondered what would happen when he was released.

Kenny approached the door to the Sanctuary, stopping to smudge. The ritual was as familiar as his morning shower, or weeding the flowerbed under Nora's office window. He took a place on a blanket on the floor, careful to make sure the dirt from his jeans wasn't tracked around. Shoes were left outside. A familiar calm came over Kenny, and he started his Gratitude list in his head.

CHAPTER 14
A CALLING?

In the midst of the silence some men began to sing and drum. We rose to our feet in honour. Their drums and resonating voices invited us to sway, and I felt the heartbeat as the song rose and fell. *It was loud. Intrusive. And fucking glorious.* Prayer.

I could hardly breathe, between here and there, then and now. Fucking glorious does that to me. I didn't want it to end, the perfect calm within heated voices, a language I didn't know. I closed my eyes and listened deeply, easily. I had a sense of home unlike I'd felt for ages.

Soon it quieted, and then silence — a calm, expectant waiting. Folks started to stir, shuffle into quiet again. Ben sat, so I did too. After a few minutes, Nora picked up the feather, and handed it to a guy on a blanket.

"Today Kenny can start us off in a good way. We welcome Beth to the circle this morning. She'll be moving in next week for three or four months," she shared.

Kenny sported clean jeans and a very-white T-shirt; his eyes were calm, his face relaxed. He brushed little bits of dirt from his clothes, collecting them in a pile on the corner of the blanket, but even that was calm, reflexive. Then he welcomed everyone with a deep, resonating voice. And later, he gave me permission to share his words.

"Thank you for the feather, Creator. It's taught me so much about trust and patience. Thank you for the wonderful song to honour our Ancestors who join us today. Thank you for this morning, for the weeds that I pulled and the many more to go. Thank you Ben, for bringing Beth, and for everyone else here." He paused, looking up. "I hope I'm open to learning from what they share, and staying present when they speak. May I learn patience as I wait for the feather, and be curious when I don't understand." Another deep breath or two followed.

"Today is a hard day for me, Creator. Thank you for putting me here, where it's okay to have hard days."

Then he passed the feather to his left, to the next place on the wheel, and one by one, everyone shared. It was strange, not at all what I'd expected. I was feeling calm, not edgy from being in a halfway house. Once again a theme of "Oh, how little I know" showed up.

Some folks talked for a while; others hardly at all. Everyone introduced themselves, shared a little about their plans for the day. Part way around I realized I had no idea who were workers and who were inmates. Well, not entirely true. Some were obviously inmates. The women obviously worked there. But some I couldn't figure out, and that was more than a little disconcerting. I kept wondering, "Well, what did you expect? Forehead tattoos? Do I know people who've been in this type of circle?" Which led to the thought "Holy S*%t girl, will you stay present?" I wasn't even approaching "skilled" with this circle stuff. So much for spiritual.

I was jarred when the feather came around to Paul, and I knew where I'd seen him before; he'd been at the front desk at the Remand Centre. And WTF? There was a guy beside him I recognized. He introduced himself as Frank. A part of me was relieved to figure it out, but I hoped they didn't recognize me. Imagine….

"You look familiar! Oh! Aren't you the UBC chaplain I saw at the cells downtown?" So not ready to come clean. If ever. Not exactly the "me" I wanted them to know. Ends. Means. Debates. Integrity. So fucking confusing.

When the feather reached Ben, he spoke and I got busy editing what I might share, while trying to focus.

"Good morning," he began, with a smile. He looked around. "I'm glad to be here, to be doing this. For the past bit, my work has been… empty, hard, like I don't know why I'm in the prison. I know I'm not… effective, not doing anything important in the big picture. This month, I remembered why I'm working where I am. Now I hear Spirit speaking, in spite of "the system" and CSC. And that even when I'm a really small pawn, sometimes I'm a good one. Having the chance to work with Beth and you all will be good for me. It felt good this morning to know I am doing the right thing, to come here, and see my boy, and get to be in circle, spend the day. Thank you everyone. Thank you God." He glanced over at me, and smiled, then looked up to the sky.

"I don't know where this path will lead Beth, but it feels important, so I'm glad to honour it." And then he handed me the feather. My heart raced, and he looked at me. Really looked. All I could hear was the not-speaking, and without even realizing it my pounding heart helped me find words. Silence, and my presence deepened; I could feel the caring coming my way across the circle, urging me to calm. I opened my mouth, honestly not sure what would come out. A squeak, maybe.

"Wow. Thank you all for letting me be here and thank you to Dr. Neufeld and Ben and Nora." I looked around the circle. "Well, for all of you, really, for giving me this chance. I hope I can help out…make a difference. I never really thought about prison, and justice, before last month, but now it's all I think about. I don't know what I expected, but it sure wasn't this." I heard snickers of laughter. "Everyone has been amazing. I hope I get to know you all." I felt like an idiot, so I just passed the feather to the next person. Then I realized I couldn't even name everyone in the circle. *God, I have to get better at this!* Another prayer, BTW.

People shared about anticipated visits, anxiety about a job interview, happiness at a letter received, a call from a child after a long silence. Some men were going to leave the site during the day to work elsewhere. I wondered about the stories behind the faces, and if I might get to know some of them. *How do you ask for a story?*

After everyone had shared, the circle ended with silence, everyone on their feet, joining hands. The Roster, a quick list of where everyone would be, what chores were to be tackled, meetings, visits, everything was read. Cook shared plans for the weekend, and what today's meals would be. We ended the circle with a short prayer.

Ben and I headed out for a quick stroll, and ended up on the dock. I was surprised when tears threatened.

"You okay?" Ben asked, offering a clean handkerchief.

"I'm fine." My answer was undercut by a tremble. Damn. I wiped my eyes. "I just didn't want it to end." We sat down at the end of the dock, and I kicked off my shoes and socks, and rolled up the bottoms of my jeans. When I dangled my feet in the water I almost shrieked, and he chuckled.

"Yeah. Mountain fed streams. COLD in winter. Year round, come to think of it. The fish are a bit slower than usual right now." I pulled my feet out of the ice bath. My baby toes were just a little purple, right?

"What do you think?" he asked after a few minutes. I pondered. It was nice to be allowed to ponder.

"I don't know, but I think my soul is happy. Like maybe I'm meant to do this now," I said. "Or something." I shrugged. The water flowing past lulled me back to quiet.

After a few more minutes, Ben tapped me gently on the knee, and I jumped, tingling. Well, parts of me were definitely tingling. Embarrassing! I worked hard not to blush, and focused on that cold pond. And when he started talking, I knew he had no idea. None. I didn't know whether to be relieved or a little pissed off.

"It's a wonderful way to start the day. Sometimes I miss living in community, my time in the monastery."

Wait. Ben was a monk? Is a monk? Are monks priests? I think they're celibate, either way. Something else to think about. I smiled a neutral Anglican smile.

Cold water dripping on my head made me turn around. Cook laughed, offering me a drink from a not-quite-full water bottle.

"Watch those re-entries, Angel," he said, averting his eyes. How long had he been there? "You don't want to burn up." I chuckled, shaking water from my dark curls.

"Nora asked me to show you the kitchen, an' I need help with lunch, okay? She'll talk wit' you after we eat." I scrambled to get up, grabbed my shoes and socks, hopping, drying my feet as we headed inside. Then we chopped vegetables, baked, shared recipes while laughing. A lot. Also unexpected.

Lunch was chunky vegetable soup, and croissants from my Nana Beth's recipe. Ben arranged veggies and dips on a tray, and Cook laid out some cold leftover chicken. He warmed the soup, and had time to help us set tables, find ingredients, get serving trays together, and generally run the show. I think he was even doing some dinner prep.

"I swear, the first time anyone tries to help in a kitchen they are nothing but a liability. You sure are a gracious host, Cook!" I shared.

"Are you kidding? You can bake. And cook. You're helpful. Some of what passes for 'help' around here is miserable. Folks send imbeciles to the kitchen to punish 'em, an' only I suffer. You can help any time!"

People started to wander in. They lifted chairs off the wall, and were milling about the sideboard, plates in hand. People jostled, teasing each other, catching up on progress with the chores, making promises (or not) to help each other, and I recognized the sacred quiet of the circle was done. I felt a little outside the group again, until Cook let them know I'd made the croissants. Then they all wanted to be my friend.

"Hey – can these become a regular at lunch time?"

"Do you give doggie bags?"

"Something this rich has got to be sinful, right? Or at least bad for me? I knew you were an evil temptress…." Paul was smiling at me from behind his bangs. I felt just a little uncomfortable. He winked. Did he know?

"Yeah, right, Paul. Because you can't find your own trouble…only guy sent back to prison for refusing to leave a halfway house…." Ben called out, and I smiled at the chuckles around the table. That was a story to be asked for. I wondered if I'd dare.

Lunch was hearty and delicious, and the best part was that cooks didn't do clean up. Cook took a coffee to the back deck and put his feet up, and Nora called me into her office. Ben headed to the stables, and told me he'd touch base soon.

"How are you doing, Beth?" Nora began, and of course, I answered. "Fine."

She stopped rearranging the papers on her desk, and looked at me.

"How are you doing, Beth?" Hmmm. No ducking allowed.

"I'm good. Really. The circle was amazing. I love the space here. And Cook lets me bake. I just hope I can actually be a help."

"You already are. Just being here. Being you. It mixes things up in a good way for everyone."

She handed me some papers, and reminded me about the upcoming AVP workshop. Next weekend, in the medium-security prison. I was to stay at *Just Living* so I didn't have to commute. Bring food. All that stuff.

"Do I need to take anything with me? Notebooks or pens or anything?" I asked.

"No Beth. Nothing in. Nothing out. The facilitators will give you everything you need. Photo ID, and your car keys. Dress to cover yourself; loose clothes, elbows to knees covered, okay? Flaunting bodies doesn't help." She smiled at me. "I don't really think that's an issue for you, but they say it to all the volunteers, even the elderly women who visit for chapel services."

I wondered out loud who would be facilitating, and if I could be of any help.

"A volunteer, Claire, will be facilitating with three of the 'inside facilitators,' men who are trained. Ben will be there, too. Another person will join them, I'm not sure who. As for helping them, well… first you participate, then you go through quite an extensive process of learning how to lead the exercises for others.

"These guys know what they are doing. Some of them have been facilitating for decades, and they know more about group work than most people, inside or out. A part of modeling equality is that everyone starts in the same place. Show up, be open." Nora smiled and she moved away from the desk. Ouch.

"Beth, prison is a whole new culture…a different language, different cues…don't assume you know what's going on. And remember – you're safe. These men would rather die than put a volunteer at risk. Literally."

She followed that little lecture with information about being at *Just Living*, what I should pack and bring. I was glad I'd stay over during the workshop, so that I didn't have to commute when we had such long days. We decided Friday would begin my "residency."

She covered internet use. I would be allowed to use her computer from time to time, but there was no cable internet or wireless router. I asked about getting my own USB access.

"I'm not sure you will need it that often Beth. You'll want to watch your email, of course, but you can do that with your phone. If you need to download documents or something, come ask me. It just makes it easier for me to monitor."

"You'll be monitoring my Internet while I'm here?" My hackles rose. She laughed.

"No. But some of the men have restrictions as a part of their parole, and if we have fewer access points in the house it's just easier to monitor. My office – I have a stick. I take it home for Kate and me to use at night." Hmmm…Kate and Nora? Maybe I don't have to feel jealous….

"Kenny is allowed online, and he uses it to research information for his gardens. The ones who are allowed to use it don't really want it all that much – maybe because they've never had it.

"If someone asks you to use your phone, tell them you aren't allowed, and if they push, ask them if they want you to ask me. It'll just make things easier."

I flushed. Of course there were restrictions. I couldn't imagine all the stuff I didn't know. And as my mind started imagining why guys wouldn't be allowed to access the Internet, I really started creeping myself out. Who were these people?

Nora sent me back to the kitchen, and Cook took a break from dinner prep to show me my room. We climbed the rough wooden stairs at the back of the Lodge and he opened the first door in the hallway.

I grinned. The room was small, with a single bed covered in a fuzzy blue blanket. A table was pushed under the window that overlooked the garden and the Sacred Grounds. An old, comfortable chair would work for reading, or sitting at the table. A small bookshelf, and a few drawers were built into one wall. This was simple living, and it looked comfortable. A couple of reading lamps completed the décor –nineties thrift shop. I sighed.

"Perfect," I said.

I would share a small washroom with Sally, a woman who looks after the housekeeping; Cook said everyone uses a larger bathroom down the hall, but because I'm new I get privacy. I hadn't even thought about sharing showers with ex-prisoners...I suspect being female has something to do with it, and in light of the internet restrictions, I'm just fine with the arrangement.

"On a day like today, you can see the pasture out there," he said. I had a door to the balcony on the back of the building, and some Adirondack chairs were grouped around small tables.

"I'm out here most nights after supper for coffee," Cook said. "Feel free to join me. My room is on the other side of the hall. Sally is beside you. The others are doubled up further up the hallway. That bathroom you share? Keep it clean. Sally's a neat freak."

Note to self – put down the lid, and toss out my Q-tips! Interesting that we could only get to the bath from our rooms – there was no hallway door.

"This is a really nice room," I said, running my hand over the blanket, touching the table under the window. "It must be one of the nicest in the place! I don't want to be taking this great space from someone else."

Cook grinned. "Enjoy it while it lasts! They'll boot you in a heartbeat," he said, winking. If only I'd known.

By mid-afternoon, Ben reappeared and suggested we head back to avoid the worst of the traffic.

"Do we have to?" I whined, trying hard to sound like a four-year-old. I did have a grin on my face, and Ben laughed. At least he got my humour.

I hugged Cook as we left, surprising myself, as Ben ducked into Nora's office to say goodbye. We headed to the Corolla.

"There is a great coffee shop in town. I'll drive you by the prison so you can see it, and we can stop and get a latte for the road," he said.

Coffees in hand, he loaded a tape of Gregorian chants and their richness filled the air (no CD in this model!). I was exhausted, and relieved when we settled into a quiet trip back into Vancouver. Quiet on the outside, at least. Inside, I couldn't forget about Paul and Frank, and my stupid trip into the Remand Centre. What the hell had I been thinking?

That night, I called Glenn

"I don't think I can do this, Glenn. Really. I know Paul saw me and recognized me. Maybe Frank, too." I was freaked.

"So what? It's not like they know you shouldn't have been wearing a collar. They just saw you sitting in the waiting area. Really, Beth. Settle down. You have to trust God. He wouldn't send you into harm."

A few minutes later, I hung up. My stomach churned. There was something ominous about ignoring the situation with Paul and Frank. I had until the weekend to decide.

Maybe before I move in, I'll figure it out. Hopefully. Prayer.

OMG. Oh My Grace. I hope I can live up to their expectations.

I don't remember feeling this "right" during nursing training, or even in church. Maybe I just don't remember. But terrified, too. I'm trying to remember what I learned about "discernment" and all I can remember is I'm supposed to look for concrete stuff to back up my feelings. I wonder if them being okay with me coming is a concrete sign?

Today I wanted to pray for the people in the circle; Intercessory prayer, I guess they call it. Do You respond to begging?

I really want You to be kind, and wise, and loving, and good. And I'll try to be those things too, 'kay?

But is this REALLY what you want me to do?

CHAPTER 15
IN SERVICE

Claire put down her trowel and wiped her forehead with the sleeve of her garden jacket. She knew January was too early to be digging in the soggy earth, but she had hoped she might escape the memories of what had chased her from the Order. This time it wasn't working, though. Maybe because of the time she'd spent in the lock-up at the protest, perhaps because of the people she'd encountered there.

Claire knew she presented to the world as a white-haired do-gooder who volunteered in prison and cuddled babies at the Indian Friendship Centre. And that was certainly one piece of the truth. Some people even knew she used to be a nun, a Grey Nun, to be precise. But blessedly most people assumed they knew why she'd left the Order. *Thank Goodness.*

Bishop Patrick had called yesterday, said, "because of her experience with Aboriginal people in prison and on the street," he would like her to train as a listener for the Catholic Church, with the Truth and Reconciliation Commission, an attempt by the "settler population" to make sense of the past horror of Residential Schools. Claire kept trying to figure out if he called because of her volunteer work, or if he knew enough about her past to know that it still haunted her.

Her heart heard his request as a Call from God, and she was wrestling to decide if her body was up to it, if she was worthy of God's request. She had hoped to hear God more clearly in the garden over her guilt and doubt and heartache, for all the children, for all the men and women, for those who had gone on to hurt because of what had been done to them – all in the name of God. Could she listen well enough?

Claire sighed, and tugged at the wet gloves on her swollen fingers. She left them in the mud room off the kitchen and sighed as she climbed the few steps. Perhaps wrapping her hands around a hot mug of tea would help.

As she waited for the kettle to boil, Claire glanced around her small kitchen with its yellow plywood cupboards, and wondered again if she deserved all this. She couldn't believe she was able to rent this little house on this small plot of land with her teacher's pension and what the government provided folks over 65. The church didn't support ex-nuns, but she had been able to work for fifteen years in an elementary school. Thank the good Lord, because she didn't think she deserved this warm, snug little house and her quiet solitude.

Tea in hand, she curled up on the faded couch, pulling an afghan over her knees. Maybe today she would be strong enough to bear the shame that followed the memories. Would there ever be a day she could work with the men and not see them as little boys in her early classrooms, crying, afraid, shaved heads and hungry bellies? Did she want to?

Claire had felt her calling to the convent early, and entered at 17, right out of high school. Her family had been thrilled. She'd attended teachers' college from the downtown mother house, and graduated early at 20. By 22 she had taken her vows, donned her habit and found herself living on the shores of James Bay, working at a residential school in a tiny town surrounded by Aboriginal communities. And she had truly and wholeheartedly believed in the goodness of the work she was doing.

It wasn't just that these children, by all measures, were struggling with cold and hunger in what she thought were horrid conditions, or that some of their parents struggled with addictions and abuse rampant in the community. She believed she was sent by God (and her Mother Superior) to save these savages from the clutches of Satan. That her presence there was going to make life better for these children, and their families, and bring them into the 20th century, so they could live and work amongst the civilized in the south of Canada. And onward into Eternal Life.

The shaved heads had startled her at first, reminding her of photos of prison camps after the war, but they didn't bother her as much as the lice and bedbugs that infested everything. When the little ones sobbed into their pillows at night, she thought it was a short-lived necessary suffering that would lead them toward a more enlightened path, a modern path, an educated path. When the little family members begged to see one another, she knew it would only hold them back, a chance to speak their language and talk about who knows what from their past. Maybe even plot to escape to return home to the mud and squalor of their parents' lives. She believed in the vision the older nuns shared with her, didn't question the wisdom from the church that had welcomed her, nurtured her and made her promises of a meaningful life, well lived.

Some of the older boys had done their darnedest to get the better of her. They acted up in class, refused to eat the food the Brothers provided, wouldn't participate in the daily services that brought her such comfort and joy. She learned to deal with them, watching the older Sisters and Brothers disciplining the children. At first she cringed when she had to send the boys to be whipped, but no one else seemed to be bothered.

All too quickly, she knew now looking back, she had come to accept that this was necessary -- a way to punish those boys who resisted learning. And, on days she was able to be especially truthful, she could admit that a few times she relished the thought that they were being whipped because they made her classroom an unruly mess, and then she got in trouble with the older Missionaries. Surely they would understand how necessary this was once they spoke English and understood maths and geography and European history? Surely, at some point, these unruly boys would come to thank her?

But then there was the electric chair. She never knew who built that thing, or really understood its purpose, but at the time she'd wanted to think it was some new scientific method of retraining their primitive brains. She didn't often participate when the children were electrified, mostly because it wasn't thought to be seeming for a young nun to witness this, but once or twice when dignitaries from Ottawa or the church were visiting, really young boys were taken into the room where it was, and she had seen their little bodies dancing from the electric shock when they were strapped onto that metal chair. Their legs bounced and heads jumped, sometimes they wet themselves. And while she hadn't sought it out, the watching, sometimes when she had been asked to serve tea to the visitors in her morbid fascination she hadn't looked away. And now she had to ask herself – what the hell was wrong with her?

And it would be wrong to just blame the Church. If she was honest, she would admit that there was always a part of her that knew it was wrong, the disciplining, the bad things the Missionaries did to the little boys when the lights were low and they were alone. In fact, to be really honest, she had admired the oldest nun who was the head of the girls' side of the school. She was ruthless in her approach to order, whipping boys and girls alike for perceived infractions. Claire had admired her strength of purpose and clarity of mission. And she hated herself for it now.

Eventually, Claire had been called back to the mother house in Montreal, sent out again, until finally, in the mid-seventies, most of the residential schools in Ontario closed for good, and she was sent to teach at an orphanage. She worked hard to avoid contact with the other teachers she had worked with in the North, to forget the screams and tears, to pretend that their mission had been good, and true, and holy.

And finally, in the eighties, she couldn't face the demons any longer. The Church denied the horror that they had visited upon Aboriginal Peoples in Canada, and the denial infiltrated the very lives of the Nuns. And finally, she left the Order and moved out west where she hoped the demons would leave her alone.

She was startled to find that even into the eighties, residential schools were still open in BC, at least one on the Island and one here in Mission. And like a moth to the flame, she felt compelled to settle here, to watch as the school was closed and Aboriginal Peoples struggled with the pain and suffering they had endured for nearly 120 years at the hand of the Church she had once adored.

As a fumbling attempt to both understand and make amends, she had joined the local Catholic Church and begun to volunteer in earnest. Some heard she had been a nun, and thought they understood her unrelenting need to contribute, to love and serve and do charity as a consequence of that calling, knit into the fabric of her being and something that could not, should not, be excised.

She became known as someone who had a soft spot for Aboriginal children who struggled. She would support their addicted single mothers, arrive with groceries for their children, make allowances for the children's weak attendance records, and the parents' inability to come into the school for community events or parent-teacher interviews. And her colleagues just thought she was kind.

Then she retired and turned her energies to working with even more vigour in the prisons and halfway houses that struggled in the Valley. She'd head inside to help with an AVP workshop this weekend, while sharing only a small piece of her broken heart with the men. And she got away with it because, what the hell – she'd been a nun and was exalted in their eyes. She often felt like a fraud, but kept going, relentlessly bringing the ideas of healing and resilience and kindness into those dark places. And sometimes, together, they uncovered a dark patch in her heart, and Light reflected to the darkest corners.

Now she was being asked to be a listener, to hear the stories of meaningless abuse and torture the children had suffered. And the stories of the anguish the parents left in the quiet villages when the children were rounded up. Could she bear their pain, too?

Thank God for Ben. He seemed to "get it," having left his Order. They had talked about what they missed, and what they didn't, and even though they never spoke of the horror, she sensed he understood. Maybe she would go to him and tell her story.

Could she confess out loud to the sins she had committed? Could she listen, could she hold the pain and suffering and relive the agonies of the children and their parents without making it about her debt, the horror of her actions, the tragedy of the pain she had willingly caused others?

Could she even consider saying no?

CHAPTER 16
VISITOR ACCESS GRANTED

Two days later, the phone rang in my apartment, and because the ringing seemed innocuous, I answered. Silly me. Mom was on the other end, asking if she and Dad could come up. My gut clenched; I recalled one other "visit" from Dad, and I still had regrets about that one. Mom assured me they just wanted a visit. I asked for ten minutes to get ready. I should have asked for a week.

Oh dear Mother of God

Will I ever get over this? Used to it? Okay with it?

Why do I feel like the sky might fall every time I'm with my Dad?

Jesus, did you feel this way around Joseph? Or your other Dad?

When will I grow up?

Will finding "a meaningful life" help with that? (Sigh.)

Beth

While they climbed the stairs, I applied myself to what Glenn and I called "the Fundamentalist clean" – it's all okay on the surface, but don't ask too many questions or open too many closets. I was shoving stuff under beds and couches, into cupboards. Three of us in a small space weren't exactly keeping house. Dirty pots were relegated to the oven, dishes into a sink of soapy water to hide them. Would I always be working to "pass muster" with my parents?

They arrived with scones from Tim Hortons, like bringing coals to Newcastle, and I put the kettle on for tea, all very civilized. Soon we were in the living room and there was a palpable presence with us; I just wasn't sure of the shape of the current elephant. Dad spoke first, of course.

"Bethy, I spoke to the Bishop, and he tells me you aren't doing your practicum in an Anglican parish. Have you decided to finish your degree with coursework instead of a practicum?" he asked.

The elephant was quickly taking form, but I grabbed the tail, and thought I knew its whole shape.

See, one of Dad's greatest fears is that I will take up a different faith tradition. God forbid I become a Roman Catholic (like there is ANY chance of that). Or, gasp, a Lutheran. I didn't want him to know it was more likely I'd become a Buddhist. He's obsessed with his congregation's opinion, a priestly variation on the common theme of "What will the neighbours think?" I wish he cared more about where Spirit is leading me.

I should have chosen my words more carefully, but I didn't even take a breath before blurting. Classic Bethism.

"Oh, don't worry Dad. I'm not leaving the Anglicans. I'm thinking of going to work in a prison." In retrospect, that might not have been a great strategy for comforting Mom. Damn. I'd almost decided to pack for an adventure, and I *so* didn't want Dad's opinion.

Mom's jaw-drop should have clued me in that she wasn't...well... enthusiastic. But I was so all-fired about figuring out how to make my life matter that I ploughed on, explaining my new future as if it was a done deal. Dad's cough slowed me down, and I realized that somehow, over store-bought scones and a cup of tea, I had to convince my parents that I knew what I was doing. I decided to take the spiritual offensive, a best defense?

"Dr. Neufeld and I spent a lot of time talking and praying about what my next steps should be. Really. Then, he remembered this important work, and thinks I have a lot to offer. I know I have a lot to learn. I'm really excited, Mom. I don't know what God wants from me, but I knew you'd be happy that I finally have a sense of calling. And you know the university wouldn't support any agency that wasn't safe and secure. Did you know more injuries happen in a hospital than this type of setting?"

Ha. Argue with that one, Dear Parents. I have God *and* statistics on my side.

We finished our tea, and they left before Steve and Sarita returned. I felt happy again, but this time I knew why -- I'd decided. In a few days I would be driving out to *Just Living*, and the day after I was going inside to do the AVP workshop. With Ben. Life was getting very interesting indeed.

Maybe that was a resounding *Yes*. I won't let Dad know it was his influence that helped me decide.

Dr. Neufeld arrived a couple of days later to drive me and my stuff to *Just Living*, and I was *very* ready to go. My backpack, suitcase, and a box of books and other special things were quickly loaded into the back of his little truck. He shared a coffee with Stephen, Sarita and I, and after hugs all around, we were off. As we headed out the door, Stephen whispered in my ear.

"Have an amazing time, Bethy. We'll see you soon, eh? Is this the guy turning your crank?"

I looked over, stunned. And the alarm meant I didn't whisper, unfortunately.

"Stephen! This is my prof! No, this is not *the* guy. Besides, what guy?" I was sputtering. Dr. Neufeld looked back and forth between Stephen and me.

"Are we ready to go?" he asked, and I grabbed my stuff. Off we went.

Once we were out on the highway, Dr. Neufeld let me know he wasn't going to let it go.

"Look Beth, we need to talk. You're an attractive young woman, wise in many ways beyond her years, and somehow…well, naïve. Do I need to know what Stephen was talking about?"

I took a moment. I wasn't really sure what Stephen was talking about. I mean, I was clearly flustered by Ben, or perhaps the idea of Ben…or maybe my reaction to Ben. But HE hadn't done anything. He hadn't even noticed me, and I didn't want his reputation questioned because of a crush. I didn't know how to talk about it. Or if I really wanted to. Silence is like no, right?

"Okaaay," Dr. Neufeld continued, "I don't need to know what your brother was talking about, but I need your reassurance that nothing is going on that shouldn't be. The men at the house have lived in a really over-sexualized and unhealthy environment for a long time." I must have looked sufficiently stunned to convince him I was mortified at his suggestion. I sputtered.

"So, first, we are away from the University. Call me Aaron, okay? We'll be colleagues in a few months, and I don't really embrace the 'Doctor' thing." I was remembering other students calling him Aaron, and I felt chuffed, like I'd made it into a special club. And then I was thrown by what he said next.

"Second, and more important, your Dad called."

What? Dad knew Dr. Neufeld? I'd protected my life at Seminary, hadn't wanted to share it with my parents. I didn't trust Dad, and didn't realize it until that moment. Incredible, eh? And, in the moment, I think I found something in myself. Not sure what yet.

"He said he had heard out about your practicum plans. He was upset. Which is his problem. But something else bothers me, Beth. I've decided I need to tell you, and let you decide if I need to do something." Okay, *now* I was confused. More confused. Aaron smiled at me.

"And I was going to talk to you even before that thing with Stephen. Really." Aaron hunkered down in his seat.

"Your dad told me he didn't think you were a good candidate for this practicum, that 'becoming involved with a bunch of thugs' wouldn't be good for you."

Dr. Neufeld used one-handed air quotes. Really. One hand on the wheel.

"He said you're young and vulnerable, in spite of your years, and how he still felt it was 'his job as your father' to guide and protect you." More air quotes. Sigh. I live in a backwards universe where brilliance and pop culture collide.

"I told him your decisions were grounded in good discipline and sacred practice, that you had treated the choices with maturity and sincerity, that I was convinced that you were entirely capable of deciding." Aaron grinned. "I don't think he was pleased. I didn't even get near the whole 'Who's judging thugs?' question." He pulled over into a rest stop.

Tears of frustration threatened to spill over. Well, *very* awkward. He handed me his handkerchief, and his water bottle. I looked up, and his eyes were shining too.

"He kept trying to convince me. He told me what happened when you were seventeen, how, 'without him guiding you,' you would have 'ruined your life.' He talked about your passion for 'the underdog' starting with strays, and kids being bullied."

My blood began to boil. Damn. My father had done precisely what he had forbidden me to do, what he promised he'd never do. He'd convinced me to never speak of what had happened and I'd been obedient. Mostly. Except for a few really close friends who I trusted. So much for that.

"He told you?" I asked, and Aaron nodded. "About Jesse?" More nodding. "Did he tell you about Chaos?"

"I don't know," Aaron replied. "He didn't use names. You can tell me if you want, but you don't have to."

"Chaos was our baby...Jesse's and mine. Dad convinced me that we weren't ready to parent, babies rearing babies, he'd said. He forced me to have an abortion."

I'd replayed that event in my mind a thousand times, a thousand times a thousand, with no one to talk to about it. I squirmed in my seat. We sat for a while in the car, me staring out the windshield at the greenery, Aaron watching me. The silence felt good.

"Beth, what your Dad did was wrong. And I think he was motivated by love and responsibility to you. What troubled me was that he's proud of what he did back then, and thinks you still need his guidance now."

My brain was firing a mile a minute. WTF? Dad thought he needed to intervene for me? And worse – he was proud of what he did? In a corner of my mind, I knew that I needed to get my shit together. I was heading out to a practicum where people were going to judge me on my professionalism. I was heading into prison, and supposed to be contributing, not showing up a mess. Aaron wasn't done, though.

"And, good intentions aren't an excuse. So, while what your Dad did was wrong, I wonder what he's afraid of."

We sat. He wondered. I was still outraged.

"You're a bright woman, one any father should be proud of." We sat for a bit, and I thought about fathers and their kids. Stephen and Dad were far from close. Was there a father alive who didn't mess up his children? Or dead, for that matter?

Had God messed up his Son? Maybe that was the legacy, even if I wanted to believe in rainbows and unicorns. There must be an incredible father somewhere, right? And I thought of Glenn, and smiled. *There* was a guy who understood his sons.

"We've got to get going, get you into the prison in time, and you can decide after the weekend if this is the practicum for you," Aaron looked right at me. "We'll figure this out."

"No. Not a problem. I SO want to do this," I said emphatically.

"I thought so. I just needed to hear it from you."

"You did the volunteer training last week, right?" he asked, and I nodded, thinking about it.

I'd read about "life inside" in a desperate attempt to prepare for *Just Living*. Watched TV shows about prison. And in the whirlwind of preparation, I received an afternoon of volunteer training from the Correctional staff in the prison. I learned that prisoners, on the continuum of intimate partner to stranger should be treated with more suspicion than stranger, because they had done something very wrong, indeed (like we hadn't...?). There was advice about who I'm to listen to if things go wrong ("Does that happen often?" I wondered.... "Never!" Aaron told me later. "No volunteer has ever been hurt by a prisoner in a Federal prison in more than 25 years. No one remembers farther back than that, but I've never heard of anything.") Who not to trust (inmates). What to watch out for (contraband, information) and who to report it to (staff). And again, I wasn't to carry anything into or out of the prison. Got it. Check. Conflicting messages. SO not prepared.

I'd left the training, walked zombie-like to my car, drove down the long driveway, and burst into tears. I prayed all the way home. Question prayers, for a change.

Dear God,

What are we thinking? What are we doing? How can we do this to each other? Or more precisely, how can men do this to other men? The cages. The inhumanity. The barbed wire, and steel bars clanging, the concrete everywhere. There is no hope for life in those spaces, no hope for change.

And the hurting just keeps on keepin' on. Layer after layer of hurt and betrayal and lashing out...leading to hurt and betrayal and...well, You know, don't you?

Are you in those spaces, Dear God? Why can't I feel you there? And more important,

Why don't you stop the suffering?

Tonight, I'm just, Beth.

Confused Beth.

So imagine my surprise when my first legal experience inside was more profound than almost anything I'd ever lived, and I became more real as the three days unfolded. I was longing for a spiritual experience, and found it in a prison, not a church. Or maybe in a church in a prison.

I *really* didn't think I'd feel comfortable being left alone in a room of convicts with only three other "outside people," even if one of them was Ben. I admit I didn't completely relax for a couple of hours. Which seems so weird now. Coming through the main gate, having our property (even our jackets and shoes!) X-rayed like at the airport was weird.

"No talking! Stand back until I call you!" I get it, Mr. Prison Guard. You're serious. I guess I get it; we were going into a prison and all, but really? *I'm a becoming-priest, for heaven's sake.* Also a prayer. I got the feeling he would be happier if we would all just go home. Ben was amazing.

"How are you this morning, sir?" Ben asked, putting his CSC-issued photo ID on the counter. The duffle bag with materials for the workshop went on the X-ray scanner.

"There should be a gate pass for these materials for the weekend; we are in to do AVP." The guy didn't exactly scowl, just an almost-scowl.

"I'm the chaplain here," Ben continued, and the fellow began to thaw. Marginally. He looked through a huge binder and finally found the magical piece of paper that granted us passage. Ben's copy didn't count. We received black light ink stamps on our hands.

First, a sliding glass door, followed by a moving gate on a fence (after a locking glass door, and the metal detector). Wow. I felt a little guilty, and judged (and I'm not sure why; I didn't bring anything in!). Another glass door, and a scan of our hands under the black light, and we were inside, with only one more building to walk through to gain access to the compound and chapel.

As we walked the corridors and outside walkways towards the chapel, people – mostly men – were checking us out the whole way. First uniformed guards in the Admin Building, and then after more iron gates were slammed behind us, the prisoners. Gauntlet much? I felt like an animal at the zoo, and wondered if they did, too.

The chapel stood in the yard, and nearby was a covered area where some logs were being carved, shavings of yellow cedar ankle deep around the men whose heads were bent in concentration. I'd only seen finished poles at the university before, never anything like this, and it was amazing to see it here. I wondered about the huge knives and chisels and mallets the guys were using; it didn't seem to make sense. But no one seemed afraid, so I decided not to be either. It was curious though, with what I'd heard in training. Logic would be welcomed, folks.

There was already a lot of activity in the chapel. My eyes were drawn to the stained glass above the simple wooden altar, and the windows reminded me of the glass in the Sanctuary at *Just Living*. One was a picture of a plant climbing up a branch with a dove taking flight, a sunrise in another, and a third one a lovely lotus flower on water. Beautiful.

A couple of couches along the wall, chairs in a circle, a wooden screen in front of a couple of offices to the side. It was a great space, easily transformed from workshop to worship. I thought of a couple of churches that could learn from this design; no fixed pews here.

Two burley guys were making coffee in a big urn, a few were rearranging the chairs, and another was setting up a flip-chart. Everyone wore jeans and white T-shirts, green jackets and sneakers, except for one pair of leather loafers. With tassels. Weird.

Two men grabbed Ben, and said Claire was waiting in the office. He joined them, after passing me off.

"Beth – can you hang out here with Bill while I do a little prep work with the team?" he asked an elderly man who welcomed me with a huge fist shaking mine. Bill guided me towards a chair without laying a finger on me. Skill.

"Welcome Beth. Good to meet you. Let me get you some coffee," he said, and we were off into unexpected banter.

"Are you a cream and sugar coffee girl?" he asked, grinning at me. "Double double at the drive thru?"

"Milk if you've got it," I answered, and he laughed.

"You can have white from a jar, or white from a jar, or black," he said, and I figured out that "cream" meant creamer. Cheap artificial petroleum by-product. And "sugar" meant horrid pink packets of sweetener.

"I'll just have a little whitener," I answered, imagining the coffee was going to be God-awful. Good assumption, I thought later.

"Great. I'll get that for you right away, in about 20 minutes when it's done," Bill teased. He'd been having me on.

"What did you do to get sent here?" he asked, grinning.

"About four months," I replied, "should be out in April." He chuckled.

"So parole's already on board?" he joked.

"Oh yeah. As long as I'm well behaved, it should be fine," I shot back. Before I knew it I was edging towards comfortable, probably about as comfortable as the rest of us waiting for "the team." Glancing around the circle, not wanting to stare, I noticed at least twelve of the men from inside were squirming. Like even more uncomfortable than me. A few latecomers drifted in. And then the team came out and we began.

And then I really saw Claire, the other volunteer, and my stomach set off again. She was Claire, Julie's friend from the Remand Centre. Argh! I might as well shout it from the rooftops: *I impersonated a priest to break into a jail!* I played back Glenn's voice. "Trust. It'll be okay." Maybe she doesn't know I don't wear a collar. Sigh. But I think she recognized me right off. Looked right at me.

And she didn't look happy.

CHAPTER 17
EXPECT THE BEST

So, I didn't expect I'd be transformed that weekend. But I was nudged along in lots of ways, shown stuff I've never seen. Yes, there was apprehension because of Claire. And warm fuzzies from Ben. But I also sat across from a man I've never met and we shared about stuff that matters. Back and forth. Five minutes, and I'd shared more with this inmate than I'd shared with my parents. Or friends. I felt seen. And got to know these guys in ways I hadn't anticipated. AVP really did work to change me. And the guys talked about how they hadn't felt heard in years.

Some things I never thought I'd do that weekend such as trust an offender with the dawning realization that maybe I had to share some responsibility for Chaos' death. "It's okay," he said. "I've done worse. Not that it's a competition," he added. And I realized it wasn't a competition for redemption either.

Mildly freak out when a prisoner whipped out a knife to open a juice box.

Watch a middle-aged woman hug a young man who dashed into the chapel during a break. A hug that didn't end. Later she said, "He's like a son to me." Then I found out her daughter was murdered. Sigh.

This is an amazing place, where amazing things happen. And I am just a little fucking confused. Prayer.

Saturday night we finished about eight o'clock, and Ben drove me and Claire home. On the way, we stopped for a coffee. He sat beside me in the booth, and I felt an exquisite warmth when we brushed against each other. He even smiled at me once, and I swear it wasn't just a friendly smile.

Ben tried to drive the conversation, inviting me to talk about myself with Claire. But Claire wasn't buying it. She kept bringing the conversation back to their volunteer work inside.

Maybe she was debriefing the workshop, preparing for the next day, but it sure didn't seem like it. She kept commandeering the conversation, chumming with Ben. I found out she's an ex-nun, so they have that in common. But she's thirty years (at least!) older than him, so I hope it isn't a crush...for his sake.

Anyhow, I'd hazard a guess that Claire doesn't like me. And I'm not going to broach the whole "I met you in prison before" conversation. I have no idea where to go with that. Anyhow, the mocha was delicious and I only got distracted by foam on Ben's upper lip once.

Okay, twice.

When I got home, the lights were off in the kitchen, so I tiptoed upstairs to my room, dropped off my stuff and headed out onto the back porch. It was dark, and quiet, and delicious.

I could hear Sally inside, trying to reason with Ricky, a new arrival. The quiet of the evening meant voices travelled easily, reminding me that even with the sound of the rain on the roof and the waterfalls falling off the mountain behind us, there was little privacy here.

"Ricky, here are the things you brought with you. You can unpack them now. I really think the rest of your stuff will get here tomorrow. No, I don't know what the holdup is." Sally was saying. I couldn't make out Ricky's words, but his tone was whiney. Oh great. Sharing space with a whiner.

"Ricky, if you take the time to unpack these things, I will make sure we look into where the rest of your things are in the morning, okay? I know it's hard, new place and all. Are you hungry?"

A little more whining from Ricky, and I could hear Sally opening and closing drawers, helping Ricky unpack. I started to wonder if I should go inside and inject a little support into the situation. I was still really unclear of my role in this place. I must have sighed, or something.

"Angel – that you over there?" I heard Cook whispering. He was further along the porch, and we were tucked under the overhang, avoiding the rain.

"Yeah, Cook. It's me. How are you?"

"I'm good, Angel. You gonna help with breakfast? What time you got to be on the road for the workshop?" he asked.

"I'm here to help you, Cook. I can get up whenever you want. What's for breakfast? I think Ben and I are leaving at around eight o'clock."

"We usually have the food out around 7:15. Coffee at 6:45 for the early risers. Breakfast tomorrow is oatmeal, and some eggs and toast and stuff. Mostly people get their own. Might add croissants to the menu one of these mornings if I knew where to get some."

"I'm happy to bake croissants, Cook. Just let me know when. Meet you in the kitchen at 6:15?" I asked. A comfortable silence grew between us. Once again I heard Sally's voice as she tried to work with Ricky.

"Ricky, just give it one night. I'm sure I can scare up some cookies and a warm drink for tonight. You can take an apple and some snacks into your room. Don't worry, son. It'll be fine. Tom is in the next room. You remember him, right?"

Ricky seemed to be getting more upset. I couldn't tell what the problem was, other than he was being unreasonable. I sighed again.

"Don't worry, Angel. He'll settle down. Sally knows what she's doin' – she's been settlin' guys for years. Addin' us to the mix will only make it worse. You just relax, girl." How did he know I wanted to intervene?

"I can't tell if I should help or not. I guess I'll figure out how to figure it out," I said, and he chuckled under his breath.

"You just ask. You can help me any time. Some of the others are better left on their own, though." I wondered if that was because it was a job for one, or Sally liked to work alone. In a few minutes I heard them heading downstairs, no doubt for cookies.

"Cook, can I ask you something? I've never been in before." I said. I wondered if this was what it was like to hear confession – disembodied voices sharing with each other.

"You're doin' fine, Angel. Jus' be yourself. You treat everybody good, so no problems. You didn't ask why they're in, did you? Don't expect them to tell you. And I promise they won't ask you about the worst thing you've ever done either. It's jus' like in the grocery store. Treat em' well, an' don't pretend you know 'em."

I put my head back and imagined stars where the clouds were. I really wanted to talk to him about Claire and Ben, but I didn't want to admit to my earlier capers with Glenn.

"Can we talk tomorrow night too, Cook?" I asked, realizing I should really let him get to bed because morning would come early. I had lots more to think about before I'd be sleeping.

"Sure, Angel. Don't worry about tomorrow mornin'. You sleep in and get ready for the workshop. Next week's soon enough to help. I'm good. See you downstairs for breakfast," he said, and I heard the door to the hallway open and close. Ricky was coming back upstairs, and Cook bid him goodnight on his way in. Ricky's door slammed, and I heard Sally sigh as she headed to bed. A few minutes later I made my way back to my room, locking the screen door on the deck and grinning at the irony of locking myself in with these guys. I knew the alarm would be set soon, though, and I didn't want to trip it my first week.

I lay in bed thinking about home, and wondering where that was for me. This place felt at least as good as any other.

Dear God, I know I asked for this. And now you seem to be delivering. I'm scared, though, that I won't find my meaningful life. And I think about "be careful what you wish for."

And I'm glad you'll be going with me tomorrow. I'm feeling you beside me again, and it's weird, but I'm glad.

Thank you, God. Goddess.

Or maybe both.

By the end of the weekend I was spent. Tired. Exhilarated. Jolly. And I had encountered Spirit. People taking Light into a very dark place, exploring how to be courageous enough to change. And the finest tools were laughter and play.

I didn't expect to play with Tinker toys with grown men. To feel pushed while role-playing. To let them carry me around on their shoulders in silence. With my eyes closed. To have them challenge my "perfect little girl" persona, and challenge me on all the ways I treat other people horribly. *Or to feel my world crack open just a little bit and let the tears leak out. And the Light shine in.* Yes, Leonard Cohen is my prophet.

I left there wanting to know more about AVP. Good God – if those guys can commit to change, surely I can, too? And I was glad for Cook that night, too.

After Sunday dinner, Cook and I sat outside again, smelling the rain and watching a fire below us in the Sacred Grounds. I think the guy named Al was out there, and maybe Tom, too. Or Paul. We'd feasted on a hearty stew, and I felt sated, and tired, and happy. A cuddly barn cat was curled up on my lap purring.

"How'd it go inside?" Cook asked. Sighing is an adequate response, right?

"Yeah, I thought so, Darlin'," he said. "Just watch out for re-entry. Again, it can be a bitch," he offered.

That got me started.

"What do you mean? It was amazing. Really. I never imagined being so open with people. Especially people I just met. Especially there." Have you ever had an experience, and realized midway through it would be life-changing? It was this weird hyper-awareness that (cue spooky voice) "this is important." I wondered if I'd just had...*a mystical experience.*

Cook chuckled. "Really? Maybe it's *because* you don't know 'em. In other words, some of 'em are still assholes," he said, and I was a little shocked.

"Blasphemer!" I whispered, smiling only a little bit. "It was amazing!" But he got me thinking.

"Just don't be surprised if it don't stick for all of 'em," he continued, and I knew he just wanted to prepare me for disappointment.

"You mean, one weekend workshop won't turn them all into Pollyannas?" I joked, and he snickered back. The cat was kneading my lap and purring, and I was carefully trying to pull some of the small mats from her long fur.

"Yeah," he continued, "the real work starts when you try to make it stick in everyday life. Really. Six 'simple' rules, but they ain't easy." I thought about the "six rules to live by"– six agreements from the workshop.

No put-downs. (Even of ourselves.) Honour confidentiality. Everyone has a right to pass. Affirm yourself and others. Listen – don't interrupt, and volunteer yourself only.

Simple rules, applied simply. I had decided I was going to try them in my life – which would be easy, because they were guides at *Just Living*, too. Along with no drugs, no alcohol, no violence, I mean. I found out that Cook was right; simple didn't mean easy....

"One interesting thing happened during a break, Cook," I told him. "A group of guys hung around out front of the chapel. I guess they heard I'm staying here, and they wanted to know what it was like."

"Yeah, watch out for them. They gotta do AVP to get into here, and sometimes...well...jus' be careful," he told me. Cook resisted saying anything bad about anyone.

"Yeah, I suppose. They were really skeptical; no one seemed to believe it's run like a 'house' and everyone has a say. I think they were checking out the stories they'd heard."

I scratched the cat under his chin. The men had seemed curious about the set-up and the grounds, how much work they had to do, and what kind of work. Some asked about how far it was for visitors.

"One asked about having to work here, and I didn't really know. Do the guys have to work? He seemed to think it was sorta like slavery," I asked.

"Ah. Rumours. The guys, they gotta contribute. They ain't used to it." I thought about that for a bit.

"One really shy fellow asked about Ricky. He seemed relieved to hear Ricky's doing okay."

"I guess Ricky did have a friend or two inside after all." I heard his smile.

"Cook?"

"Yeah, Angel?"

"I think I might have pissed Claire off, and I don't know why," I lied. "She thinks I'm a flake or something."

"Ah, Angel, that's just Claire. She's grumpy sometimes. I don't know why, but don't you worry. You're safe here as long as we're around."

"Really?" I said, thinking about that for a few moments. "I feel all warm and fuzzy now," I joked.

"Yeah. Just don't piss us off," he said, chuckling. "Keep the croissants comin' and you're good." I smiled into the darkness.

When I got ready for bed that night, I thought again about how hard it had been to leave the workshop, and the men inside. I didn't know if I'd see them again, and realized I'd never be with exactly that group, and that was sad. It got me thinking about stuff I take for granted. Seeing my family whenever I want. Eating what I want, whenever I want. Picking friends. Spending time with Kenny and Cook. Not so much Ricky.

The following week was spent in a whirlwind, really meeting people, and figuring out how to be helpful in this amazing place. Ricky and I had an official tour; Nora had spoken to us and everyone else about her expectations for him, and the restrictions and limitations that were a part of his orientation and welcome. I think I heard it 20 times. No this. Yes that. Not there. Maybe not. We'll see.

So Monday, the rules were printed up, and I put them on the front and back of Ricky's door, and in the bathroom and kitchen. I found out that Ricky is "developmentally delayed," which I think is the current politically-correct term. I didn't know then that he was also brain injured – a gift from his time spent inside at the insistence of the Queen. Quite a gift from Royalty.

Ricky found his place in the cattery, working with the strays. He loved cleaning cages, petting the kittens, and didn't seem to mind the occasional scratch when he was over-enthusiastic. He seemed to get along with Kate; they were quiet together as far as I could tell. He steered clear of the barn and pastures, I noticed. Maybe that work was too hard.

I found my place, between the comfort and ease of the kitchen with Cook, and the wet, dirty muscle strain of winter garden clean-up with Kenny, the gardener. We pruned fruit trees, raked wet leaves, pulled the leftovers from the vegetable gardens. I loved Kenny's humour, and we delighted in doing anonymous random acts of kindness. Sometimes, he snuck in and mucked the barn before Tom got there.

Once, he left a fresh pot of tea in Nora's office, sneaking in while I distracted her. She didn't find it before it turned cold, so we laughed that the joke was on us. The next time we put it right in the middle of her work. On Cook's day off, Kenny cleaned the ovens. He even washed my sheets when I wasn't looking. Which was only moderately creepy. Not. I love the guy. At least he enlisted Sally's help.

And boy, is he funny. Kenny is outrageously flamboyant; I don't know how he survived inside. Frank told me later that sometimes it is easier for "real gays" to survive in jail, because they're accepted more than those who are "institutionally adjusted," slang for those who participate in same-sex "relations" while incarcerated.

"They don't mind having a reputation as a 'fag,'" Frank explained. "That takes away a whole bunch of power from name calling." I kind of understood. Not looking for things to make sense, just to understand the way they are. I don't know if Kenny was "out" in prison. And I still don't know if he's still under warrant, or an employee.

I delighted in his presence, and became one of the safest people for me to hang around with. No problem, he won't find me attractive. I didn't have to explain Jesse, or Chaos, or my growing interest in Ben to him or myself. I so needed to laugh. And he was wise.

When I didn't understand Nora's reactions to Tom, Kenny gave me context; Tom rails against women in authority. When I felt sheepish about using the word "goof" (Who knew? Worst name-calling in prison culture...a child molester), Kenny assured me it was more startling to people than a relationship-breaker. Did brand me a "fish" though...and he taught me what that meant, too. (Think of the similarity between a gold fish and the dropped jaw of a newbie in jail.) Kenny propped up my sanity that first week, I think, so that I was ready for the more intensive work to come.

I added the men in the workshop to my prayer list, and said a special thank you for our community. Some of them had said being in the workshop was like "getting out of jail for the weekend," and I was glad. That weekend, I began living "fully alive" and "loving wastefully," two prayers that were a part of my daily devotions. Funny that I had daily devotions now.

May I live fully alive,
Love wastefully,
Be true to who You are in me, living authentically,
Following Your teachings, leadings and will.

And I confessed to God about my lie to Cook. I knew why Claire was suspicious of me. I just had to figure out how to own it.

Or if I wanted to. Ends. Means. Shit. There they are again. At least Chris is alive.

Drifting to sleep, I wondered what it would be like to have an intimate relationship as profound as the platonic connections I'd built inside. Intense. Real. Honest.

That led to all kinds of wishing and dreaming about Ben; I wondered if reality would measure up, but now that I've imagined a deep connection, it'd be hard to settle. Who knows what the real deal will be like...but I'm working up the guts to find out.

It just might be an essential part of my "building a meaningful life" project.

A prayer if ever I heard one. An anthem, really.

Like that sacred chord. *Hallelujah*, like kd lang singing it to Leonard Cohen.

CHAPTER 18
SUPPORT AND ACCOUNTABILITY

Bob closed the spreadsheet, and shut down the laptop. He'd been able to update the current receivables and cut cheques for all the outstanding bills, so Nora could sign and send them in the morning. He was a little concerned that *Just Living* was ahead of its budget in the year-to-date column, but noticed this wasn't uncommon looking at previous years. Somehow Nora and the crew would make it work until April 1st when more funding was promised.

It had been challenging, learning all the ways charities were different from real businesses, but Bob was starting to get the hang of things. He'd been doing the books since he'd arrived last fall, and clearly they'd never had a chartered accountant set things up before. He was proud that the Board had allowed him to reconfigure things so they made more sense for the annual audit; he hadn't been sure they would trust him. Bob liked putting order to the numbers, showing (at least two ways) that what the columns said accurately reflected the financial reality of the organization, and that because of the careful work he'd done people who *didn't* love accounting could actually understand his spreadsheets and make responsible decisions based on them.

Of course, some guys didn't understand why Nora and the Board trusted him with the money. Writing cheques – even if he didn't sign them – was pretty close to the finances, he had admitted. But then, they assumed he'd been in because he'd been caught with his hands in some giant cookie jar. I mean, what else could accountants be in for, right?

And he'd let them believe. He'd been so ashamed of what he'd done, and tried hard to learn how to manage the "urges" he'd always felt. He was glad he'd looked into organizing a Circle of Support and Accountability before he'd left the prison; the people in his circle seemed to care. Now he was off to meet with Anna, the big boss down at the CoSA office, and then to see some of his supporters. It felt weird even thinking he had "supporters," but he liked having coffee with them every week. Because who else would talk to him? He wondered how they'd help him next year, when he'd be moving out of *Just Living*.

Maybe Nora would let him continue with the books after he left. He knew he owed them for letting him in, and he liked that he was fooling everyone. That is, except Nora and Frank, his counsellor.

"I'm heading out, Nora. I have a meeting with Anna, and then the clan," he called over his shoulder as he grabbed his coat from the back of the door. He'd heard the taxi on the gravel out front, come to drive him into town. He'd put in a full day's work already.

"No problem, Bob. Anything I should know before tomorrow morning?" she asked, but he was already gone. He didn't like to keep anyone waiting, to rock the boat or speak his mind, Nora thought. She shook her head and wondered how long it would take him to trust.

Bob sat in the back of the cab, tapping his fingers on his corduroy pants and watching the trees go by. The cabbie tried to strike up a conversation, but Bob didn't bite. He was glad he still had enough money to take taxis. That didn't obligate him to chat.

When they arrived at the strip mall, he paid the cab and then waited until it left before he took the stairs to the CoSA Office. No sense *anyone* knowing why he was here, he thought, and then wondered if he'd be mistaken for a volunteer or a worker rather than a "core member," as they called him. He smiled at the idea flying under the radar. After all, he didn't look like one of *them*, right?

Anna, the Director, welcomed him, and pulled up a chair. After polite back-and-forth, she told him why she'd called him in.

"Bob, one of your circle volunteers saw you last week at the bus stop outside the library, and I just wanted to ask what that was about. I thought you'd agreed take cabs around town," she said.

Once again, Bob was caught off-guard. Yes, he'd been at the bus stop. He'd had to go down to the Social Services office to find out if they were going to find space in a care home for his Mom since he wouldn't be living with her any time soon. Turns out, he needed to talk to someone in the health authority. Afterwards, he'd decided to catch a bus to the pharmacy about a mile away just to save cab fare. He hadn't even thought to tell anyone, and didn't appreciate being interrogated.

"Yes, I took the bus. What's the big deal?" he asked. Anna reminded him of the contract he'd signed.

"You know, Bob, all of this could be avoided if you were more trusting. It has to go both ways. Jean-Guy was worried because he thought you might have been online in the library right next door. A lot of folks are working to keep you on track, Bob, but you have to work with us. Otherwise, you'll have to go back inside until your warrant expires. We can't risk any more children being hurt by you."

Of course. He hadn't even thought about that. Now he understood why they were a bit freaked out. Accessing the Internet was strictly off limits, and he guessed even on a weekday there would be children in the library, another reason he couldn't go in the door. No rec centre, no pools, no parks, no schools, or other public places where children gather. If he needed to shop, he was to go in, get what he needed (in this case his hormone suppressants at the drug store) and leave – no loitering in the candy aisle.

Bob apologized, and promised again to do better. Anna looked like she only halfway believed him, but let him go because his circle volunteers were waiting next door. Besides, the day was over, and she was heading out.

It took him a moment to find his friends in the dimly lit café, but there they were in the back booth. Three of his supporters were here – that was unusual; usually only one or two met him for after-dinner coffee.

Gerry stood up and hugged him, and made room for him in the booth. Annie and Chuck, a husband and wife team, sat across from him.

"How're you feeling, Bob?" Chuck asked. Annie looked up as the waitress stood by their table.

"I'm good. It's been a busy week. We're getting ready for CSC's fiscal year end, and it's the end of our quarter, too, so I've been busy," Bob said, hoping to deflect the question.

They paused to give their orders, and then returned to the business at hand.

"Bob, really. How are *you* doing? Not just 'how's work?'" Chuck said.

"I'm okay. Really. I like it at *Just Living*," he answered, his voice falling.

"Then tell us about the bus stop," Annie said, and she patted his hand. Damn Anna for telling them, Bob thought, then remembered it was one of *them* who'd told Anna. Or maybe told the police. He hadn't really thought about being watched.

Bob sighed and told them about his week. The call from his uncle because his Mom had been found wandering the streets again, this time wearing only a blouse, pants, and her slippers, in the middle of a BC winter. He was lucky a neighbour had seen her and called an ambulance, because when the police went to lock the house, they found the stove on and a burned dinner. The smoke detector may have been what drove her outside. At least the place hadn't caught fire, Bob said.

His current parole restrictions allowed him to visit her once a week, but she needed round-the-clock care to live on her own, and he wouldn't be able to move home for a while, even in the best case scenario. Something needed to change with his mother.

The circle listened to Bob and started asking questions. Had he talked to her doctor about getting her into care? What about his siblings? Maybe they could get homecare to help her? Could they afford to pay a care aide to move in? What about neighbours looking in on her?

Bob patiently answered their questions, but none of this was new; he'd thought about every one of their ideas, and either pursued each to a dead end, or dismissed them. He felt a little like they were testing him to see if his story was real. Then Gerry changed the tone entirely.

"Bob, it sounds like you've really been wrestling with this for a while." Bob nodded. "How did we fail you?"

"You failed me?" Bob's eyes snapped to Gerry's. Second time he was surprised today. He didn't like surprises; they knocked him off guard.

"Yup, we have. You've been struggling with a really serious concern, and you shouldn't have to carry that alone. That's what we're here for – to help you. I want to know how we've failed you, because you didn't think you could come to us," he said. "We have to change how we're doing things if you can't use us for support. Maybe we need new volunteers," he said, looking at the others who were nodding.

Bob was amazed. He hadn't wanted them worrying about him and his problems. He'd grown used to being a loner, taking care of himself. His time inside had strengthened his resolve to be independent; it'd been a matter of safety, mostly his.

"God, I don't know what to say," he mumbled, his first complete truth today. "It's not you guys, it's me. My mom. I thought she was my responsibility since my sister won't talk to us anymore. She got pissed when Mom visited me inside." He paused for a minute, holding his hands palms up.

"The social worker is trying to get her connected to health care, but it could take a few weeks. Maybe a month. I'm trying to get over to see her, but it's really expensive taking the cab across the river and back all the time. And I only get passes to go unescorted once a week," Bob explained.

As they finished their meals, Gerry, Chuck and Annie pulled out their calendars.

"Let's get this figured out, and we can dart over there tonight, okay Bob?" Gerry said.

"I can take him Tuesday and Thursday afternoons; my parish can do without me," Annie chipped in.

"I work nights next week. Maybe a couple of mornings when I get off work I can head up and get you and take you to see her," Chuck said. "Don't worry, I won't bring the squad car." He smiled, and Bob felt a weight lifting off his shoulders. "I'll also connect with the other volunteers and see if they can help. I think Andy lives near your mom. We'll get this figured out, Bob." He took a breath, and continued. He knew Bob didn't like taking orders from a cop, but it was time.

"You have to tell Nora and Frank, Bob. Really. And share the stress. When you're healthier, your ability to stay healthy and make good decisions goes WAY up. *This is what we signed up for, remember?*" Chuck reached over and touched Bob's arm. Bob tried not to pull away.

"Our goal here is *no more victims,* Bob. We want to help you learn to live in our neighbourhood and you have to trust us and let us know what's going on for this to work. Okay?" Bob glanced at the cop he never thought he'd like. "Okay?" Chuck repeated.

"Okay," Bob said, and he was embarrassed when tears pooled in his eyes. He hadn't been able to rely on anyone for years, and this was so different. He wasn't sure if he would get used to it, or if he even wanted to.

They left the café, and he hopped into Gerry's car. They drove over and spent half an hour with his Mom, and Bob hoped she'd remember Gerry because he'd promised to take her to the shops the next morning. Bob felt a hundred times lighter as they left his childhood home.

"Thank you Gerry. I can't believe how much better I feel just knowing she's fed and safe tonight," Bob said. "Somehow a phone call isn't the same as seeing her."

"That's great, Bob, because when you feel better, so do I. Learning to ask for help, one step at a time, okay? Really, it's what we want to do."

During the drive back, Gerry reminded Bob he would need more support than he was asking for at *Just Living*. He reminded Bob that the seminary student, Beth, had offered to help, and he suggested Bob actually get to know her. Then they strategized about all the ways he could include his circle volunteers in his life without telling anyone there that he was a skinner, a goof, a baby-diddler, the most reviled of all criminals inside the prisons or out. And that way, they'd all work at keeping children safe. And him, too.

CHAPTER 19
THE RABBIT HOLE

"It was much pleasanter at home," thought poor Alice, "when one wasn't always growing larger and smaller, and being ordered about by mice and rabbits. I almost wish I hadn't gone down that rabbit-hole—and yet—and yet—it's rather curious, you know, this sort of life! I do wonder what can have happened to me! When I used to read fairy-tales, I fancied that kind of thing never happened, and now here I am in the middle of one! There ought to be a book written about me, that there ought!"

Oh dear God, I can't even think up my own prayers anymore. Thank you for Lewis Carroll's Alice in Wonderland. And Leonard Cohen's Hallelujah. And all the other wise people who encourage me to think great prayers. Because it's no surprise I don't have any great words myself.

Maybe that's a next thing I'll work at. Right after I understand Adoration a little more thoroughly. Physically, like. I get the idea, but the closest I get to Adoration as an experience is when I look at Ben.

And I don't know that you'd really approve of those prayers, God.

The transition to *Just Living* was easier *and* tougher than I expected. I LOVED my room, my private sanctuary. I'd settled my stuff the day I arrived, and moved it around a bit, but felt really at home from the beginning. I did spend lots of time walking the grounds alone, looking for signs, hoping to be replenished. Or directed. A how-to on building a meaningful life.

Anyway, by week two, things got better, but I spent great chunks of "imagination time" playing a "what if" game about Ben and me. Parts of my private journal from that time are NSFW. Good thing I don't believe this is sinful; I only had the moral dilemma of working through an attraction to my mentor, who may or may not be a monk.

After my second week, Nora asked me to spend time with Al and Paul in the Sacred Grounds, to help them "with their relationship." She also mentioned that they host a group of Aboriginal youth for ceremonies, and it helped if they had a woman with them as a chaperone, because, well, co-ed.

I'd met Al in circle during my first visit. He's a big fellow, I guess about fifty, with long braids and an ever-present red bandana rolled into a sweat-band. He's a man of few words, and little patience. Paul helps with sweats and other ceremonies but mostly he's with the animals. Al has an amazing voice, and when they drum and sing together, there is power. But I've never seen them talk to each other.

Al hadn't paid much attention to me since I'd arrived maybe because I was someone who got in the way and didn't know a whole lot. Turns out there isn't much about the church Al appreciates, and when I heard his story I didn't wonder why. During that first week together, though, I thought it was all about me…of course.

I wasn't allowed in the tipi, or the sweat lodge. Couldn't chop wood ("Women don't need to do that when I'm around," Paul said.) Couldn't carry wood or water (same reason), wasn't allowed to watch the carving they were doing, or help build the carving shed. No talking while they were carving. No going near the medicines, or the fire, or just about anything else.

All I *was* allowed to experience was their animosity towards each other. They didn't fight with words, but they re-did tasks the other had completed, or went off and did something in a different way than they'd agreed to. One would sweep, the other would come and rake. One unwrapped the drying sage so it was in the wind, the other would cover it up with cotton to keep out the pollen – in January. It was like spending time with siblings who don't get along, but won't yell either.

By the third day, I'd heard Al complain about CSC's view that all Indians are the same (Pan-Indianism, apparently), and learned a little about the differences between Interior BC First Nations (like Al, from the Lil'wat Nation), Plains Cree (like Tom, from Alberta), and one or two Coastal bands of British Columbia. And Aboriginals who'd grown up in cities, like Paul, who didn't know anything about being an "Indian" (his words).

I received some teachings (graciously and humbly, I hope) about sweetgrass and how it's used to invite good spirits into a space or ceremony, and dried sage burned is used as a smudge, a different kind of prayer of cleansing. I heard stories about Aboriginal justice (more helpful than reading books, even if *The Way of the Pipe*, and *Returning to the Teachings* are really good). But I didn't win any gold stars in building caring relationships or even tolerance, for that matter.

Paul kept looking at me like he was watching me, like he knew my secrets. I kept avoiding his glances, shaken by his watching. What exactly *did* he remember?

On Thursday, Cook asked me how it was going, and I think I mumbled fine, but I'm sure looking at me told the real story. I missed spending time in the garden with Kenny. Cooking and baking. Even doing chores in the cattery and kennels with Ricky and Kate had allure.

I was heading back out, and he gave me some reading from Nora. I folded it under my arm, afraid I would burst into tears, and ducked into my room to look at it. It was from Dr. Martin Brokenleg, and boy did I feel dumb because I'd actually taken courses with him at University – of course, I hadn't thought about actually applying what he'd taught me.

Nora was suggesting his work with youth, reclaiming their spirits, could be useful to me. Duh. Circle of Courage, and it's really good stuff. I had to stop making everything that happens all about me, and figure out how to help. I knew this stuff, damn it, from textbooks and lectures and stories. I guess I just don't recognize it when it's happening in real life. I suck at this.

First step -- Belonging – well, I think they had that wrapped up. They seemed confident in their place at *Just Living*. I definitely didn't feel belonging yet, but…it wasn't about me. Next, Mastery. Maybe they'd believe in themselves if I could show them they were good teachers.

Just before dinnertime I headed back out to the grounds, and asked Al if I could lay a fire to "show him he'd taught me well." He sent me to a far corner of the Sacred Grounds, away from where he and Paul were not working together. He told me to go crazy trying. "'Jus don't set the place on fire." I wondered how, in the absolute sogginess of January, I would do that, but for once I didn't blurt the question. He even offered a couple of matches. I didn't let on I'd taken a whole book from the pantry in the kitchen just in case.

I spent about an hour gathering rocks for my fire ring, and some dry underbrush from the nearby woods. I hauled a bucket of water and dragged a log over to sit on. By supper time I was ready to start my fire, and decided to forgo food; I didn't really feel like being with anyone. I lit my fire, offered some tobacco in prayer, and began to sit, and be. And suddenly, it *was* all about me.

Belonging. What an incredible idea, feeling, belief. I thought about all the ways I belong. In my family, and my little apartment home with my brother and Sarita, and the babe on the way. To my church, which was a surprise. With classmates at school. My friends, both spiritual and worldly. Glenn. Trish. To the AVP folks, a belonging all shiny and new. The first blush of relationship with Ben. And then I thought about how

I belong in much bigger ways. And how much work I had to do to get to Mastery.

Inexorably connected to the earth, to Spirit. Inexorably – a word that I love. Ah, thank you, education. I sat staring into the fire like my ancestors have done for millennia, and then I was leaking silent tears. In gratitude, for where I already belong. In sadness, for those places where I'm disconnected. Where my inadequacy keeps me from connecting with Paul and Al. And my Dad.

Then on top of the sadness, I felt fear, wondering how I would ever "belong" in a romance; I couldn't bear that I might not. Then I noticed at the edge of my consciousness all the privilege I carried but hadn't really understood before now. All the opportunities I'd had that these men hadn't.

White. Educated. Middle class. Two professions. Loved as a child, a part of a family. Canadian. Healthy. In all the ways possible. *Damn near spoiled*, and that was a prayer, too. *May I do something meaningful with all this damned privilege*. I had to figure out the obligation and not get resentful that my life had been easy and so I was under huge pressure to make it meaningful. *Fuck, this was hard.* Prayer. Really.

Sometime later, I washed my dirty hands with water from the bucket, and cupped the clear water to drink deeply. Then I thought about how I was connected to the world by this water. Some of it might have been the very water Jesus drank, or Gandhi bathed in; maybe it cascaded over waterfalls in Africa. Or more likely, maybe it was the water an unknown child in the Amazon drank just before she died of a treatable disease. Last year. Or water from piss that an ancestor had tossed into the street from a chamber pot a few centuries ago, a servant to the wealthy. *Water. We are water.*

My eyes were drawn to something over by the fencepost. On the edges of darkness, I made out the profile of a cat – large, but not so big that I thought it was a cougar, *thank God*. Prayer. And when I noticed him, I swear he spoke in my mind.

"Well, that's all well and good, Princess," he said sarcastically, "All this connection...what are you going to *do* about it?"

"*Jesus. Who are you?*" I prayed in a quiet whisper, wondering if Satan could be a cat. Or if I believed in Satan.

The cat started rubbing himself on the fencepost. I'd read once that cats rub their saliva to spread their scent and mark territory. Somehow, this cat was reminding me I was in his territory, not welcoming me as family. I knew I wanted to make a meaningful life. And that this was a cat, God damn it. Maybe a real prayer was in order?

I didn't want to feel sorry for myself just because being with Al and Paul was hard. Paul wasn't around that much because he worked a ton with Tom and the four leggeds, as he called them, so really, I was being a bit dramatic. But I did want to be effective. Belonging. Mastery. Generosity. Independence. How could I help without coming across as trite, privileged, and oh, so white? (Especially when I was trite, privileged and oh, so white?)

The tabby sauntered off (I really don't know how else to describe it), and I sat on my log and listened. Waited for a message. Then I remembered that I'm not very good at that kind of prayer. Sigh.

Well, beating myself up wasn't working. Maybe I should focus on being helpful. I started to move around, and kinda disengaged from the fire, and noticed I was hungry. As I started looking for the water bucket, I heard footsteps and jumped. It was Al, and from his profile I could tell he was carrying something.

"Join you?" he quietly asked, and I nodded, looking at the flames. He reached out, handing me a plate.

"Cook sent this. Thought you might be hungry," and he placed a miracle into my hands -- my favourite comfort food -- and crouched down. A toasted bagel with cream cheese and tomato. I vaguely remembered mentioning it to Cook. How did he know? How could he not?

After a few minutes, Al asked how I was. Or rather grunted "You okay?" into the fire.

"Sad, I guess. I want to be helpful," I said. "I don't want to be a bug, Al. Really. To you or Paul. I'm learning so much from you. I just wish there was something I could give back," I said. We sat for some time together, sharing the chore of fire-tending.

"At least you didn't build a white-man's fire," Al said, chuckling.

"What's that?" I knew not to look at him.

"A big one. So big they have to sit way back, and spend all their time searchin' for lots of wood to burn. Then they get cold in the woods, and make it even bigger," Al answered. I thought I noticed a gleam of teasing in his eyes. I softly laughed.

"I'm too lazy," I said. Some more time passed and Al asked if I was ready to go in. I glanced at the kitchen and noticed all the lights were off; even the offices were dark. I thought I saw Cook sitting on the balcony upstairs.

"Yeah, soon I guess," I answered. Together we started to pull apart the fire, letting it burn itself out.

"Hey Beth," Al started. I looked towards him, without making eye contact. "I'm learnin' too, 'kay? I've never spent time with any ladies except my Mom and Aunties, and sisters growing up. Well, and the kind who aren't ladies. Even Nora and Kate and Sally steer clear of me. The only things I know about ladies I learned from television, or women visitors. And you don't seem like a nun, a uniform or a hooker," he said.

As I looked at him, tears were pooling in my eyes. That was more than I'd ever heard Al say at one time. He held out one arm and I fit my body next to his warmth. His big, painted arm draped casually over my shoulder, and I put my arm tentatively around his back.

"Grab me like you mean it," he said. "Else, how will I catch you when you fall down the rabbit hole?"

We crossed the field and garden together, letting go of one another at the door to the dorms. I still don't know if he's ever read *Alice in Wonderland*. There are lots of rabbit holes at *Just Living*, I was finding.

I headed to my room, washing up on the way. I decided to catch my breath on the balcony, and see if I'd missed Cook. I wanted to thank him for the bagel.

I stepped out into the darkness, and saw him sitting quietly in one of the chairs, head back, eyes closed. I decided to sit, without disturbing him. I spent a few minutes imagining what the stars might look like behind the ever-present clouds, when he quietly said, "You okay, Mugwump?"

"Only because you didn't let me starve to death," I replied, inferring thanks, I hoped.

"Your brother called to make sure you'd landed. We chatted and in the end I convinced him you were fine, just busy. He sounded kind of protective, so I decided I better send you food so that you didn't die. For my own protection, you understand." He peeked over at me through one cracked eyelid. At least now I knew where he'd picked up my family nickname, Mugwump. I chuckled.

"Yeah, smart thinking. Steve's scary."

More time passed.

"You met Timex yet?" Cook asked. He wasn't opening his eyes.

"Who's Timex?" Cook chuckled.

"The resident spook," he answered. "Kind of mangy looking, one ear half torn off. He's the one who really runs the place. Has Nora do the paperwork."

"A cat?" I asked. Cook nodded. "I think I met him tonight on the Grounds." Cook chuckled again.

"Unnerving little fellow, eh?"

It was my turn to nod.

"Al brought him out of the woods one day about a year ago. He looked like hell, don't really know what happened to him. Covered in open sores, big infected snarling mess. Burned, maybe. Anyhow, he fought us all the way, and we have the battle scars to prove it." Cook rolled up a sleeve, and I saw a faint trace of a scratch in his ink. Maybe.

"You've never seen such a bunch of sissies, all of us doting on that damn cat. After three months or so, Kate convinced us he was as ready as possible to be adopted, so we did. Convinced Nora we needed a mouser, but she only agreed if we didn't let him in the buildings because some folks allergic. Not that it's a problem. Timex don't go inside. Sometimes he holes up in the barn with the barn cats, especially if there's a new rescue moved in."

A few more minutes passed, but I'd stopped keeping track. I finally got up the nerve to ask.

"Why'd you call him a spook?" I understood that was a derogatory word for a black guy...and the cat was an old, grey tabby.

"If'n you don't know already, you will soon enough," Cook answered. That was as close as anyone came to acknowledging Timex's "mind power," as I called it. Later, Kate admitted that she had never seen the men so silly about an animal, nor an animal so resistant to help. I asked why they'd called him Timex.

"Takes a licking, and keeps on ticking," she answered. I smiled

I found Timex to be the most unnerving creature at *Just Living*. And everyone made *way* more allowances for him than deserved. They had more loyalty to that curmudgeon than to most of the people who come through here, and he treated everyone equally -- with disdain. He ate whatever, slept wherever and kept company with whomever he pleased, whenever he wanted. I tried (unsuccessfully) to steer clear of him because he's such a freak. I don't think he liked me. And it's all about me, right?

Cook and I turned in shortly after. As a gentle rain began to fall on the steel roof, I found myself being lulled to sleep, happy for a closed door that even Timex couldn't pass through. I slept well.

And sometimes, Creator, my prayer is found in the rising of the yeast, the kneading of the dough and the feeding of the masses.

A little differently than the loaves and fishes of your time, but I must admit, I imagine it's just as satisfying. Feeding bellies. Feeding souls.

Life is rich and good.

Thank you for the elasticity of the dough; in a politically incorrect way, thanks for the gluten. Grin.

CHAPTER 20
MAKE NEW FRIENDS...

Contemplation: deep or full consideration, thoughtful observation. Prospect or expectation.

My foray into prayer has led me here, to a place of wanting to understand my connection with You more fully, more...currently? And so my mornings and evenings have been looking and feeling like this:

Space. Silence. On the page I think it looks like this. I listen without "hope or agenda." And when my mind wanders (like it is right now) I gently release the thought and bring myself back to this.

Somehow, after just the right amount of time I feel closer. I understand more fully. And I'm readier to faithfully face the day.

Thank you for helping me understand Us more fully.

I had lots more learning opportunities, and things were easier between me and Al. Paul stayed aloof, but I started to notice he was aloof with everyone, even Tom. So the moral of the story: It really isn't all about me.

Thursday evening my getaway driver touched base, asked me if I could meet with him on his way to his placement in Pemberton.

"Sure, but why aren't you travelling through Whistler? Wanting the boys to spend more time in the car?" I asked, smiling.

Glenn adored his boys.

"Nah…I'm going up alone for now," he said, and I could hear tension in his voice.

"What? What about Donna?" I blurted.

"I'll tell you about it. And about what's going on with the protesters at UBC."

Shoot. I'd forgotten about them.

"How's Monday?" he asked.

I couldn't wait to hear what was going on.

"See you then, Glenn. I'll let you know if there is a spare room, and what the room will cost you."

I signed off, and mentally added Glenn and Donna to my prayer list. The list of intercessions grew. Continued begging.

Friday, around lunch, Al began cleaning up the grounds, gathering wood and stacking the "Grandfathers," large rocks heated for the sweat lodge. He wouldn't let me help directly, but at least Sally let me know why.

"Thinks it might be your Moon Time, Beth," Sally said at lunch.

Because it was, I told Al I'd steer clear of the ceremony.

I spent the afternoon at my firepit, and about a half-hour later Hugh, our Elder, asked if he could join me. Of course, I said, reaching in my pocket for the rose quartz I'd been carrying. I offered it to Hugh, and he graciously accepted, throwing some sage from his pocket on my fire.

"You know, my Grandmothers taught me that a woman's Moon Time is the Creator's gift of purification," he began. "We men purify using a sweat lodge, but women were gifted with the power of the moon and the flow of the oceans to cleanse her. It would be disrespectful to the Creator to suggest that our human ceremony is more purifying than the one given by the Creator."

I started to feel special, instead of excluded.

"I have a favour to ask," Hugh went on. "Ben is bringing out five or six young people from the Friendship Centre. You know some of them: Justin, the young man who's been helping you and Kenny, and a couple of others. Anyhow, I know he won't think to ask the girls about this."

I waited.

"Al tells me you are learning some crafts," he added. I showed Hugh the beadwork I had started, couching a Celtic pattern onto some fine, sturdy cloth.

"I'm better at this than carving," I admitted. "And I've learned a little bit about leatherwork and weaving cedar bark."

"If any of the younger women are on their Moon Time, would you do some crafts with them in the Great Room during the sweat?" he asked.

I reassured him that I'd be honoured. "See you next week," he said, with a gleam in his eye. Maybe I do belong. Maybe I have moments of being helpful, after all.

A half hour later I found myself building a little fire in the fireplace with Agnes, a young woman of about sixteen. I received instructions about soup-stirring and bread-baking from Cook, who was joining the sweat. I watched amazed as people congregated; only Ricky and Kate in the kennels, Sally and Bob (the administrator who DEFINITELY wasn't Aboriginal) didn't participate. I wondered how everyone would fit into the small lodge Tom and Al had constructed over the willow frame; it couldn't have been more than about ten feet across, maybe twelve, and no more than three or four feet high. It was covered in hides and tarps, and kind of shaped like an igloo, I thought, with the door flap facing east (like the tipi) towards the open fire pit heating the Grandfathers.

In the Great Room I showed Anne my beadwork, and explained how Al had taught me to couch beads. He did his work on leather; fine, detailed work, even with his big hands. She asked me about the pattern I was tracing.

"It's a labyrinth," I said. "This is a copy of a huge labyrinth on the floor of a cathedral in France."

She wanted to know more, so as we set her up couching beads on a leather headband Al had cut earlier, I told her about the labyrinth as a spiritual tool.

"I thought it was some kind of weird Medicine Wheel," she said, and I admitted that I'd noticed that too.

I asked her what she knew about the Medicine Wheel, and she talked about the four directions, the four colours of the races, and the gifts and symbols associated with each. We shared easily and comfortably, working beside each other, our conversation peppered with lots of silence. We could smell the hearty soup wafting over from next door; Sally was taking care of it.

I shared with Anne some of what I had read about the Circle of Courage from Rev. Brokenleg, and she listened for a time. I asked her if she knew of him, and his teachings. Turns out he visited the Valley regularly, and Anne had attended his workshops. I was grateful to hear her perspective and told her so.

Anne shared a little bit about Justin, that young man who'd been around. I think he'd had a few run-ins with the law, but was turning his life around. Anyhow, Anne seemed a little more than interested in him, and it was fun to talk with her about him, and what her Grandfather told her to look for in a man --someone who is hardworking, and sober, and knows who he is.

Before long, darkness was falling. People began to drift away from the Grounds, and into the kitchen, gathering quietly to share the light meal. A calm had settled over *Just Living*; even Ricky was subdued. Anne and I offered to bring in the horses, and found out it had already been done. The easy fellowship was as delicious as Cook's feast.

As Ben got Anne and the other youth ready to head back to town, I curled up in front of the fire in the Great Room reading, my beading beside me. I was disappointed that I hadn't gotten more time to spend with Ben. Before they left he tracked me down and asked if I'd be interested in a coffee in town later that week.

"Yes, but I have plans to meet a friend on Monday, I think. He's going to call me and confirm," I said, cringing, and hoping Ben would be flexible so I could fit in both visits, and that Nora would be okay with me being away from the house for two evenings.

"Should I be jealous?" he asked, casually touching my arm, a gleam in his eye.

My heart began to pound.

"God no. He's married. Kids. Moving to a new parish – we just want to catch up before he goes. That's all," I sputtered, turning bright red.

"Don't let him talk you into joining him," he said. "I want a chance to state *my* intentions," he whispered as he snuck out the door to drive the van back to town.

He seemed awkward, which was weird. And made my heart pound even more.

Then, Kenny came looking for me, offering a cup of tea. I was well cared for by these men.

"How you doing, Beth? It was weird not having you in the sweat," he admitted. He knew I liked to be included in stuff.

"Moon Time," I said, and all was explained, it seemed. "And I got to do some beading with one of the young women. We're in sync, apparently," I said, raising my eyebrows.

He chuckled.

"What is that?" he asked, pointing to my beading, and I was explaining again about the labyrinth in Chartres. He was tracing the pattern with his finger.

"Is it a maze?" he asked, and I explained there was only one path in, and it was walked in prayer, a time of moving inward, and then after some time in the centre, a time of returning to the world by the same path.

He was intrigued.

"And people walk on it?" he asked.

"Well, in real life, the one in the cathedral in Chartres is a lot bigger than this one," I said, laughing. Mine was about six inches across. "It covers the floor of one wing of the chapel, I think."

We shared our tea, and Kenny headed up to bed.

Later, on the porch, I replayed the conversation with Ben in my mind over and over, wondering if I could have been reading more into it than he meant. The only sounds around me were the birds and coyotes settling for the night. I decided to keep imagining that he was as interested in me as I was in him. Then Cook joined me.

"This week, I'm going to the pub. I'm going to meet my friend Glenn," I reminded him.

"Glenn, Glenn...who's he again, Mugwump? Should Ben be worried?"

I reached over and swatted his arm.

"You remember. He's a *married* friend of mine. And what are you talking about Ben?" I thought I'd been cagey.

"Oh, I don't know. But you've asked me every question I could think of about him and hardly any about anyone else, except Claire. And I don't think she's as interestin'," he answered, and I blushed as we hugged in the hallway, heading to our rooms.

Nora joined me after breakfast the next day and asked how my time at *Just Living* was going. I didn't know how to answer her.

"Hard. Incredible. I feel lucky to be learning so much. Blessed, really." I saw Nora flinch at the religious talk. "It's like I've landed in a foreign land, and I'm not sure if the foreign-ness is because of prison, or restorative justice."

She smiled. "You've got the whole weekend to think about it," she said. "We expect one shift in the kitchen."

(Dishpit! I thought. Or maybe I'd bake some scones...or croissants!)

"And an hour or so helping with the animals. The sign-up sheet is in the office; it's time to pitch in. You sign up under 'helper' not 'leader,' okay?"

I chuckled, knowing I wasn't even much help yet, but again feeling a little more welcomed.

"I have no trouble mucking stalls or walking dogs," I added.

"And go to town, even just to Mission, to a coffee shop or the library, okay? You've been hanging around here a lot, and it's important to remember there's a whole world out there. Kate and I are going to town Sunday if you want a ride."

I told her about my plans to have coffee with friends next week, and she seemed pleased.

The weekend was a delicious time, a time of rest, and work, community and solitude. Saturday I spent writing in my journals, and walking dogs. Some time in the vegetable garden turning the wet soil. I read some stuff about trauma recovery and groomed a horse or two.

Saturday night I wrote a letter to Ben, and an entry in my practicum journal. Didn't know if I would send the letter, but after an edit or two, it looked like this:

"Dear Ben,

I missed you this weekend, everything from your steady presence to your insightful, probing questions. I've learned tons, miss Steve and the family, and worked hard. In some ways, this feels like vacation, biding time until I can get on with my life. In other ways, this luxury of space to seek insight feels like a perfect gift. I've been reading about and practicing different kinds of prayer...still have lots to learn if you have any insights to share.

I wish we'd had more time to talk when you were here for the sweat, and I'm looking forward to coffee sometime next week. My buddy confirmed he's coming out on Monday, so if we could meet a different night that'd be great.

I'm learning to trust that whatever it is I'm supposed to be doing with my life will come clear if I'm patient. These past few weeks have opened my eyes to the possibility of having my heart's desire, of finding service and even personal relationships that bring me meaning and bliss. This is new to me, and exciting, as I let go of the idea that my life is to be grudgingly, not joyfully, lived. Is it only because I'm exploring living while bringing the integrity of values and beliefs into my actions more fully? Or could it also be because of the relationships emerging in my life at this time?

Trust. Patience. I'll try to follow Sister's advice, and not be attached to outcomes, but I'm noticing possibilities I want to believe are Spirit-led (and besides, they are delicious. Better than a warm mocha in a cold car.)

Wishful thinking? Hope not.

A rookie, at best,

Beth."

There. Hopefully that will give him something to think about.

"Beth! Can you help me with this?" Cook was shouting up the stairs.

I was pretty excited about seeing Glenn for coffee, and had spent all day helping Cook with meals. I groaned, grabbed my wallet out of my sock drawer (original, eh? In a house filled with felons...) and ran down the stairs to the kitchen.

"What do you need, Cook?" I asked. Every surface was covered in flour, and the ovens were hot. I could smell bread baking.

"I'm not feeling great, Mugwump, and I just wondered if you could watch the bread for me while I go sit for a bit. It's just rolls for lunches for the next few days," he said, and I looked more closely at him.

He was grey, and I was used to Cook looking robust *and* rosy cheeked. I didn't like this.

"Oh my God! Look at you – sit down!" I said, as I moved into baker mode.

I quickly donned an apron, ran a sink of hot water, checked the buns, and (most importantly) put on the kettle for a quick cup of tea. I even snuck into the pantry to call Glenn and let him know I'd be a little late and he should order food for both of us, and then called off my taxi.

I was able to wash up the counters and dishes, and pull the buns from the oven before the tea was steeped, all the while listening to Cook.

"Not a day goes by, Darlin', that I don't thank God you came here," he said, eyes closed, as he leaned against the cool window. "I feel so crummy and tired, I ain't felt really great since that sweat last week. But I just couldn't burn them buns."

Cook had issues with waste, so getting halfway through a yeast adventure and leaving it unbaked just wasn't in his repertoire.

"Your buns are in good hands." I cracked a smile as I put the cup of tea in front of him.

"Go on up to bed once the tea is done. I'll put them away when I get home," I reassured him.

"Where you off to?" I could see Cook trying to remember if I'd told him my plans.

"Going to meet Glenn at the pub, remember? Let me rebook the taxi," I said, heading into the pantry. It was not only the most private place for telephone calls (so even had a comfy stool), but also, for some obscure reason, had the best indoor cell reception.

"Darlin' I've told you, you don't have to pay for a cab. If you don't want to borrow the *Just Living* truck you can use my car," he said. "Just pull the keys off the wall by the door."

I hated to take advantage of Cook, but I was running late. "Really? You don't mind?" I asked.

He waved me off with a curt "I ain't huggin' yah today, Mugwump. One of us has to stay healthy," and I was off in the blink of an eye.

"Don't worry about the buns, Cook. And I'll get up and do breakfast, okay?" I could totally do that without his help, I thought, which surprised me. I pulled off my apron up and tossed it over the cooling bread, and headed out. Maybe I was getting this after all.

I started the engine, and thought, "I might not even be too late." I concentrated on the wet road in the dark; it wouldn't pay to be even later because I was stuck in a ditch.

As I drove down the road towards the pub, my mind wandered to Glenn. I'd met him when I was in first year of theology school, he'd been in his second, and we'd become study buddies, without the sex or Adderall. Last year he'd graduated and started working as a Deacon just outside of Vancouver, so we didn't see each other much anymore. Except when I talked him into helping at the protest, of course. He was brilliant, and one of the kindest men I knew.

I knew he'd hated commuting for hours to his parish, and that he wanted to serve a church in a community where he lived. Donna liked their neighbourhood in South Van, but had told him she'd move when his position was "more permanent." Being a Deacon was like an internship, so I hoped his move to Pemberton was to be a permanent congregation. I was really looking forward to catching up with him, but our phone call had me worried.

Dear Mary,

Whichever one of you is listening. Or maybe Mary and Martha both....

I think I'm realizing that sometimes service is prayer...if I do it with enough intention. Attention. Focus.

I helped Cook tonight, and as I danced into his kitchen and took over baking the bread, it was as if my body was made for that act in that moment...and there was nothing else I could be doing. Even as I did it I was aware that I didn't want to rush it, nor to prolong it...the service was enough.

Enough focus.

Enough work.

Enough love.

Thank you for helping me notice that prayer can be a physical conversation with Creation.

Today I felt joy in the baking. I hope that happens again.

CHAPTER 21
FAMILY MATTERS

Veronica took the corner just a little too fast, her mind on her destination, not the journey. She reached out and braced the stew on the seat next to her as she slowed down; the last thing she needed was a wet-cleanup all over the passenger seat. Between working, volunteering, and taking care of her yard, she was busy enough. And, she had her commitment to Kenny on Thursday afternoon to talk about spring garden plans.

Heading to her daughter's for a family potluck, she was pretty sure she was heading into an ambush of epic proportions. She expected her son Jim, who hadn't spoken to her in two years, had decided the family should get together "to talk." She smiled, realizing she'd rather be going to prison, or *Just Living* for an afternoon of garden design.

She pulled over to the curb just for a moment and closed her eyes, deciding she needed a minute to calm down. She opened the car window, and breathed in the cool air. Driving the back roads always settled her, and she smiled, thinking of the grandchildren who would certainly be happy to see her. She was still enchanted with being a grandparent, and felt some sadness that Bert wasn't alive so they could grandparent together. He would have liked spoiling the girls, playing sports with the boys, taking them fishing on the river. She smiled, feeling his presence steadying her. After a few minutes, she put the car in drive and headed up the street towards Brenda's.

Veronica nudged open the side door, and as she reached down to pick up the dinner she heard raised voices pouring out of the kitchen.

"I don't care what she says. She'd have to be crazy to be doing what she's doing. We *have* to intervene. Do you know what the relatives are saying?" Yup. Jim was here. Veronica sighed, tired before she even got inside.

"She's an adult, Jim, and quite a bright one at that. I don't think you get to have the final say about what she's doing." There was Terry, Brenda's husband. Veronica sent up a prayer of thanks for his support.

"You have no idea what she is doing! She is spending time up there *with him*. This just isn't safe. And wanting to hang out in that place tells me she isn't all right upstairs, if you know what I mean." Veronica grinned, and didn't rush into the kitchen. This was far too interesting.

"Oh Jim, it's not like that. You have no idea. You've been listening to crazy Aunt Ruth again. Mom is fine, really. She is happier than she's been since Dad died. You should try listening, really listening." Brenda turned and was heading towards Veronica on the stairs, so Veronica coughed to alert her.

"Mom, is that you?" she called as she headed towards her mother.

"Yes dear. Where are the children? I expected them to meet me out front."

"They're at the school for movie night. They'll be home later. One of Stephanie's friends' parents took them."

"Well, that gets them out of the way for this heated conversation, anyhow," Veronica smiled at her daughter, her eyes dancing.

"Mom, I'm so sorry! I had no idea Jim was going to be crazy about this. I actually agreed to this dinner because, well, Easter's coming and I hoped for some family peace. I had no idea he was in a snit. I'm so sorry."

Brenda dragged me into the garage and opened the freezer to retrieve an ice cream creation she had moulded earlier in the day.

"Don't worry honey. It'll be okay. If Jim tries to have me committed hopefully some of my friends and family will intervene," Veronica joked.

Brenda looked so worried that Veronica wondered if that was what Jim had threatened. Veronica reached in and hugged Brenda. "Really, honey, you aren't responsible for your brother's attitude. It'll be fine. Let's go in," she finished.

When the women entered the kitchen, platters and casseroles in hand, Terry leapt to his feet to help. John, who had been quiet until then, took the casserole and slid it into the oven for his sister. He took Veronica's hand and pulled her into a hug.

"Hi Mom," he sighed. "How are you? I'm glad you're here," he said, and Veronica knew that that was a loaded greeting.

Jim and John had fought since they were boys. Jim saw opportunity, John saw oppression. Jim knew black and white, and saw very little grey, and John's world was complex, colourful and usually viewed from many angles. She loved her boys and reached across for a quick kiss from Jim.

"Hello son," Veronica said, pretending it had just been last week that she'd seen him. "How are things at home? I hope the customers are treating you well at the bank," she said, hoping small talk would fill some space and carry them to dinner. "That stew will be ready in a few minutes once it's warmed through. Can I help you with the table, Brenda?" She hoped she didn't sound like she was babbling.

"Mom." That was all Jim said. His air-kiss on her cheek hadn't really landed, and in a breath Veronica decided to change her tactics and meet his attitude head-on. Jim didn't like being the one answering questions.

"So Jim, have you heard? Corrections have nominated me for an award as a volunteer. And I've been asked to speak during Victim Awareness Week in April. Can you come?"

"Oh Mom! That's wonderful! Dad would be so amazed!" Brenda was always enthusiastic about my volunteer work.

"How can we support you?" John asked.

"Well, you can come, of course. I'd love to have all my family there. It's going to happen in a theatre in Mission, and Roger will be presenting with me if the Warden approves his passes. Jim, I'd really like it if you could come and hear me speak. It'd mean a lot. Maybe you could bring

Ruth. Don't worry, you don't have to let me know now. I'll get the details to you, and reserve tickets for you closer to the date."

Veronica busied herself checking the casserole.

"It's not normal, what you do!" Jim sputtered. "It's not right. And it's true, Brenda, Dad would be amazed. Mortified, maybe. Mom, have you talked to Fr. Patrick lately?"

Of course, Jim was comfortable reminding his mother of the conservative Catholic priest who had baptized her children, even if *he* hadn't been to see Fr. Patrick in years.

"No, I haven't. I go to the Lutheran church now, Jim. You remember – Fr. Patrick wouldn't bury your Dad. Have you been to Mass lately?"

Jim had the wisdom to look sheepish.

"Jim, really, I know we're all dealing with the fallout from your Dad's murder. It wouldn't be normal if we all reacted exactly the same way. So at least, if you don't want to hear my perspective, let's leave it alone. I promise not to bring it up again if you don't." Perhaps he'd settle for an unholy truce.

"Now, let's have dinner. My grands will be home soon, and I bet they'll be hungry!" Veronica bustled around setting the table, not really sure if they'd be hungry, but not willing to spend another moment arguing with her kids.

Everyone pretended not to notice when Jim made excuses and snuck out the side door. They heard his car back down the driveway and head down the road, maybe just a little too fast.

CHAPTER 22
THE OTHER, GOLD

When I walked into the pub, Glenn was in a back booth, nursing a beer. Frankly, he looked like hell. His skin was pasty, his expression drawn, and he was peering into his glass; I presumed it wasn't his first. His eyes had that "I haven't slept in days, and don't think I will tonight, either" look. I seemed to be plagued by pasty guys tonight.

Dear God, what is going on here?

"Are you waiting for me to begin?" I asked, trying to set a light tone as I slipped in across from him.

He kept looking at the light foam on his glass, avoiding my eyes.

"I'm not sure," he answered. "I'm not sure of much anymore."

I reached out my hand and wrapped it around his.

"What's up, Glenn?" I asked.

"I don't even know where to begin," he answered, sighing.

"I've got all night. Doesn't really matter where you begin because I'm happy to hear it in any order. We've got time…." As I looked right at him, his eyes met mine briefly, and then he looked back into his glass.

"I got a parish," he began. I had expected the announcement would be coupled with eager anticipation, not dread.

"I heard. Up north, right? And…?" was the only response I could think of. How clever.

"I'm heading up there now. A little town near Pemberton, lots of travel, at least three rural churches…I'm going to go up and check it out. The Bishop assured me it's mine if I want it."

"And…?" I repeated, searching his eyes for some clarity.

"It's exciting, new, all of that. I should be ordained at Easter."

The waiter, hovering, intercepted and asked what I'd like.

"A Blonde," I said, tongue in cheek. My mind flipped to Ben, whose curly hair was definitely dark brown. I blushed as the waiter left the table, order in hand.

"Remind me to ask what that's all about," Glenn chuckled, and I blushed more. Dang! He knows me too well.

"So, tell me what's really going on with the new parish, the ordination, and all, which, I might add, should be exciting."

Glenn sighed, and looked at his beer again. "Donna's not coming," he said.

My beer arrived, finally.

"What do you mean, Donna isn't coming? What about your family, the boys? I thought she was supportive, understood all that." My voice trailed off.

"When I told her about my meeting with Bishop Tom, she told me we had to stop 'kidding ourselves.' 'I don't think I can keep this up, Glenn, pretending I'm a part of this. I really don't want to move to the Toolies, leave my community, be a Priest's Wife in some economically depressed town with all the depressing shit that comes with that…I'm a part of something here. I love Vancouver, the community centre, the day care…all of it. Mom and Dad said I can move into their basement suite next month.' She'd had it all thought out, all planned. I didn't even see it coming." Glenn took a long, slow draw on his glass. He looked right at me and his raw pain leaked onto me.

"God," I said (not a prayer). "I don't get it. I thought she was into this. She has a spiritual connection, I thought...." I was grasping to make sense of things, overpowered by his pain.

"Yeah, she does, still does, I think. But she says she doesn't really feel connected to the church anymore. Doesn't like how I have to do what the Bishop says. Thinks it is all 'old school' and 'becoming irrelevant.'"

"But I thought she knew we all agree with all that, but want to work to change things from within...keep what is working, change what isn't and all that...." My voice trailed off as I realized I was debating Donna's point of view with Glenn, who already agreed with me.

We sat in silence for a bit, nursing our pints.

"God, what are you going to do?" I asked.

Glenn had always been the family guy, a Dad who loved his wife, really in love with her, and the boys, the yard, all of it. I couldn't imagine him single.

"Well, it seems I'm going to Mount Currie. She doesn't want to work on the marriage even if I turn down the appointment, so I'm going to check it out, maybe find a place to live. I just wanted an evening of company on the way. Some things I think I've figured out, others I'm still working on. In some ways, it's a relief. It's been hard for her to bite her tongue about stuff, and now she doesn't have to."

He didn't sound nearly as resentful as I wanted him to be. But maybe I was just remembering what a bitch I'd been when I'd asked for a divorce from my quickie wedding.

We ordered our food, and another beer each. I found myself distracted by the TV, by conversation at the next table, anything nearby...I was having trouble staying focused and said so.

"I'm sorry, Glenn. I'm being a flake. It's like everything's connected to me, but not. Maybe I'm just not ready for this job." I was looking for an out, I admit.

"Not ready? Seems to me if it's in front of you and you recognize it, Spirit might think you're ready. Not ready, or not willing?" Glenn challenged me, bringing me back. He always did that.

"I don't know," I lied. "You said you'd learned some things?"

"Well, when she told me, I was really fucked up. I mean, when I married her, I MEANT for better or for worse, right? And I thought she did, too. Maybe she did at the time. So this sucks, because I can't even really figure it out. What it says about me, about us, about our family, about my word. I'm not really angry, or anything, but I did ask her and all she would say was that she had meant the vows at the time, but things had changed and she believed God's will for us had changed, too. I'm trying not to see that as a cop-out."

He took a slug of beer and as our food arrived, he asked for another. Hmmm. If he kept this up, he wouldn't be driving anywhere tonight. I chuckled when I saw our waiter's eyebrows rise…I wondered how much higher they'd be if he knew we were becoming-priests. So much for stereotypes. Glenn was intent on "tying one on," which was okay; I was willing to look after him, and so I stopped drinking so I could get Cook's car home safe, with both of us in it. Glenn continued.

"I couldn't get my pride around a divorce, and I didn't understand what Donna was saying. I know she's done. But I couldn't understand how to just walk away from a promise I made to God. Not that I'm being given much choice." He snorted.

Our burgers smelled delicious, and we started to eat. *Such communion* I silently prayed. As close as I got to public grace nowadays.

"So, what did you do?" I asked around a mouthful.

"I called Al Steiner. Do you remember him?" Of course I did.

"So, you have a marriage problem wrapped up in Christian theology, and you reach out to a gentle, gay, social-rights activist, who is Jewish. I get it!" I joked. "Makes perfect sense." Glenn laughed. "What did he say?"

"Well, you know I think he's brilliant. I remembered that he had just ended a relationship when we saw him. I didn't want legal advice, or even Anglican advice. I was hoping he'd say something that would stretch me. I was being pretty self-righteous, and…well, I can be a bitch to live with when I'm self-righteous. Don't even like myself, which wasn't helping with Donna.

"To make a long story short, I learned a little about why I make promises I clearly can't keep. Maybe I just want to have all those promises of rainbows and unicorns, and forever-unconditional hope and love…but by adding love-making, it was physical, earthy, and not just mystical."

My skin began to tingle, my hair lift on my arms and the back of my neck.

"Um hum," I said.

"Well, Al thinks we yearn to have the qualities of our God-relationship in our human ones, like I said, so we make these promises with every intention of living them out, but our human imperfection just doesn't make it easy, or sometimes possible."

I sat back for a while reflecting on that. It tugged at my consciousness, and I couldn't figure out why. And I couldn't even blame the beer.

"How did that help you?" I asked.

I was mostly curious but a small part of me was messing with him. He was getting more and more tipsy, so his answers were getting more fun.

"Well, once I started seeing human-Donna, and then human-me, too, things just got softer. I gave up being a four-year-old, stomping my feet and screaming 'But you promised!' Then I thought how it would be if she stayed because I guilted her…NOT. 'Cause the best fun is all about obligation, right? And then I had to admit," he said as he looked me square in the eye, "that things sucked at home. They haven't really been great for a while."

I sat back, hands around the base of my glass, and sighed.

"So falling in love can be delicious and energizing and consuming because, well, we think the other person is perfect, like God."

"Wait a minute," Glenn slurred. "You in love?"

"That's not what I'm thinking about," I lied. "What about original family relationships? We never really 'divorce' those. I carry all that baggage with me, even when I try to dump the relationship. I'm wondering about my Dad, and our relationship. I think I'm just starting to 'get' that one," I answered.

"You're totally dodging the 'You in love?' question," Glenn teased. Maybe he wasn't that drunk after all. "But keep going. I knew you'd help me." He paused, and sat back. "It's good to talk about it. You don't try to fix it, or tell me just to suck it up, like my hockey buddies." Glenn really did play hockey...but not in a league that bruised each other.

"Well, I've been trying to figure out the crap I've sold myself about my relationship with my Dad, trying to be a little more honest. I want to know, really, why I've been happy to play the compliant, obedient daughter all this time, while whining about feminism at the same time. Why can't I grow up?

"I think you've just shown me a part of it. I wanted Dad to be a perfect father, and expected him to be all knowing. I've never really been honest with him about any of it. Maybe I didn't want to be vulnerable. It was like I was being the bitch-daughter -- he hurt me once, and I wasn't going to give him another chance." I munched on a few fries.

"I think maybe he's just been trying to be Dad in a way that makes sense to him, and he's not measuring up to my standards, but has no idea what I want from him...he's just Dad but I expect Perfect Dad. And that lets me write him off as old and irrelevant. I've got lots more to think about, but I'm getting tired."

I drained my water glass, and looked up. The waiter brought us each a coffee, and I was glad because I knew driving up that dark road tonight was going to take some focus. Glenn was staring at me, glassy-eyed.

"You are amazing," he said, and I laughed.

"We seem to have figured out many of the problems of the world, so, what now?"

"Ask me about the students!" he said, re-energized.

"So what about the students?" I said, grinning.

"You won't believe it! They're doing great. They've started a lecture series about the history of campus protest, and citizen rights. They've partnered with a couple of social media groups to stay connected to environmental stuff. Anyway, they have this big plan to stop the pipelines. It's kinda cool to see how well they've organized.

"The law students are working on the legal aspects, and the sociology group is working on some of the more political stuff. First Nations groups are getting involved, and that's sparked some stuff with the law students again, supporting the First Nations legal injunctions." Glenn seemed great when he wasn't talking about his family, but he stared at his beer again. I didn't want him to get teary-eyed – maudlin Glenn isn't fun.

"What about Julie and her boyfriend?" I asked, trying to keep him distracted while I got the bill.

"She's great. I don't know about her guy, except he recovered. I guess it was touch-and-go for a bit, but he's fine." He took a sip of beer, the glass almost empty. "The experience seems to have…I don't know…Julie's just more serious. Focused, maybe. Anyhow, I had to talk to her a couple of times about keeping quiet about what you did. She thinks you deserve a fricking medal or something," he finished.

I felt a little panic rise in my stomach. She had to understand that being right and being legal don't always match up.

"Thanks for that," I said. "What now?" I asked.

"Short term, or long term?"

"Well, short term you can come up to *Just Living* and spend the night. I'm sure we have space."

"Did you check? It's not like it's your place. You aren't running the show."

I thought about that. It actually felt more like my place than anywhere else right now. Stephen and Sarita were in my apartment, and from our phone calls I could tell they were making it theirs, which was great. Mom and Dad's house held memories, but hardly felt like "home."

"Actually," I said, "it is my space, and I know no one will mind because you're important to me." I was kicking myself that I'd forgotten to talk to Nora about it, but surely it would be alright. This was Glenn, right?

We finished our coffees, I settled the bill and we headed out. Glenn grabbed a few things from his car and we were on our way. Luckily he didn't puke in the "Cookmobile."

Cook was napping when we arrived back at *Just Living*, and I tried to assess him under the yellow porch light. He looked kinda sickly. Yellow, maybe. Fancy that, under a yellow light. One eye opened and he peered at me.

"Don't want you to think I'm keepin' an eye, Darlin', but, well, good you're home safe," he said, and I noticed I kind of liked that he was waiting up for me. And his car. And it did not escape me that I would be throwing a tantrum if it had been Dad. Hmmm. Interesting.

"Cook, Glenn. Glenn, Cook. Glenn's a little under the weather and couldn't drive so I brought him home," I said, a smile in my voice.

Cook crossed his arms, and closed his eyes again. "Good to meet you Glenn. Welcome. Darlin', I presume he has clearance?" The one eye opened again, once more peering at me. He smiled, and it was pretty clear that Cook knew he didn't, and I blanched. "Don't worry, Mugwump. We'll figure it out. Of course he can stay...let me think up somethin'."

In no time we'd checked with Tom, and fashioned a bedroll in the tipi...and Glenn was fast asleep, outside the perimeter alarm.

"I hope he doesn't freeze to death out there...when he agreed to come I think he imagined an indoor bed, at least," I said, grateful for the help. Cook chuckled again.

"He has lots a anti-freeze on board, and this is the Fraser Valley, not Edmonton. Spring's already on its way. He'll be fine. Tom put a couple of hot rocks from the fire by his feet. He's toasty," Cook reassured me.

"You bagged the rolls, and laid out breakfast already. You feeling better?" I asked.

"Yeah, I am. The strength came back after a few minutes of restin'. Sally looked in on me, and we played a little crib, and things righted themselves. But thanks for cleanin' up," he said.

"Oh Cook. I'm so happy to really be a help," I said, and gave him a big bear hug. I loved that his belly jiggled when he laughed. "Anyhow, thanks for your help with Glenn. Sorry I was so stupid. I'm heading upstairs, 'kay? See you dark and early?"

As I climbed the stairs I started berating myself for being a fool. Of course, this wasn't "my home." I'd been here six weeks, and I still didn't get it.

What was I doing, presuming anyone could visit, especially overnight? Thank God for Cook who caught my mistake, then rescued us. I knew he'd bent the rules even letting Glenn on property, but I was tired, and glad I didn't have to drive back into town to find a motel room for him.

It was as if Cook could read my mind. He called down the hall after me, "Don't worry, Mugwump. We can say he was visiting the tipi...how were we to know he'd fall asleep?" I ran down the hall and hugged the burly man again and thanked him, starting to get just how much I'd fucked up. Maybe not a prayer. Cook'd need to be rising in four or five hours to start breakfast, and had stayed up waiting to make sure I was safe. Now he was compromising the house rules for me. On a night he was ill. I owed him.

He chucked me under the chin as I turned to leave.

"Don't worry, Bethy," he said. "I never sleep that deeply or for too long anyway. Too many dreams." He must be talking about nightmares. What kind of system do we have that leaves men so broken they can't even sleep?

I stayed up half the night feeling ashamed of myself for being presumptuous and naive. When would I grow up? I wrote to Aaron about it, needing to bare my conscience and confess my stupidity. I explained with humour that I had forgotten that the rule "Nothing in, nothing out" included priests, and I felt like a foolish schoolgirl. As I sent the email to him, with an apology, I cc'd Ben. Because a part of my sleeplessness was about wondering if I'd wrecked things with him before we'd figured out if there was a thing. My heart beat picked up when I thought of being close to him, and my heart was aching for being stupid. Either way, it was easier to admit up front what a fool I'd been than tell him in person later, I decided.

Confession: a formal admission or acknowledgement of sin or sinfulness. Or a crime.

Tomorrow I'll have some confessing to do, God, to Nora and the others. I've messed up and I want to make it right. Sigh.

Perhaps being public about it will help keep me honest. And humble.

And yes, I'm thinking about the thing with the costume, too.

If confession is good for the soul, who, other than you, do I confess that one to?

And why have we stopped confessing in person to the priests? To what end, not admitting our faults, our "transgressions?"

Did we throw the baby out with the bathwater when we pushed back against the authority of the priests?

Could I please sleep now?

CHAPTER 23
FACING THE MUSIC

Creator,

Al and Tom and Hugh have been tutoring me on the Seven Teachings, and Paul still ignores me. The more I think about the Teachings, the more I'm blown away by how wise they are. I could throw away most of my expensive theology texts and study these for a few decades to get closer to You, Great Spirit.

And this morning I need to be reminded of humility. I keep thinking I have something to bring here, that I'm educated and brilliant and all that, but I forget how much I don't know. Tons of stupidity, which brings lots of shame.

Like how I shouldn't just be bringing friends here, and treating this like any other apartment I've lived in.

Humility. That's what I'm working on today.

Alongside the other six teachings. Wisdom. Courage. Truth. Respect. Honesty. And of course, Love.

Thank you for these Teachings, Creator. And to think my ancestors thought your ancestors needed schooling. I am ashamed of that, too.

I guess I'd best go face the music, and own my mistakes.

I overslept the next morning, up half the night tossing and turning and writing that email. I knew I'd feel embarrassed when served the well-deserved reprimand from Nora or Kate. Then I remembered that I had to drive Glenn back to his car, so I mustered my courage and headed for the kitchen. Besides, my stomach was getting growly.

Cook greeted me with his usual bear hug and "Morning, Mugwump," and pulled up a chair in the alcove. I was glad he was looking hale and hearty. He set a mug on the table for me, and heated a bowl of oatmeal in the microwave.

"Sorry, Darlin', but that's all there is left. Glenn had an unexpected appetite. Guess the fresh air overnight did him some good. He's out talking to Tom...believe it or not, they hit it off. I think Tom might a' took pity on the obvious hangover."

Cook gestured out the window towards the Sacred Grounds, and I could see Tom and Glenn walking around, talking. From time to time it seemed they both fell silent, but I wasn't close enough to be sure. Maybe they were listening to Timex.

I ate in quiet, watching Cook build lasagnas for lunch or dinner. Finally, I admitted I couldn't postpone the inevitable much longer.

"Where's Nora?" I asked.

"Oh, she's around. Kennels, maybe, visiting Kate. Why?"

"I'm sure she wants to talk to me...." I hedged.

"She said somethin' about catching up after lunch. She and Kate chuckled when Glenn showed up for breakfast and they heard about last night. Kenny mentioned he could use your help turnin' the compost when you got up."

That was our secret code for "let's go for a walk, to talk." No one turns the compost in January, even in the Fraser Valley. It's just too damned wet...but then, the men seldom talked about anything important inside the buildings. Too many years of electronic ears meant I was used to strolling outside when someone wanted to talk. The one exception was the Sanctuary; they seemed to feel safe enough in there. No hidden spaces, with open rafters, solid walls without outlets meant no hiding places. I was pretty sure Al still checked it for bugs after guests visited, though. Old habits and all of that.

After clearing my dishes I headed out to find Kenny, and walking from the front of the house to the back didn't turn him up. I headed for the Sacred Grounds to ask if they'd seen him. Getting closer, I saw Kenny was sprawled on his back in the tall grass, and Timex was there too. Glenn held his finger to his lips in the age-old sign for "Shhh!"; so I pulled up a stump and sat, content to listen. Al was, as usual, eavesdropping and tending the fire.

Tom had scratched the outline of a Medicine Wheel on the ground with a stick and was sharing some Teachings. Al chipped in from time to time, and I realized he was actually adding to what Tom shared, rather than correcting him. Hmmm. I smiled. Glenn was pointing to the silk-screened picture of the Chartres labyrinth on his T-shirt, and talking about it. After a few minutes, I saw what they were doing.

Glenn was telling them what he knew about the labyrinth and they were mentally walking its quadrants while exploring the Teachings of the Medicine Wheel (which were actually much more complex than I had gleaned from my academic readings). Kenny, meanwhile, was lying deep in the grass (only Kenny would do that in January; he was so connected to the earth he even loved cold, wet grass.) He kept asking about the practice of walking the labyrinth, and building them. They were deep into the conversation before I arrived, and were able to follow one another's thoughts. I wasn't, so didn't try.

Timex was curled up beside Tom, who occasionally rubbed the fluffy smug cat. The feline seemed to be daring me to say something, and of course, being chicken, I didn't. Glenn paid special attention to what Al was saying, as if Al was a part of it, but separate. Al never sat down with the other men.

A while later, the discussion broke up with Tom taking Glenn into the tipi to get his stuff, as Kenny and I strolled around to the north end of the dorms. Al had wandered to the wood pile with a big axe to split some more rounds. Who knew where the damned spook went.

"Shall we turn the compost?" I asked, and Kenny chuckled. He had stopped on the 'lawn' and was pacing off the field that lay between the building and the hill and trail that led up to the forest.

"Yup, it would fit well here," he said, and the penny dropped.

"You called me out here to tell me you want to build a labyrinth, right?"

"Actually, I called you out for something else, but what I want is for *us* to build a labyrinth, with stones, and plants...we'll see. I actually called you out to thank you for bringing Glenn home last night, and that was even before he started talking our ears off about the labyrinth."

I was flummoxed. I'd screwed up royally, and Nora wasn't waiting to chew me out, and Kenny was thanking me. I didn't get it.

"He's heterosexual, you know," I teased, hoping Kenny would explain.

"No kidding! But when I see you forget that this place is a halfway house, and treat it like your home and us like your family, I can almost forget, too. Thanks for that; you did my imagination good."

I didn't know what to say, so I just reached out and hugged him. "You are so welcome," I whispered in his ear, covering my welling tears with the hug.

"Enough that you'll help with the labyrinth?" he asked.

"Keep talking...." I said, and we did, until lunchtime, when I had to drive Glenn down the mountain and say goodbye to him.

It wasn't easy, and I said so. He promised to keep in touch, and I promised myself I'd hold him to it.

"I'll be back in a bit to make my decision, and visit the boys. Maybe we can get together," he said wistfully.

"Maybe we can go on an adventure. There's some amazing waterfalls around here," I said, planting seeds.

I really did wish him well, but I worried at the sadness in his eyes when he talked about his boys. He vowed to stay connected to them, but it was hard with him living far away, and them so young. I wondered if he wasn't making another wish-filled promise, like "I do." I hoped not, for everyone's sake.

When I got back, I mustered my courage and found Nora to apologize for my lapse. She graciously accepted my apology, but admitted that she was going to have to spend some time figuring out "the ramifications" of what I did. Her brow was furrowed, and she shuffled papers. Nora never shuffled papers.

"Beth, this is problematic. Our taking you on was supposed to be relatively work-free and stress-free. I'm fairly certain there wasn't a breach last night, but I need to figure out if I am going to report Glenn's stay. I need to be seen to be completely above-board, and I admit, his being on-site without my awareness has put me in a pickle. I'll let you know what I decide."

On the way out of the office, I turned and asked her, "Why aren't you mad at me? Why don't you yell?"

Her disappointment was written all over her face.

"What would be the point? You knew you'd made a mistake the moment Cook said something, and you took steps to put things right. It's not like I'm worried about you doing it again next week. It's just I have to deal with the outfall. Mad won't fix it. We can all tell you stories about a time we forgot we weren't just some hippy commune. The first forms Kate and Frank created to allow some teens from 4-H to work the horses neglected to mention what we do here, for example. We all make mistakes; that's why we're here helping each other, like Cook did last night. There's too much for one person to remember…just spiritual beings having a very human experience."

I smiled at her oft-repeated phrase, and again tears were welling up in my eyes.

"Let me think things through. Glenn did pick up clearance forms to send back to me, in case he wants to visit again," she said.

Life was good, even with my worries about Glenn's sadness, and Cook's health, and Nora's "ramifications." And, I still had coffee with Ben to look forward to. Friday night, he'd promised.

Which seemed to take forever to arrive, but then went too quickly. And not according to plan. He'd asked me to meet him in Mission for dinner and I hoped it wasn't because he was uncomfortable picking me up. Right? Anyhow, Cook figured out we were "going on a date," and when I said I'd get a taxi, he offered his keys. I love that man.

We dined in a little café with an outdoor garden – almost secret – and it was lovely. I was feeling all shy and awkward, but he didn't seem to notice. He talked about his work – the guys inside I'd met, and other chaplain-y stuff. Not exactly romantic, but I suspect I could listen to Ben read a phone book, if there was such a thing anymore.

I remembered not to order soup (I always wear it), so enjoyed a simple cheese and veggie sandwich with my coffee. He flawlessly finished a delicious-looking bowl of homemade fish chowder. We didn't talk about us; I told him about my conversation with Nora (his brow furrowed), and gushed a little about how much I was learning, and how incompetent I still feel. He accused me of fishing for compliments, and we laughed.

I did ask him a little about how he figured out his path, because I'm not getting any clear messages from God or the universe yet. He said something cryptic about a winding path, while stirring his soup, and then looked at me and declared that I had nothing to worry about, I'd figure it out soon enough.

So. Not. Helpful. Anyhow, I said I might talk to Aaron about it, and he thought that was a good idea.

Then, of course, all I could think about was how much he might be thinking I was fishing for encouragement about us. But then I don't think so. He seemed uncomfortable, and a little distracted. I hope he doesn't think I wanted him to pledge undying commitment or anything. Especially with what happened next.

We sipped our coffees and shared an AMAZING piece of cheesecake. The conversation went back to his work, and some of the projects the men are involved in: a Pow Wow this summer, and some were getting passes to grow vegetables at a local cooperative, and donating the proceeds to crime victims, which I thought was kind of cool.

"The men always support the AIDS network by doing the AIDS walk inside, and collecting donations from one another," he said. I remember smiling, thinking, "How nice for them to get involved, when they have so little money." I know AIDS and Hep C are real problems in prison.

And then Ben said something that made me throw up a little.

"Yeah, they can't give much, but what they give matters. And now they want to support a new agency this year as well, so I'm investigating that."

"What?" I asked.

"The Pro-Life Society. The guys want to raise some funds to help them."

I choked.

"Really?"

"Yeah, the Inmate Committee suggested it, and as the Catholic Chaplain, it'd be hard for me to disagree. Lots of the chapel volunteers are really enthusiastic. I think it would help boost the attendance at some of the services," he continued.

I guess he couldn't see I was dying inside.

"It surprises me that all that male energy is being funneled towards an agency that wants to decide for women what they should do with their bodies," I continued, trying to figure this out. I really hadn't expected this for our first date! Few issues would separate me so clearly from a guy.

"Well, that's one way to frame it, but it'd be hard to come down against this," he continued.

He wasn't getting it. Duh. Monk. Men's prison. Male church. Things were starting to feel a little tarnished, and I didn't know if I could polish them up. Anyhow, Ben didn't get how much I was bugged by this.

He paid our bill (so much for feminist principles), and we headed out. I was ready to head home, but needed to say something before we parted ways.

"You know, there are lots of people who might not look favourably on men in prison engaging in the misogynist power imbalances inherent in the abortion debate. I'm surprised the powers that be in CSC think it's okay to get involved in this hot potato."

Did that sound detached enough, academic enough to encourage him to think again about this? I wasn't sure, but was glad I'd said something.

"Really? Maybe I should talk to someone else. Aaron, maybe," he said.

I suggested the Quakers. From what I'd read they seemed really liberal. He chuckled.

"Yeah, worshipping in silence doesn't mean I really know them well. I could do that after Meeting this week, I guess." I felt a little better; maybe they'd be more adept at showing him what a colossally bad idea this was. He walked me to Cook's car, and I wasn't really disappointed when he didn't try to kiss me. He told me he'd "be in touch." Sigh.

Driving home up the dark rural roads, I took my time and thought about whether or not it was worth daydreaming about Ben any more. I mean, really, what would he think of me if he knew about Chaos? And I said a little prayer of thanks that I trusted Aaron not to share my secret. I headed to the barn to give myself some time to think -- no one expected me to be home so early.

The horses came to greet me, then went back to munching their hay, or sleeping. I decided to spend some time in Buttercup's stall, to give her some love, which she patiently, *almost* willingly accepted.

After some time listening to the horses breathing and scratching Buttercup's warm flank, I was feeling more settled. Animals do that for me. Note to self: remember this.

I sat with my cheek to her neck, sitting on her manger, and heard a quiet noise beside me. I didn't want to startle, so slowly turned to see what was there, half expecting a rat, I think. The orange barn cat that cuddled in my lap in the evenings had taken up "residence" in one corner of Buttercup's roomy stall, bedded down in the sawdust, and was getting up to turn herself over. As she did, I saw a miracle in the dim light of the night barn.

She was lying in a bed of kittens! Little furry balls, eyes barely opened, began to mewl as she stood and stretched. She dashed out of the stall – probably to go find a meal, I thought. The kittens settled down together in a bundle to keep warm, except for one that tried to follow Mom. She was a delightful calico kitten, with large splotches of colour and clear, golden eyes. As she left the nest she quickly sensed that Mom was gone, and she couldn't keep up, and started to cry out in protest. As I eased off of the manger to peek around the corner to look for Mom, I distracted her, and she pounced on my bootlaces.

We played for about ten minutes, Topaz and I; I knew right away that was her name. I didn't know how old she was (Kate later told me she was about three weeks old that night) but she quickly tired and I scooped her up to cuddle her. She settled under my chin, purring as I stroked her soft fur. I was in heaven, waiting for her Mom to return so I could re-introduce her to the nest. My eyes drifted shut. Within moments I heard Timex's voice in my head.

"You shouldn't handle ones who are so young; their mothers might reject them if they smell like you."

I opened my eyes, doubting myself. I sensed he was teasing, though, and chuckled.

"Want me for yourself, do you?" I teased back, and he lifted his tail high in the air and left, nose raised. Maybe I was starting to understand Timex. I kept on cuddling Topaz.

Mother Cat returned shortly after, and the kitten was happy to return to her brothers and sisters. Mom didn't want cuddles today, but she didn't seem phased by my presence either. Topaz soon forgot me, and I thought about her all night. And other stuff, too. New life – Steve and Sarita, Chaos, kittens -- it always feels to me like the veil between this world and God is thinnest with new life. And screw ups, too.

See, when I joined Cook on the porch that night he told me Frank had been looking for me after dinner.

"Why?" I asked.

"I'm not sure. He and Claire and Veronica were talking about something after the volunteers meeting tonight. Then I saw him talking to Nora, and he asked me to tell you to find him tomorrow mornin'. I'm sure it's nothin', Darlin'."

My spidey senses hummed. First the screw-up with Glenn. Then Claire talking to Frank. Sigh.

No sleep again.

Oh Dear God,

I think I've really blown it this time. Fucked up. I know I've done that before, but this time...I don't know. It's about waaay more than me. It's about fucking up this path you offered. It's about screwing up in ways that might get in the way of me really knowing how to make a difference.

You know when there are paths in a wood? Somehow I feel like I just messed up enough that one might have just grown over. And I'll never know what a difference I could have made.

Fuck.

Will "I'm sorry" be enough?

For You?

For them?

CHAPTER 24

FLASHBACKS

Six months later...

As the sun rose over the treetops and the forest began to wake, the Addict admitted that he might as well start to move. His body was shivering even though he was warm enough. His guts were cramping, and staying here in this god-forsaken hell wasn't going to help. Not that he'd kid himself that moving would change his hell.

He started to brush the leaves and pine needles from his body. He'd burrowed into the soil last night, trying to disappear, bury himself. At least he'd stayed warm. But still, the shaking. And he was thirsty. And was that a dog behind that tree, waiting to grab him by the leg? He lifted his throbbing head into his hands, and forced his body to sit. Every time he opened his eyes, the light drilled into his brain. Fuck. Why didn't he have a fix?

Oh, right. Memories flashed towards him. This wasn't a planned trip. The horror he'd seen, he'd lived, he'd created, came crashing back. The gurgle of the Priest as he'd breathed a last breath.

The forgiveness he'd spoken.

The horror pummeled his brain but he chased those thoughts away. Staying here wasn't going to help. He had to figure shit out. He just wasn't sure what shit that was.

One next step. That's what the Counsellor always said. Just find one next step. A good one. And the Addict decided. Go get his damp T-shirt off that bush, and put it on. He shivered again, but when he put his jacket on over top, he felt better. In control.

And then he saw her. That fucking bird, announcing to the world that he was here, tormenting his fucking brain.

"Skreeka! Skreeka!"

He held out his hand, but she didn't land. Fuck. Of course she wouldn't land. It wasn't her. An imposter bird, sent to fuck with him.

A part of his brain was glad, because he didn't have any morsels in his pocket to offer her today. She kept screaming at him, an intruder in her world. And then the Addict smiled. Maybe this was that nun, here to remind him of his sins one more time?

One next step. A good one. To the stream. To catch something to eat. To drink, at least. He stumbled through the forest towards the sound of the water, and tried to remember last night. How fast was the river up here? Or was it a stream? Were there fish in it? What would he eat? Just thinking about it made his stomach lurch.

And then he was through the trees, standing on the bank of the river. He remembered climbing over the bank last night, and looked around. In the sunlight he could see there weren't any creatures around, which wasn't surprising the way he was crashing around. He quieted his breathing, and looked down into the water.

Stepping in, he saw small fish, but he knew they'd be too fast for him to catch, especially when he was Jonesing like today. He cupped his hands and took a drink. His stomach clenched, but he didn't throw up. He smiled.

Looking around, he saw a frog on the bank, and was surprised when his hand darted out, fast and steady enough to catch it. He brought it up to his mouth, but it moved in his hand, struggling, and he couldn't bring himself to do it. The thought of biting into its cool flesh made him hurl, and he tossed the frog away as his stomach emptied once again– mostly bile and the water he'd just swallowed.

He sat on a rock, wiped his face with cool water and thought about his *next* next step. The Counsellor's face filled his mind. And then the Manager's, the Chef's. Even the Aboriginal Brotherhood, and he didn't like them. But they paraded through his mind, tormenting him.

Focus, he thought. Next step. Drink some more. He did, and it settled his stomach, which settled his mind. He looked up, noticed the breeze through the trees, and the sounds returning to the forest. A squirrel yelled at him. Birds started talking again, worried at his intrusion into their nesting areas. And then it flashed in his brain again.

Drinking from his hands, he looked down and saw the water dripping off of them, catching the light, reminding him of the shimmering with blood. Sticky, shiny, red blood from the Priest, and he tried to back away from his hands, thrusting them deep into the water, cleaning them off again. And again. Slowly, he calmed his body and mind, and focused again on one good step.

Plants. Spring, early summer plants were all around. He would find some to eat, like a salad. It would help, he knew. He thought back to his Uncle, who had taught him well how to be on the land, to hunt and fish. And eat plants. Girl food, his Uncle called it, but it would work for the Addict today. He drank again, and felt his bowels turning to water. He lowered his pants and shit in the stream, glad that the water carried his mess away, away from him, away from the dogs he knew would be searching. He cleaned up as best he could, and drank some more. Upstream, he thought, chuckling.

Heading back to the camp, he saw some blue Camas growing in the underbrush, and dug up some of their bulbs. Brushed them off, and thought about whether he should start a fire and roast a few, or just eat them. He decided he couldn't afford the fire, and nibbled slowly on the bulbs, tasting their bitterness, the earth that clung to them. And his body settled. If he was honest, he was half hoping he'd misidentified the bulbs, and that these were the toxic cousins, ready to kill him. But he knew they weren't.

The Addict spent the rest of the day making his "hole" more hospitable, collecting greens from the forest floor, heading to the water to drink now and then, chasing the horror from his mind when it intruded. And thinking of Little Sister, and one next step.

As the evening darkness drew closer, he was relieved and distressed that he'd avoided detection, that the decisions for his life were still his to make. Sigh. It would be so much easier if they just found him. And as Grandmother Moon rose in the sky, he thought again about the teachings he'd learned from the Elder, and the Elder's wife...and gazed on the Medicine Wheel he'd had inked on his arm so the teachings would always be there.

He felt comfort as the darkness grew, choosing to think of all the nights he'd spent outside in the Sacred Grounds, sweeping, making fires, just sitting on a log hanging out. And he chose not to think about the terror he'd felt in the darkness of that cupboard in the church so long ago, and he sighed. He'd worked hard to teach himself how to think the good thoughts, not think the bad ones. And he wondered – where had it all gone wrong?

As soon as he thought that question, his mind remembered the living room, the Priest, bleeding everywhere, gushing, gurgling in his throat. And the knife, and the stabbing, how surprised that man had been to look up and see the Addict coming at him...how resigned he'd looked when his life had left his body. How was it that the Addict remembered how to think good thoughts, but couldn't remember not to go crazy and kill the Priest? How many priests had he killed? How many would be enough?

Then he admitted that he knew. It was the smack. The speedball, the out of control feeding of the Devil inside him. Not the Devil who'd hurt him, but the one that grew in his heart, put there by God knows who. Not the Creator. And the shame he felt made his head hang, and his chest collapse. And he wept, but just a little.

Fuck. He needed to decide. One next step. What the hell?

Was he really just going to live, cold and hungry and Jonesing, here in the woods, waiting for them to realize what he'd done, where he was? Could he?

He might as well go drink in the river. Into his soul. His lungs, his being. That might be one good next step. But he'd sleep on it. He said his prayers to the Creator, and cried his shame and his apology, thought of all the people he'd disappointed. The men he'd killed. And he prayed that tonight he would sleep without nightmares or flashbacks or too many DTs. Not that he deserved even that much grace.

The next morning, the birds woke him early, and he knew he'd become a part of the forest again. As he started his morning prayers, to the Father Sun, and the Grandparents all around him, his mind brought him back. Again. What he'd done to his people. And then he imagined it.

They'd get a call that the Priest was dead, and they'd have to try to make sense of it, without answers.

Because he would walk far into the bush upriver before he'd breathe the water. He'd fill his pockets with rocks, snag himself on a tree underwater, and they'd never find him. He'd just disappear. They would never know. Maybe that was best, he thought, trying to convince himself.

He ate some more greens, washed his hands again, cleaned himself up, washed the blood from his hands again, never really drying out or getting warm, some kind of penance for the horror he caused. And as the afternoon began to intrude on his morning, he stopped kidding himself.

He wasn't that guy. That guy who walked far upstream and breathed in water, and escaped while longing for one more fix. He used to be that guy, but he wasn't anymore.

He was so so sorry for the fucked up mess that he was. He didn't deserve those people, the Elders, the Teachings. He didn't deserve any of it. And then he heard the Elder's voice.

"It isn't because we deserve it. It's just Truth. The Seven Teachings are just there."

Then the Addict knew what he would do. He shivered as he thought about calling the police, turning himself in, heading back to Kent, to the hellhole he'd once lived in. Would again. Forever.

Because his people deserved answers. Deserved to know.

Deserved to see who he was -- that even though he knew better, sometimes that wasn't enough.

Sometimes the Devil in him won, even when he didn't want him to.

For that reason, he wasn't to be trusted. But he knew the goodness in their hearts, their souls deserved to know.

That it wasn't their fault. And the Priest had said so.

At least Kent would be warm. Dry. And the food, believe it or not, tastier than Blue Camas bulbs in the spring.

They'd help him through the Jonesing. The people paid to cage him. He was pretty sure he didn't deserve any of that, but he just couldn't bring himself to breathe in the cold water today.

So he started to walk out of the bush. One next step after another. All good ones, he told himself.

And he almost believed that it wasn't because, underneath it all, he was a coward.

CHAPTER 25
NATURAL CONSEQUENCES

Eight months earlier...

Morning has broken

Like the first morning...

Dear God, that is one sappy piece of crap. I hate guitars in church, in case anyone's asking. But this morning, I'm humming it because I'm feeling fucking broken, too.

Fuck. What am I going to do? I'm really sorry I brought Glenn over. Because how was I supposed to know they'd freak?

Except for that 'nothing in, nothing out' litany. Sigh.

Should'a paid more attention.

The next morning, I woke up feeling tired and groggy and grumpy. I wasn't sure why Frank wanted to talk to me, but decided I'd better go face Morning Circle and find out. A quick washcloth to my face, and I put on my big girl pants and headed out to the Sanctuary. Morning Circle had become second-nature, and I remembered what Kenny and I had talked about last week -- how do we find another space in our future that is held together by circles like this?

Anyhow, circle was short and sweet. A storm warning was in place, so Nora had dispatched chores to everyone that would help us prepare. At the end of it, Frank came and found me just as I was planning to head back to the Sacred Grounds with Al.

"Beth, can I talk to you for a few minutes in the office?" he asked, and he sounded SO serious. In total Beth form, I just followed him, like a prisoner to the gallows. Soon enough, we were sitting in Nora's office on her couch, the door shut. Which was weird -- I'd never seen anyone in her office without her present, and certainly little was done with the door closed. Bob had given me the stink-eye as we had walked by his desk.

"So, Beth, Nora asked me to talk to you because she had to go to Regional Headquarters. I hope that's okay," he said, and I nodded. Like I had a choice.

"A couple of things have come to our attention, Beth, and Nora has to rethink her ability to have you stay here at the house. She doesn't think she has the time and energy to do proper oversight."

My stomach dropped, and my head started to pound. I was being kicked out? What was I going to do? And just when I thought I was getting closer to finding my calling. Nora was so angry she couldn't even talk to me? My face turned bright red, and I couldn't look Frank in the eye.

"I'm sorry, Frank. Whatever it is I've done, I'll try to do better," I stammered.

"Well, Beth, it's clear you need more training before you understand how important security is here. You can't really be blamed for not understanding. People usually come volunteer or work here after spending time in a prison or traditional halfway house. Usually a substantial amount of time. You came directly from university, so I don't think there is a way we could have prepared you better. Past students have been local, so no one stayed here." Frank paused, rearranged some stuff on Nora's desk.

"Nora is okay with you continuing to work with us during the day. You're just being asked to live off-site for a while until we work some things out."

"What things? Is there a training I have to do or something?" I asked. I kept on going. "I'm guessing this is about Glenn coming overnight last week. I realized I really messed up. It won't happen again."

I ran out of steam at that point. Frank looked at me, and I felt indulged. You know the look -- one a father gives his son when the boy admits to breaking a window with a baseball.

"Well, Beth, that's not all. In fact, it's not even the most problematic, although it is indicative of your lack of training. Claire and Paul told me about your adventures at the Remand Centre, and while I don't remember seeing you there, I trust their memories. Is there something you want to tell me?"

I launched into the story of Julie and her boyfriend Chris, and I admit I tried to put a positive spin on what I'd done. And halfway through the story I heard that I sounded incredibly defensive and just a little like I imagine prisoners sound when they try to justify their law-breaking. My voice petered off, and I looked at Frank.

"You're right. What I did was wrong, and now I know just how wrong it was. I was just so caught up in helping; now I get there are a bunch of other options I had, but on the day I just didn't see them. Didn't really try." Yup. I continued to sound lame. And we both knew it.

"Well, if anyone finds out, *Just Living* is at risk. I have to believe Aaron didn't know what you'd done, so I'm not going to take it up with him. But really, the optics, and the risk, are just too high."

My mind was going a million miles a minute. How the hell was I going to get here every day? Would I have to move home? I was starting to get just how serious this was.

I really needed to get this practicum done to get my degree.

Could I salvage the building of a meaningful life? My meaningful life? I was working really hard at not bursting into tears, but only kinda succeeding. Evidence was leaking down my face. Frank put his hand on my shoulder.

"It'll be okay, Beth. We have a plan. And I hope the learning about the importance of your word and your actions lands solidly. Really. You can't think of working in law enforcement or corrections --the legal system, really -- without leading an absolutely exemplary life. I mean, you can do it other ways. But the personal toll is enormous. On your health, but also on your soul. You don't want to be worrying about this stuff, really."

I caught my breath, trying to take it all in. Did he say a plan? He didn't stop, but I couldn't keep up.

"Is there anything else we should know about, Beth? Anything else that would affect your ability to keep your security clearance?"

I was trying to think about all the small and huge ways I'd fucked up in the past.

"I had an abortion when I was 17," I mumbled.

Frank put his hand on my shoulder again, and looked square at me.

"Last I checked, that wasn't against the law," he said.

"I dated a guy -- the father really -- who might be in jail now. But I haven't seen him in almost ten years," I added. What else? There must be more.

And then I knew this horrible pit in my stomach was because it wasn't really coming clean if you just owned it once you'd been caught. Would everything have been different if I'd offered the information up front? Would I have even been allowed to come? And why did one mistake, doing one thing wrong bring my whole life into scrutiny? Fuck. I'd made lots of mistakes, done a ton of things wrong. I just couldn't think of them right now. But my face kept on flaming.

God, I wanted to talk to Glenn. What the fuck had we been thinking? Or rather, if I was going to be brutally honest, what the fuck had *I* been thinking? He hadn't thought of breaking into the Remand Centre while impersonating a priest. Sigh. Is this what "being held accountable" feels like? My mouth was dry, and my face was burning.

"So, we've arranged for you to stay nearby with a volunteer, Veronica. Have you met her before?"

I had, briefly, so I nodded. But really -- she was willing to let me live with her? Amazing. What about my car? Stephen still needed it for "the impending miracle." Veronica lived nearby; maybe I could bike. Rainy, but possible.

We ironed out a few wrinkles -- Veronica would pick me up later that afternoon, and take me to her place to check it out. Until then, I was to work with Kenny, Cook or Sally. I wasn't to go near the Sacred Grounds, or the other residents. I was to move out before next week. The sooner the better. Sigh.

This was serious. I headed up to my room, and started to pack; no point in putting off the inevitable. I would go if Veronica would have me. I could go home to Vancouver on the weekends, if need be.

A few minutes later, there was a knock on my dorm room door, and it was Cook, with two mugs of tea in hand. He gestured to the porch, and I joined him. We pretended it was night-time, and my heart broke just a little more when I realized I wouldn't be learning from him tonight. Or any other night.

"So, Darlin', I hear you're movin' on," he said.

"Yeah. I really fucked up, Cook."

"Welcome to the club," he said, and I smiled. "Don't worry, Darlin'. We do fuckups well around here. We'll figure it out," he assured me.

Only I still felt like shit. I started blubbering.

"Oh, Cook. I was so stupid. I didn't mean anything. Really. I just thought I was helping…." My voice trickled off as he started to chuckle. And after another uncomfortable moment, I needed to own it.

"Okay, it was kinda cool, gettin' away with it. That was a trip." I was smiling at the memory. "But I didn't get that it could hurt anyone."

He kept chuckling, sipping his tea, his big belly rising and falling.

"Oh God. I knew it was wrong. I just thought it'd be a lark," I said.

"Didn't think you'd get caught, like so many others," he said, and I knew that he understood in ways lots of others wouldn't. I had to get my shit together if I was going to figure out how to finish my practicum, how to find "meaningful."

"What am I gonna do, Cook? I can't imagine not being here," I said. "You guys got under my skin. I feel like I'm being kicked out of the club."

"Well, you're gonna take your lumps," he began, reaching across for my hand. "And then you're gonna show 'em that they need you as much as you need them."

We sat for a bit longer, watching the horses in the pasture playing with something that I suspect was Timex. I'd even miss the spook.

"How long you gotta be away?" he asked. And I told him I'd still be around during the day, just not living in.

"Well, that sounds great," he said. "We can do afternoon tea instead of evenin' tea. Maybe I'll get more sleep." His smile was contagious.

"I just wish I knew what to do," I said. "I can't figure out who to tell what to. Nora asked that I just tell folks I had to move out because of regulations. But that doesn't make sense."

"Unless it's the truth," Cook said. "Maybe there are regulations about people livin' here who haven't taken the security course, or somethin'." That sounded realistic. I thought about it.

"But what about Ben? I have to tell him. And my family. Maybe even Aaron." God, this was way more complicated now that I thought about it. Who did I come clean to? Glenn for sure. And Ben. Aaron was a tough one -- I'd talk to Frank or Nora about that. What if this meant I got kicked out of school? I could just imagine the bureaucracy now.

"You should have thought of that before you did it," they'd say.

We talked it through a bit more, and then I realized something else.

"Cook, how did you know what I did? I never told you," I said.

"Oh, Darlin', there's a underground information pipeline I'm still a part of. I tried to stop it. Really. Paul knew from day one, he just didn't know it was wrong. He'd never rat you out. But, boy oh boy, you must have somethin' going on with Ben that's real fine."

Now I was confused.

"Ben did it? How'd he know?" My mind was trying to follow a trail I really didn't get. And the breadcrumbs were invisible.

"He didn't. Claire. She seems to think she needs to protect Ben. Or somethin'. He's real important to her, I think because of their church stuff."

And I knew I had underestimated Claire.

"Oh God. I never realized," I said, just trying to figure out this new layer. A few minutes later, Kenny came up and gave me a hug.

"Veronica's downstairs. You want some help?" he asked, and unlike when I arrived, I didn't have to carry my bags.

"Looks like I'm getting my wish, Beth. We're going to work together on the labyrinth," Kenny told me. Well, one thing was working out, at least.

Veronica was gracious, and kind, and her place was lovely. And I was really messed up around her because I didn't know what she knew. If she knew. Fuck. *Is this what it's like when you're busted? I've never been busted, God. But I guess I'm supposed to believe You always know. I guess if I thought you were a judgy Guy, I'd feel like this around you all the time.*

I'm glad I don't think You're judgy, God. Because this sucks. Who do I tell what to?

Veronica lived in the house where she'd raised her family, and warmth oozed from the walls. I was moved into her daughter's room -- all her kids were grown up, so I made myself at home. I didn't know how much she'd been told, and I wasn't sure how much I should share, so I just told her again and again how glad I was. And periodically, my face got all flame-ish again.

"So, for now I'll drive you into *Just Living* in the mornings for circle. I'm working on the labyrinth with Kenny, so we can get an early start. Someone there will bring you home at night."

They were taking care of me, but that just seemed to add to my shame. Before we settled in for the night, and I baked some scones for the morning. At least I knew I wouldn't fuck up the baking.

Holy God, I am so not worthy. What am I going to do to work my way back? What does Grace look like? Amends? I better study grovelling next...'cause this feels like shit.

I wonder how the men do it. And how awkward it would be to ask them. I wish I could talk to Cook. Sigh.

Later that night, Ben called me on my cell phone.

"Hey, Beth, how are you?" he asked.

I didn't really know how much he knew, so I spent a little time telling him about my day, swearing him to secrecy. On the one hand, it felt good to share, but on the other hand I was still feeling really ashamed. Anyhow, he knew, and reassured me that in the grand scheme of things, while he understood Nora's reticence to have me staying on site, he didn't really think I was unredeemable. I was still a little weepy, though. I'd never really fucked up something I wanted. Maybe because I'd never really wanted anything. Why had stuff always come easy?

Sigh. Then he totally sent me for a loop.

"Thanks for the advice about the pro-life stuff. My Regional Chaplain was completely against the guy's involvement; sometimes I think I'm totally out of touch politically. Anyhow, you saved my skin. And I have kind of an awkward question, now that you're on the phone."

Silence. I was actually amused by his social awkwardness, but it went on so long that it stretched even my comfort level.

"Yes?" I asked. "It's okay to just ask, you know," I continued. Now my imagination was working overtime, and I was feeling a bit better.

"Well, I know we've only gone out once," he said. "Yes," I thought.

"I'd really like to spend some more time with you away from *Just Living* and everything. And a friend has offered me his cabin for the weekend. For some reason, before I got on the phone I thought this would be perfect – a retreat together, sort of. Now I realize it's really inappropriate." His words were rushing out. I laughed out loud. Really. Lol.

"Oh, Ben, you are so delightful. One second I'm thinking you don't even think about me and the next you are inviting me on a tryst!" I said.

"Oh my! I never thought of it like that!" he said. "That's not what I meant!" He was so flustered I kept giggling.

"Ben, don't protest too much or I'll think I'm unappealing," I teased.

"Oh my God! That's not what I meant either!" he said.

I was giggling so much I couldn't talk and I could hear the panic in his voice rise. I had to tell him to breathe.

"Ben, you are delightfully bad at this," I said. He exhaled. Audibly. "Please, don't change. I'm enjoying this way too much." I let a moment pass and then I said, "I'd be delighted to go on an adventure with you, Ben. But I don't know if *your* virtue is safe with me." Was that a gasp?

A few minutes later, we'd made plans. Ben would meet me at the barn next Friday night, and we'd head out for two nights, arriving back on Sunday before he had to work at the prison in the afternoon. I was pretty excited, even though we'd agreed to separate sleeping bags.

Ben had been visiting around more often, which I liked, helping out around the grounds and even washing a few dishes. We'd even stolen a few "looks" at one another in the kitchen when no one was watching. If this is romance, it is molasses romance, I swear. At this rate I'll be old and wrinkled before we even touch each other. I may have to get crazy bold and graze his arm or something. This weekend would give me a chance.

Life had taken a hard left, and I was reeling. As I laid in bed listening for God, I couldn't help but be distracted by thoughts of Claire, who had worked so hard to keep Ben and me apart.

How's that workin' for you now, Claire? I thought. Getting caught hadn't exactly added to my ability for compassion, I admit, God.

We'll work on that, right?

This teaching about Love. What is it? What does it mean?

Is it an idea?

A feeling?

Just biology?

I think for now I'm going to just focus on doing love. Being love. Serving love. Forget the notion of romantic love.

I remember the other night reading a little about Quakers (grin) and I came upon this quote. I'm gonna use it, God, when I go over how my day went, where I felt alive, and what I plan to do tomorrow.

"Let us see, then, what Love would have us do."

I think it was George Fox who said it. Or maybe William Penn.

Maybe thinking about it will get me closer to my "meaningful life"....

Or at least let me be a little more compassionate....

CHAPTER 26
ORA ET LABORA

Ora et labora.

In all things, prayer and work. There must be wisdom in that; the Benedictines have advocated it for centuries...although my studies tell me they also advocated a thorough dose of reading. Is it cheeky to think I've got that part covered?

There is a secret place of prayer-in-all-things the mystics tell me about, and I yearn to visit there. Repetitive work – a place to seek it...and perhaps it will keep my mind off the crap I'm in right now. Or even give me an insight.

God, I could use some insight. I've got some fixing to do.

And yes, that's a prayer.

It turned out that after sleeping an hour or two, I hardly slept that night and it wasn't just because of thoughts of Ben and the cabin, and how I was going to put things right at *Just Living*. That weather alert had turned into a huge storm that pounded rain on the steel roof at Veronica's all night. A small part of me was glad I wasn't at *Just Living*, couldn't leave my warm bed to go check on animals, or residents. Thinking about my friends there, I was glad they'd heeded the warning. Al and Paul had taken the canvas off the tipi; the wind would whistle through the poles but it wasn't likely it would topple. If it did, I knew he and Tom could raise them again in an afternoon with Paul's help. Kate and Ricky had worked to make sure the kennels were as snug as possible, and Tom had bolted the doors on the stable.

The next morning, Veronica and I drove to *Just Living* early. We met the others in kitchen before Morning Circle, and everyone was bleary-eyed. I guess no one had slept well, and they were up early surveying the damage. I went out with Kenny to check which trees had lost branches and how much stuff had been blown around. He was upset to find his wheelbarrow blown into a garden; some plants he adored had been crushed. He shook his head. We headed to Circle, which was quick. Nora assigned people to help out with the most obvious damages. I was put to work with Kenny. Of course.

We were collecting branches into a big pile on the north slope when I heard a car drive up; curiosity got the best of us, and we snuck around the side of the Lodge to see who it was. I guess there was a part of me that was hoping it was Ben, but I was surprised to see Dad! We did introductions and everyone was glad to meet him. Except I was panicking because, well, here he was and he wasn't cleared.

"I heard about the storm, and I thought about you out here, and I just got curious, I guess," he said, and Al and Tom set him to work helping clean up the pasture. Be careful if you show up looking able to pitch in at *Just Living*; you will probably get your hands dirty. He acted like he belonged, which stirred up some interesting feelings in me. Especially since he hadn't asked me if he could visit.

I ducked into Nora's office to let her know that a SECOND visitor of mine was here without clearance, but she was expecting him. My breathing steadied. Later, I walked him to the car (after a quick tour of the facility – including stopping by to get clearance forms from Nora in the office for him, Mom, Steve, and parishioners Carol and Scott, who were thinking of volunteering on site).

"Thanks for dropping by, Dad," I said, not even convincing myself that I meant it.

"I was curious about this place after Steve mentioned it was growing on you. He talked about it with Glenn, too. And Steve mentioned they were always looking for volunteers, so I decided come get clearance forms. Ben thinks there might be a role for me in his chapel, so I'm going to go get trained. I hope you don't mind," he finished. I sighed.

"Well, it is a Correctional Facility, and you need clearance. I just hope they don't come down on me because I didn't explain that to you before," I said, thinking, "Can't you just leave me alone to do my work?" Blessedly, that stayed in my inside voice. I totally didn't come clean to him that I'd moved out yesterday.

"I'm sorry, Mugwump. I'll get the clearance in as soon as I can. Anyway, I did check with Nora first," he finished.

WTF? Why does he keep going over my head? First Aaron, now Nora. And did he know I'd been kicked out?

One crisis, at a time, I thought, glad Easter was still three weeks away.

"I'll see you at Easter," I said. "I'll be home for that weekend, 'kay? Steve's coming up next weekend, I think." Dad agreed, and I waved as he drove away.

Soon, we gathered for a hearty lunch, to talk about the damage the storm had caused. The barn had lost a substantial number of shingles, and Frank would bring some in the morning. Moving horses back and forth to Shalom was put on hold to give us time to prepare for the roof repair. The horses had been spooked by the storm, and it would be good for them to calm down before working with kids.

The kennels were fine; their concrete construction defied the elements. The dogs, however, had been terrified and some had torn up stuff in their kennels. Others hadn't gone outside all night, preferring to use the indoors as a doggie bathroom. More than one of the kennel doors had been blowing open and shut, which likely further scared the poor beasts. Nora, Ricky and Kate had spent the morning giving the place a thorough washing and repairing some of the hinges and clasps.

It seemed the wind had stirred up everything, inspiring a spring clean. We were energized, pumped up about getting rid of everything that was collecting dust, and putting the whole place to order. Tom was even talking about a new coat of paint on the fence around the Sacred Grounds, and I thought about my hope for repetitive work. Hmmm. Frank was going to bring paint out tomorrow as well, and I offered to do the painting if the dry weather held.

The next day we kept cleaning. I was getting used to the routine of sleeping at Veronica's, spending days at *Just Living*; she had dropped me off today and not stayed. It was almost like living there. And then, Nora decided it was time I learn something new. Again. I was really missing Cook and the kitchen, but no.

I'd love to say that I enjoyed the honour or pleasure of learning about patience and tolerance from Ricky, but in reality he was an irritating soul who is a ton of work to be with. What I did learn from Ricky was about *the need* for patience and tolerance, even when it's really hard.

Nora had had to go to town that Friday for meetings with CSC, and Tom was busy on the barn roof with Frank. Kate was working over at Shalom with a couple of new clients, without their horses. Cook, with hot oil and boiling water, wasn't a great match for Ricky's temperament. I was asked at morning circle to include him in my work, in my care. A chore, and a gift. *Ora et Labora.*

When they asked, I thought – why not? What could be so hard? Contemplative physical work as prayer -- Ricky and a fence. That would give me a chance to transcend, right? I offered us up to paint the unending stretch of simple three-rail fence that separated the back garden from the Sacred Grounds and the pasture, and the weather was predicted to hold for a couple of days; spring was really upon us and the earlier storm had brought some nice breezes on its tail.

Seven or eight weeks of *Just Living* had changed us, but I wasn't thrilled with Ricky's evolution. When we arrived, he'd been a terrified soul who walked along walls, peeking out, occasionally whining. He was about my age, I guessed, maybe a little older. I had never seen him with his guard down, and his sleep was still punctuated with screams. That was one part of living at Veronica's I wasn't missing. He'd evolved into a less-terrified soul who was whiny and lippy. Oh joy.

I knew *Just Living* had wrestled with whether or not to welcome Ricky, not sure they had the capacity to meet his needs, in part because he'd been brain injured while inside. In the end, they decided that maybe his needs were wrapped up in theirs. Or mine. I had spent my wide awake nights wondering whether or not they'd made the right choice. Sally, Cook or Kenny looked in on him when the night terrors visited. I was only mildly pissed that he'd stayed when I'd been asked to move out.

After morning circle, Nora told me that Ricky had been scheduled to have a day pass with his family, but they had called and said that they couldn't cope with him anymore. Ever. And I heard a mixture of compassion and anger in her voice.

Which is how Ricky became my companion for the day; Tom and Frank offered to keep an eye on us from the roof, Cook from the kitchen. Al and Paul were re-tying the tipi, and cleaning up the Sacred Grounds, but they weren't a good match for him either way.

We gathered our scrapers, rags, brushes and two buckets of white paint, and headed across the garden to the fence. That morning I got the full force of Ricky as whiny brat. I carried both buckets that morning. And all the tools.

"I shouldn't have to do work today, cause I'm was supposed to be with my family. It's my day off," his nasal voice proclaimed. Did I mention that now Ricky talked non-stop?

"It's not fair," he said again. I heard that a hundred times a day from his lips, and clearly today would be no different. He bitched about the house agreement, the judge, the work, the food, the universe. It was tedious. Later, in thinking back, he had never once bitched about his family. I can't figure out if that's because he was loyal, or because he had written them off.

As we walked through the garden, I got tired of reframing Ricky's ranting.

"So what I'm hearing you say, Ricky, is you are angry that you have to use headphones when you play your loud music and Tom is around."

"If I understand you right, you can't think of one good thing the Warden ever did."

"So you think Cook made oatmeal this morning just to piss you off." It was always about Ricky. Ricky this. Ricky that. Poor Ricky. Argh!

After some time I decided to just listen to him without judgment, mostly in surrender. I stopped listening to his words, and started to really hear Ricky. I became, for the first time, a vessel for his story.

I noticed that Ricky's voice was soft when he talked about the animals he helped with, or any kindness that had been shown him. It only became strident when he talked about prison, or any extension of it. Including me. He didn't track his thoughts in a linear way, and he seemed to forget what he had said earlier. I'm pretty sure this was from his brain injury.

We decided to paint opposite sides of the boards, starting near the sweat grounds. That way we'd be into the pasture around lunchtime, when the horses were inside. I faced the sweat grounds, and Ricky was inside them, looking at the Lodge. We started scraping and then painting one section at a time, and I tuned out Ricky's voice.

"I shouldn't have to paint today. Why should I have to keep this God-damned system going? This isn't my responsibility. Tom should be down here. I thought he was responsible for the buildings. He is such a slacker. Where is Bob? Why can't he do this work?" I tried not to be affected by him.

I let my body move into the repetitive physical movement of the work, striving for the meditative state I'd decided to experience. Sort of elusive like "don't think of elephants," I discovered. Anyway, I tried for contemplative, occasionally rising out of it to nod, or grunt. I hoped I was showing compassion. Sigh.

After a while I realized I had left Ricky behind, and looked back to see why he was taking so long. I'd like to say I looked back with curiosity, but truthfully? I was frustrated. At least he'd stopped ranting.

I marched towards him, intent on drilling into him how much we were going to get done by lunchtime. And when I got closer, I slowed down and watched in amazement at what was unfolding in front of me. Each time Ricky came upon a spider, a caterpillar, a bug on the fence, he stopped and picked up a piece of grass, coaxed the bug onto it so that he could gently move it from fence to the meadow. And there were a lot of bugs. Again and again. Bug after bug. After bug.

Ricky lived "interconnectedness" and "Sacred Grounds" in a very, very deep way. Perhaps just a bit too literally for me, though. It was incredible to watch his patience. He seemed to be meditative in a way that had eluded me.

I came up to him quietly and asked him why he didn't just brush the bugs off with his hand if he didn't want to scrape them away, and he floored me with his answer.

"Because I don't know if they want me to touch them."

I took a breath and thought about that while a lump rose in my throat. *Because I don't know if they want me to touch them.* Wow. He quietly went back to saving the bugs, and then slowly scraping and painting the fence. As I watched him I felt tears falling from my chin, so mumbled that I needed some water. I stumbled towards the kitchen, towards Cook's warm, strong presence.

Cook took one look at me, and put the kettle on. He made us tea, brought a plate of cookies to the table so we could keep an eye on Ricky through the window. I told him what I had seen, witnessed.

"He said he didn't know if the bugs wanted him to touch them," I finished, wiping my cheek with my paint-splotched finger. Cook drank a sip of his tea, and began.

"I can't tell you Ricky's story, mostly 'cause it's his story to tell, but also 'cause I don't really know his story. He did get his brain injury inside, beaten with a weight bar in the pit by a group who didn't appreciate that sometimes he fought back. Left him for dead, and sometimes I think that might 'a been more humane. Ricky must still have some teachings to share with us on this earthly walk, though. Unlucky, I guess, that he was more agreeable to 'em after his beating." He took a drink of tea and looked at the cookies.

"What's I can tell you is what life was like on the range for a young fellow named Bill when he first graduated to a federal pen from Juvie. He had been a biiiig deal in Juvie, B&E master who rose to armed robbery for holding up a 7-11 with a knife." Cook chuckled. "This was a few years ago now. Well, more 'n a few. Bill got to the joint on his 18th birthday, on a Friday night, and was told to go to his house and 'keep his head down' 'til Monday when there'd be more staff around who could help him 'learn the ropes.' That was before inmates were assigned to do the welcome tour. Well, it wasn't pretty." Cook shook his head.

"After the guard left the range, Bill got thirsty and curious, and filled with hisself and how big a deal he was, and made the mistake of headin' into the common room for a drink. Should have stuck with the water in his house. All seemed quiet, so he went for a stroll, checkin' out the guys playin' crib, an' the showers and laundry room. Before he knew it, there was three big guys around him wearin' colours, with a fourth at the door keeping watch. To make a long story short, they put some loud music on a ghetto blaster on the shelf, and made him dance and strip. They bugged him: 'Girl'; 'Shake it'; 'Look at that nice bald ass, just like a pussy'; 'Get your hand off your piece, man.' Didn't notice, or prolly didn't care, that there was tears streaming down Bill's face, how scared he looked. The hardest part for Bill was watchin' other guys from the range walk by the door and look away. He didn't know 'til later that they was only doin' what *they* had to do to survive.

"They broke him and then they took him, there on a table, one after another after another. He barely whimpered. He learned about 'The Taker' that night, a guy who 'took' all the new kids. And when they were done with him, they dumped him back in his house, where he puked and bled all night." Cook was staring into his tea cup. He took a deep breath.

"They left him alone for the rest of the weekend, but let's say the damage was done. Bill flinched every time he heard someone in the hallway, jumped every time someone brushed against him. It became a joke to see how high they could make him bounce. There ain't much to entertain you in prison, so 'Let's see how high we can make Billy jump' became the game.

"Well, Bill learned to do what he had do to survive. He made friends with his cellmate, who became his 'Uncle' and kept him safe in return for being his girl." Cook snorted. "Safety."

"Bill took to the gym like a frog to water, and started pumping weights, takin' juice when he could get it, workin' out hard. Within about a year, a year and a half he decided he could defend himself. He left his Uncle, and decided to grow up and become independent. Things were great for a while.

"But there was a big fat ugly guy who'd been on 'im for a while, who kept buggin' him. He tried to warn the big guy off, tell him to fuck off, leave him alone. Ugly guy wouldn't take no for an answer, so Bill started carryin' a shiv. One night he told the guy no, and the guy didn't listen, Bill showed him that his no meant no.

"Only one of them got back up, and Bill got a Life bit for that. Came in on a six-year sentence for armed robbery, and ended up doin' Life-25. They didn't even consider manslaughter because he'd been carryin' his shiv, and he couldn't afford a lawyer. 'For a jail-house killing? Why bother?' they said. I guess the only good part is that after that everyone left Bill alone." Cook snorted again. He took a big gulp of tea.

"'Member, Beth," he continued, "Rules and the Man inside can't protect you any more than Laws and the Police can on the outside. It's all just retaliation and punishment until you choose to stop hurtin', stop fightin' and start carin'."

He raised his big body from the table, collected our cups, brushed the crumbs into one, and took them to the sink. "Sorry that was so graphic, Mugwump. Gotta get lunch ready now, and you got a fence to paint." I hugged him again as I left the kitchen.

Walking across the garden, I was boiling that such brutality happens inside. My outrage only increased when I thought about a system that cages the brain injured, the vulnerable who need medical support. Who could I write to, who could I get to fix this? By the time I reached the garden I had stoked quite a head of steam. This fence wouldn't take very much time to paint if I used my indignation wisely.

When I reached the meadow, I found Ricky was sitting in the first grasses of spring with Timex draped on his knees. They were both purring in the sunshine. "He likes me," Ricky whispered. He kept patting and scratching the languid cat.

"He asked you to touch him, I see," I whispered back. Ricky chuckled.

"He sure did. He nearly knocked me over with asking." Timex sneered at me through one half-closed lid, and as he turned away from me, I swear I heard that cat ask me, "What exactly is the point of blame when there is so much healing to be done?" I'll think about that in my next essay to Dr. Neufeld.

Oh dear God, Why look back, if not to punish?

CHAPTER 27

BLESSED SOLITUDE

Tom laid the reins across Tex's neck as they headed off the central trail into the bush.

"See you later, Tom. Enjoy your time. And I'll enjoy mine," Frank called, and as they parted ways, Tom grunted back, and tipped his leather hat.

Frank was glad to be working with Tom; supervising from afar would give him two days off himself, to spend in retreat, relaxing in a cabin alone. Ah, self-care.

Tom's heart beat fast, and his eyes darted from left to right. The sun dappled onto the rain-soaked underbrush and he wondered how long he could ride before the sun began to set and he had to find a space to camp. He focused on slowing his breathing and slowing his mind so he would enjoy this time. He couldn't believe that for the next two days, he didn't have to answer to anyone.

Frank would be staying in that cabin nearby, and twice a day Tom had to call him on a cell phone, receive a code and enter it into a GPS tracker he had with him. Nora was monitoring the GPS, and as long as he stayed in-bounds he wouldn't be bothered (ten miles any direction from this point, easy as long as he remembered how to use the GPS).

Of course, it wasn't a foolproof system. Everyone knew that. He knew that if he wanted to, he could beat it, but why would he? His life was better now than it had been in years.

He was so glad Nora, Frank, and his parole officer worked had together to find a way for him to have this time alone. It was a miracle, their Christmas present to him.

He hadn't been alone in the bush for 25 years – at least. Tom remembered riding the fence line in Alberta when he'd been a young man. He'd had a job working on a ranch just outside the reserve, and he'd enjoyed his "time in the saddle."

For this trip, Ben had offered him Tex, and he had a bedroll and some food in a saddlebag from Cook. He honestly didn't have to really talk to anyone for the next two days, and when he thought about that his breath slowed and he and Tex calmed down. The rocking of the saddle and the cracking of the small branches underfoot all reminded him of how much he hoped that one day he'd have his own horse to take out whenever he wanted. And that he'd be free enough to do that.

Tom steered Tex between trees, heading slowly uphill, visually mapping out switchbacks as he climbed. He'd spent days poring over geological maps of the area that Ben had brought him, and having memorized them he had a good idea both where he was and where he was going. There was a small marsh he would travel through to a space just above the tree line where he wanted to spend the night. He wanted to be close enough to the forest that he'd be able to find fuel for his fire, but far enough away that an animal wouldn't be able to stalk him, or more importantly, Tex. Keeping his mount safe and sound was his first priority – that and finding grass for Tex to eat, clear water for both of them to drink.

The moon was going to be out tonight, "full" in a couple of nights, so he was confident that if the clouds held off, he'd have time to make camp, and then he'd be able to light a fire and cook his dinner by moonlight. This was turning out to be his best day ever.

Four hours later, Tom was calling Frank to get the code. His fire was warm, and he had some wood stacked nearby. Tex was grazing on a lead not far away, and Tom rubbed his growling belly. He'd enjoy those beans and the buns Cook had packed for him. He knew he'd be sleeping in no time.

Two hours later, resting his head on his saddle pad, Tom had plugged his phone into the battery thing Frank had given him, and was snoring. Tex wasn't moving too far away from him; the night sounds didn't disturb the gelding as he hung his head and slept. Their food and dishes were suspended up in a tree, and all was quiet.

Tom woke to the sound of birdsong and checked the time on his phone. He was surprised that it was already 6:30; usually by this time he was awake and dressed with coffee, heading to the barn to turn the boys (and Buttercup) out into their pastures. He couldn't remember the last time he'd slept so deeply; he was sure it was the fresh air.

Luckily, even though the dew was thick, it hadn't rained overnight. He climbed out of his bedroll and sat by the fire pit watching the sunrise. He offered prayers to Father Sun, and wondered what today would hold. He thanked the Ancestors for his life, for this day, and he asked that whatever was offered, that he would use his time and the gifts given well. It was satisfying to begin his first day on his own in 22 years in a good way, and he was glad.

And then it was time to get moving, so he scrambled to his feet and began to roll his bedroll, and fold the tarp that had covered his blanket. He gathered wood to start his morning fire, and remembered to check in with Frank and Nora. He strolled down to the stream to grab some water, and he put it on the fire for coffee and porridge. He was amazed that by 8:30, he'd done all his chores. Tex's rain sheet was off and stowed, his fire was out, and he was tacking up for a day of riding trails just for the hell of it. Before he mounted, his eyes scanned his camp, and he was pleased to see that other than a few hoof prints and horse apples, there was no evidence that they'd stayed the night. Leave only footprints, he thought, as he swung into the saddle. Footprints and fertilizer.

Tom stayed below the tree line for most of the day, enjoying a quiet path through the woods. He dismounted every couple of hours to let Tex rest. He knew he didn't want to ride the poor beast for more than about five hours, but within that "plan," he mostly gave Tex his head, let him lead them up and down the mountain, and just stayed aware of where he was so he didn't accidentally step out of the ten-mile radius. He ate cheese and bread in the saddle for lunch, finishing with an apple that he shared. His canteen was filled with fresh water every time they stopped to water Tex. The easy day was good for his soul.

He thought about how this solitude was feeding him, and couldn't help but contrast it to how the solitude of segregation had been so brutal. Constant noise, but no one actually talking to him. Constant light. Hard surfaces. And nothing alive in there. He'd spent 15 months straight in seg at one point, and nearly lost his mind. Or maybe he had, it was hard to tell.

He smiled when he remembered what helped. The Elder visits. Yoga. He snorted. Him. Doing yoga like a girl. Calisthenics. More and more reps every day. Pacing his cell. Four steps. Turn. Two steps. Turn. Four steps. Turn. Two steps. Turn. Count 1. Then 18. Then 247. That had been his life day after day. Monotonous. Terrifying. Boredom and demons and then realizing that this existence was his new normal.

It was interesting how being alone wrecked him for being with other people, but too much solitude made him dangerous. And now he didn't know what helped. At least, he hadn't before this weekend. This definitely helped. But he wouldn't want to do it all the time. He knew that, too.

In the late afternoon, he stopped again and made camp back in the field he had slept in the night before. He didn't remember ever feeling this calm and relaxed. Ever. Tex was untacked and on a long line, grazing near the stream. As Tom gathered wood for the fire for dinner, he remembered the bundle that Hugh had given him to open during his "time apart" (as

Hugh called it). When he unpacked his food for dinner (a tinfoil packet of stew that Cook had made him to throw on the coals), he reached the bundle at the bottom of the saddlebag and pulled it out. It was larger than a medicine bundle, and he was a little uneasy about opening it.

He didn't think he was smart enough to even understand the bundle, and that made him nervous. Hugh had never embarrassed him before, but now this. Maybe he'd lose the bundle on the way back to the trail head tomorrow. But curiosity won.

He unwrapped the cloth, and laid out what was in it. He found some sage, an abalone shell, and lighter to light it, so he did, smudging himself and offering his prayers to the Creator. He watched the smoke from the sage rise, and imagined it carrying his prayers upward.

Then he spread out the simple blue cotton and laid out the other items Hugh had sent in the bundle.

A beautiful red sandstone rock.

A big chunk of BC jade.

A small leather roll tied with a leather cord.

And a piece of hardwood – maybe red oak.

And as he looked at the bundle, he started to imagine spirits being liberated from the stone and wood, and he smiled. Maybe this would be his medicine. There was nothing scary here; he'd been borrowing the other men's tools for too long, and he guessed Hugh had heard about it.

As he unrolled the handmade leather tool pouch in his hands, he noticed how supple and soft the leather was. He wondered who had used the pouch before him, and smiled. There were some files and a few small chisels and other tools, six of them in the pouch that would hold up to ten. His fingers caressed the tools, and even though they were used, Tom let out a small whistle that made Tex perk his ears.

"Sorry buddy. It's all good. I just never seen anything so beautiful," he said in a quiet voice.

The tools were old, and really well cared for. They had recently been cleaned and oiled, and Tom examined each one. He was grinning from ear to ear, thinking about how he'd take really good care of them until tomorrow when Hugh would ask for them back. And he picked up the wood and started to carve.

Before long, he smelled his stew and wondered if he'd burned it. He looked up and was surprised that the sun had set and he was sitting in a heavy mist that was threatening to turn into rain. Tom slowly sat up, his bones creaking, and pulled the stew out of the fire. He dug in the saddlebags for Tex's rain sheet, and put it on the horse. Then he covered his tack and spare blankets under a tarp. He unrolled the tinfoil from his dinner and tucked in. It tasted great, up until he reached the charred bits on the bottom. He smiled as he rolled that up and hung his garbage and food back in the tree, swearing he would ditch the garbage before he returned to *Just Living*. He didn't need Cook teasing him for his "reheat" abilities. Before he settled back to the fire, he checked in with Frank, and they made arrangements to meet up late the next day at the trail head with the horse trailer. Tom felt good, and he told Frank "even if the heavens open, I'll be happy sleeping outside tonight."

Soon enough he was back at carving, this time with a headlamp on. It wasn't really raining, but he was sure it would before morning. As he watched the mama otter and baby emerge from the wooden block, he focused on what was in front of him, and the bad voices and memories in his head left. It wasn't until much later when he was wishing he had sandpaper and oil to finish the carving that he realized he hadn't thought about his murdered brother, or crack-addled street-walking sister for hours.

And as he crawled into his bedroll, he still felt calm, and that felt uncomfortable. He wondered if he was being disloyal to his brother because he hadn't thought of revenging his death all day.

The next morning, Tom was awake again before the sun rose, this time chuckling because he was remembering a dream that had woken him. Some might consider it a nightmare, but he knew why he dreamed that the staff at *Just Living* were chasing him down the hallways in the Lodge, and peppering him with questions. He remembered, shaking his head, the night ten years earlier, his first release to a downtown Vancouver halfway house. He'd gone over to his "girlfriend's" apartment one evening, and fallen asleep waiting for her to put her kids to bed. Because she was angry, she just "let him sleep," and he woke up at 12:30, a full ninety minutes after his curfew.

He'd phoned his buddy to see if he'd been reported yet, and found out he hadn't so he'd crept into the backyard of the house and was trying to squeeze in a window when a staff member caught him breaking *into* the halfway house. Needless to say, he was sent back to the prison for a "tune up" – and hadn't made it back out for eight years.

He'd learned from his mistakes. The first time out, he'd partied hard and lived large, and didn't bother to pay attention to his health, his "criminogenic factors," or taking the simple steps that helped keep him on the right side of the law. This time he wasn't going to make the same mistakes again, even if that young mother from the Friendship Centre made his heart pump. Given time, he might even ask her out for coffee.

The day passed too quickly. He ate the rest of his food, saving only a granola bar for lunch. It was too early for berries, but new shoots of some of the plants looked familiar and were safe to eat, so Tom knew he wouldn't go hungry. He packed up his gear, and tacked up Tex. He kept his carving gear in a pouch on his side; he wanted to be able to start working on the sandstone this morning. He wanted to release the swirling circle he'd imagined overnight before he had to give the tools back.

All too soon, it was time to head down the mountain and back to the trail head. Frank arrived shortly after he did, and he emerged from the woods slowly, with a huge smile. Yes, it had rained. He'd want to heat Tex's oats tonight to thank him for his steady work. Yes, he was fairly drenched. But boy, oh boy, was he feeling good. Without even speaking to Frank, they untacked and loaded Tex, and in the cab of the truck before they knew it. Frank reached across the console and offered Tom a hot black coffee. Tom smiled across the cab and wrapped his huge hands around the paper cup.

Later that evening, after he'd settled Tex, cleaned Ben's tack, and started a load of wash with all his wet gear, Tom went to search for Hugh.

"Cook, have you seen Hugh?" he asked as he scrounged for a cookie or two in the kitchen. Dinner had been hearty, but Tom still felt hungry.

"He's down at the Friendship Centre with the youth. Said he'd be back around ten if you wanted to show him anything. Should be back soon," Cook surmised. "I put a bunch of food in the pantry for you. Thought you might come back hungry," Cook said, clearly pleased that Tom was enjoying his baking.

Tom rummaged in the pantry, and headed up the stairs with a mug of coffee and a plate of rolls and those ginger cookies he loved.

"Thanks, Cook. This is delicious," he called back, and Cook wondered if Tom had ever said so much to him in one evening. He smiled. Time alone had helped the cowboy.

Ten minutes later, Tom heard the crunch of Hugh's pickup tires on the gravel out front. He headed outside with the leather tool pouch, and a cloth with the otter wrapped up. He hadn't finished the sandstone carving yet – working in sandstone was trickier than he'd imagined – but he wanted to thank the Elder and return the tools. Maybe he'd be allowed to borrow them again soon.

He approached Hugh on the deck out front of the Lodge, and took the old man's pack to carry.

"How was your time?" Hugh asked. Tom looked over at him and smiled.

"Real good," he answered, and as they arrived at Hugh's room, Tom was invited in. He thought it was weird that Hugh stayed some nights at the Lodge, and went home some nights, but he'd heard Hugh's wife was going visiting for a while. He was glad Hugh wouldn't be alone.

Tom put Hugh's things on the bed, and turned to show him the otter he'd carved. Earlier this evening he'd found some sandpaper in the barn's tool shed and the otter was as smooth as glass now, but warm and soft from the oil he'd worked into the wood. He'd worked hard to show the coat on the faces and the paws of the mother and kit, and he thought he'd done a good job. He held out the carving in his hand, and gently placed it in Hugh's palm.

"Thank you, Mushum, for lending me the tools. I used them. I hope you like what I made for you," Tom had to stop because he was out of breath. That was more than he'd ever said to the Elder. Hugh chuckled and held the otters up close to his face to examine.

"These are fine, son. Good use of your new tools. You should save this carving, to remember your time in the forest." Tom was confused. He'd never seen Mushum turn down a gift before. Maybe he'd done something wrong. He shrugged, and put the tool pouch on the bed. Maybe the otters weren't that good. Maybe they had offended Mushum. He slunk out of the room.

"Tom!" Mushum was calling him back. Tom turned, but didn't look at the man. He felt ashamed, and awkward. Looking at Elders was never good.

"Son, come here. You don't understand. These tools are for you. Some of the carvers at the shack I go to put the kit together for you. They said they were sorry they didn't have more tools for such a good carver," Hugh said to the man. "I can't take them back. They will be offended." Hugh was smiling.

"Mine?" Tom said. He had a puzzled look on his face.

"Yes, a gift from the carvers upriver. And that is why I can't accept your first piece done with those tools.

"This is a beautiful piece. I feel the spirit of the Mama Otter and her kit here. They look happy together. The Creator is happy you have found them, and revealed them so well. But it is not for me. It is for you, son. You have done very well, and I am glad.

"One day soon, when there is a good reason, you find an old stick in the forest and carve something precious just for me. Maybe you could show Angie from the Centre these creatures that you've carved. She asked about you tonight," Hugh said, sneaking a sidelong glance at Tom.

"Really, Mushum? The tools are for me to keep? How do I thank the carvers?" Tom asked. He was blushing at the mention of Angie.

"Well, in the summertime, the carvers carve paddles for the children who are graduating from school. Maybe you can help with that. And in the fall, they collect donations of artworks and carvings to sell at a sale to raise money for the children at Christmas. Maybe by then you will have something carved that you are tired of and you can donate it," Mushum said, putting his hand on Tom's shoulder. His smile reached his eyes.

"Really, son, you have a gift. I want you to save your first pieces, and ask yourself 'What do I think about when I carve?' and 'What is in my heart?' and 'What is the Creator asking me to do here with this spirit trapped in the wood or stone?' Pay attention, and think about that for your first five or ten pieces. Then we'll talk again. Maybe I'll introduce you to a master carver."

Tom couldn't believe it, and certainly couldn't find words. Hugh picked up the tools and put them back in Tom's hand.

"It's okay, son. You should rest now. Tomorrow will come soon enough."

That night when Tom lifted his prayers to the Creator, he felt the truth in Hugh's words. He surprised himself by sleeping well; he felt like a schoolboy at Christmastime, home with his family for the holidays. Or at least, he imagined that he felt like that. He'd never been home from school at Christmastime.

CHAPTER 28
SOMETHING'S IN THE AIR

Dear Father God, Mother Goddess,

I am in awe of your ability to sit back and allow us "free choice," the capacity to inflict so much pain on each other. I want to believe I couldn't do it, if I saw a child (or an adult, for that matter) suffering I'd intervene.

And I admit I'm a little bit pissed about Your role, okay?

I mean, in my head I understand. But really? Ricky deserved this future?

And my head gets that it isn't about fair.

But really?

Why not?

Later that night, in my bed at Veronica's, I thought about my time with Ricky and Cook. Then I remembered that when Cook's brother called, he might have asked for Bill. But did it really matter? Whether or not Cook is Bill, he is a testament to the possibility of healing. He is walking, talking, and hugging proof that anything is possible. I hope for Ricky's sake that the brain-injured can heal, and I know that if it's possible for Ricky to find healing or peace, *Just Living* might be his best hope.

And I thought a little bit about who is responsible. When a guy gets so hurt he lashes back, who *is* to blame? And where does the buck stop, when it comes to keeping prisoners safe? I mean, we cage them. We abuse them. And we let it happen? Why don't we care? When they get out, they do become our neighbours. And, I was surprised to find out that in Canada more than 99% get out.

These are children we worry about when they are sad foster children (or at least we say we do). But if they grow up reacting all over their lack of childhood, of love, end up addicted, and rip us off, we want to punish them hard. Sigh.

Cook mentioned once in circle that no one was ever healed, that we are all just healing. I'm beginning to get it, I think. Humans are humans, doing the best we can with what is in front of us. Sometimes we get hurt. Sometimes we hurt each other. Sometimes a lot. But all our behaviour comes from somewhere.

I still don't know if Cook is staff or a prisoner. Maybe he's both. Maybe we all are.

For the rest of the week, I tried to sleep, but was distracted by Ben. We still texted every day, but I hadn't seen him in way too long. And at night, when I wasn't wrestling with ideas and prayers about justice, I was sweating between the sheets thinking about that weekend coming up.

Oh Beloved Goddess,

Thank you for love. And that most delightful of carnal pleasures…anticipation.

And it would be okay if, for just a little time, I was able to focus on something other than daydreaming about my time with Ben.

I've spent this week reading and re-reading the Songs of Solomon. I think average folk would blanch at the beauty in the writing, the juiciness of its words…but I've got them going around like a mantra in my soul.

"My beloved spoke and said to me,

'Arise, my darling, my beautiful one, and come with me.'
His left arm is under my head, and his right arm embraces me." 2:6
"I said, 'I will climb the palm tree; I will take hold of its fruit.
May your breasts be like clusters of grapes on the vine,
your fragrance like the apples.'" 7:8
Somehow, I think it's more like this with Ben:
"If you do not know, most beautiful of women,
follow the tracks of the sheep and graze your
young goats by the tents of the shepherds." 1:8
He's more a naïve shepherd than a conquering King, I admit.
And I'm kinda liking that. Thank you for Ben.
And for the Songs of Solomon – for convincing me that really, hot steamy sex between consenting adults is…wondrous.

The next few days were spent vacillating between bliss and terror. Steamy notions of us in the cabin would be uprooted by realizing I had to come clean with him about my abortion if I was ever going to relax around him. Not coming clean didn't work for me anymore.

Then, questions about "What am I thinking, a relationship with my mentor?" would creep in. Followed by "He's a colleague. Dr. Neufeld is really my mentor, right?" I couldn't figure out any of it, so decided that if our plans were illicit or immoral or even just lacking integrity, Ben wouldn't have suggested it. Then my brain would go to "A relationship with a monk? But…you abhor the Church…." And then my feminist self would get all uncomfortable with *that* perspective.

Life with Veronica had fallen into a gentleness I hadn't had at *Just Living*. She made dinner, and I arrived home and ate. I cleaned up, and baked for the next day or two. Then, we might share a tea, but mostly I'd head upstairs, feigning homework.

The hours journaling about my relationships with Dad, God, Nora and Ben didn't help. Rereading, I know it's self-absorbed drivel, with a touch of Pollyanna. Not particularly productive, but at least I approached the possibilities with awe, a naïve hopefulness for its beauty and rightness. Or some other crap.

I did remember to check with Nora if it was okay to go away (and noticed I didn't mention where or with whom). She acted like I didn't get it -- she wasn't responsible for my weekends any more. Sigh. So instead I told Cook a little bit about what was going on. I swear, that man could get secrets from a priest.

Oh wait. He just did.

Friday morning, Kenny and I started clearing for the labyrinth, staking it out, dreaming and planning as we went. A couple of times Al or Tom walked by, and we talked about how to integrate some Medicine Wheel teachings that honoured each practice. Paul even gave us his advice at one point.

Al admitted that no matter what we did, or how honouring we tried to be, some people would be pissed off. I knew he was right, and decided to talk to Hugh about it. Maybe he had some more wisdom he could share.

Friday afternoon finally arrived, and I waited in the barn with Tex and Thud, visiting Topaz and Buttercup, who was getting friendlier. I'd packed my backpack at Veronica's and stashed it in the tack room that morning, and Kenny had lent me his bed roll. I needed the calm from the animals; I felt like I was dancing on the sharp points of possibilities over and over in my mind – and not all of those possibilities were of starlit romance. Some felt dark and gloomy.

I heard Ben's car pull up, and soon he was there, stroking Tex's nose, starting a weird conversation about our trip, first sounding all happy and excited, and in the next minute asking me if I was sure I wanted to go. I cringed. Was he talking himself out of spending time with me?

"You know this isn't going to work, right Beth? You have such potential, your life in front of you...being with me will only upset all that. I think we should just call the whole thing off. Why even go there? Who even knows if we'd get along? Let's just get over it now, and it'll all be good." I couldn't make hide nor hair of what he was talking about, so I called him on it.

"I have no idea what's up, what you're talking about. We're just getting away for a bit. Are you ashamed of me? I know you want to "keep me safe," but I'm kinda safe…and really, I can look after myself. Big girl, and all of that. And besides, we did say we want to spend some time. No big commitment, just have fun. Keep it light. Right?" I sounded confused even to me.

"I guess I'm uncomfortable," he admitted.

"With what? Being alone with a woman, or being alone with me?" Suddenly I knew he may not have ever been with a woman before, which, I admit, made the whole thing even sexier.

"I just started thinking about it on the way out. Really. What am I thinking, you're a student, for heaven's sake, and I'm a chaplain."

"And?" I let the awkward silence hang for a bit. "You know I'm almost 30, right? I've even been married. Grown woman, able to make adult choices," I pointed at myself for emphasis. My stomach started to hurt a bit; I'd left out a really big disclosure. Maybe ending our not-yet-relationship now would save me having to share about Chaos.

"I know," he said. "I'm worrying about what Aaron might say. I'm not really worried about what we're doing, but more about the appearance of it. Especially since you're staying at Veronica's now." Ben was rambling.

"So…poor little me is being dragged off against my will by the big male mentor?" I joked. I wanted him to be comfortable, but I was disappointed. WTF? Had I fucked up this, too?

"No! I'm not saying that. It's just that I agreed to help supervise your practicum here, and now, well, it feels uncomfortable. That's all," Ben answered.

"Okay, I get it. You told Aaron you'd help him by touching base with me and helping with the day-to-day, right? And it's not like I even get a mark for the practicum – it's pass/fail. And no one fails. Did Aaron ask you for input on my marks?"

"No…." Ben got all flustered.

"Anyways, let's back up a bit," I said. "We're not off for a torrid weekend of illicit sex that leads down a path of moral turpitude! You offered a weekend in nature. Some time alone to get to know each other. That's all. Let's not make this into more than it is...please?" I finished almost with a whisper. "Besides, you're the first guy I've even noticed in forever. And I've had a rough week. I don't know what it'll mean. But dang, I'd like to talk to you without a million people around."

Ben still looked like he was in pain. He was really uncomfortable with all of this. I suggested he talk to Aaron about it, and he disappeared into Tex's stall to call. A few minutes later he came back, looking sheepish. "He says to get over myself, enjoy the weekend, and I'm off the hook as your mentor."

"He called Nora? Or you did?" I was surprised, I admit.

"Nah. He says he checked with her this week to make sure it was all going okay, and she was happy with how things were going, how graceful you've been about moving out. I guess she likes your baking," Ben said, smiling.

"So we're good? We can head out?" I asked.

"Yeah," he said. "He took my hand, and we headed off to his car. My heart was pounding.

We headed east out of town towards Harrison Hot Springs, and the cabin. On the drive up we talked a little more about my time with Ricky, and how things were going at Veronica's. I mentioned working with Hugh, plans for the labyrinth, and how we were integrating the Medicine Wheel. About a half hour in, I knew it had all been about me.

"What about you, Ben? How are things?" I asked.

He talked about work, and some of the guys inside. Soon we were back to me, and I was a bit uncomfortable about that.

"Let's play a game called 'Get to know you.' 'Kay?" I suggested.

"How'd you play it?" Ben asked, looking sideways at me. I think he knew I was making it up.

"Favourite colour," I said.

"Green," he said.

"Orange. Favourite book."

"Other than the Bible? Maybe something by Anne Lamott. Or Matthew Fox," he said.

"Hmmm...*The Hour I First Believed*. Wally Lamb. Or Lamb. Christopher Moore. Favourite food."

"My mother's mac and cheese. I don't get it anymore," he said, sounding wistful. I made a mental note to figure out why it was special, and make it for him.

"An amazing crab cake I had once," I said. "Or East Coast – fresh-off-the-docks lobster." We kept on for a few more rounds, and then started talking about *Just Living* again. I elaborated on the plans for the labyrinth.

Before long, we arrived at the trail head for the path to Eric's cabin, and Ben pulled a large backpack out of the trunk. When I chided him about it, he reminded me that I had better be nicer than I was being, or I might find myself hungry. He was packing in the provisions! I hadn't even thought about eating. Fail! Considering how much time I'd been spending in the kitchens it might have occurred to me. I'd packed precisely two chocolate bars and six muffins; we'd have been some hungry if it'd been up to me.

We donned our packs, and headed up the trail. The day was overcast and nippy, but it didn't feel like rain. The path was narrow enough that I followed behind, enjoying the view. I realized after a few minutes that other than a quick hug in the stables and holding hands to the car, we hadn't touched one another. Which was kind of cool; I really didn't feel any pressure, even though I felt the electricity between us.

After an hour of hiking, some of it fairly steep, we reached a small clearing and Eric's cabin. It was a small A-frame, with a covered porch, and it looked snug and dry. Our next hour or so was spent opening shutters, sweeping out cobwebs (and large spiders!), clearing a nest from the chimney (which happened quite dramatically when Ben opened the damper on the wood stove) and making the space ours, for now. I had glimpses of "playing house," and kept noticing I was smiling.

Ben laid a fire, and it was after eight o'clock when he suggested dinner; I admitted I was famished. He prepared it while I took my stuff up to the loft and laid it out for later. I wasn't sure what our sleeping arrangements would be, so I carefully unrolled my bedroll and shoved my stuff to one side, leaving lots of room for his stuff. As I lay down on my bed and listened to Ben puttering below, I found myself looking across into the darkness of the forest through the large windows. This place was glorious.

The cabin was simply furnished. There was no water except a pump outside, and the "plumbing" was a pit toilet out back. There were a few chairs and a table downstairs, all made out of the wood from the forest around the cabin. A few rough bookshelves held religious texts and plates and bowls; a pot lived on top of the woodstove. I felt happy, content in ways I hadn't expected. And did I mention hungry?

After about twenty minutes, Ben served a hearty bowl of minestrone soup, pâté, cheese, and French loaf. Wow. He does know how to "pack it in." We followed with a huge pot of tea from water he'd had in his water bottle. I couldn't believe it was the same stuff at *Just Living* because this tea tasted out of this world. What is it about fresh air that makes my taste buds come alive?

I ate everything offered, and we settled into the evening, sitting in deep chairs reading our books on either side of the stove. Soon, I was yawning and the candles and kerosene lamp really weren't enough light to read by.

I rose to brush my teeth, headed up to the loft and fell asleep watching Ben read beside the stove. God, is he cute when he's pretending to read. I'm not sure I saw him turn a page. Maybe one. I fell quickly and hard into deep sleep; good food, a hike, and all the sleepless anticipation had caught up with me.

The next morning, I rose, and saw him flaked out in front of the fire, laying on his sleeping bag, still wearing all his clothes. He looked adorable, and I guessed from the warmth, he'd woken a few times and stoked the fire. I stayed upstairs watching him. Creepy, I know, but I couldn't help myself.

I hadn't spent time the night before doing my usual "spiritual practice" of recounting the day, reminding myself how I was "doing," and spending some time giving thanks for all the things I was intensely grateful for. So when I remembered, I did it. God gives allowances for "better late than never," right?

And ten minutes later, as I said prayers for each of the men, for Chaos, Jesse and my family, I noted yet again that even with all that had gone on, I lead a pretty charmed life. *God, I am lucky. Really, really fucking lucky.* Prayer.

I couldn't postpone a trip to the latrine any longer, and wanted to brush my teeth, so I snuck down the loft stairs. As I opened the front door, I noticed Ben stirring, so I hurried out. By the time I got back, he was outside priming the pump to clear the lines of brackish water, and fetching fresh spring-fed water to make oatmeal and more tea. More yum.

We chatted over breakfast, about everything and nothing. I told him again how excited I was about the labyrinth/Medicine Wheel. He told me about the upcoming AVP workshops. We talked about a new book by a favourite writer expected in the spring. And yes, being Canadian, we talked about the weather.

After a bit, we were both chomping to get outside, so I got up and started to clean up. I cleared the dishes while Ben stoked the fire and brought in wood to dry. A few minutes later, the pot on the stove was full of warm water, and Ben brought it to the counter so I could use it as a sink. In no time at all, the food was cleaned up, and stored in the bear-proof cooler. It wasn't cold – there was no ice – but at least it was safe from critters!

Doing the dishes together, few as they were, gave us a chance to be "near" each other, which was nice. Who knew I like doing dishes? And once they were washed and stored away, Ben pulled me toward him, and then we were hugging each other, sharing some warmth and a sigh of contentment. He raised my chin with his fingers, and a slow, languorous dance began. As I opened my lips to invite him, his breathing became charged, and after a few tentative advances of each of our tongues, he pulled back, and then held me close again. A fire had been lit and I wasn't sure I was ready to either fan the flames or be caught in the inferno.

Ben chuckled. "On the one hand," he said, "this is delicious. You are delicious. Um..." he hesitated. "We are delicious? On the other, I am quite aware that this is dangerous." He didn't need to elaborate, my heart was pounding. After a couple of more minutes, we agreed to a hike with a picnic; Ben said he had a surprise for me. He quickly packed some food and water in a day-pack and off we set, heading further west into the rain forest, dripping with life and the promises of spring.

Have I mentioned life is good?

"You, whose day it is, get out your rainbow colours and make it beautiful..." – Traditional Nootka Song

Dear God,

Hugh told me the other day that the longest journey we make is from our heads to our hearts.

This prayer flew to my heart today.

Thank you.

CHAPTER 29
WATERFALLS AND HEARTBEATS

Wandering up the path, again enjoying the view, I started to think about my readings this week on Integrity. It seemed fitting.

Dear God,

With Ben being a Quaker, or at least hanging out with them, I read about their Testimonies last week. Seems testimonies are actually "ways to live," not stories of salvation. They have five they try to live by: Simplicity, Equality, Peace, Community, and Integrity. Wow.

This is what Wikipedia told me about Integrity:

*"**Testimony to integrity and truth**, refers to the way many members of the Religious Society of Friends (Quakers) testify to their belief that one should live a life that is true to God, true to oneself, and true to others.... For example, Friends (Quakers) believe that integrity requires avoiding statements that are technically true but misleading....*

"The essence of the Testimony of Integrity is choosing to follow the leading of the Spirit despite the challenges and urges to do otherwise.

"This testimony has led to Friends having a reputation for being honest and fair in their dealings with others. It has led them to give proper credit to others for their contributions and to accept responsibility for their own actions."

That's profound. And I'd better tell Ben about Chaos soon.

You will stay with me while I do that, right God?

As we hiked up the path, we settled into another conversation about relationships and theology. I wanted to know what were we doing here, and, maybe more important, where were we heading, so I asked.

He turned, took my hands, and looked right into my soul.

"I haven't a fucking clue, but I'm open to being surprised," he said, and I knew this could be fun. Remember that thing about relationships being intentional and vulnerable like AVP? There was a hope.

But I had decided who I wanted Ben to be…and wondered if I would like the real Ben as much as I liked the fantasy version I'd created. Hmmmm….

I reached up and kissed him quickly, giving him a low growl. My curiosity and those kisses had my body on a low simmer.

"How long 'til we get where we were going?" I asked.

"Almost there," he whispered. I wondered if he was talking about the walk.

We wound our way upwards, until I heard water. Ben sighed and looked up; as he slowed down (and I nearly bumped into his back), I saw why.

In front of us was a small, steaming pool, fed both from an underground hot spring and a clear waterfall, cascading off into a small stream. Water dripped from branches of cedar trees above us, as the steam lifted skyward towards the ceiling they created. We just stood, breathless, holding hands. After a few minutes, Ben said, "This is one of my clearest experiences of God," and I fell a little further.

I bent down over the water. The pool was about ten feet across, but I couldn't tell how deep. I bent to dip my fingertips in.

"Hey, take care," Ben quietly cautioned, as I dipped my arm in deeper. "Sometimes it's really hot." I smiled up at him.

"I'm going to take off my boots, and soak my feet," he said, and I noticed his voice was still hushed.

"Mind if I join you?" I whispered. Soon I pulled up my pant legs and dangled my feet off the rocky edge. Looking around, I saw the rocks had been carefully placed, like someone had "created" this pool. It felt soothing, smelled of sulphur. Ben told me about it.

"This hot spring opened up a few years ago after a small quake, years after Eric had bought the property as a hermitage. He was a monk, too," Ben explained. "When he left the monastery he didn't want to completely leave the disciplines behind, so he retreats for months at a time, living in solitude, praying, and writing. He's in India for a year, and asked me to look after it. And yes, he knows you're here; we keep in touch by email." I felt lucky to be invited.

"When the water bubbled up and made hot mud, Eric dug it away and made a larger pool. Then one weekend, we lined the pool with rocks from around here. He guards its secret pretty carefully because he knows that if people find out about it he'd either have to share it or fence it, and he doesn't want to do either," Ben continued. "So, if you tell anyone, I'll have to kill you." His dancing eyes belied his sombre tone.

"No worries," I laughed. "I don't think I could find it again."

After another couple of minutes, Ben took my hand, and I expected him to suggest we leave. The sun had crossed over the small opening in the trees, so I knew it was afternoon, but heck, we hadn't even eaten yet. Instead, he reached for his bag, and pulled out a candle, lit it and placed it on the rock.

"Beth, is it okay if I share a bit? You've been so friendly, it feels a little awkward. It's kinda why I brought you here."

I smiled, hoping that would reassure him, and squeezed his hands, while squirming about Chaos-shaped gaps in my sharing. He reached into his pack and grabbed our picnic, and we broke bread. When we were done, I leaned against him, enjoying the feel of his sweater on my cheek, and looked into the pool.

"You know my roots are Catholic, right?" I nodded. "I was raised in small town New Brunswick. Papa worked in a mine, Maman stayed home with me and my sisters and brothers, and we went to Mass a couple of times a week. Life was happy for the first seven or eight years, with all my Aunts and Uncles just down the road. Cousins to play with after school, street hockey in the winter, swimming hole in the summer. It was like the perfect childhood – some hard work, lots of fresh air and good food, and plenty of love.

"I didn't even really know there was a bigger world, because we didn't even have television." I looked up at Ben, and his face was flushed. His hands were fidgeting at the zipper on his jacket.

"Then, when I was about eight, the mines expanded and the town grew. Some folks came because they had jobs, others hoping to be hired. Hard times, and many were homeless. Our life changed overnight.

"Papa's cousin started hanging around, asking for work. He helped Maman with the yard work, sometimes got day labour from neighbours or the township. He always gave me the creeps, but Maman told me he was family, and explained his French sounded different because he was from Quebec. I was to 'be welcoming and charitable.' His family was struggling, I guess, living in an abandoned cabin."

I started to shiver a bit, more because of the story than the temperature. My legs and feet were warm, but my back was cold. Ben put his arms around me and held me close. I leaned in, smiling.

"Well, over time he began to do more and more. After a couple of months, he told Papa I was his 'best helper' and Papa set us up to work building a playground at school, a rough ball diamond and backstop, that kind of thing. We had an old shed that had been dragged up there to store our tools. Then one afternoon, when we were left alone, he took advantage of me. I didn't even know what we were doing, my life was so innocent. But I knew it was wrong. He threatened to hurt my sisters if

I told anyone, so I didn't." Ben took a deep, ragged breath, and leaned back against a rock, pulling his feet out of the pool.

"You don't have to tell me this if you don't want to," I whispered. He chuckled.

"Believe me, I have wrestled with how much to tell you, when to tell you, what to tell you ever since I drove you up to *Just Living*. It seems to be all I think about." He took a deep breath. "I *want* to tell you, Beth. Then we'll see. I understand. I really do." He paused for a minute, stirring the water with his feet.

"I want to be honest. You've been so up front sharing your journals, and about everything at *Just Living*. I'm going to trust you. I know you won't betray me; no one else knows of my past except one counsellor, and a couple of folks back home. My old Priest," he finished.

I nodded, feeling overwhelmed by his revelation. And kinda dirty with what I hadn't shared. In fact, truth be told, a part of me was a little baffled; I didn't want Ben to be any less than the perfect guy I'd imagined him to be.

"Wait. I need to tell you something," I blurted. "Later, I mean." And as easy as that, I'd chosen my path. After a moment or two Ben continued.

"Well, this guy abused me on and off for a couple of years, and as you can guess, my behaviour got bad. I was really confused, too, because sometimes it felt good." He stopped, checked out my reaction. I hoped I looked neutral.

"It's weird. I felt betrayed by my body, and acted out. My parents were baffled, and the Priest told them I was testing them, to discipline me harshly. I became more and more resentful. When I was about 14 the guy finally left; I don't know why but I was sure glad. The little boy that I had been was long gone, but I thought I was doing a good job hiding everything.

"I hope my younger brothers and sisters were spared; I never had the nerve to ask them. Anyhow, after some particularly bad behaviour when I was sixteen, I was asked by Papa to leave town. I left, went to Montreal, and a few years later, joined a seminary. I lived in the monastery for about ten years. I only went home once, for Papa's funeral, and even then my family didn't speak to me much. Maman keeps in touch, so that she knows I am fine. I kinda hope she is proud of me, of what I've done."

My heart was breaking for the little boy who had been hurt. I hugged Ben, determined not to let go. I started to say how sorry I was, telling him it would be okay, when he told me he wasn't finished.

"I need to tell you everything, okay? It's really important. When I was sixteen, and totally a mess, I started targeting younger boys at church camp, and I even abused two of them; they were about 13 I think. It might not have been as serious as what had been done to me, but I don't want to minimize what I did.

"At first, when the Priest told my Papa, they tried to write it off as 'normal curiosity,' and 'boys will be boys,' but my anger and hate for myself grew and I was afraid I would really hurt someone. So one night I went to the park to burn down the sports building; it was bigger than the original shack, but wasn't much more than a two-room wooden building with a bathroom. Luckily Papa caught me, and put out the fire before there was too much damage. He asked me to pack my bags that night."

Ben kept on confessing, and I felt worse and worse.

"I graduated from high school in Montreal a year or two late, but with straight As, so I went on to Seminary on scholarship. Père Joseph supported me, which made it easy to build a wall around my sexuality. I was afraid I was gay. So, I became asexual...which worked well for my story of being called to be a monk.

"After leaving the monastery I started at the prison, and issues started to bubble up again for me. About two years ago I met a chaplain doing serious violent offence mediation, and when I asked questions he figured out I had been abused, and had abused others. I've been going to counselling for about two years, and think I am starting to heal.

"I couldn't do mediation with the creep who hurt me because he died about five years ago, but I did write letters to the boys I had molested, and apologized. They were really kind, and willing to accept the letters, and I haven't heard from them since. My counsellor says they are doing fine, some guilt that I was sent away. He reassured them that I'm good. I told them in the letter that I was sorry, and willing to make amends in a way that made sense to them, but they didn't ask for anything. Maybe they're being kind.

"Anyhow, Maman still doesn't know why I left unless Papa told her, and I don't want to tell her if he didn't because I don't want her to feel responsible – for either the leaving or the abuse. One day I want to go back. I have nieces and nephews I haven't met."

We sat in silence for a while, my feet dangling in the water. Ben sighed. I imagined him around his family's table, eating macaroni and cheese.

"I guess I'm saying I don't have a great history with women. Any history, really. And I don't really know how I'll react to this, to affection. I sure don't want to hurt you. I do care, but I feel like I'm fifteen, and just learning about stuff, except that I have all the junk from my childhood right there putting questions and 'bad tapes' in my head." He sighed.

We continued to sit, and I was swirling the warm water with my legs, leaning my head on Ben and stroking his chest through his fleece. I listened to his breathing, shallow, guarded. I tried to find my voice, but I didn't know what to say, and was struggling with a huge inclination to try to "make it better," which was ridiculous. I finally got up the nerve to say something.

"I don't really know what to say, Ben, except I'm sorry it happened. Really. It sucks. And I'm still really glad I'm here." He squeezed my hand. "I know Frank told me when I'm listening to someone, I'm not supposed to tell my own story."

I didn't want anything less than an honest and equal relationship between us, but I held back. Working with Frank I knew enough to know that I know very little, and that counselors with a lot more experience were already on it. And I needed to come clean about my abortion, but no rush. I decided to ask a few questions.

"What would help?" I was remembering I shouldn't ask a question I don't want to hear the answer to. I really didn't want to hear he wanted to stop seeing me.

"I'd like to dip in the pool. I always feel like I need to wash after I think about all this. You can come in if you want, but I need some space, 'kay?"

My fantasy was certainly not this, I thought, as I slowly peeled down to my sports bra and underwear. Thank goodness I was wearing black! Ben eased into the pool and vigorously scrubbed himself in the mineral water. I eased in slowly, and sank in up to my neck. I was sitting on a rock on the bottom; the pool was about three feet deep. We sat facing each other, and I asked if I could hold his hand while I spoke to him. He gave it to me, and I took a few more minutes to gather my thoughts, and then I started.

"I'm afraid to say anything in case I say the wrong thing, and I know that chances are pretty high that I might have already done that…." I laughed. Ben reassured me he wouldn't break.

"I don't know what is in store for us. I know I want to spend some time with you, without any promises. And I do know a couple of things." I kept going.

"I think you're a brave man for facing what happened and taking responsibility for the hurt."

I kneeled in front of him, keeping some space between us. He reached for me, and I put my arms around his neck and began a gentle butterfly dance on his face with my lips. I murmured to him that I understood, and that I was willing to give him space and trust him. And I was doing the exact opposite of what I said.

I slowly caressed his face and shoulders, but stopped there, pushing away. I asked him for a hug, and he dragged me into his arms. I could feel his deep ragged breaths while he struggled to "be good," as he put it. He kissed to top of my head, and just held me.

There was wonder in that moment, under the dripping cedars, and I felt a spiritual connection.

After a few minutes, I was overheating again. Ben climbed out and I looked away as he pulled a towel from his bag and offered it to me. I told him to go ahead, and soon he was dressed and encouraging me to get out. He wrapped the towel and his arms around me as I emerged from the water, dripping everywhere and making him more than damp.

I felt so cherished. After a couple of minutes I began to shiver, and Ben encouraged me to get dressed. I told him to turn around, and when he said it was okay, I needn't feel shy, I started to peel off my underwear.

He spun around, sputtering, asking what I was doing. I laughed. "I'm cold. I'm not putting on dry clothes over wet." He wasn't looking, though, and I don't think he even snuck a peak. Darn. A few minutes later we had packed up and were heading back to the cabin.

After hot chocolate, a bowl of chili, and my muffins and cookies, we were getting ready to call it a day.

"Where do you want to sleep?" Ben asked. I convinced him that I would sleep best with him, in my long flannel jammies. He grabbed my bedding from the loft, and set us up in front of the fire while I got changed in the corner.

"Hey, Ben…without getting all 'convince me,' why did you invite me here?" Yes, I sounded insecure.

"You were amazing in AVP, with the men. Then, when you told me about what happened at *Just Living* with Glenn, and having to move to Veronica's, I realized I really care about what happens to you. I guess I liked that you told me, didn't try to hide anything." Ah, my inability to keep secrets? I didn't feel so attractive. Sigh.

It was wonderful, spending that night in his arms. I'm not sure I slept a wink, I was so happy. I kept thinking "Pinch me! I can't believe this!" I think we dozed on and off, cuddling, occasionally sharing a kiss, wrapped in one another's arms under the sleeping bags, and I almost wished the sun wouldn't rise. I had shared sleep with men before, of course, but that night the magic swirled.

The next morning we packed up our things, cleaned the food right down to the crumbs out of the cabin, and got ready to leave. I asked Ben if we could stop by the hot spring before we left, have silent worship, without swimming.

The space was just as sacred that morning, and I had a chance to tell Ben about all the things I was feeling grateful for. It was the best church I'd visited in a long time. Well, that and the Sanctuary.

I felt hugely blessed that he had chosen to share about his childhood with me. I asked him to set the pace with our relationship, taking it as slowly or quickly as he wanted, as he thought God wanted. We agreed to keep talking, especially if we were uncomfortable with anything.

Ben asked me to make a wish. I wished that we could come skinny-dipping some night to the pool, and "really get to know each other." He groaned. He wished that something wonderful could come from his childhood experiences, and that whatever it was, we would share it together.

"Oh yeah…and I also want to skinny-dip," he said. Before we left, he told me that until last night he had wondered if he was gay, or dysfunctional, or would be able to have a loving relationship with a woman. He felt pretty sure after his evening and night with me that he had his answer. I was beaming.

Dear God,

I know the Catholics swear by confession, a way to cleanse, to find absolution, to reconcile with God and get access to heaven. Again.

The Sacrament of Penance, they call it.

And it's fallen out of fashion in my generation, and I understand why. If it's about giving power to the priests, or me needing an "intermediary" to access God, it loses my interest.

But soon I promise to own my sh*t, so to speak, and am hoping for Grace in return.

I want to be responsible for what I do. What I've done.

Am I finally growing up?

In any case, please stick with me,

Beth

CHAPTER 30
THE PICNIC

Stephen called. He and Sarita were coming out on the weekend for a visit; he said he needed to talk. I suggested a picnic in a wilderness park near here, with a beautiful waterfall, and some benches, and it didn't sound like it was going to rain too much.

And then Glenn called. He's coming back to pick up his boys; he was offered the Rectory in Mount Currie, and they're going out there to see it. Donna resisted, but anyways, he's taking them. So our picnic grew! I was making food for everyone, and I told Steve to borrow lawn chairs from Mom and Dad so Sarita would be comfortable. He told me she's big as a house. I told him not to say that around her, but I could hear her pounding him with pillows in the background. I was happy.

I was scheduled to go back into prison soon for the Second Level AVP – exciting! Believe me, I was learning, and paying attention, more than I ever did in school. But I still didn't know what I was going to do with my life. Or if I'd get back into Nora's good graces.

Tonight, as I was drifting off to sleep, I remembered Nana Beth singing to me when I was little. Her voice reminded me of angels...and I would try desperately to stay awake through her lullabies. I had to look up the lyrics tonight, but when I read them I could still hear her voice....

Sleep my child and peace attend thee,
All through the night
Guardian angels God will send thee,
All through the night
Soft the drowsy hours are creeping,
Hill and dale in slumber sleeping
I my loving watch am keeping,
All through the night.

I read three more verses, and although I never heard her sing all of them, I don't doubt she knew them.
I wonder what lulled the men at Just Living to sleep when they were children? And what it would take to quiet their fears and make them feel safe now?
Maybe I should start singing my prayers. THAT would be quite a legacy to Nana Beth.
Maybe some time I'll even get to sing to the men back at the Lodge.
It can only help my discipline.

As I drifted off to sleep, I thought about how I want to hang out more with Ben. I just wish I knew how to make that happen.

So that weekend I was ridiculously excited, making bunwiches and packing cookies, and apples from the big bin inside the pantry door. Glenn was coming to pick me up; he said their vehicle was filled with bedding, and camping gear and as much of his stuff as stuffable, but they would save me a seat. And they had a surprise!

We were headed for a grand adventure! I'd carefully decorated some Dalek cupcakes, and was wearing my "I love bowties" T-shirt. I knew Bruce loved Dr. Who, and hoped this would catch me some slack. There was lemonade from real lemons, and a thermos of coffee for the adults. A half-hour later, I heard the crunch of gravel, and rushed out. Cook was just behind me, standing in the doorway calling out instructions.

"Don't go too near the falls, Darlin'. People get hurt there. Some die every year," he said, and I wondered if Cook knew that some of those deaths might be intentional. Because suicide. Sigh. Cook embodied goodness.

"Don't worry, we will be," I said, and looked up to see Glenn in a shiny grey pickup truck. Not new, but certainly new to him.

"Nice wheels," I said, walking around it with a critical eye.

"It just makes sense for where I live," he said. "It was about time. We can fish and camp right out of the back of this, right boys?" Glenn wrapped me in a big hug. He seemed happier. Adam was playing with the power window, having escaped from his car seat.

"Dad, can we let Tiger out?" Bruce called out.

"Good idea, Bruce. Just keep a hold of his leash and stay where I can see you," he said, and Bruce emerged out the back door with a puppy on a leash. The puppy immediately squatted and peed, and Adam started praising him. I smiled; clearly they were working on house-training. Then I noticed Bruce looked scared.

"Good dog," I offered. "Well done," and I rushed over to meet Tiger.

"It's okay if he goes here?" Bruce asked. "I was trying to get him over there," he said, pointing to the north of the Lodge.

"No problem. Any messes he makes we can pick up, right Dad?" I said, laughing. Bruce's shoulders fell, and he smiled. "Tell me all about him!"

"This is Tiger. Adam named him," Bruce sighed. Clearly naming a puppy after a big cat wasn't okay with him. I laughed. "We've had him for a week."

"Where did you guys get him?" I asked, and they all started telling me the story.

"Daddy's friend gave him," Adam said.

"He was going to get killed!" Bruce said with some drama. Glenn chuckled. I was bending down to ruffle Tiger's soft golden fur, admiring his big ears and paws.

"What a big guy he is!" I said, looking at Glenn and wondering what the heck he had gotten himself into. He was beaming at the boys.

"He was a sorry bastard from a sorry litter born to a Labrador that was purebred. Which he clearly isn't. The guy was sneaking the dogs to the Humane Society when I offered him $30.00 for Tiger. He was thrilled. I fell in love and she's good company. I told the boys she's their dog when they visit." Clearly Bruce was taking this seriously, because he had a tight grip on the leash and wasn't letting go.

"Let me!" Adam was begging of his big brother.

"Let's let him run for a bit, with his leash on," Glenn suggested.

"No Dad, he'll run away!" Bruce panicked, but Glenn reassured him that Tiger loved them and would come back. Within moments they were playing with Tiger and a ball, running around in the parking area, and up on the dock. In no time, Tiger "accidentally" jumped off the dock, and splashed into the water. We laughed out loud at his surprise as he paddled to the edge and climbed out.

"His mom's a swimmer, of course, but I don't think he's ever seen water before," Glenn laughed as Tiger shook all over the boys. They were squealing.

In no time, Cook brought the picnic, helped by a few other guys. They were pounding Glenn's back in greeting, and Kenny was trying to lure him around the side to see where he wanted to build the labyrinth/Medicine Wheel. About twenty minutes later, the boys were into dry clothes, and we were on the road, Tiger tucked in the back between the boys' car seats.

"Adventure!" I shouted, and Adam giggled. Bruce was quiet, but I was determined to draw him out. Glenn was happy – new truck, camping gear, his boys in back and a new dog.

"Does it get better than this?" he smiled. Was there a little melancholy?

"Not today," I said, grinning from ear to ear. "Stephen and Sarita are bringing lawn chairs and blankets in case it gets too cold, but I think it'll be a fine day," I said. I had memorized a few jokes that were groan worthy, but after a bit I think I saw Bruce smile, just for a moment.

By the time we arrived at the picnic site, Adam and Tiger were napping in the back seat.

"Hey big guy, wanna help unpack stuff while the little ones sleep?" Glenn asked Bruce. Then they played pitch and catch with a tennis ball and baseball gloves. The windows were cracked for air, and the littler ones slept on. I grabbed my book and sat at the table pretending to read, watching the family have fun, and felt a little tug at my gut when I realized Chaos would be about two years older than Bruce now, if he/she had lived. I wondered what my life would have been like with a child. And if I'd ever have another.

I'm still trying to make sense of the Ben thing. I've never been 'the initiator' before. Hmmm…maybe I need to "initiate" more in life. Maybe that's a key piece in my quest for meaning. I couldn't imagine a scene where I got baby-making with Ben, but took on a new resolve to push things just a little faster to find out where our "us" might be going. Where I might be going, too.

A little while later Stephen and Sarita drove up, and unpacked my car. It was a bit startling seeing them in my old beast. I'd told Stephen to feel free to use it, but it was just weird that he was. That car had been with me for years – I'd bought it with Jesse's advice, and just couldn't let it go. Darn! I hadn't expected the sense of "Get your hands off my beast!" at seeing Stephen behind MY wheels.

The commotion of their arrival, and all the subsequent introductions woke Tiger, which woke Adam, and Glenn said he was glad because they had a lot more driving to do later. Adam shed a few tears, missing his mom, but soon was running around with Tiger, his brother and dad, playing a game of tag. Stephen joined in (Who knew? He's great with kids!) and as "the boys" entertained one another, Sarita and I put out the food. Soon we were pumping water for washing up.

Over our meal, Stephen and Sarita broke the news Stephen had been waiting to share -- they'd decided to get married! I was so surprised, but really tickled for them, too. I never imagined Stephen married, because he was so against both religion and politics (he always said it gets really clear when your work is to mend people being blown up by those things), but Sarita was beaming. Stephen wanted me there and so was giving me two weeks' notice – City Hall, be there or be square! How exciting! He even asked if I'd be his "witness," as close to a bridal party as they were getting. They needed two, and he was trying to scrounge for a second. It really HAD been a long time since he'd lived in Vancouver. I got caught up in the organizing, promising to do some baking for them.

After lunch, Sarita told the rest of us to hike to the falls while she cleaned up, but we talked her into coming, as part of her "welcome to Canada." We quickly locked the food in the truck (bears!), then headed off down the hill. From behind, I was struck by how Sarita's body moved, compensating for the babe within, and felt jealous again, wondering if I would ever feel that fullness of creation. Being with youngsters and Sarita made my hormonal clock tick like a big brass drum. So much for a jolly holiday. And of course, Chaos had been peeking around the corner in my mind for some time, probably because of my angst over how to tell Ben.

We reached the bottom, and Glenn, Adam and Bruce kept going, walking Tiger along the creek closer to the falls. Sarita told Stephen she was heading up to nap on the chaise lounge, and because we could see almost the whole way up the trail, he watched and we chatted.

Soon it was just us, and we sat down beside the creek, and I took off my runners and socks and dangled my feet in the fast-flowing (yes, freezing) water. I was so grateful I could talk to him after all these years.

"So...getting married. I must admit, I'm a little surprised," I started.

"Yeah...me too. But Mom gave me a talk that included the argument, "If it's just a piece of paper, why would you let it get between your child's mother and her family?" and I couldn't think of a good reason. Sarita's been so relieved. It's really about her dad; he's not okay with us and he's REALLY not okay with a grandchild and no piece of paper. I guess I just didn't think it was that important." He shrugged, and I understood.

We sat in silence for a bit, listening to the crashing water, punctuated by the boys upstream, throwing sticks for Tiger, and watching the pup crash through the underbrush. There was a lot of laughter going on, and I remembered again what I'd given up with that damned abortion.

A couple of minutes later, Stephen poked me a little more.

"I saw how surprised you were when I drove up in your car. Are you sure you're okay with me driving it?" and I burst into tears.

It was, for some strange reason, all too much to admit to my big brother that I felt possessive of a car because of a baby that hadn't been born...but there it was. I could hear the boys upstream still laughing, unaware of our tension. And so I decided to really 'fess up.

"I guess with Bruce and Adam, and your upcoming excitement, it's all come back to me. And I'm trying not to stay mad with Dad because, well, ten years, right? And Mom. You know." My voice trailed off.

"I don't even know what to say, Mugwump. You're so brave." So I told him about staying at Veronica's...not feeling successful at *Just Living*. Swearing him to secrecy with Glenn -- I didn't want him feeling responsible. Wondering if I'd ever feel competent at anything again. And then I decided there was one thing I could do to feel better about myself.

"You know, Stephen, I've thought a lot about what you said when I told you about Chaos, and I think I need to come clean." He raised his eyebrows when he looked over at me. "I remembered that the nurses did get me alone and ask if I wanted the abortion, and I definitely consented." We sat for a few more minutes, and my mind was swirling.

"It was still a shitty choice for me, but I'm gonna have to remind myself I made that decision, even if Dad led me there," I finished. He hugged me, arms around my shoulders, as we sat on the side of the creek.

"I get it, Mugwump, but I'm still pissed at him. He never should have suggested it to you as a choice. I mean it."

"Hey! I'm trying to take responsibility here!" I laughed.

And then Glenn was shouting at us, and the boys were screaming. I looked up, and Tiger was being tossed towards us in the water, trying to keep his head up in the fast current. There was panic in Glenn's voice.

Without a thought, Steve jumped in, and I leaped behind him, staying on shore. Tiger was being driven right into Steve's arms, but I was worried that the impact of the big pup might bowl Stephen over, make things worse.

"Let me hold onto you!" I called out, and Stephen nodded. I grabbed his belt, my shoes rolling down the stones into the creek. River, maybe. It seemed much bigger than it had a few minutes ago.

Tiger hurled into Stephen's arms, and I held on as tight as I could – for a minute – long enough to give Steve the chance to toss the puppy onto the bank. Steve clamoured back up the rocky bank as Bruce, Adam and Glenn arrived. I was clinging to Tiger's collar, determined not to let him go, and he was shaking furiously, trying to get dry. Maybe get warm. Whatever he was doing, I was getting very cold and very wet, very quickly.

Glenn grabbed him and looped his leash around his collar, apologizing the whole time, thanking Stephen over and over for "saving his puppy." The boys were both crying and hugging Tiger, and there was general pandemonium and happiness. Stephen was drenched, even wetter than me, and I started to laugh out loud, a laughter one degree away from bursting into hysteria. Then we were all laughing and hugging, trying to dry off, and having no success. And that's how our picnic came to an abrupt end. A good news story, mostly.

Up in the parking lot I was shivering, Sarita and Glenn were packing the car and truck, and Stephen was using a blanket to dry me and Tiger. In no time Glenn and the boys were changing clothes and loading up the truck, and I was saying goodbye again. Both cars were hoping to make it home by dinnertime, so blessedly I had no time to weep, and we promised to connect in a week when he brought the boys home.

Then Stephen and Sarita were getting into my car, and I joined them, still shivering with a blanket around my shoulders. I was trying not to cry, but Steve asked if he could tell Sarita why I was upset. A few minutes later, they dropped me off at Veronica's. We promised to talk before his wedding, and I tried to reassure him that I was so happy for them, in spite of my tears.

As I headed inside, I wondered what my brother thought about me, and I knew I had further to go. Maybe I could ask Frank or Hugh about it. And, of course, I still had to talk to Ben. I really had to figure this out, come to peace with what I'd done, and maybe even forgive myself. I was supposed to be the one helping out on this practicum, but here I was trying to figure out how I could use the folks at *Just Living* to help me. So much for contributing.

And I tried not to be just a little resentful that my superhero brother was the one bringing all the life into the world, saving all the people, and now rescuing all the drowning puppies.

And then there was me, baby killer who was no closer to figuring out how in the hell I was going to make a difference in the world. Another prayer. Honest.

Tears streaming down my face, I snuck up to the bathroom for a hot shower, looking forward to dry clothes, and a warm bed.

Weeping, with wet hair on my pillow, I plugged in my headphones and let the soothing sounds of Gregorian chant fill my head. My heart.

I'll figure this out, God. I promise.

You could help me any time. Truly. I'm listening....

CHAPTER 31
A FAILED REPRISE

Glenn rolled over in bed, and couldn't believe where he was. Or rather, who was beside him. He rubbed his face, scrubbing the image from his eyes, and looked again. Yup. He wasn't alone.

What the hell was he doing?

Yes, he'd bought a double bed, but he *really* hadn't envisioned this when he'd bought it.

It had all started around dinner time. He'd run down into Vancouver on Friday and picked up the boys; they were SO excited! They were coming to spend six days with Dad at the new house, and Glenn had big plans! Spring Break! The picnic with Beth and her brother had begun the holiday.

The boys' room was set up, and the house was well furnished. Okay, well, furnished for three bachelors. Yes, they still ate off of a card table in the dining room, and the TV hadn't been hooked up yet, but really, had they needed it? They were happy to pile into his bed in the evening to watch a movie together on his laptop. Last night it had been *Train your Dragon*. Again and again. Glenn didn't mind; he loved hanging out with his boys.

Every time he was surprised at how they changed, even with just two weeks between visits. And it mostly had been just two weeks. A couple of times Glenn had driven into town and taken the boys to a motel. Once they'd crashed at a friend's apartment, but Adam and Bruce had been uncomfortable, so they hadn't tried that again.

Now, Glenn brought them to his little space in Mount Currie. They were creating "home," and Glenn loved it when they were with him. Even his congregation loved having them; on the weeks when they weren't with Glenn, the congregants always asked about the boys. These visits, with phone calls between them, well, this was okay, Glenn thought.

Mrs. Moore, a parishioner, took SUCH good care of them when he had to work. She was like a grandmother, in the ways their grandmas weren't. She baked with them, and let them run free – within reason. To the park and back, to the corner store for a treat. Bruce took such good care of his little brother, who was also growing up. Next year they'd be in Grade 1 and Grade 4; so hard to imagine.

Glenn missed being married, but only a little. Truth be told, not having to deal with Donna's drinking had been a relief. He'd had a lot more energy to do some great things at work, to build some friendships with a couple of guys in the community (yes, he WOULD be fishing this year!) and even to reach out to the Aboriginal neighbours and build bridges with the church. It was fun meeting the Chiefs and Elders, remembering how to respect their wisdom. Every band was just a little different, he was learning. He loved his life.

He was looking forward to having the boys for Spring Break; he intended to buy them bikes to ride on the mountain. There was a series of trails, and they were going to shred them. He didn't know what kind of bikes to buy, but he had an appointment this morning at the bike shop.

So how the heck would he get from here, in bed with her, to the bike shop?

Sunday evening, he'd tucked the boys into bed when there'd been a knock at his door. Unusual, but not freaky or anything. He'd tiptoed out of the boys' room and headed to the living room to look out the window;

he was shocked when he saw Donna on the stoop, looking terrific. Like she'd really worked at it.

He opened the door with his finger on his lips, willing her to be sober *and* quiet. He didn't want to have to do bedtime all over again. She giggled, and stepped quietly over the threshold. So much for sober. They headed to the kitchen at the back of the house, and he put on the kettle.

"What brings you North?" he asked, and folded his arms over his chest. He wouldn't easily forget how much she'd hurt him.

"I just wanted to see how you boys were doing. And there isn't much to do at Mom's house," she said.

"We're fine, really. Watched *Train your Dragon* three times tonight. Ate beans. Hung out with Tiger, our puppy. All good guy-bonding stuff," he answered, still confused. WTF? Why was she here? Once the tea was ready they headed to the living room to talk. He put the tray with the cups and teapot on the camping trunk that was serving as a table, and saw that Donna had curled her little feet up under herself in the corner of the couch. She was wearing that purple top that somehow both fit her like a glove, and conveyed modesty, which was such a turn-on.

"Whoa, boy," thought Glenn as he poured her tea, adding just a spot of milk to her cup.

"I presume you still take it this way?" he asked, and her laughter was light, like a crystal bell.

"Yes, Glenn, you do still know me," she added. And over the next few minutes, he told her all about his plans for his week with their sons. And she really looked like she cared. A few minutes later, Glenn remembered she'd have to use the bathroom, and he ducked in and wiped all the surfaces – not that they looked that bad. But really, he knew those things were important to her, and he didn't want to give her any reasons to try to take the boys back. He still couldn't figure out why she was here, so he decided to ask, pointblank. He steeled himself and headed back into the living room.

"So, really, Donna, why did you come? If it was just to see how the boys were doing, you would have asked ahead of time," Glenn surmised, and noticed she at least looked sheepish when he said it.

"I don't know, Glenn. I miss you. It's hard looking after the boys alone, and Mom and Dad don't really help out as much as I thought they would." Glenn grinned. He knew his mother-in-law wouldn't enable a divorce – she'd told him she thought her daughter was making a "bad decision."

"Anyways, I was supposed to go out tonight to a show with a girlfriend, and she cancelled on me. I couldn't bear to spend one more night alone in that dank basement. On a whim, I decided to drive up here. I didn't even pack a bag." She sounded a little pathetic, and Glenn almost pulled her under his arm. Almost.

"I decided to head up here to see my two favourite boys, and my favourite ex," she said.

And Glenn thought for just a moment, "Hey – we're still married." Followed by, "Wait, I think she wanted me to think about that." He knew Donna was really clever, some of his buddies said manipulative. At least she didn't seem too drunk.

They talked for a while, although the next morning, Glenn couldn't really remember about what. Nothing important, he knew. He'd told her about meeting with the Band Elders, and working with them and the students from UBC to try to stop a pipeline that was supposed to go through the area. He was passionate about this work, but saw her eyes glaze over.

And then she started touching him, and he was lost. At least he had gotten them into the bedroom before he started taking his wife's clothes off. It was the best loving they'd had in years, but somehow it felt to Glenn like a smile that didn't quite make it to his eyes. And now, he had no idea what to do; the boys would be awake in a few minutes, and he didn't want to mess them up even more than the separation had.

In a flash of insight, he grabbed his sleeping bag from his closet and his pillow from the bed, and went back into the living room, unrolling the bag and unzipping it a bit, punching the pillow so it looked like his head had been there a few minutes ago. Then he headed for the shower.

When he got out, there was Donna in the kitchen, wearing his shirt and nothing else, making coffee and pancakes and talking to the boys.

"Well, I missed you guys so much, I decided to come up here and help you go shopping for those bikes!" she said. Darn. That was supposed to be a surprise, Glenn thought. Soon they were jumping up and down, and he was trying to get them to focus on getting dressed and brushing their hair. Before long, the pancakes were cooked, and they were sitting down together, eating like any other happy family. Donna poured herself a coffee, and leaned over Glenn from behind, whispering in his ear. "I'm going to go get dressed. Just know that I can't bear the thought of dirty underwear, so I won't be wearing any today." He sighed, presuming that she wanted to tie him in knots. He was darned if he would be manipulated again.

"Great! You go get dressed, and we'll head to the bike shop. I'll pack some sandwiches because we're heading right for the trails," he said, making it clear that his time with his boys was THE top priority. She pouted as she headed for the bedroom.

"Mom doesn't like the woods, not like Beth." Bruce said, matter-of-factly.

"I know, it was good to see Beth, and I want to do the woods with my boys again today!" He realized his cheerfulness sounded forced. "Mom can stay here if she wants, or head back to the city," Glenn said. He wanted to be clear that Mom didn't live here. "We're gonna leave Tiger at home until we know the trails, 'kay? Mrs. Moore said she'd drop in and check on him." Hopefully he'd sleep outside all day.

"Mom's pancakes are good," Adam said. "And she knows how to make happy faces on them," he added, and Glenn felt just a little deficient in the Daddy department. And here he thought he was doing so well.

"I like yours better," Bruce declared, deciding male solidarity was more important than tasty pancakes. Anyhow, a few minutes later, it was decided that while Donna would come to the bike shop with them, she would stay home during their inaugural adventure back-country biking. Glenn felt relief as he made peanut butter and jam sandwiches, and packed some cans of fruit juice for their ride.

They arrived home four hours later, and the kitchen smelled wonderful again. Donna had baked macaroni and cheese with bacon, just what "her men" needed after a hard day's work, she said. She brought the boys inside while Glenn parked the bikes, visited Tiger in the back yard, and took their helmets and stored them all in the garage. By the time he returned to the kitchen, Adam was in tears, explaining his grazed knee (and torn jeans) and the bruise on his elbow.

"Don't worry, little brother," Bruce kept saying. "The jeans are okay. They were old ones of mine. I think that hole might have already been there." He kept looking over his shoulder at his mother, anticipating an outburst, inserting himself between mother and brother. Glenn was trying to talk himself out of what he saw, but decided to intervene anyways.

"Come on, partner, you're my responsibility right now," he said, taking Adam by the hand into the washroom. He carefully undressed Adam's leg, making sure the jeans didn't hit his knee again on the way down. Soon, Adam was sitting with his foot in the sink, gulping air, and trying to be brave while Glenn washed his knee and elbow with warm water. Soon he had cream and a couple of BIG Band-Aids on the knee, and had put Adam's soft pyjama bottoms on him. He carried his little boy into the kitchen, and found Bruce washing the dishes from Donna's cooking.

"Where's mom?" Glenn asked, not wanting to sound too worried.

"She's in your room," Bruce answered, his voice tight. "I just thought I'd clean up in here while you were looking after Adam." Glenn wondered at what age he started to notice chores that needed doing in his house, and he knew it was a lot older than eight or nine.

"That was fun this morning, eh?" Glenn asked, wanting to refocus. "Why don't I set you guys up in the living room with a game, and I'll go see how Mom is," he said, and both boys were jumping. They didn't get to play videogames in the afternoon very often, but Glenn figured after the morning of hard work and many tumbles off the bike, Adam was ready for a little *Mario Kart*. As he set them up, he reminded Bruce how proud he was of how much he thought about his brother in these games, hoping he'd let Adam win at least one round. He headed for the bedroom, knocking on his own door, and realizing how ridiculous this situation was.

When he heard Donna scrambling behind the door, calling out "Just a minute," he knew what she was doing in there. She had clearly travelled with a micky in her purse. He decided not to wait, and opened the door catching her taking one last slug.

"So, they're busy with *Mario Kart*. What's up that you need to wash this morning down with booze?" he asked, hearing the judgment in his voice and not really liking it. After all, he had not only married Donna, but had made love to her last night.

"I don't know, Glenn. I just thought you'd need me, you'd miss me as much as I missed you. And when Adam went with you and you looked after him...I just expected him to want me, that's all."

"Do you know Bruce was out there doing the dishes?" He was grilling her now. "Dishes. He's eight. What the hell, Donna?"

"He helps out now. He's growing up, and he's a big boy! It's okay that he helps his mother," she said. She was looking way more pathetic this morning than she had last night. He wondered how much courage she'd had before she'd driven the deadly Sea to Sky highway last night, and was grateful the boys still *had* a mother.

A little while later, they emerged from the bedroom, and Donna started gathering her things, preparing to leave. Glenn had been clear: until the drinking stopped he wasn't interested in being with her again, but he wouldn't proceed with the divorce either, unless he felt he needed to have the boys full-time and he needed custody. He thought at that point, he'd at least need a separation agreement. Or something.

The boys barely looked up as she headed out the door, his "child support" cheque in her fist. He walked her to her car, and as he shut her door, he begged her not to drink again before she got home to Vancouver. She promised, and they both thought of all the promises she'd broken over the years. It was the last promise she ever made to him.

CHAPTER 32
GETTING TO EASTER

"True self is non-self, the awareness that the self is made only of non-self elements. There's no separation between self and other, and everything is interconnected. Once you are aware of that you are no longer caught in the idea that you are a separate entity."

– *Thich Nhat Nanh*

Dear God,

Interconnectedness. Relatedness. Togetherness. One-ness. I'm falling in love with these ideas. Or maybe I'm falling in love with Ben. And I bet that's inter-related too.

Thank you for giving me this chance to explore prayer, and consciousness, and practice. I read somewhere this week that when my consciousness changes, so does the collective consciousness that may be related to you, or more specifically what Anglicans call The Holy Spirit.

I bet there's lots of change in heaven because of this practicum, 'cause there sure is here in me. I'll figure it out....

And I'm excited, but I admit more than a little uncomfortable, too. It'd be okay to keep the squishy bits that are hard down to a bare minimum, 'kay?

Thanks.

Amen.

Life continued at *Just Living*, and at Veronica's. She's amazingly chill. I was carried along on little sleep and much distraction like everyone in the first throws of…whatever? Now that I'd spent some time with Ben, a little didn't seem like enough. At all. We started checking in with each other by phone every day, and I was a bit obsessed by those calls. Luckily, Cook and I had started hanging out together again on the back porch after lunch, which was good for me.

"How's it goin', Mugwump?" he asked one rainy afternoon.

"Really good. Finding my stride here. Getting over living at Veronica's. Having fun on weekends," I answered. "How're you feeling?"

"Fine. Real fine. Back in the saddle, so's to speak. And likin' how things are goin' round here." I laughed. Sally had been hanging out more and more in the kitchen, calling Cook "Chef." It made him blush.

"She's a fine woman, Cook. And I think she likes you," was all I had to say.

"How 'bout your man?" he asked.

"He's a source of fun." I smiled with my hand over my face, hoping I hid my crazy grin.

"That's good. Good man, that one," he added, and then we sat, both of us, just being happy. We seemed to have the same conversation every day, and after the third one I thought "so this is happiness," and I realized how different it is from what I imagined. It's really not about everlasting fireworks and excitement, but for me it seems to be a good friend touching base, sitting outside in the fresh air, protected from rain by the cover of the overhang.

Then, lo and behold, I went to a wedding! Wednesday, a week before "Holy Week," Dad came out to fetch me, and we drove into town for

Steve and Sarita's "nuptials." They had decided to get married before Easter and the craziness that is Holy Week for Dad. It was a simple, beautiful ceremony, "performed" on the seawall in Stanley Park, heartfelt because they shared vows they'd written, and glorious because it was surprisingly sunny. Steve seems to pull that kind of good luck out of nowhere. Every time.

Steve said the best part was that it was cheap (Dad knew a JP who did it for almost nothing) and over in 20 minutes. Of course, Mom and Dad and I were there, and Steve had even scared up a couple of friends from medical school who somehow got some time off mid-day to witness with me. Everyone, especially a VERY pregnant Sarita, looked happy. Afterwards we all went out for an expensive, and early, dinner (okay, only the family – doctors gotta save lives, after all), and then Steve and I tucked Sarita into bed in the apartment, and he drove me back out to the Valley in my car.

Ben and I had talked about taking The Beast back from Steve, but really...what if they needed it to get to the hospital quickly? I had gotten over him driving it, but was amazed at how much I missed having access to transit. Ah, Valley life. Anyway, as soon as I got into The Beast, I knew something was up. It was clean. Like REALLY clean. And it was purring. Steve fessed up on the drive home.

"So, guess what, Mugwump." Um...yes?

"Last week I was so bored, I searched out Jesse for you." Wait. WTF? Did I ask for this?

"For *me*? Really?" I squeaked. Oh, such wisdom.

"Okay, busted. I felt bad about not being here for you when you needed me, so somehow I thought it would help if I found him." Again, really? Did I ask for this?

"And?"

"Well, he's doing great. He has a garage in East Van, and tuned up The Beast. Was surprised to see it. He said to say 'Hi.'"

"You guys talked about me?" Maybe a little strident, so Steve got all defensive.

"Well, not really. He recognized the car. I wasn't trying to meddle! I just remembered what you'd said about him maybe being in jail, so I thought I'd check out the garage and see if it was your Jesse. It was." His voice trailed off, and then I barely heard "I'm sorry. For not being here, and for doing this." I laughed. It was SO different hearing him apologize. My "always doing the right thing" brother! Of course, I let him off the hook, which, it occurred to me, could be exactly what he planned.

"So he's doing okay?" The relief in my gut was palpable. I think I had been a little worried I'd run into him inside – good to know I didn't have to worry. "Did he say anything else?"

"No, I kinda pretended to be amazed he knew you, so…well, there wasn't anything to talk about. I actually cleaned up his office while he was working on it and he's doing good." I swatted his arm while we cruised down the highway.

"Detective Doctor now? I can't believe you did that!" I do not know how he gets away with this shit.

"Well, it started with just sorting, then I decided to clean up and did some filing. He was actually happy I did it. I even separated out the accounts he still has to collect on," he said, again, just a little defensive.

"Creepy. And I'm glad he's doing okay."

"Oh! And he's married, with children." I looked out the window -- the forests had started to show up between the malls. "Kinda like I will be next month! I mean, with a baby! I am married." Steve blurted. He sounded surprised, like "How did this happen?" and I laughed again.

Soon we were driving into *Just Living*, and I was giving him big hugs and kisses at the door. Some of the guys came out to meet him, and share congrats. Kenny and Cook even gave him big hugs, and teased him about driving his sister around on his wedding night. Which led to more laughs when he tried to explain Sarita's need for rest…I do love being a part of this motley crew, and that my peeps are their peeps. Cook had baked some pastries for Steve, to take home, to make the "honeymoon" special, he said. I suspected they would be frozen for post-babe. Grin. A few minutes later, Kenny drove me back to Veronica's, and the three of us planned the upcoming days' work on the labyrinth, and the spring garden.

The rest of the week was spent helping Kenny prepare the space. We were looking for some funding for stones and plants, and he was very keen to get the path staked out and the grunt work of creation started. Al agreed, because it was almost spring, and the time for planting and creating new projects. The talk around the table was turning from "What do you hope to do this year?" to "How do you plan to do it?" I needed to start thinking about that myself – a new form of the familiar question *"What the hell am I going to do with my life?"* Prayer. A plan wasn't hatching, but maybe a next step. At least, I thought, I can help build the labyrinth. And wait for the babe…and then it happened.

Oh My God. Oh My Grace. Oh My!

Before I know it, I'm waiting for Ben to come get me to drive me to the birthing centre because I'M GOING TO BE AN AUNTIE! I'm startled by how excited and nervous and happy I am.

Steve called about two hours ago to let me know that Sarita and he were heading into the hospital; Sarita wanted to give birth at home, but she was nervous about her progress. The good news…I trusted them. Doctors having babies.

Talking to him I was aware how discombobulated he and Sarita are; they have delivered hundreds, if not thousands of babies in difficult conditions, and yet…I smiled. AND I hope it all goes well. And gently. Is that a thing?

I spoke with Nora about going home to be with family, and she reminded me that I was going home in two days for Easter, so I might as well combine the trips. She let me go pretty easily, and I'm a bit rattled about that, considering I only have about a month more at *Just Living*. I'm still disposable.

So I called Ben to get me, and I ran around saying goodbye to everyone, including the horses and cats. The knowing looks I got from some of the guys reminded me that they were used to being left, had come to expect it. I wasn't entirely comfortable with being cast into that role. Even when it's the truth.

Now here I am, sitting in a deck chair on the front dock, hanging with Cook. He brought me some cookies to bring home to Sarita and Steve, and a casserole to add to their freezer. God, I love that man. We decided to enjoy the break in the rain to sit out front for a change, and drink tea and wait together. I am so comforted by both the easy quiet, and his big galumphing body on the next chair.

"I'm gonna miss this place, I think," I admit, maybe to both of us.

"It's gonna miss you, Mugwump. But don't worry. You ain't done here." He comforts me still.

"Only four more weeks, though," I answered, trying to make clear that this is the beginning of the end. And I knew it.

"Like I said before, you ain't done here. No worries, Angel." He seemed pretty clear about that. Maybe I need to start imagining my future with *Just Living* as a part of it. I was suddenly struck by what that would be like. Lots of possibilities, maybe.

"You mean it?" I asked. "You think I'm not done here for good next month?"

"You're done when it's time, and I don't think it's time yet," Cook continued. And knew in a whole new way that in a month or two, I was going to graduate, and I'll get to call the shots.

I think I've been pushing against something. Resisting becoming something. Denying what I will be. Declaring what I won't. And maybe not thinking about what I *can* become. It's time to start thinking about what I *will* do instead of what I won't.

And it's quite appealing to think that maybe, just maybe, I might do this kind of work full time. Wow. And then, of course, I am flattened because *I am not ready yet.* I have no confidence that I have skills or even basic proficiency in anything related to this work, but I did feel giddy when I thought about learning more so that I can be useful. Then I felt inadequate again. Beyond humble to totally gobsmackingly insecure.

Something to think about. But not right now, because right now I'm thinking about my brother, and his family-becoming and then this weekend. And Ben. Blessedly, before I knew it, he drove up. Phew. Saved me from myself.

Cook and I shared a never-ending hug and loaded the packages into Ben's car, and we were off. We stopped by Veronica's to pick up my pre-packed bag, and soon were retracing the drive we took weeks ago that first brought me to *Just Living.* It's amazing how much has changed for me since then – the people, my fuck-ups, and the many teachings. Mostly what I've learned is that I have a lot more to learn.

"Excited?" Ben asked, and I looked over at him and smiled.

"Um, yeah. Really excited. And a little nervous. You?"

"Me? It's great to see you. It'll be good to see you for the next few days. I'm not sure Steve means for me to be included in family time, though," he answered. And I laughed.

"I don't even think he wants *me* hanging around, honestly. I want to go and celebrate with them, but then I'm not sure what I'm going to do. I think they deserve to have a few days alone getting to know their baby with no one bugging them, right? Maybe I'll see if Mom and Dad want me home.

"I promised them I'd go to the Easter sunrise service on Sunday morning, and then to dinner at their place later. I might even go to the Good Friday service too," I admitted. Ben chuckled. "I also have a service to go to Saturday evening. Glenn is being ordained," I reminded myself. That's a lot of church, but then…PK, almost priest. It happens.

"Being displaced from your own home? By a baby that isn't even born yet? I admit, that's funny," Ben said, chuckling.

"What are you up to for the next few days?" I asked, trying to figure out how to steer the conversation.

"No plans, really. I have to go to the prison on Sunday afternoon for services, but I've left stuff for the men so they can lead their own Good Friday services, or do devotions in their cells. I feel like I'm playing hooky, I admit!"

"I know," I agreed, "I think that's a part of why I feel so giddy. Five days with no obligations except visiting my niece or nephew and a couple of church services. The rest of it I get to plan," I said. I couldn't really be any plainer, right?

"Wanna hang out?" he asked, and my heart actually did a double-beat.

"Um, yes?" I admit I sounded tentative. "Hang out like drink coffee together, hang out like go hiking together, or hang out like…I don't know…*hang out* together," I asked, looking at him out of the corner of my eye.

"Well, my week is quite free. Let's start with heading to see the family together, and then I'll cook dinner if your family doesn't have plans for you. If you're worried about where you should stay, I have a couch in my apartment you are welcome to crash on," Ben finished. He looked sideways at me and smiled.

"No pressure, though, okay? I mean from me to you, or you to me?" It hadn't occurred to me that he might be feeling awkward about this, too. When I thought about it, there wasn't really any part of our relationship that I thought Ben *didn't* feel awkward about.

"That feels delightful," I said. "And if it gets awkward or we change our minds, I have friends I can call and crash with." I was thinking of Trish and her husband, who I'd love to see again.

"That feels good," Ben said, and I giggled a bit.

A few minutes later Steve called, and I found out they'd been sent home from the hospital in "early labour" and now were well on their way to having this baby in my apartment! I suggested that Ben and I go and keep Mom and Dad company, and come by later once they were ready for guests. Steve sounded so relieved that I felt like I'd made my first good decision as an Aunt. He promised to keep in touch with texts, and I promised to pretend it was all a surprise when he phoned Mom and Dad. Grin. We're still colluding.

We dropped my luggage at Ben's place on the way to Vancouver, had a quick cup of tea, and I tried not to look like I was casing the joint. Then we headed for Mom and Dad's.

The four of us had fun eating lunch at a pub, and I even teased Mom about how often she checked her cell phone. Of course, I was surreptitiously watching mine under the table as Steve kept me up to date.

Dad wanted to learn more about circles. Seems he'd been following the Anglican response to the Truth and Reconciliation Commission and residential schools. Who'd a thunk? I was impressed, and said so. He was going to come out for one, to participate. Which wasn't as scary. Especially since I came clean about being kicked out of The Lodge. Although, maybe they're happy I'm not living with thugs....

Looking over at Dad, I wondered what it was like for him, becoming a grandpa. I'd never had a grandpa, so it was hard to imagine.

And then I thought about Dad, and the differences between us, theologically. And prayer, and Easter, and what it all means.

Dear Jesus,

I remember when I was a teenager, the stories of Good Friday, and you "hanging on the cross" were told to us again and again, and we were supposed to be grateful to you for suffering for us.

And I couldn't help but think about all the suffering over the centuries -- Africans stolen by slave-traders and carried like bricks in ships for weeks to the New World. Dying and being dumped overboard after weeks of suffering.

Families ripped apart by World War II, taken to concentration camps where they either endured suffering and experimentation with less care than we give rats now, or dying in the ovens, swiftly and with a crassness I can't even imagine.

Even the babies born today into places in the world where clean water and nutrition are a daily challenge that sometimes ends with suffering and death.

And now, I have to add the First Nations Peoples of Canada, who have suffered for generations **in your name.** *Why now? Because I've only learned about them now.*

And I admit I freakishly wonder, in a quiet place in my brain, why your suffering was more notable, more important, should make us feel more...well, guilty, I guess. Because none of them asked for the suffering. Hell, no one deserves that kind of suffering.

And around Easter, I always think of it again. How I'm supposed to be eternally grateful that you chose to die "for our sins," whatever that means.

And I'm afraid I'm more thankful (if there is a ranking for thankful) for how you lived your life, the gentleness and compassion and equality and simplicity you engendered.

We all die.

Lots of us suffer along the way, in unimaginable ways.

I just fail to see the miracle in that....

Sigh. How can I consider being a Priest if I don't even believe in the Story of Easter? Or maybe it's just that I don't see how it's an Important Story.

Can you tell me if I should be a priest, Jesus?

Would you want me to be your priest?

And I wondered, in that pub, what I'll be doing in a year. And if it'll matter.

CHAPTER 33
EASTER MIRACLES

And then it happened! Sitting in the pub, Mom's phone rang, and then we all knew -- Steve and Sarita and the baby – Daya, we learned -- were all healthy and happy and good! I had a brand new niece! I was overwhelmed with a "take my breath away" feeling of gratitude.

We paid our bill with a generous tip for the occasion, walked away from half-finished pints, and drove to the apartment. And there they were, Sarita wrapped in her pyjamas and a robe under a blanket on the couch with the most gorgeous and delightful baby in her arms. Steve and the midwife were cleaning up, putting things away, doing laundry, and doting on Sarita and Daya. And everyone was beaming, the four of us included.

Ben took a seat in a corner, not wanting to intrude. I made tea, and asked Steve and Sarita if they wanted to eat. Of course, they didn't, so I prepared a platter of fruit, nuts and cookies I'd brought, and they were devoured quickly with tea. We just kept the food and warm drink flowing while we heard their birth story again and again. It was a lovely story.

Soon, their energy was flagging, and Daya needed her Mom and Dad and some peace and quiet to get used to this new world. I started shuffling Mom and Dad out the door with Ben's help, and the family started to argue over where I should stay. Ben put his hand up in the universal sign for "Stop!"

"Beth has a couch to crash on. We've already dropped off her stuff, and I know she'll be in touch," he said gently but clearly. I backed him without inviting conversation, and we got everyone out of the house. Later that night I texted Steve to ask if there were any groceries, whims, heartfelt desires they had that I could provide them with in the morning, and he assured me their lives were perfect. I suspect their fruit juice won't last forever, watching Sarita drink it in volumes, so I will at least drop by with some of that tomorrow. And then we were back at Ben's, alone with no obligations to anyone but ourselves. *And Truth.*

I felt at home in his space, and I felt at home with him, too, which was lovely. He made tea and a simple stir-fry, and we settled in for a few hours together, curling up on the couch with books and computers. The conversation between us was sparse and easy, and then I knew that what I really wanted was to put down my book and computer and really be with Ben. A few minutes later he put his stuff on the coffee table, got up to pour more tea and bring baking "for sustenance," and when he came back he sat right beside me, put his arm around me, and soon we weren't struggling to keep to ourselves.

It was a glorious night, getting to know one another, exploring the newness of adoring each other's bodies and souls, and the adventure that was between us. It was like we were living in our own creation: clean linens, fresh fruit and croissants, candlelight and the musky aroma of each other. And even the next morning was untainted with regret or awkwardness; we stayed with each other easily enjoying our time separate from the world.

And what a lover! I thought, because of his experiences, he might be clumsy, even "adolescent." Ben was careful and tentative, enthusiastic and patient. Every time we made love it was as if our souls were relearning a familiar dance, and we didn't hide from one another or show shame in our sharing. It was a glorious coming together, and the memories made my breathing shallow and my breasts heavy.

We did leave to visit and love Daya (and her parents), and we attended services together at Dad's church over the weekend. I went to Glenn's ordination, and it was beautiful. Even his boys were there, all gussied up in their best clothes. They looked so cute, and we played peek-a-boo. We agreed it was a good thing Tiger didn't come.

Going back to church felt like coming home after a long trip, and I wondered how I had changed when the church hadn't. It was spooky, maybe what Thomas Wolfe meant when he wrote "You can't go home again." I sort of got it.

Being in the pews was comforting, and miraculously, I enjoyed listening to Dad preach; he spoke about the idea of serving one another and even put it into the context of a recent visit to prison…how he thought he was going to help others, and ended up helping himself.

He preached about betrayal, and I knew he was speaking with an authenticity that comes from experience. And he talked about the dark night of the soul we sometimes experience, and how we can be drawn back into the Light of the Resurrection. It was powerful and felt relevant to my (our?) situation, and my recent time at *Just Living*. I wasn't sure if I had changed, or his preaching had…but I knew I would have a chance to talk about it with him, as a colleague and a student. That felt new.

And the space! The dark stained glass, the incense, the sombre music of Good Friday spoke to me, and the light and joy of Easter morning, the lilies, the bright white vestments and gold glimmer of the embroidery all felt sparkly and new. And I thought about how much I appreciate how we Anglicans express the inexpressible. The outward signs of the inward transformations. Or potential transformations. Or something. And Ben came along, and he sang beautifully, and prayed fervently, and sat attentively. Holding my hand. Trish and I shared a smile across the aisle, and a coffee in the hall afterward.

I tried to explain my time at *Just Living*.

"I think I may have found it, Trish. The thing I'm supposed to be doing. But I really fucked up by inviting Glenn to stay." I still wasn't owning the Remand Centre debacle. It was just too complicated.

"I really have a ton to learn about security, and stuff. But sometimes I think I'm making a difference. There's a guy there who has started asking for time with me; he's…" and I couldn't talk with her about Bob. Still learning. Still incompetent. *Oh dear God, help me*, I thought as my voice petered off. "I can't really explain it, but I think I'm helping." Even to me, I sounded weak. Trish laughed.

"I really don't understand, but that's okay. I wouldn't be comfortable working there, and really, Glenn is like the least security risk of anybody I know. If they can't see that…." Trish's voice trailed off. I didn't try to explain the rules; I guess I was starting to understand them.

And after the service, I went over to Mom and Dad's for Easter lunch with Steve, Sarita and Daya while Ben worked at the prison, and over dinner we talked about the sermon, and he told me about how he prepares them. Mom fussed over us, bustling back and forth from the kitchen with platters tall, and then Steve and I dealt with the dirty dishes. Again. Together. It was fun.

We talked about "my future," and I told Dad I was feeling led to work in this field of justice, but I really didn't know what that meant. And we all adored the beloved babe in our midst, and tried to do as much as we could for Sarita while she recovered from the birth. I even managed to change a diaper!

Dad's parish wanted to help out at *Just Living*, but didn't know how, especially because of the distance. I planted a seed (get it?) about funding the plants and stepping stones for the labyrinth. We talked about connecting the Anglican Church in Mission with his parish, and it felt good to be tossing ideas around and just chatting, without spending energy judging everything he said, or wondering what he was thinking about me.

And I was daydreaming about getting to Ben's place, so shortly after lunch, when Steve suggested Sarita and Daya were tired, I jumped on that bandwagon and we all headed out. Another glorious evening with Ben…. *Thank you Goddess.*

Monday morning I had a chance to connect with Julie for an early coffee, and I heard she'd broken up with Chris. She got upset just telling me about it; somehow he was angry about how things turned out during the protest. Julie said she thinks he's really warped – pissed off we rescued him, wanting drama, not help. I wondered if he was a bit embarrassed about the whole thing.

She seemed pretty broken up about it, until she started to talk about Glenn, and going up to Mount Currie. Seems they've been talking, and they're planning a meeting between one of the First Nation bands up there and the UBC students, maybe even some law students, to figure out how to stop the pipeline.

Anyhow, it was great to see her, and hear about the plans, but it seemed so…insignificant? I hope Chris is doing okay, that he's getting his head together. I feel somehow connected to him because I helped him. Weirdly connected.

But also…it was hard to relate to Julie, and for the first time I kept thinking "Really? That's what's important to you?" I don't know who's changed, but somehow the things I think about seem more…real? Important? God, that sounds judgmental, and I don't mean to be. Maybe change isn't good or bad – it just is.

I wasn't upset that I had to make it a really quick coffee, so I could get back to Ben's (and no, I didn't tell her about Ben and me). It was good to say goodbye to Julie, and we didn't make any plans to see each other again.

As Ben and I packed to head back up the Valley, it was clear neither of us wanted this time together to end (Can time end? Begin?). Ben went to the deli and brought back mochas and bagels for lunch, and we shared them in bed, and made love one last time, realizing that in a few hours we would once again be "of the world," and that would change how we could be with one another. Slowly, as the realization became more fully formed, Ben became more awkward with "us," and maybe I did, too.

Our drive back to *Just Living* was awkward and weird. Ben was quiet, and I was trying to figure out how we would be with each other. Then, he startled me.

"Hey, Beth, I remembered the other day that when we were at the cabin, you started to tell me something, and stopped. Do you remember?" And in a blink of an eye, it all changed. I didn't even see it coming.

"Oh yeah! Thanks for reminding me. I did want to tell you something." And I headed straight off a precipice I didn't even see. "When I was just finishing high school, I started dating a guy who was older than me, and I really liked him," I began, and before I knew it, I was telling him all. Sort of.

"It started in high school. Dad and I didn't get along much. Stephen had moved away, and I made some really bad choices." Well, there goes nothing. I plowed on.

"I was so upset at my Dad about something that I ran headlong into a marriage afterwards. How young and stupid is that?" I knew I'd have to come completely clean about everything, but was trying to figure out how.

"What did he do? He seems like a good guy," Ben said, glancing at me.

"It's complicated. I told myself he did something, but really, I'm just now getting that he was supporting me. I was in love with Jesse, a guy Dad didn't approve of. He was a good guy," I started. Ben's brow was furrowed. I wasn't making sense even to me, but this was a new telling of the story. The miles were passing under our wheels, and we were getting closer to Veronica's where Ben would drop me off. Ben pulled off into the rest stop Aaron and I had talked in. I kept talking.

"See, I really liked this guy, Jesse, and we got pregnant. In high school. And Dad suggested an abortion, and I went along with it. I told myself for years that Dad had forced me into the abortion, but to be honest, I told the clinic I wanted it." I stopped and a tear trickled down my cheek, while I explained about Jesse and Chaos.

"It was a really bad choice for me," I lamented, "and I've felt awful about it ever since. With Daya, and everything, I'm trying to make sense of it all. I mean, I feel awful, but I can't imagine where I'd be if I had Chaos. I think it was the right choice. For me. At that time." It was the first time I told the story that way.

Ben put the car in gear, and headed up the road. He got really quiet, and he stiffened when I touched his arm.

"Ben? Are you okay?" I asked, but it was clear he wasn't.

"I don't really know what to say, Beth. I imagined you telling me lots of different things, but I didn't imagine this." We drove a few more minutes, "Is this why you were against the guys raising funds for pro-life?"

"No! I mean, I guess maybe a little." My voice drifted off, and before I knew it and I was home. At least as home as I would be for a while.

I'd naively presumed Ben would be as forgiving and tolerant as I'd been with his confessions, but in the end, my abortion was a deal-breaker for him.

"Beth, I don't know what to say. I think I need some time," he said, looking at the driveway in front of the car. He couldn't even turn to look at me.

"So what does this mean? How do you want me to act around you?" My heart was breaking all over again. I couldn't help but think of the sweet love we'd made only hours before, of our trepidation at re-entering "the world."

"I guess just as if I'm your mentor. It really isn't anyone's business, is it?" I gathered my bags, and stumbled from his car.

"Okay, then." I was starting to get angry. "I guess my legal act is too hard to get over." I let out an exasperated sigh. "Men," I let rip quietly as I slammed the door. I hoped he would get out and we could talk, but he slowly backed down the drive and left me. My tears returned, with a new intensity.

My life was a roller-coaster, unrecognizable. It had taken only nine weeks to fall in love, grow up, get rejected, be changed. And not just because I was Auntie Beth now.

Dear Jesus,

Transformation. Transmogrification. Transposition. All those other trans words.

And in a birth, I was changed.

And in a pregnancy, I was changed, too.

And no doubt, I was changed by Nana Beth's death.

Transformation. Becoming changed.

Maybe that's the Easter story.

I still don't get the emphasis on suffering, though.

Especially bits about comparing suffering.

Because, really. It's all suffering.

I've heard Jesus was a Buddhist.

Let's not get attached to it.

CHAPTER 34
PLAYGROUND MISCHIEF

Debbie sat on the bench and looked down at her phone again, occasionally glancing up to see her son Donovan and his cousin Blair play tag around the playground. She tugged her pumpkin-coloured sweater around her shoulders, and picked some cat fur off her trousers. She smiled, remembering how happy she was the day she'd found the sweater on sale at the thrift store; she felt elegant in it, even at the park. And who knew who was watching? She was only a block or six from the coffee shop where she'd run into that cute guy last week.

The clouds had stopped leaking this morning, and Debbie had jumped on the chance to get the boys out to run off their sillies, as she called it. She was smiling. They seemed to have endless energy on these rainy spring days, and she loved them to bits, but really, who could contain all this in the small apartment she and Donovan shared with her best friend?

Debbie was glad to look after Blair on the two days a week she wasn't at work. Of course, the money her sister paid her helped out, but really, having Blair helped keep Donovan busy. And she loved that the cousins were building memories; she hadn't known her cousins growing up and had missed that. At least, she thought she did. Hard to miss what you've never had.

The melancholy when Debbie remembered the big Sunday dinners with Scott's family returned. The four brothers, all young fathers, still roughhoused with each other, and played tag football before the big meals. Sometimes they sat around watching football or hockey. The adult girl-cousins (well, and wives) looked after the babies, and swapped stories about their week.

The cousins had grown up together, their parents were brothers and sisters who still lived in the neighbourhood they had grown up in, so that their children would be playmates, the grandparents gathering everyone home for Sunday dinners. Even though Scott's temper had gotten in the way of a marriage, she still missed those meals. She was glad Donovan got to go to those meals with Scott now, even if it was only a few times a year. Donovan would understand how important family is, Debbie thought. And she was glad he played with his only cousin from her family, Blair, at least a couple of times a week.

A bonus of her babysitting Blair, she had to admit, was that Jane would always look after Donovan at the drop of a hat. When Debbie had a date or got called into work on the weekends, she could count on her sister to help out. Debbie was struggling to make ends meet, but she was determined to spend as many days a week with her son as possible. Being a mother first had always been important, especially early on when Debbie had been a "teenaged-mother." She hated those hyphens. Teenaged-mother. Single-mother. Welfare-mother. She was determined to do right by her boy. Next year, maybe, she'd take on a couple of more days at the shop, once the boys headed to all-day kindergarten. Then, she thought, she might be able to go shopping for some more new clothes.

"Hey boys, look over here!" Debbie called out as she held up her phone to take a picture. She'd post this to Facebook, and tag her sister so Janey could see her happy son from the front desk at the physiotherapy office where she worked. The boys hammed it up on the slide, Blair pretending to photo-bomb Donovan. Debbie snapped a shot, and waved at the boys. Looking down at the photo on her phone, she realized there was a man in the background, leaning on a garbage can and watching them. He was smiling. Debbie looked up to see the man look over at her. He waved, and headed on down the path. That was one of the reasons Debbie liked living in this small town; people cared about the kids here.

Debbie posted the photo and spent a few minutes looking at her newsfeed. She sipped the coffee in her travel mug, and spent a few minutes texting with a girlfriend. The boys were happy to race each other up and down the slide, so Debbie let them have at it. A few minutes later, she looked up and the boys were gone.

"Donovan! Blair! Where are you?" she called, smiling. She knew hide-and-seek was a favourite of theirs, especially when it got closer to lunchtime. They'd be having to head home soon, and she'd make them their favourite -- Kraft Dinner with ketchup. And a hearty dose of mixed vegetables to appease her healthy sister. But they'd milk the park visit for every possible minute they could get her to agree to. Those boys!

Debbie stood up and started walking towards the trees just past the playground. The park was at least six full city blocks, and there were paths, and creeks, and a dog park at the far end. She knew where those boys would head. Either into the water, or by the tennis courts where the dogs played.

"Blair! Donovan! Time to go!" She kept calling, heading up the hill, phone in one hand while she kept up her text conversation about that guy she'd met at the coffee shop. An elderly woman with a small white dog stopped and pointed up the hill towards the dog park.

"I think I saw them head up there," she said, grinning. "Boys. They stopped and petted my Misty on their way by. I thought that guy following them was their Dad," she said. "He had a nice little terrier," she added. Hmmm. That fellow at the garbage can. Did he have a dog? Debbie didn't think so, but she really wasn't sure.

"No, they're just up to mischief. I'll find them. You are right. Boys!" Debbie put her phone into her purse, and jogged up the path towards the dog park, more for show than because she was worried. Once she was out of sight of the old lady, she slowed down again, calling their names once more for effect. Five minutes later, she had checked under the footbridge over the creek, and around the parking lot, and was getting angry. She had other things to do today, and those boys were being brats, running off without permission. Her calling became more strident.

"Donovan! Blair! Where are you?" Maybe it was time to get worried. Her heart started to pound, and she started scanning the park. How could there be no one around? Where were they? She noticed something white under some trees, and ran over to find Donovan's baseball cap. Things were getting freaky – he never took that hat off. She picked it up, banged the pine needles off of it, and tucked it under her arm. She kept calling.

And then, as she crested the hill near the dog park, she saw them. They were talking to the fellow with the Jack Russell terrier, completely oblivious to her calls. She smiled. They didn't mean to aggravate her, they were just little boys, interested in the world.

She saw the young guy and waved, pointing to the boys. He got their attention, and pointed to her. Before she knew it, they were running towards her, arms outstretched. She waved a thank you to the fellow in the off-leash area. Smiling, Debbie pulled out her phone and took another picture of the boys to send her sister. Their smiles and laughter were infectious; even the guy in the dog park was laughing and waving. She'd talk to the boys later about running off, but she was glad she lived here, where kids were safe, and you could trust people to look out for each other's children.

After their Kraft Dinner, she sent the boys to the bedroom for some quiet time and they decided to construct Lego vehicles. Debbie knew that would keep them engrossed for a while, but cringed when she thought of stepping on pieces tonight on her way to bed. She put the kettle on, thinking about how weird some people were about her sharing a room with her son, but it really wasn't so bad when she knew the savings meant she could take the boys for park adventures a couple of days a week. She sat down on the couch with her tea, and checked her email. She was so excited when she saw she had a note from Terry, that young guy she'd met at the coffee shop.

She smiled as she opened it. This was the best day ever.

CHAPTER 35
THE ACCIDENT

Dear God, Look over him. Keep him safe. Bring him back to us hale and hearty. I've just found him; I'm really not ready to lose him.

I will do anything. Honest.

Remember my promise about studying prayer? Here I am, using what I'm learning about Intercession.

But you know what God? I'm learning from Al, and Tom, too, all about the interconnectedness of life, and I'm realizing even when I'm "interceding" for someone else, it's also about me...it's always about me.

What's it like, God, to have Created beings who are SO self-absorbed, and at the same time so filled with love (and hate, and courage, and hurt...)?

That's what I'm thinking about tonight, God. But mostly keep him safe.

In Mary's name,

Amen

I spent the next two days learning about "boundaries." I cried myself to sleep at night, and then showered in the morning, put on a happy face, and went to work at *Just Living*. And worked really hard to not show that

I was crumbling inside. Only Cook figured it out, and he just gave me an extra hug and didn't pry.

Then it happened, the weekend after Ben and I broke up, and everyone at *Just Living* was prepping for a party. Tom's birthday was on the Thursday, and Paul's was Sunday, so we were going to celebrate them together Saturday night. Then Dan, a new guy, said he'd never had a party and didn't really know when his birthday was; none when he was really little, and then, well…Residential School. Nora looked in his old CSC file, and found out he was listed as a January 1 birthday, with a guess at the year, and we knew he needed a party. He was kinda down on the idea, so we geared up for a massive celebration to show him how great a party can be. Tom and Paul were grudgingly accepting, in their own way. The plans grew.

Saturday was Cook's day off – but that morning he was in the kitchen, and the birthday cakes were cooling on the table, waiting for icing. "They can't share a cake!" Cook declared. "They each need one!" The kitchen smelled like Nana Beth's house, and I had done some extra baking as gifts for the men. Everyone kept sticking their noses in, because, well, ginger and cinnamon.

When it happened, Kenny and I were outside dreaming up plans for the labyrinth while we planted spring veggie seeds with Veronica and Claire. Yes, Claire was hanging around. I didn't know if she knew Ben and I had split up. In fact, I didn't know if she knew we'd been together. Sigh.

In the kitchen, Cook was moving a huge pot of creamy fish chowder (Dan's favourite) from the stove-top to the grill to keep warm when a handle broke off one side of the pot, and the bubbling, thick chowder spilled everywhere. Well, actually, half the chowder, because Cook was able to save some, but he got horribly burned. Hot, creamy stuff sticks! His right arm was splashed, and quickly blistered. His right stomach, hip and thigh were also burned. Luckily, his apron saved parts of him. Dan ran in and doused him in cold water from a jug, which helped, but really added to the mess.

When we heard Dan's yelling, we came running. He was pouring more water on Cook, and Nora and Sally were woman-handling him into the wash-up area. Cook was protesting that he was fine, and to stop fussing, but even his protests were weak, and we could tell he was hurting. And he was getting grey again, which was scarier than the burn.

"Grab some rags," Kenny said, and we started cleaning up. Veronica got the first aid kit from the pantry. Nora was barking out orders from the washing up area.

"Dan, you mop. Get a truck, someone. We'll have to take him to town. Where's Kenny? He has advanced First Aid."

"Beth was a nurse," he reminded Nora, and we joined her in the washing up area. She was being efficient, but a little over the top. Dan grabbed a mop and called for Frank to get the truck. The next moment, Nora was hurrying us out of the washing up area with a grin on her face. She was trying not to laugh. Sally, who had spent years working up north with "the guys" was hollering.

"Well, darn it, if you'd wear underwear you wouldn't have to pretend to be so shy! Get over it!" We heard Cook's shoes and jeans hit the deep washbasin, one at a time. Sally stuck her head in the kitchen asking for wet, cool towels, which I grabbed and rejoined her. We gently wrapped him in the cloth, covering his burns and his modesty. Frank pulled up his truck, with its large bench seat, and Sally told Frank to "Get a blanket – we got to go!" They left in a hurry, Cook wrapped in a blanket over the cold, wet cloths. Al, Nora and I were left to clean up the mess in the kitchen...Kenny and Tom had disappeared. Nora made some excuse about phone calls. I was glad Al didn't bail, too. *God, I appreciate that man,* I prayed. Gratitude.

Before they returned, the kitchen was clean, the chowder moved to a smaller pot and Nora and Kate had arrived on the scene to finish decorating for the party. I made some extra fish and chips in the oven, determined that we would be well fed. I even coerced Kenny into blowing up and hanging some balloons with Kate; of course, it became a competition and I had to stop them before the whole ceiling was covered.

"Nothing will prevent this party from happening!" Nora had declared, and I saw that under Dan's bravado and Tom and Paul's feigned indifference were three little boys prepared to be disappointed. Again.

We had fun. The dinner was wonderful, and Cook even joined us for a short time, although he was obviously tired from the many tests at the hospital, and was still in pain. The doctors had decided to investigate the "greyness" as well as treat the burn; turns out maybe Cook's ticker is working overtime. No surprise, it's so big.

No one has ever heard more enthusiastic renditions of "Happy Birthday" sung three times with gusto, with 40 candles or so each to blow out. Once the dinner was cleared and cleaned, we started into board games and storytelling around the table.

Later some of us headed for a bonfire on the Sacred Grounds. I laughed until I cried; I heard stories of the men inside brewing homebrew under guards' noses, or having it explode all over them in the night from a warm air vent where it was stashed, unvented, in garbage bags…young inmates building a makeshift swimming pool from soccer nets and tarpaulins one summer on the sports field…guys pitching in to support The AIDS Walk or Special Olympics. I was reminded how much community exists inside the walls of the prisons, and thought about my AVP guys.

The men seemed tickled with the gifts people had made for them, which led to more stories, this time about Christmases inside, and the decorations and gifts the men had shared even when they'd had to make stuff for each other out of scraps and garbage. It was so amazing to hear about hardened prisoners making toys for each other.

Kenny gave them little bonsai trees he had cultivated; Frank gave them some leather-worked belts. And a few tools so they could do more leather craft. Nora had put together photo albums of their time at *Just Living*, and Sally had given colourful knitted scarves (she must have a stash.) "So I can keep track of you on the grounds," she said. Kate gave them secondhand coffee table books about the PacificNorthwest. The pictures were gorgeous.

Al added something to their medicine bundles. There was sweet grass, and seeds to grow more from Hugh, and I had hacky sacks from Guatemala that I was thrilled to pass on. I hoped it made up for what they wished they'd had as children. Someone shared a tape of a CD that was loved (yes, resistance to tech advances is strong with prisoners.) Ricky gave them each a chocolate bar from his "stash."

Then we gave them each a card with some cash; we had "passed the hat," and I think some made it in from Nora's "discretionary fund." Or maybe from "friends" -- volunteers. The instructions said that Tom's was to put towards a "a good saddle," and Dan's was for "starting out." Paul was to spend his on "school" -- he wanted to learn more about storytelling.

The money clearly touched Tom; he had been saving for his own saddle and tack for years, but it is hard to save much on a prisoner's "salary" of about $4.00 a day. Tears welled in his eyes as he opened it, and exclaimed, "Thanks, guys. I can order it next week, and I even have enough for stirrups!" It was the friendliest I ever saw him.

It was good to see so many people honouring him – his roots, and even where he is now. He dreamed out loud about helping Kate and the Therapeutic Riding School with fences and lessons, decked out with new gear. He talked about his trip last month, sleeping under the stars, and even though I'd heard it all before, I never tired of how animated he became, talking about the trust he had been offered.

I was asked by Nora to sleep over, so that I could get breakfast out the next morning. My face must have looked shocked, because Veronica offered to drive me back early.

"No, it's okay," Nora clarified. "I was going to talk to Beth this week about moving back in, if she wanted. Now we really need her," she said. I told Veronica I'd come by tomorrow and pick up some of my things, but would get by until then. And it was that easy; I was back in the Lodge just like Cook said.

I remembered what he said about me taking my lumps, and I guess I had. I went to bed that night thinking about how much I care about these people, even after such a short time. And how much they care for each other, funny folks that they are. And I realized how much I've changed since I got here. I even started to get over Ben. Not over over, but I started to think about how there was nothing I could do to change his mind. And I really didn't need to apologize. He'd get it. Or not.

And if he didn't, well, I didn't want to be in a relationship with him.

I worked really hard to be nonchalant about coming back, and I figured out that I'm more a part of this community than I imagined I'd be in just a couple of months. My circle of friends at *Just Living* is smaller than in Vancouver, which might explain why I get overwhelmed with people there.

Some folks here treat me with not very veiled skepticism (perhaps outright disdain). Cook is my refuge, my soft place to land, and Kenny my co-conspirator in Fun 101. I'm learning the most from Al, Nora and Frank (not to mention Aaron) although mostly from watching them, paying attention to how they "do" and "be" in this world, which leads me to wonder about "why." *Every one of them is a blessing.* How do they keep it up? And of course, I'm learning from Ben, too, both from what he does to my heart, and all the ways he mangles it.

During Morning Circle the day after Cook's accident, Nora welcomed me back, and said I'd take over the kitchen chores, with help from Sally. She's going to rally the rest of the troops to share the cleaning and other housekeeping that Sally usually does – I agreed to keep the laundry room clean, but I have to admit it's rarely dirty. Only Ricky is being loud with resentment; he seems to think the change has really affected who he gets to work with. I think maybe any change is hard for him.

That night, under the overhang, I was staring out at the Sacred Grounds, watching the shadows in the fields, and I recognized how familiar this view is, even in the dark. And I started to weep quietly, both from relief that I was being welcomed back, and because Ben hadn't reached out. It's weird how relief and sadness can feel like different shades of overwhelm, and I decided to let the tears come.

And a few minutes later, Cook was beside me in his chair, offering some Kleenex and a warm hand. Which made me cry harder.

"You okay, Mugwump? I missed you," he began. "Not enough to pour hot soup on me self, but I was thinkin' 'bout the silver lining." I grinned out loud.

"Oh Cook, you are so sweet. How're you feeling?" I asked. "Really."

"A bit sore, I won't lie. And kinda small, watchin' y'all take over so easy," he admitted. And I felt a little less smug, walking into his role.

"Well, I've survived most of a day," I said. "And I'm weeping," I added. "Just wait until I have to make an order, or actually cook something rather than just heating up what you've already got in the walk-in." We sat for a bit.

"It does feel good to be here, though. Good to be back."

"So good, y'all are weeping," he said, not asking the question. I chuckled.

"Yeah. Feelin' sad, Cook. Ben dumped me. I did something a long time ago and I guess he's not okay with it," I explained. "I was young, and in love, and got pregnant." I didn't feel like I had to explain any more.

"Oh Darlin', I'm sorry. For all of it," he said, and I knew he meant it. I sniffed.

"Yeah. It sucks." We sat a little while longer, and I felt him fidgeting in his chair.

"Cook, you need to go inside. It's cold out here. You need to rest," I said, and at that moment, Sally stuck her head out the door.

"You comin' in, Chef? You'll freeze to death," she said, fussing.

"In a minute," he called out. The door closed. "She's takin' care, but jeesh," he said.

"I know. It's nice until it's too much," I said. "But she's right. You need to get in."

"Not sure I can get up, Mugwump." And I chuckled again.

"Let me help," I said, rising and offering him my forearm. At least the lifts I'd learned in nursing school were still useful. I braced myself and helped him. I gave him a minute to catch his balance, watching him wince in pain. And then he grabbed me in a bear hug.

"Don't you worry, Darlin'. He'll either come to his senses, or he ain't worth it," Cook said. "An' at least he has the good sense to make hisself scarce around here," he added. "Kenny and I'll take care of him."

And in a heartbeat, I was reminded that I was loved. And valuable, and worthy. And that if I'd never been vulnerable with Ben, I would have had a whole relationship of being careful "not to talk about it," and that would have sucked. But damned, I miss him. And it's hard.

So, here we are, nearly two weeks later, and I've cooked and cleaned more than I could have imagined. I'm really helping! It was so delicious to move back into my room upstairs, visit Cook every afternoon, and appreciate every minute that I'd been welcomed back. It was so much more this time around. I kinda missed working on the labyrinth with Kenny, but at least Dad's parishioner Carol and her son Scotty come out each weekend. It's getting done.

I had no idea I could cook for many; it's so different from cooking for just myself. Simply quadrupling recipes doesn't seem to work, but I've called Mom and together we've figured out how to convert some of Nana Beth's recipes for a crowd. Cook has taught me a ton from nearby when he's propped up by the window. I don't think I'm doing too badly, and I'm spending less money too, which Nora likes. Some of Dad's parishioners even sent some food out, which was nice. Weird, but nice.

Sally is caring for Cook, and running interference, trying to keep him upstairs resting and healing at least some of the time. I have introduced a few more vegetables, and some of the men are pressuring Cook to come back to the kitchen sooner rather than later. Nora, Kate, and Kenny seem to like it though.

I'm spending more time with Bob, too. We have tea, share, and I'm trying to figure out how to help, but he says I am. Really, I'm just hanging out with him.

Presence, Frank reminds me. *It's important.* Who knew? I can have tea with the best of them.

And Topaz is glad I'm back. I get to duck out to the barn more, after work, between meals. She crawls into my jacket and snuggles in, and in deference to obedience I don't smuggle her into my room anymore. Sometimes I let her be my listening ear, and I cry on her shoulder. She just purrs. I love her. Tom steers clear when he hears me mumbling, which really is best for all of us. Even after almost three months, he still squirms when I'm around.

I've settled back into a gentle routine, and everything is running smoothly. I may be overachieving in the kitchen, but I'm just filling my time so I don't think too much about Ben, and what we had over Easter. At first I was hoping for redemption, but I've given up on that. And I'm tilting back to right, because, really, there's nothing I can do. I'll believe it if I keep reminding myself. Right?

Yes, I made a bad decision ten years ago. But a part of me is glad I did.

And I've done what I can to make things right. Sigh. I hope it's enough.

Dear God,

Thank you for looking after him, keeping him safe, and helping him heal.

That was scary. I'm a bit stunned by how much I care about him. I don't ever want to let him go.

I'm so glad for Sally, and this group of people who embody looking out for each other. Community. Caring.

We may come with quirks, and warts, and whining, but we're here, adding our piece to the puzzle of life here. I'm glad for your grace that's letting him get better.

I love him, and know that feels rich. I'm so glad.

Sigh.

CHAPTER 36
STEPPING UP AND OWNING IT

Roger turned his back on the other guys in the gym and pretended he didn't hear their comments about his "choices." Staff talked about "choices" all the time, but lately his troubles were with the other inmates, not the staff. So now he *was* choosing to walk away. He knew lots of them thought his nose was brown, but they hadn't lived what he had. Besides, now that he was in a minimum, he wasn't going to react all over them and get sent back up. They didn't get it, but that was fine. They didn't have to.

He went back to working out, because sweating was one of the few good ways he had to deal with the anxiety building up. Today he had to decide whether or not he was going to apply for a pass to do a "public speak" with Veronica, the wife of the guy he'd killed. And he was going crazy trying to figure out what to do, but time was ticking if he expected to get the pass from the Warden in time. He needed to figure this out.

It had been horrible, realizing he was capable…responsible…for killing someone. When he found out what a great guy he'd killed, it just got worse. After being found guilty of second-degree murder, he'd heard the Victim Impact Statements from Veronica and two of her children at his sentencing hearing. He'd had to stop thinking about them or he knew he'd self-destruct. He'd gotten life-7.

So he'd put his head down, so to speak, and done his time. The first three years or so were a bit of a shit show. He'd stayed cranked a lot of the time, and fed his need for adrenaline in every way possible, including mouthing off to staff, pissing off solid guys who were just doing time, and working out. A lot.

Then he started to realize that if he didn't shift something, he'd be doing life-means-life. A forever bit. And he wasn't too far into his sentence before he really started missing the simple stuff. Going to the beach. Watching cartoons with his niece. Eating dinner at his mom's place with his sisters and brothers. Real maple syrup. Dill pickles. Vegetables. Yes, vegetables. Good ones. Fresh. And yes, hanging out with women, enjoying their company. So, about four years in, he started to look a little more closely at what other guys did that worked, and asked a few questions.

This thinking back wasn't helping him decide whether to ask for the pass, so Roger racked the free-weights, and grabbed his gloves to take on the heavy bag. He'd be lucky to find someone to hold it for him. And then he was back to thinking -- about the guys who had shown him not only how to do time, but how to get out. He thought about what they'd do in his situation. He'd learned a lot from watching them; some did school, others – often the ones who did have brown noses – hung around staff, liked programs a little too much. Some guys hung out in the chapel, and they weren't all Christians.

The chapel had different services each week, for Buddhists, Muslims. Sikhs. Even witches. And some men hung out with the Elders at the Sacred Grounds and followed the "Red Road" and got involved in Aboriginal programs. Even white guys like him.

Roger had decided to do school, and attend chapel occasionally. And lo, and behold, there were some amazing volunteers he connected with, a couple who "took him on" and visited him every couple of weeks.

He had to admit, he hadn't met people who "gave" just for the sake of giving before he went to prison, but there really were people like that. Who knew? He thought about whether or not he'd ever be one of them. Doing something because it was right, even if there wasn't anything in it for him.

Then he'd found spirituality. Of many kinds, and they all kinda worked for him. Buddhism first, then he started going to sweats, and they started to change him. At school, he finished his GED, then got his full diploma. He kept going and did two college courses before he ran out of money for the correspondence work.

Then, about year five, he met a guy from outside who came to chapel every Sunday, who played guitar and his music was amazing. He sang of drippy love, but of struggles, too. And he brought other volunteers sometimes, and Roger started going because, well, for just a little while on Sunday afternoons he could feel like he wasn't in prison. That was worth the price of admission – the other inmates thought he was crazy, but he got a little sanity for a few hours once a week.

At that point, no one from the street talked to him. He couldn't remember the last time he'd contacted a family member, and his friends were long gone. It was pretty lonely, but the volunteers helped, and he was making new friends inside, guys he thought he might actually like to hang out with when he got out. If he was allowed. Parole conditions, and all of that.

He couldn't remember when he started doing hobbies, carving and painting. Maybe four or five years in. He learned from some Aboriginal guys, then he took it back to his "ancestors" and started drawing and carving wizards and dwarves and wolves and occasionally medieval knights and horses and Celtic knots and stuff. It was popular stuff because almost everything else was First Nations, and the work was amazingly good, but it was only one theme – First Nations. He developed his craft and soon was being asked to teach other guys how to do what he was doing. Sometimes he showed a few young guys, but mostly he kept to himself, and steadily did clean time. He carved, and sometimes donated his work to charities.

About six years in, a guest came to the prison and talked about forgiveness and how his daughter had been murdered, and this guy'd decided to get to know the murderer. Work with him. They'd met, and he'd decided to pray for the guy who'd killed his daughter. Really. No shit. Roger and the other guys couldn't believe it, but anyhow, Roger kept on thinking about something the guy said.

He'd said most victims want answers, information about the crime they can't get from anyone except someone who'd been there. And Roger thought about the people who'd written those Victim Impact Statements. Around that time, he'd started his heavy "programs" – after the one on substance abuse had actually helped him get clean.

So when his Violent Offender Program started a couple of years ago, he was ready to learn some things, even if it was just for parole. By then he'd been in more than eight years on his life-seven bit, and he was starting to figure it out. He'd gone to the program as willingly as he could imagine being, and the facilitator told him that understanding what he did, and why, would help him understand how he could make sure it never happened again, and he thought again about the woman whose husband he'd killed.

Then he'd noticed a pamphlet on the Victim Offender Mediation Program in the chapel, and he'd picked it up. A chance to meet with the person he'd "harmed." On a lark he'd spoken to his Parole Officer about it, and applied for the program. In time, he met with the facilitators, and they made him think about why he wanted to meet with her, and what he'd hoped to get out of it.

Damn it, it was the hardest thing he'd ever done. They reminded him that she would be responsible for deciding if and when they met, and what questions she'd answer, if any. He started to really think about the impact this crime might have had on her.

He talked to Jagdeep, one of the facilitators, about going ahead, and Jag said he'd approach the woman, but that Roger needed to be really sure this wasn't about trying to manipulate her for parole. And Roger had had to come clean to himself.

One reason he wanted to do mediation was because he heard all the time from guys coming back from parole hearings that the victim impact statements had stopped them from getting parole. Really. And Roger didn't think he could manipulate the woman to write a good one, but if he were really honest, he wanted to know ahead of time what the victim impact statement would be like. If it was a brutal letter, he'd withdraw his first application. Because even though he'd been eligible after seven, he didn't *have* to apply at any specific time.

A couple of months later, he'd worked with Jag, and talked to the Elder and the Chaplain, and everyone decided they should go ahead, and about six months later Jag got hold of him and told him the family was ready. Or at least the wife was. He'd been in almost nine years.

Now, as he pounded the bag, Roger remembered how hard he'd worked with the Elder to get control of his anxiety. He'd had to learn all over again how to breathe, and he never really did get control of his blushing; he'd turn a few shades of red every time he thought about how ashamed he was of what he'd done, and what a shit he was for ruining these people's lives. But if meeting her was going to help her, then nothing was going to stop him, he decided. Even if she wanted him to postpone parole. He was that committed, and he did intend to ask her.

They'd met, and she'd asked lots of really hard questions. And she cried, and so did he, if he was being really straight. She missed her husband, who had been a great guy. And Roger knew if he could take one thing back, relive one moment in his life, he'd skip showing up that day on that construction site. Towards the end, she asked him if he wanted forgiveness, and he choked up. He said he didn't deserve it. And then he asked her if she was okay with him applying for parole.

And she gave a most surprising answer: she'd said he was free to apply for parole whenever he felt ready. She just wanted "meaningful evidence of change" she said. Whatever the hell that meant.

"How can you convince me there will be no more victims?" Veronica had asked. Her answer got him thinking right up until his parole hearing later that year. He'd applied for, and received, escorted passes, and he'd used them to go to church, and visit his M2W2 visitors. It was expected he'd get full parole to a halfway house this fall.

And here he was, almost two years later, having to decide if he was going to get up on stage with her and talk about the day they'd met, the hardest day of his life. Well, after the day he'd helped kill her husband. Bert, his name was. But Veronica had asked him to do this event, and he figured he owed it to the memory of Bert.

He never wanted to forget Bert's death, and if doing this hard thing was going to help him remember, and help Veronica heal, he *had* to say yes. Even if he would turn twenty shades of red. In public.

Even if this might be the second-hardest day of his life. Or third, maybe. After the crime, and the mediation.

He'd created this shit; he might as well try to clean it up. And he had to admit, since he'd started to do that, he cared a whole lot less about the idiots in the gym who thought he was a brown-noser.

'Cause he knew they didn't have nearly the courage he did.

Or Bert's family, for that matter.

Maybe, just maybe, he was starting to be a guy who does the right thing, even when there's nothing in it for him.

CHAPTER 37
FOUR DAYS LATER

He's gone. Just like that. I can't believe it, and this place is in complete chaos. We all want to grieve, to either be with each other or be alone, but the bureaucracy of CSC has kicked in (not to mention the rabid media), and it seems we won't even have a chance to "be" with it. People are freaking out.

"He's not gone, love, he's just found the strength to get to a place where it doesn't hurt quite so much," Sally says (through her tears). I love her perspective; it's helped me keep mine. Until now I haven't worried myself much with the practical ideas of "after-death theology" or those big "what ifs?"

"God questions," Ben called them when he came after it happened. To visit. Not me, but everyone else. He still can't look at me.

I know I believe something lives on. I hope it's better than what his life on earth. It was so hard for that little man to even glimpse happiness since I've known him…I can't imagine what it was like before he came here.

Thursday morning, Tom went out to the barn to say good morning to the beasts, and to turn them out, and found him hanging. He'd used some rope and a beam – classic. Tom said he knew something was wrong right away because the horses didn't nicker "Good morning." Maybe they understood the quiet sadness that had settled around them.

Ricky must have left the Lodge in the night, after we were all in bed. No idea why the alarm didn't go off. Looking back, none of us knows for sure why now, but Cook said Ricky did take a call that afternoon on the kitchen phone, and from Ricky's half of the conversation it sounded like his family.

I can't (won't?) imagine what was said this time…disappointment, anger, frustration, desperation…. They're all understandable possibilities. And Kate did tell us she found one of the kittens from the litter he'd been nursing had died. Ricky hadn't told her; he'd just buried it in the bedding in one of the cages. But it's really hard to say what took him up the ladder.

I know he was working towards going in front of the Parole Board for passes…but to where? His family couldn't even invite him over for a few hours. I can't imagine what it must be like to be a mother to a brain-injured "criminal," so no judgment, but…surely some love, some compassion, a little hospitality? Clearly the environment that produced Ricky wasn't a great one for alleviating his torment, either.

He left a note he'd written in kindergarten scrawl telling us it wasn't our fault, and he just "couldnt tak it any mor." He said he was glad for circle, and likes us all "even you guys who don't like me bak." He said he hadn't meant to hurt the kitten, but Kate reassured us there were no signs that he had; the kitten had just died from being too young, too fragile in spite of Ricky's attention. And, she said she thought it had lived longer than it would have without him.

I didn't even know Ricky could write, and he'd left us a beautiful note -- all positive stuff, worrying about us, apologizing for making a mess. It didn't offer any real clues as to why he was hurting this time, but we didn't need any. We knew Ricky's life was really hard. I feel bad that he couldn't reach out to one of us, but maybe whatever it was that night was just too…much.

Maybe I was partly responsible, somehow, but I don't want to be full of my self-importance. I hadn't really connected with Ricky, and hadn't worked to stay in touch after our episode with the fence. And I knew I should have. I kept hearing, "I don't know if they want me to touch them," and then would smile through my tears. As an almost-priest, surely I should have noticed something. And more than one of us commented that he'd chosen to end his life surrounded by the animals he had once been so afraid of. He'd gotten almost comfortable with the horses the weeks since we'd arrived here. So much progress, so much tragedy.

I needed to learn first-hand some of the harder parts of this work, of this life. We gathered in the Sanctuary the first night, keeping space in darkness with only one candle. We shared some of the hurt in our tender places, and Nora talked about working hard to remember that she needs to stay compassionate and caring, bringing dignity and love where there is so little, that it seems a constant struggle…that her judgment and second-guessing of herself needs to be as gentle as she is with everyone else. I tried to remember that when I had surges of anger towards CSC and the media, and when I started to blame Ricky for all the chaos here now. Really, Ricky had no capacity to imagine what his suicide would unleash, so it was CSC and the media's fault.

And then I'd remember that blame is a waste of energy.

Since the moment Nora called CSC to report what had happened (after calling 911, and helping the coroner, who came to remove his body, and the police, who had to investigate for "foul play"), I felt like our sacred space, the place we called home, had been infiltrated by an outside world I don't want to be a part of.

"Fault" and "liability," "risk assessment" and "emergency protocol" -- all of it became a part of the daily conversation over lunches that we willingly shared with those alien bureaucrats. *Dear God, help us.*

We shared our bread, and they shared their protocols, oblivious to how they were slowly killing us with their determined effort to keep a distance from the pain. I confess I had a bias, but the only one who seemed genuine and compassionate was the Regional Chaplain, Peggy. She showed her support again and again, and had gone to bat for *Just Living* repeatedly since it opened. From the practical "Who do we release the body to?" to the "How could this have been prevented?" I felt a bit like Alice must have felt down the rabbit hole.

Hello! Prevented? How about looking at Ricky's childhood, and addictions, and HIS EXPERIENCES OF TRAUMA IN PRISON! No one so much as whispered those things out loud. Chaining him to his bed would not have prevented his agony, his hurting, his death. It could only have prolonged it, I knew.

With the focus on "Cover Your Ass," people seemed more concerned with asking on whose watch the tragedy happened, rather than really feeling or even opening to the possibility of the pain, of that much suffering. Or their own hand in it.

The bureaucrats infiltrated our very being, and every aspect of our life together was changed -- I hoped not forever. Finally, Nora put her foot down.

"If you want to eat with us, we welcome you. But we won't talk about business in the dining room. This is a time for us to relax, check in with each other and connect. Business sometimes gets in the way of that."

They seemed to get the message, and there has been less "We'll just squeeze in this interview, form, investigation, report, procedure, whatever we can because we are Busy, Busy, and Important People."

Their attitude reminded me of Sisyphus, and the stone they bear is Policy and Procedure. I was sick of them, and they hardly even interacted with me (I was the inconsequential young person, not quite real because I hadn't graduated yet, was neither on payroll, nor a bothersome lawyer or vocal advocate.) I felt like furniture around them, but don't want to say anything to "draw their heat," as Al would say. I didn't envy them, mostly because they worked so hard to keep from connecting, from feeling, from being, and I sensed a quiet desperation. Or I was full of bullshit, and projected what I wanted to believe.

The most interesting and sad repercussion of their being here was how quickly the men donned their masks. Cook became a little too affable; Al, quiet and invisible, acting the part of dumb Indian (right!); Kenny rarely came indoors; Tom was sullen (even more so than usual); and the others shovelled in their food and disappeared. Bob tried to anticipate Nora's needs, and hovered, helping. Dan was so invisible, I wondered if they didn't even want CSC to know he's here.

No one hung around at night to chat, or suggested walks in the fields with the horses. Everyone's focused on "doing their work," but less is getting done. The wind has been knocked out of this place, and I don't understand it. When I headed outside, Kenny, bless him, remained true to himself, and was still funny and real…but with a sharp edge, an attitude of "just try to fuck with me and what we've created" -- his leprechaun had a dark side, definitely. Which made me inordinately happy.

After a couple of days we figured out how Ricky got out without tripping the alarm. Hugh had been staying over, and decided to leave to go home in the middle of the night. His wife had called and told him her flight was coming in crazy late, and he wanted to be home when she got there. He thought he'd reset the alarm, but, clearly hadn't. Or at least, that's the story being shared.

I decided I wanted to figure out what was going on with the men, because clearly there were private signals being shared that I didn't receive. Nora was overburdened, Kate was totally focused on the kennels and the barn, Sally became "the invisible maid"; so I went to Frank for help. He and Ben were in the stables, dealing with some chores and taking horses to Shalom because the men aren't allowed to interact with the public for a bit. Ben left when I walked in. Sheesh. Ouch. It still hurts. I asked Frank for help.

"Well," he told me, "the men here were starting to believe things can be different. Trust is a long time coming. They don't want to re-engage until they know there's a chance things will turn out okay." It was the first time I saw the real gravity of the situation, and it took me two days to get there. The men got it in a fraction of a second. Wow.

It was the most obvious and in-my-face evidence of institutionalization. I was grieving Ricky and thinking (in my self-absorbed way) about what I could have done differently to change things (what if?) and the men, in a nano-second, understood that everything that had been built – from buildings to relationships -- was threatened. Investigations, recommendations, "It's for the best," new policy, involuntary transfers, friendships, therapists, group work, even teachings from Elders – it could all be swept away on a whim by a stranger, a bureaucrat, and at any time. Nora had been talking about working to be independently sustainable, and now I got how important that was.

I sat with Buttercup, cuddling Topaz, thinking about the ripples that had been cast on the peaceful waters here. First, my relationship with Ben, brief as it'd been, had blown apart, and now this. I wondered if this was how life went for people seeking meaning.

I know I don't I understand it all yet. It's like we're in an illusion of control over our space, our lives, our being. I thought it was real, and now I feel so naïve. I'm realizing that when any group "chooses to sleep with the system," as Nora says, they sell their control, and what they create is always fragile, vulnerable. I feel so silly. And I wonder what it means when the "system" is the Church. I really want to talk to Glenn about it.

I contemplated control while hanging out with the animals, with Topaz and the horses. I am, at the same time, grieving not just Ricky, but also my connection with the other men, this place.

I couldn't go back to being numb, to existing without caring. I refused to make protocol more important than a hug. Wherever I end up working, whatever I do, I need to put relationships and people, and even animals first, before commitments to rules, before my needs for stuff or personal accolades.

That's how I'd honour Spirit, and Love, and Connection. And I wanted to find the courage to do it.

The next morning, I pulled up my bootstraps, scrubbed my face, and put on a smile before breakfast. I wanted to chase down those men who were hiding behind their masks, and reach out to them. I wanted to remind them that while we are being infiltrated and possessed by these weird creatures, I HAD (HAVE?) A RELATIONSHIP WITH THEM THAT WAS REAL AND IMPORTANT TO ME. I wanted to show them my mettle, as Nana Beth would say! And I expected them to step up to the plate and be real with me, even if they could only show glimpses. Or else.

I would call them on it.

I would remind them what they were in control of, and how strong we were, together. Of course, I may have been totally off-base, they could have bounced me out of here, but I knew I had to try.

I was going to ask Nora what else I could do to help, to suggest a couple of things. I know Dad and his parish are setting up some formal support; maybe it would help to go a bit public with that? Or would that hurt the project? I felt green in the field of media and political savvy, but was ready to learn.

After strolling around with my beloved kitten in my arms, I took her back to the barn, and spent some time there with the horses, and Ricky's Spirit. We had a little conversation, and I told him that even though I still have moments of blinding fury towards his decision, I don't want him to carry any guilt. I know he was doing the best he could, and I was learning lots about myself, and life, and political strategy because of everything going on. No one here blames him. I'm starting to view it like fall-out after a bomb. And, when I leave behind the judgments, it gets much clearer that I have to focus on helping to make things better. And I am trusting that a caring clean-up crew will arrive soon.

But my plans were pre-empted. The next morning, Nora mustered us for a morning ride before the bureaucrats arrived. There weren't enough mounts, so some of us hiked to the clearing in the woods behind the Sacred Grounds. Peggy (instead of Ben?) joined us. We gathered, shuffling in a standing circle. People weren't looking at each other. Then Nora spoke.

"I want us to work together, and each of us, to get over our resentment towards Ricky. We have to figure this out, and I really need your help. I've decided I'm not going to lose myself or this place because of this, okay?" Her steely eyes scanned the eyes that were looking back at her. I believed her.

"It's really easy to be in an 'us and them' place with them. We have one or two more days with them here, and we have just that much time to show them who we are and help them to see why this place deserves to survive," she finished.

We all talked about what had happened and what it meant, and then she talked about some strategies we agreed to. Education campaigns, communications with supporters, asking them to help. Revising how we look after each other, living our "policies" and declaring some new ones so we can show everyone that we have been affected by this, and plan to do things differently from now on. Not because it's mandated, *but because we care.*

Kate will reach out to Ricky's family, and coordinate a memorial gathering. Frank is writing up a case study to share what we learned with others. Peggy will give a safe ear to the men (she doesn't have to report to anyone.) Nora talked about her open door, communicating openly with the Board and CSC, and keeping track of planning, of what's working and what isn't. Kenny seemed to reclaim some lightness; he promised to bring some fun.

Sally and Cook will be "models of hospitality." I will interface with some of the outside agencies and supporters, and write more publicly about my experiences here. Tom will take on more of the "work chores" as he called them, and Al and Hugh will continue to offer sweats, teachings, and hard physical work for anyone who wants to spend time in the Sacred Grounds. Dan offered to finish the fence painting that Ricky was doing, as a memorial. I think he's dealing with some demons, because he wasn't always kind to Ricky. I'm also going to suggest that Dad's parish might help, but not yet.

We're going to meet again after dark in the Sanctuary to talk about our progress, and every night until our community feels more solid. Then we ran back to the kitchen and greeted our guests as they arrived for breakfast. I think they were a bit concerned when they got here and no one was around, but muffins and warm scones were on the table. We greeted the day with a smile. I hoped that surprised them. Or that at least that they noticed.

Dear God,

I found a poem on the interwebs today, written by Rabbi Joseph Meszler. Thank you for letting me find it. On HuffPost, no less.

It helped.

"Prayer at the Funeral of Someone Who Committed Suicide"
Let there be no whispering, no secrets here:
Our hearts are broken.
Ricky took his own life.
And even though it might appear
that he died by his own hand,
no one does this without great, coercing pain,

inner suffering that seems to have no end,
even though we wish
he knew that no agony is forever.
Source of compassion, help us to cry out loud,
to hold each other gently,
to live with unanswerable questions,
normal feelings of anger and guilt,
and this gaping hole of loss.
Help us to reach out to others who are suffering,
to show them our love, to say the kind word,
and that this is not a choice we condone
or is worth imitation.
It is hard to see the divine image in the lives of those who suffer.
The sun sets and rises.
We put one foot in front of the other.
We hold our hearts in our hands.
We lift them up to You, God of eternal peace,
and to each other.
Help us live each day.
Amen.

CHAPTER 38
LEARNING AND TRANSFORMATION

I am beginning my days with the Sun Salutation...heralding each morning with some simple yoga. And yes, I topple. And I'm not flexible or strong enough to do it and look graceful.

But you know what? It feels good. And I'm improving, I can feel it.

So you know what else I've decided, God? I'm going to get better at it. I'm starting to tell myself I'm not flexible or strong enough YET.

I like that word a lot. I'm moving towards something, and I know I'm still learning, but I can honestly say I've learned something, too. How to say YET.

Thank you for that word....

The days following had moments of sadness ("Ricky's Mom isn't coming to the memorial; I think she just is glad to be free of the connection to CSC," Kate reported), and bushels of frustration here and there, but overall it was much easier to make sense of who we were, and how we should be with each other. I would love to be able to say that there was an immediate reversion to the way we were together when Ricky was physically with us, but we've changed and so has this place.

The men still seem to be grieving, in a sadly familiar way. I think on the outside we all think we're in control. We "manage risks" and make "to do" lists, and decide where to eat and what to eat and with whom, and we ditch some people, and befriend others, and we have this illusion that if we just keep on working and staying on top of things, we will be in control. Ducks in a row. And a Mack truck can get us any time, or cancer, or we end up pregnant, and then we make choices, and our Dad helps us and we end up hurting for a long time. So much for control!

On Friday, Dad came out to visit. Of course, he arrived just before lunch, and the guys, happy to see a familiar face, flocked around him and asked him to join us. Okay, Kenny, Cook and Bob asked. Dad's smile was so big when they did. He knew what we were dealing with; Ricky's death had been all over the media. And apparently he'd been in touch with Nora.

As lunch was ending, he asked if his parish could help with things from time to time, and Nora asked what he meant by "help." She wasn't sure about a bunch of people she didn't know hanging around; there had been trouble in the past with journalists trying to find the "sensational" stories, and everyone was a little leery of "voyeurs," especially now.

Dad reassured her quickly; he had a list that he whipped out of his pocket. They wanted to assist with funding the labyrinth (and he produced a cheque, to Kenny's delight), and to help provide some household goods or food. One fellow in the parish was a veterinarian who offered to help with vaccinations, and such, if he could bring out vet tech students from time to time. Kate was thrilled; there was a vet in town who had been helping, but she was becoming overburdened, so Nora knew the help would be welcomed.

Dad confessed that some of the women had even baked some bread for him to bring, which he had left in his car; seems they weren't aware there was an excellent cook and baker on site. He offered to drop the bread at a soup kitchen if Cook didn't think it was needed. Turns out Cook was actually pleased to have the bread; his burns weren't healing as quickly as he would have liked, and less time on his feet was still a help. Maybe he was being gracious. He did tell Dad that he would cook a big pot of soup for the parish as a thank you some time soon.

As we cleaned up the kitchen Kenny and some of the others headed back outside to continue with yard work. Nora went to her office with Dad to find brochures and pamphlets about *Just Living*, the riding academy, and the animal shelters for his parishioners, and I tagged along. She started to complain about how out-of-date the brochures were, and Dad suggested he talk to a young graphic arts student in the parish about updating them.

Listening from just outside the door, I realized they were on fire, and it felt so right. Nora finished up by emailing him some old brochure copies, and the mission statement and annual reports. The CSC folks were just returning from their lunch in town with the Regional Deputy Commissioner, and it couldn't have been smoother.

I walked him back to his car to pick up the bread, and he shared greetings from Mom, Stephen and Sarita. He gave me a long hug, and then surprised me.

"I am so proud of you, Beth. You are so courageous! I'm trying really hard to pay attention to what you're doing. I know I've been a pain as a Dad, but I'm trying. Be patient, okay? Even this old dog is learning new tricks." He stepped back, and I brushed a tear from my eye. "Hey Mugwump, are you okay?" he asked. I shrugged.

"I'm just not used to hearing you say you're proud of me, or maybe I just haven't believed you before," I said. We were starting fresh with our relationship, and it felt real, and grown-up. Life was good.

Three more weeks and I was scheduled to leave this place. I was already starting to pull back, and working to resist that. If only I knew… anything! Things were still a mess with Ben. I wasn't sure about work, about my calling, whether I'd be ordained, about where I'd live…if this was living in the present, it wasn't easy.

Later that night, talking with Cook on the porch, he reminded me that tomorrow night I'm going out to hear Veronica speak for Victims Awareness Week.

"It's too much for me to go, so tell me about it after, 'kay Darlin'?" he asked, and of course, I agreed.

The next night, listening for someone else really sharpened my attention, but she and Roger were so inspiring, I asked her if I could have a copy of her talk because even with my listening ears, I knew I wouldn't capture her story for Cook well enough.

Afterward, I curled up in the kitchen while he baked, and read it to him. Here's what Veronica said:

"September 12, 2004. I bet none of you know what you were doing that day, but I can tell you everything about my life that day.

"I was a stay-at-home mother of three children; one of them was in college and another one was old enough to be, but was mostly hanging around on the beaches of Vancouver. Especially Wreck Beach. (There was laughter.) I had spent the morning pruning my berry bushes and digging up the vegetable patch, what was ready to be dug up. I went into the house at lunch and cooked tomato soup and grilled cheese for myself and my husband of 22 years, Bert. He was stopping by for lunch on his way to a meeting; he worked as a construction supervisor, managing a couple of job sites. We lived a good life, we were happy. I had my garden and went to church on Sundays, and I was planning to sew my daughter's prom dress that winter. Bert and I were planning a winter vacation to Hawaii, something we'd never done with just the two of us.

"Anyhow, as I was making the grilled cheese there was a knock on the door. I turned off the frying pan, and wondered who it could be. I thought it must be missionaries or something; we didn't even get packages delivered to our rural property. I was stunned when I answered the door and two RCMP officers were there, asking if I was Mrs. Veronica Steveson, wife of Mr. Robert

Steveson. Of course, I answered that I was and they asked if they could come in, suggested that I might want to sit down.

"After that it's a bit of a blur, but I do remember they asked me if there was anyone I could call, and I called my friend Wanda to come over. She's here tonight.

"Anyways, they told me my husband, my best friend, my warmth and companion had been shot that morning at a job site. I went to put on my coat, assuming we had to get to the hospital and then they told me he hadn't made it. Just like that. He hadn't made it. And my world collapsed." She stopped and took a drink of water, dabbed at her eyes, and seemed to be embarrassed by the emotion, I told Cook.

"Seems that morning he'd dropped by an old job site they were thinking of re-opening. Bids had been flying to finish a building that had been abandoned when the economy fell apart, and he thought he should drop by to check on its condition. He didn't tell anyone else where he was going.

"Anyhow, from what they could figure out, he must have walked in on something. There was evidence that there were at least two guys, two guns, and he'd been shot by both of them. There was lots of blood on the scene, and it wasn't all his. Ballistics identified two different kinds of bullets. Before Bert died he was able to call 911, and that's how they'd found him, bleeding on the ground, surrounded by hundreds of pot plants, an industrial sized grow op that had been set up at the abandoned job site.

"In that moment, my life changed forever. I had to start thinking about how I was going to tell my 16-year-old daughter that her daddy wouldn't drive her to band practice that night. I had to figure out how to find my bohemian son, and whether I had to call my other son home from university in Alberta. I wanted to see Bert, touch his body, but I wasn't allowed because the police weren't finished with it yet. Seems his body was now evidence in a criminal case. But they did want me to go with them to identify him. Even though they had the picture from his driver's licence and they assured me there were no mistakes, that it was him who was killed, I still needed to positively ID him.

"So I went that day to the morgue and I was able to see my husband's body through a window, but I wasn't able to touch him, to hold him, to scream to God about what was happening, and so I wept quiet tears. Wanda picked up my daughter from school, and took her home to her place, and they waited for me there.

"The police found my younger son. They had been looking for him to see if he had an alibi; seems when people are killed it is most often because of family. I guess they thought maybe John's lifestyle mean t he was a part of the grow-op, perhaps had let the growers know of the abandoned building. Anyhow, they found him, and he had had an alibi, and it was clear he wasn't involved so they drove him home. And together we called Jim, my eldest, and got his Residence Coordinator on the phone, and together they arranged to get him to the airport and he flew home the next morning from university and we tried to make sense of the rest of our lives.

"It took some time. Ten days later the police finally released the body, and we arranged to have it cremated because so much time had passed. And then our very conservative Priest wouldn't perform a funeral for my husband, which suited me fine, because I was fed up with the Catholic Church." Uncomfortable twittering laughter. "I told him if God could resurrect a man filled with bullet holes, he could certainly resurrect him from ashes. I was angry. And tired. And sad. And confused. And a little scared.

"You see, the police started speculating that Bert had been responsible for the grow-op and had died in a gun fight with a rival gang. Bert! A gang member! It was preposterous, I knew, but then again...a small part of me couldn't believe he'd been murdered, so...? Life went on, even when it was really hard.

"Then, four months later, just after we'd had our first Christmas without my husband and my kids' father, there was another knock on the door, and the RCMP were back. There had been a break in the case, and they had two men in custody, and they had no ties to Bert. He had just been in the wrong place at the wrong time. I was able to get a job at the local library to support the family. They were really understanding when I asked for time off every time the case came to court.

"In 2006 two men pled guilty to second-degree murder, and were sentenced to life-7 and life-12. They also were charged with drug offences and weapons offences, and over the course of the next few years I followed their cases. I knew when they were up for parole, and when they finished programs. But mostly, I felt safe because they were behind bars, even if it was too close to my home. I had to figure out how to move on with my life, doing all the things I had always done and all the things my husband had done to build a family and keep a home. Life wasn't easy, but it wasn't impossible either. Lots of people helped us.

"Then, four years later, there was another knock on my door. My new minister and a second young fellow were on my porch, asking if they could come in. I made tea and they told me a story.

"It seems one of the men who was responsible for Bert's death had contacted them because he wanted to talk to me. He'd found God, and wanted a chance to apologize to me. I didn't even know this was possible, but I learned a lot that day.

"I was curious about this man who had shot Bert and I had some serious questions for him about the day Bert had died. Questions the police didn't answer. Questions I didn't even know who to ask. Like what had Bert's last words been? And why hadn't they just let him go? Why did they leave him there, and not call for help?

"Anyhow, a year later I met with Roger for four hours one afternoon at the prison. Two facilitators went with me, and I took out my scribbled piece of paper with my questions and I asked them one after another. And mostly, Roger and I cried and he tried to answer them. And he told me he was sorry, and that he wished there was something he could do to make it up to the children, and me.

"We met two more times over the next few months, and I was able to slowly get to know Roger. I heard about his addictions, getting involved with a gang, how he was security on the site where Bert had shown up that morning. He'd been fighting with another gang member when Bert had tried to intervene, and in their surprise everyone shot everyone. Except poor Bert;

he didn't shoot anyone, of course. Roger got a bullet hole in his upper arm, and the other guy ended up losing a few fingers when Roger shot the gun right out of his hand. In all the shooting, they shot Bert, too. More than once.

"They were kids, really. Scared, dangerous, tripping kids who were literally playing with fire. Weapons that fire. And my brave Bert tried to talk them out of it, and he got caught in their crossfire."

Veronica had taken a deep breath and scanned the crowd.

"She was crying a little bit at this point, Cook. And her kids were there sniffing too, all three of them," and I told him the rest.

"Then she sat down and Roger got up. Really, Ben, you could've heard a pin drop. As she passed him the microphone, she hugged him.

"Anyhow, Roger stood up and said something like this:

"Hi everyone. My name is Roger Franks, and I am responsible for Veronica's husband's death. I didn't get up that morning planning to hurt him, but I am just as responsible as if I had.

"I'm not going to make excuses, how hard I had it as a child or I've figured out all of why I did what I did. I don't know if I'll ever have all the answers. But I'll tell you one thing.

"Meeting this amazing woman and talking to her, answering her questions was the hardest thing I've ever done. And I think it saved my life. Because in the end she asked for one thing other than the answers to her questions. She asked me to change my life, and to make something of myself. Make sure it never happened again.

"She said, 'Roger, I forgive you. I think Bert would want me to. But so help me God if you ever hurt anyone again like you've hurt my family, I will kill you myself.'" Everyone laughed. It was like a balloon popped. He just shrugged his shoulders, and his voice cracked when he said, *"How could I not change? I mean, she asked me for 'meaningful evidence of change,' and she's kinda scary right?"*

"Then they hugged again. There wasn't a dry eye in the house. Peggy got up, the Regional Chaplain, and told us the goal of the serious violence offence mediation program is to help crime victims. Help them get answers, help them understand things, help them feel safe. And that they don't emphasize, or even talk about forgiveness. And then Veronica got up and shamelessly asked for donations for the program because it is woefully underfunded, more crime victims and offenders want into the program than there's funding for. I got to meet one of the facilitators – a guy named Jagdeep. He was cool."

Cook sighed.

"Thanks, Mugwump. It's good to hear about Roger," he said as we made our way to bed. Roger was a friend of his, and that's what he'd been curious about. Who knew?

Dear God,

Remember when I wanted to learn about prayer, and got in the habit of praying every night, sometimes asking for things, sometimes praying for other people?

I thought prayer was like begging, right? Because it kinda was. But lately I've noticed something....

I'm still "researching." Yoga. Buddhism. Some great prayers.

And I still do "prayers" for other people. Nightly praying. Morning meditation, yoga.

I have a discipline! And I'm realizing this discipline brings me closer to You. I notice You during the day, in a picture, or a plant, or the way we gather in circle, talk to each other. You are there, too.

Maybe that's what "praying unceasingly" is about.

Rejoice always, pray without ceasing, give thanks in all circumstances, for this is the will of God in Christ Jesus for you. 1 Thessalonians 5:16-18.

CHAPTER 39

NAPPING WITH CONTENTMENT

"I'm jus' gonna lay down for a bit," Cook called down the stairs to Sally.

"That's good, Chef. Rest up. See you at dinner, and not a moment sooner." Cook smiled at Sally's nickname. He knew he'd always be more of a hash slinger than a chef, but he felt taller when she called him Chef. And he couldn't believe how lucky he was that she thought he was special.

He put his head on his pillow, pulled up the throw she'd left at the bottom of his bed, and sighed.

"Pinch me," he thought. He couldn't believe this was his life, and his heart grew with gratitude. So many things to be grateful for, when he thought about it.

His place, at *Just Living*. Support while he healed from his wounds. Little Beth, who treated him like a hero. Nora, who saw his potential. His PO, who seemed to believe in him. His brother, who still talked to him.

As he rested, he smiled remembering Sr. Nima, who first showed him what life could be like if he just let go.

It would be easier, more familiar to focus on what was wrong, what was hard, how unfair his life was, but he knew it just didn't help. Going to sleep to memories of Sr. Nima was still one of his best strategies for avoiding the terrors.

He thought about that first time, sitting in a circle in the chapel of the Max. He had squirmed through the whole meeting with the Buddhist nun; he'd never even been in the chapel, except for that one memorial service for a guy. This time his buddy Jasmir had dragged him along – yes, a Muslim going to a Buddhist service. But Jasmir was calm, and God knows, Cook had wanted to be calmer. He hadn't been Cook then, but he didn't like to remember that.

That day, he was introduced, and Sr. Nima took his hand in hers, and looked at him. And didn't look away. He felt her love wash over him, and pulled his hand back to cough. She touched his arm.

"Thank you for coming today. I know there are many things you could be doing, and I'm glad you came here," she said, and he was hooked. He beamed at her, feeling like a schoolboy with a crush on a 60-year-old Buddhist nun wearing maroon robes and the most beautiful saffron coloured sash. Although he had just thought it was gold back then. Cook smiled thinking about basking in her presence.

She had talked with them, to them, about what their struggles were. She read from a holy book, and they talked about fear, and attachment, and peace. They meditated for a while, maybe 20 minutes but it seemed like hours that first time. Before long, there were bells, and she was saying goodbye, pulling her big coat around her shoulders. She left Cook with a book – *Peace is Every Step* – and his life was changed. Or at least changing.

He learned to let go when guys told him he was a freak. He learned to let go when guards literally rattled his cage – walking by the bars in the middle of the night with their sticks banging to waken the prisoners so they'd move, and the guards knew they were alive. He let go when they lost his grievances, or applications for work, or training. And he fell in love with Sr. Nima. She came every month and visited, and he carried her bag, and let go of his grudges.

Until she couldn't come any more – she'd gotten sick, and they didn't want her inside if she was sick. He missed her bald head, but remembered. He had to let go of her, too.

Slowly, he had started to find happiness. He noticed the birds that visited the exercise yard when he had his time outside. He smiled when they landed on the razor wire, and didn't get hurt. And the staff started to notice that he didn't growl quite so much, and they started to get onside, working to move him to a medium security prison. He took a program or two, and started to believe he might actually get moved. And then he looked up, and it had been a year, and he had no "institutional charges" and the solid staff actually believed in him; he got transferred.

It took him a while to get used to the Medium. More movement. Double bunking. A few guys he knew, but access to the gym every evening and free time in the chapel helped. He fed the stray cats, and they started to accept him. But he'd never say they liked him. He took a job doing work in the "prison factory," CorCan, where they built furniture, and started to make a name as a reliable worker. He steered clear of prison politics, and hanging out in cliques, and just did his time, slowly and steadily. Not favouring particular inmates. Or staff. And then something really magical happened.

He met Butch, a guy who worked in the kitchen and taught the prisoners how to cook. A staff member who didn't remind them all the time how useless, how bad they were. Who actually treated them like regular people, and respected them. And so he respected Butch back.

Butch saw something in him that no one else saw, and encouraged him to take courses and come to work in the kitchen. The first time he heard the name Cook from the inmates, he felt proud. Real proud, not fake proud. He found what he needed – a reason. His purpose. Feed people well. Healthy food that gave nutrition when the ingredients sucked.

Over the next few years, he became Butch's right hand guy. He did the ordering, the meal planning, and made sure the kitchen was clean and well stocked. He looked after the meal prep, made sure guys weren't assholes, and that food didn't create unrest. He even convinced the gardeners to grow fresh vegetables for the kitchen. And herbs. The Warden came down once and thanked him, and asked him to consider heading up the Inmate Committee. No thank you. That's a heat score, he told her.

Still meditating weekly with the Buddhists, he started to have more good days than bad. That keeping his head down, cooking tasty meals, rescuing bad ones, and baking lots of cookies actually made him happy. That he didn't need to move on to be happy. And then the kitchen thing changed.

Someone somewhere (rumour had it someone who wanted to make money with the scheme) decided to move the cooking off-site, to another institution. And he died a little inside, because really, some bureaucrat in Ottawa thought they could make tasty, more nutritious food elsewhere and ship it and food *wouldn't* become an issue? So his heart wasn't in the reheating, and Butch and his IPO decided to get him moved to minimum.

It had happened amazingly fast, he thought, once he applied; so before he knew it he was living in a pod with other guys on Vancouver Island, cooking for his house (and sometimes other guys too) and settling in. Life was again really good. The joint was known for some innovative stuff – a live theatre company, a newsletter that was shared internationally – but none of that mattered to him.

He just wanted to walk by the water, hang out in the long house, and cook for his people. Add to the Feasts when the Elders came. And it didn't take long before Nora heard about him, and started visiting, filling his head with ideas and questions about how to make the kitchen at *Just Living* work.

He smiled, as he drifted to sleep, knowing that every step since his first bit was a surprise to him, but the ones in the last ten years were all good surprises. Something he hadn't had enough of when he was a boy. And he smiled when he thought about Beth, that delightful little lady who had stolen his heart. If he ever had had a child, he'd want her to be like Beth.

And he didn't know what was around the corner for Beth, but he bet the surprises would be good, and bad, but that either way they'd get through them together, if she just stuck around.

He was glad she'd moved back in. That way he could show her how much of a difference she really was making around here. Magic, that girl. And he smiled as he felt himself drop off to sleep, and hoped he'd dream good dreams of Sally, and Kenny, and Beth.

CHAPTER 40
WALKING THE PATH

Praying the Labyrinth. Amazing – release, transform, re-enter...as a practice. As a work. As a lifetime.

I release my sense of self. I am being transformed into someone who will meet a new calling. I will be patient as I discern the path forward.

What will it look like, Creator?

Who will accompany me?

Will this be my meaningful life?

I await the Oracle...grin. And the Labyrinth.

Two weeks to go in my practicum, and I was still having an amazing time. Except I still missed Ben. I wrote to him last week. It was sort of a prayer, I think now, when I look it.

Dear Ben,

I am here, again, back at Just Living. But I guess you know that.

Life is rich and good. Mostly.

I'm still struggling to figure out some of the tough parts. Like whether I should be ordained. And why, or why not.

And whether or not this is my "calling," and if not, then what. It feels pretty "right" and I'm learning much more about how to behave, what's acceptable.

But mostly, I'm trying to figure out what parts of me I could change to make the possibility of "us" a possibility again. I don't feel like we're "done," that Spirit is finished with us. Except that might seem creepy.

Anyhow, I miss you.

And I wanted you to know,

Beth.

I really try not to get stuck in wondering "what if?" because there really isn't an "if" that's imaginable. But I did like being with Ben, and I do miss being able to ask him about stuff. Like ordination. His life. And sexy times.

Dad and Mom and a few parishioners were coming out on the weekend to help plant the labyrinth; Kenny, Sohan and I were building it so we'd be ready for them. It was interesting working with them; I hadn't had much contact with Sohan, but he's funny! I remembered him teasing Ben on the first day I visited the house; I'm embarrassed to say I'd kinda forgotten about him. He was away on course, now he's back, and I wondered what else I've totally gapped on?

The site was cleared, and Kenny and I tried spray-painting the pattern on the ground, but we keep changing it. Then Kenny added big bulges (bubbles?) off the path in each of the four directions because he hoped someone (Hugh? Tom?) would build some benches eventually. He kept hinting to Tom, who might've kill him. Except he stopped.

Anyhow, we put gravel down that packs but still drains, and we laid geotextile on the paths first so the weeds wouldn't come through. Nora arranged deliveries – first the gravel and then some really nice soil for the beds.

While Kenny and I put the last touches on the design, Tom and Sohan were edging with some nice stones we've been collecting over the past few months. It was exciting, and tiring. I couldn't wait to move the wheelbarrows full of gravel, and pack it down. One of the things I liked about the work is that it didn't need conversation, just a good back and lots of determination. And I lost myself in it.

It's all coming together with everyone helping. Frank stopped by for a bit after work. Ben and Aaron brought some AVP volunteers out to lend a shovel or two. And blessedly, the rains held off (mostly) and the work got done. We rented a small compactor to finish off the paths, and Kenny made sure there were no dips that would collect water. I was excited to see how the planting would go!

Wednesday night was the Memorial for Ricky. Ben planned it with Kate and Sally, a potluck dinner and a memorial circle in the Sanctuary. I baked (as an excuse for not spending *all* day hauling gravel and stones), and tried to add prayers with every dessert and bun I made. I made some of Ricky's favourites, which was easy, because he *loved* chocolate.

Nora started a conversation the other day at dinner.

"You know, when Ricky died, all we focused on was the tragedy. I know it's really important to think about strategies that could have prevented his death, but we don't think about all the times our work helps." She had a point. Even in the short time since I'd been here, people had come and gone, but we forgot about the successes once people moved on.

"I wonder how many folks over the years have gone on to be successfully settled because of your work," Frank said.

"I bet I could actually figure it out from annual reports. We should pay attention to the numbers in some way. *Just Living's* been here six years, in one form or another, and it's made a difference." Bob was all about the numbers.

"We can't really have a 'Wall of Honour' or anything because of privacy," Nora said, thinking out loud.

And then Kenny had a really good idea.

"We should lay a stone, or light a candle on the labyrinth for each person we've helped," he said, and then Frank and I were off.

There were flat stones from the stream all around the pathways of the labyrinth, and tea lights were so inexpensive. We had a plan. And five minutes later, Bob came out of the office.

"12,465 nights offering help to men. That's about a 70% occupancy. And that doesn't include the nights Hugh or Beth or others like them stayed. Did we help them, too? I think so." Bob kept going.

"Sixty-six men have stayed more than two weeks and gone on to the community. Of those, 14 came back for a time but went back to the street. Eight who came here went back inside directly.

"Four have died, including Ricky." Nora said their names; clearly she remembered each one.

I was amazed, both that the numbers said so much, and so little. It was hard to think of any of the men I knew as "numbers," but great work had been done.

"Do you want me to figure out the cost per man?" Bob asked.

"No, it's not about the cost. It's about the men. Thanks, Bob for figuring that out. I'm going to make a note of those numbers."

Kate looked up.

"I wonder how many dogs and cats have been cared for?" she said.

"Horses, too," Tom added.

"I think I've kept track of baked goods we've donated," Cook said.

"Pounds of produce from the garden given to the transition house and food bank," Kenny said. "There's a log in the truck with 'approximate' numbers."

It felt good to be reminded of the goodness of the work.

"I wonder how many AVP minis we've hosted," Sohan said. He loved the workshops.

"And how many youth from the Friendship Centre have come through here," Al added.

"I have those numbers," Bob said. "We have to keep track for funding the crafts."

Nora created a plan.

"Okay, everyone, tomorrow is about remembering Ricky, and probably we will be thinking of the other men who've left, too, even though they didn't die here. But next week, when we say goodbye to Beth and Al and open thelabyrinth, we're going to have a big feast.

"Maybe next month we could host a Community Open House? I think we need to capture all this and celebrate. Bob, you and I will work on it. Who wants to help?" It's true, not many people appreciated working with Bob, so I volunteered.

"Nope. You are being celebrated. Maybe I'll call your Dad, though. He said there was a fellow at the church who liked doing digital art. Maybe he has an idea," she said.

"Claire does that kind of stuff, too," Tom added. I only flinched a bit. "We could call her. And I'll help," he said. I was impressed. Tom was trying harder since Ricky had died.

"I'll get the numbers for the animals, and I'll talk to the Riding Academy too," Kate said.

"Great," said Nora, standing up. "It's decided. We are going to celebrate! But first, it's time for me to get some sleep," she said, and she and Kate left holding hands, heading out the back door to their trailer. I watched Timex stalking them through the grass, about ten feet behind. Kate turned and whistled at him, and he pounced up to them. Maybe he wasn't an outdoor cat every night!

My heart grew a few sizes when I got a text from Ben that evening.

"Thanks for the note. I'm thinking about things, too. Miss you, but not ready yet," it said. I loved that word, yet.

Later that week, I cornered Frank at breakfast, and he agreed to a morning ride. He was spending more time with Buttercup, and she'd started to trust him; he wanted to try a short trail ride. We saddled our mounts and headed off, me on Thud.

After about a half an hour, we dismounted by the creek, and let the horses take their reins a bit; Frank said if Buttercup was a runner, we might as well know it now while I was around to help him get back to the barn. She wasn't, and we settled onto a large rock in the cool shade to talk.

"So, I'm trying to figure out what to do with my life, Frank. And whether to be ordained. How do I figure it out?" I asked. We sat for a bit.

"I presume you're asking me for feedback?" he asked. I smiled sheepishly, and nodded.

We talked for a while about the consequences of this work, of the skills I had, and the skills still to be worked on. We even bounced around some pros and cons of getting ordained. I thanked Frank because I felt a lot better, and we mounted the horses to head back to the barn.

On the way home Frank kept the conversation going, though.

"Why do you set the bar so high for yourself?" he asked. I think I must have scowled at him, because he laughed at me.

"What do you mean?" I asked.

"Well, you expect yourself to always behave 'in a proper way,' to know where your next steps are, and never to make mistakes, especially with your 'calling.' Do you think there are really advantages to not making mistakes?"

I was dumbfounded, and trying to make sense of his question. Of course there are advantages to always behaving 'properly!' I was an example for others, it showed I understood my calling, that I had paid attention in seminary, that I would be loved...and I started to tear up.

"I've never thought there are advantages to making mistakes. Like what?" I said.

"Well, you get to acknowledge your humanity, for one. That's a gift." I thought about that for a while. I remembered how I felt around Ben, I realized this WAS a gift from God.

"And I get to learn from my mistakes," I said. Frank nodded, and said,

"And everyone around you can admit to being human also, and making mistakes if you're fallible. I need you to be human; I wish I had known how important it was to be human when I was starting out." Wow.

"Besides," I said, "what about sermon topics? If I spend every week extolling my own virtues, who will listen to my preaching?" I started to laugh, and Frank did, too.

"You've given me tons to think about," I admitted.

"Don't think too much; feel it and notice it and be intuitive with it. Too much head space makes Mugwump boring!"

We talked a little about some opportunities I might apply for: trainings, courses, and stuff. I smiled as we rode on. The rest of the way back through the forest towards the barn I thought about all the possible advantages of making mistakes. I wrote about them for my final journal for Aaron.

That afternoon, I decided to seek out Al; we hadn't hung out for a while, and I missed our connection. We cut some wood together (okay, he cut and I stacked) in preparation for the weekly sweat on Friday, and after some time, we sat around the fire pit to just be together.

"So, what's bothering you?" he asked. I grinned...no secrets from this man.

"I guess I'm not really proud of my work here," I said quietly.

"Like what, that's any different from the rest of us? Somehow I can't imagine that what you've done is anything compared to the stuff I've done. What – some cookies get stolen?" Al was almost sneering, and I didn't like it. I thought about my "carnal relations" with Ben, and how I might have put his reputation at risk. And of course, the Remand Centre stuff, but I hesitated, not wanting to "get into it" with Al.

"I've done some stuff I'm not really proud of. It seemed okay at the time, but now I'm having regrets." We sat for a while, and I noticed that Al was becoming increasingly agitated.

"What is up with you?" I asked, and at first he tried to dodge the question.

"Nothing – what are you gonna do when you leave here?" I told him I was trying to figure it out. And turned it back to him.

"What about you? Really, I do want to know. What's up? Any plans?" After a few minutes, he spoke.

"I went in front of the Board last week, and asked for full parole to stay and work here. Nora said I should; she wants to put me in charge of the outside of the buildings.

"The parole board said I have to go home for a while first; 'separate my roles here.' They're crazy. It won't help. Being here, it's working for me." I didn't know what to say.

"Have you talked to Nora or Frank about it?" I asked. He snorted. Yes, he assured me, both were doing what they could. Even his Parole Officer wanted him to stay around here, not the Pemberton area. I was stumped, so decided to get philosophical.

"Wonder why Spirit might be calling you home…." I mused. He snorted.

"Not Spirit – Parole Board has nothin' to do with Spirit. I think they're playing with my head. I can't go back there – even for just a few months." As we spoke, Al was getting more and more agitated at the prospect. I just held the silence between us.

"Call me if there is anything I can do to help…ever…." I said. Later, I wished I'd made more of an effort to stay connected; I wonder if I might have been able to change things by staying more involved. This is such a dance, helping and empowering…choosing not to meddle, but being supportive. I don't know if I'll ever feel like I am "getting it right."

Wednesday night, we had the Memorial Circle for Ricky. It was too bad that his family didn't attend, because I think they would have liked it. We met in the Sanctuary with candles and stuffed animals all over, because Ricky loved stuffed animals. Kate brought a kitten Ricky'd looked after from birth. We sang a few songs and passed a beanie-baby as a talking piece and told stories about Ricky and how much he influenced us, even in the short time he was here. There was sadness, and lots of laughter too.

It was a good night together, and it ended with hot chocolate and baking – lots of chocolate treats. They really were Ricky's favourite.

Rest in Peace, dear Ricky. You taught me so much.
I hope you don't hurt any more.

Then Saturday – it was amazing. By 3 o'clock, the labyrinth was nearing completion; there were five people from the church there helping, including Scott and Carol, and Dad had brought a truck-load of donated plants from a nursery in Mission and some from Mission Institution where there was a greenhouse. Kenny had arranged for those.

Kenny was beaming; it was turning out better than anyone could have imagined...and so were the relationships between the parishioners and the men. Al even surprised Kenny with a few unsplit logs, carefully chosen and cut to serve as seats. Kenny put them in the "bubbles," and sighed. He said it looked even better than he'd hoped. It was a happy time, and we washed our hands and cleaned up, happy to eat quickly so that Kenny could water things in before we walked it together for the first time.

There would be an official opening with media and everything next week, but this evening was ours. Kenny, Tom and I lit 82 candles on the rocks around the labyrinth, with four larger ones taking a special place, one in each of the four directions. Hugh and his wife Emma started us off in a good way, with a prayer, and there were amazing songs and drums shared that night, the men surrounding the labyrinth in the four directions. Hugh shared some Teachings with us, and I know Dad was humbled by them, because he told me so later.

Nora remembered each of the men who'd died, including Ricky. She talked a little about each of them. One of them had been released from the prison on compassionate grounds, and had come to the house to die; he'd had cancer, and had never dreamed he'd see fields and horses again. She reminded us that he'd lived in the Great Room for two weeks, and they'd cared for him around the clock.

Then she reminded us that each of the other candles represented someone who'd stayed more than two weeks at the house. We'd decided to honour even the men who went back inside; it wasn't about "success," but about "service." And we added an even dozen for non-inmates like me who'd stayed. We had to guess at that number, but I think we were about right. 82 candles makes a lot of light, and it was beautiful.

Later, after the folks from Vancouver left, we gathered around the fire in the Sacred Grounds, and drank hot chocolate, and sang. The men offered drums and songs, and some of us offered hymns, and it was a glorious night.

I felt sated as I drifted off to sleep. It was short-lived, because I woke from dreams around 2:00 o'clock, and spent the rest of the night "Spirit-tossing" in my bed. I thought "figuring out my meaningful life" would be accompanied by applause, or at least angels' chorus, but really the clarity came from a simple "why not?" and a feeling of it being right.

I resolved that I was going to keep doing this work…not because of my great gifts, or a "defined calling," but because I had so much more to learn about restorative justice, helping those hurt by crime, prison justice, and about myself. That, and I couldn't imagine taking any other path. It wasn't like I'd decided, but more like I gave in to it. It felt inevitable. And, I'd been reminded by Frank, I could change my path at any time.

I'd applied with Jagdeep to take mediation/facilitation training over the summer months as I waited for graduation. I would think more about ordination while doing that, I decided. There's a local agency that I hoped would accept me as a volunteer, and I was planning to explore training in chaplaincy and trauma and resiliency…I hoped the Bishop would give guidance. And I knew I could call Peggy, the chaplain, any time. Aaron might have some ideas. Even Ben. And Nora. Hugh.

I asked for a final circle with Hugh. It's planned for next week, and I feel really indulged when I think about all those people coming to help me.

Dear Creator,

You must have had something special in mind when You sent me to this amazing place. Can I live up to Your expectations?

Of course, I know maybe You want me to fail, and learn, and be humble. There's value in that, too.

Amen

CHAPTER 41
ENDINGS AND BEGINNINGS

Dear Holy One,

You created me. This place. Our coming together.

Please let me be enough. Let this be enough. Let me experience enough, learn enough, serve enough.

I want to live a meaningful life.

I hope, with Your help, to know when it's meaningful enough. Or that it even matters.

I'm on a cusp, endings and beginnings and all that. I'm glad You'll be with me for the next little bit while I figure out my path on this rocky field....

Don't leave me, or drag me, or push me, 'kay? Just come with me....

See? I have learned something. I don't have to fix everything for everybody. And I don't need You to either.

As always, Thanks.

Monday of my final week began as every Monday did at *Just Living*-- morning circle. Everyone turned out, even Frank. The room crackled, people shuffled, murmuring to each other. Al and I would be leaving; neither of us expected to be in another Monday morning circle.

Nora suggested we focus on how the atmosphere had changed since Ricky's suicide. The investigation wasn't "over," but our part was – unless there were recommendations to implement later. According to Nora "later" might mean years, or maybe never. Things were slowly returning to "normal," or as normal as they would ever be. I was reminded that "this, too, shall pass," even though I couldn't have imagined it a couple of weeks ago.

There were lots of things happening, but nothing because of official channels. Dad had started a monthly column in the paper (Religion Section), and his first was about *Just Living*. He wrote about the support from his parishioners, and how much he had learned about himself and grace from volunteering in prison. Nora thought it was helping, and I promised to pass that on to Dad and his congregation.

Nora and Frank talked about my last week. They offered a week of retreat, to spend however I wanted, in writing, and contemplative work. I wanted to spend part of each day baking for the "goodbye" celebration for Al and me on Saturday, but mostly I was free to do what I wanted. And, Cook reminded me, there were lots of treats already in the freezer, accumulating during my time there, so I didn't have to bake if I didn't want to. I did.

Frank and Hugh offered to be Spiritual Directors, and Peggy also offered her counsel. If I wanted to work, I was to steer clear of the office and garden (too much activity for contemplation), and it was suggested I could paint the exterior of the stables on the pasture side "if I felt so led." Meaning they were hoping I would. After the storm some boards were replaced and were still raw lumber. The whole thing needed of a coat of paint.

A whole week! No chores, no "shoulds," no obligations but to listen to Spirit and discern my next steps. I was still waiting to hear about my application for mediation training. I was still considering ordination in the fall, but I wasn't really sure of my future in the Church. I was excited, and a bit anxious. I knew that I was a great one for inviting stuff into my life and then having to deal with it. And I still hadn't heard from Ben. Wasn't sure if I would.

Hugh, Frank and I met and decided that I would spend most early mornings up with first light in silence, maybe some mornings with the animals welcoming the day. I did want to paint the stables, and Cook had arranged for me to have my meals in the kitchen rather than the dining room when I wanted.

"It's not that we think you should be silent, Beth. You are welcome to be as loud or quiet as you wish. We want you to be totally focused on yourself, your future, noticing both what you've learned, and how to integrate it into your life. Your calling. We can support you any way you wish," Hugh assured me.

I agreed to check in with one of them each day, after lunch, to touch base and use them as a sounding board if I needed one. I felt so spoiled, indulged!

Anyhow, my head was bursting with new ideas, thinking about how I would spend my last four days in this space, and feeling sad at the thought of leaving. Which is what makes the living so rich, right? It isn't enthusiastic living if you wouldn't miss it when it's gone. Maybe faith is trusting that the next thing will be as rich and enthusiastic.

It was clear that while four days in retreat sounded like a pure indulgence of time, it wasn't enough time to do everything I wanted (which was interesting...how much time would be enough?) I planned a list of possibilities. Like recording what I've learned, including final journals and papers for Aaron. Wondering how I could take these teachings into the world (or rather, what *did* I want to be when I grow up?) I wanted to bake a few squares for Al's goodbye gathering. Maybe paint the stables, to memorialize Ricky. And think about Ben while I painted. Do I approach him again? Or let go? And in it all, do I want to continue with prison ministry? AVP? Victims' work?

Of course, of those things, one was already pretty clear (yes, justice ministry was what I wanted to explore, and what I'd decided to call it. Or maybe trauma ministry). Two activities were mostly finished (documenting what I had learned and the baking), and of the remaining four, I hoped to be able to do something other than thinking about Ben.

The next morning, I decided to assess the painting job. There was plenty of red and brown paint, brushes, ladders and rags in the shed. I even found some dribs and drabs of leftover paint from the outside of other buildings that I thought might be useful. I got right at it.

I started with a base coat of the brown, to see what inspired me. I was thinking of Ricky the whole time, and what I had learned about abuse, and pain and healing. I vividly remembered painting the fence together, and all those bugs he had lovingly removed from the fence with his blade of grass; I spent some time gently brushing spider webs and beetles from the stable wall. I was glad this was a refreshing coat; I would be able to brush the lower walls and quickly paint them without worrying too much about "perfection," or bugs! I thought I would be able to paint the walls in a couple of days, working a few hours a day, which would leave lots of time for writing and just being. Someone might even help me.

By evening I was returning to the quiet rhythm of retreat; I was glad for the ease with which I stepped into this time, this gift. I was ready to sleep by 9:00 o'clock that evening, almost plump with anticipation of the coming three days. I felt bliss, and as I drifted off realized I really hadn't spent much time thinking about Ben; Ricky and the other prisoners had filled my heart. I slept like a log and my dreams were light, and restful.

The next two mornings I awoke about the same time as Cook, and headed into the pasture, where the horses were spending most of their time now. We watched the sunrise together, greeting the light while I sipped on tea from a thermos that Cook made. Once, on the second morning, I even hopped on Tex's bare back and we strolled around the pasture. He seemed amused by me, and he knew I was only astride him because he was cooperating. He didn't even have reins on, and a rope through his halter...well, I wasn't that good a rider. I had definitely improved over the last few months, though!

It was amazing, letting him control our pace and direction. I thought about being led by Spirit, and thought about how "the reins" are an illusion...where Spirit wants to take me, I hope I will have the courage to hold on, to be present, to feel the pulse of Spirit up next to me, breathing, sweating beneath me. I draped my body on Tex's back, and laid my head on his neck, rubbing his fur, smelling the dust in his coat and the sweetness of the grass. A few minutes later, he had taken me to the farthest corner of the pasture, and we stopped for a time with Buttercup, who was grazing nearby. I wondered if he would dump me, and decided it would be okay to walk home if he did.

A few minutes later we headed off again, and before long were outside the Sacred Grounds. I dismounted, scratched his forelock and cheeks, and took the rope from his halter. He nickered as I walked away. I decided to start the fire; it was Tuesday and I knew the men would be doing a sweat with Al, as a part of his preparation for leaving. Hugh, Ben, Tom, Paul and some others were coming to support him. I hoped I wasn't misstepping by wanting to be involved and helpful; I started the fire, placing the Grandmothers and Grandfathers in the middle, chopped some wood and said some prayers for each of the men.

Soon Frank was approaching the grounds, and I slipped away. As I left, I heard Frank call my name, and when I turned, he called "Thank you, Sister." I waved, and headed back towards the stables for my thermos, wiping gentle tears from my cheeks as I went. How would I face leaving these men, who had come to mean so much to me? Could I? I headed to the kitchen for oatmeal (prepared with apples and cinnamon, my favourite, I noticed).

When I was done painting on Tuesday, Cook suggested I head out to the fire for some soup; the men were still gathered following their sweat. As I approached I was stunned to see that Al had cut off his braid.

"I am going back to using the name Martin, Little Sister, which my Auntie called me," he told me. He, too, was preparing for his move home. I stayed a while by the fire, spending most of my time with them in silence, just reveling in their acceptance of me. I realized before too long that all of my simple needs were being met by the men before I even identified them: a mug of soup, a mug of water, refilled often, a stump to rest on, quiet, and some bread. I started to gently weep, but these were tears of feeling overwhelmed with love-in-the-moment. Corny, eh? I hugged each one and left, thinking they might want to spend some more time alone with "Martin." I wanted to head to my room to write about life and this.

I wasn't clearer in my head about what would happen with Ben and me, but I had decided a couple of things. I was really happy with my life, blessed, really. I was finding my path, and I wanted to believe I would be fine either alone or with a partner. I didn't want to become someone who couldn't survive without a "significant other" beside me, but companionship along the way would be okay, too. Not to mention the toe-curling love-making.

The rest of the week was similar -- an early morning ride, morning and early afternoons painting. I was glad the hot summer sun had yet to arrive (if it would at all? Did it get hot up here, beside the mountains?) Often, in the evenings when everything was quiet, I would bake for an hour or two in the kitchen. I loved kneading dough, rolling pastry, tasting the tart filling as I prepared it. I was baking love and good wishes into each bit of yummy. Cook and I visited on the back porch after the sun was down.

By the lunch the third day I needed a rest from painting; my muscles were tired from reaching and stretching, and besides, I was almost done. I asked to borrow Cook's vehicle, and without checking with anyone, I headed to Ben's friend's cabin. Yes, without permission. I spent the afternoon swimming in the hot pool, and snoozing curled up with my head on my jacket on the porch. I headed back to the Lodge in the early evening, rested and rejuvenated from my walk, swim, and time alone thinking about Ben. I let go.

My practicum writing was mostly complete; I had two more days to spend reading it through and deciding my "next steps." I also wanted to paint a commemoration to Ricky on the side of the barn, not too large, something humorous and light to remember him. I thought maybe a ladybug on a piece of grass; I understood from Al – back when he was Al -- that ladybugs were about family, and home, and life, and hope. He told me they could consume fear, encourage adventure. All bugs that passed through a larval stage were about transformation and rebirth. And I liked ladybugs. I wasn't sure if Ricky did especially, but I didn't know that much about his likes and dislikes. I hadn't spent much time getting to know him, or asking him questions. I wasn't very proud of myself for that, but I thought ladybugs would capture Ricky.

I hadn't asked Hugh for direction…I would do that in the morning, I decided as I drifted off to sleep Thursday night. I felt satiated, so I reminded myself to integrate retreats into my life…a time to wrestle with the truths of my past and some time to consider what Spirit was telling me about my future.

Friday morning I asked Martin (I *would* get used to that), Kenny, Cook, Hugh and Frank to join me that night in circle. I had a few questions I wanted to ask them. I finished the ladybug.

Entering the dining room for supper, I heard everyone talking about it, laughing. I was so pleased! They understood! But most of the laughter was about my artistic (in)ability . Ah well -- I hadn't thought to ask for help. Hmmm….

They were calling it an alien bug…and I had to laugh with them. I was leaving proof that I never understood perspective in art class. I gave them permission to paint over it, if they chose, and they were appalled. I realized that I was in part memorializing myself, too. That felt weird, and I spent some time thinking about the work that I do, and hoped to do, and leaving it behind. It was strange to think about it that way. Letting go…first Ben, then this place.

That evening I was honoured to be gathered around the fire. We stumbled over there, coffee and tea in tin cups, and spent some time around in silence, just gazing into the flames. When it was the right time, Hugh invited me share why I had asked them to come. What I wanted from them could be summed up easily.

I told them I had two questions. The first pass of the talking piece I asked for any feedback they had to give me…I felt so vulnerable but I wanted to grow from serious criticism. The second round I asked them for advice about my life, and next steps I should consider.

I learned more about myself that night than I expected. Their insightful comments were wonderful; first they affirmed me, my humility, spiritually congruent walk and obvious compassion. Then each of them chose one thing to challenge me to work on.

"Learn more about trauma recovery," Frank said, "and don't be afraid to look backwards in your own life as you are learning. Own your stuff. Ask yourself the tough questions."

"Don't be afraid to show some weaknesses, Little Sister," Martin said.

"Cut loose, have some fun (he wagged his eyebrows), and don't feel guilty," Kenny shared.

"Focus on listening harder, especially when you are excited about something," Hugh said.

"Show them, don't tell them," Cook said. "Live like you bake." And I knew that with the bit of sting attached to each comment (mine, not theirs), I had plenty to think about. Hugh took the talking piece and reminded me how I had invited the feedback, and what courage that took.

"We're all learning and growing all the time, if we're paying attention, Beth," he said. "Keep asking for input, but don't be afraid to sift it for nuggets and throw the rest away. We are all becoming." I smiled, and noticed the sting was gone. I also knew they were all nuggets, speaking each to a weakness I had, something I could work on. Was working on.

The advice? Well, that was simple, too.

"Follow your passion," from Frank.

"Never stop loving us," from Martin.

"Keep something green near you, always, for strength," Kenny shared.

"Be curious, not just with questions, but also in your walk," from Hugh.

"In the words of the angels: Fear not!" from Cook.

Then Frank said he had asked each of them to write out a question to send with me on my journey. They read them, and collected them for me.

After that round, I spent some time thanking them (and crying), letting each of them know how they had touched my heart, my life, how I would be taking a little bit of each of them with me. I gifted them with some polished stones I had brought with me. I knew as we finished, and Ben joined us, and that this circle time was my way of beginning to leave-take.

Ben smiled across the circle, and my heart skipped a beat. Until he left with Frank. I stood in the crook of Cook's arm, and began to understand the depths of what I would feel when I drove down the driveway on Sunday night.

What a gift this time and place had been. And I had one more day to just be with everyone and "deal with icing the cake," I thought as I headed upstairs to sleep. And read the questions. And I heard them as a prayer.

Who do you want to surround yourself with?

How will you know when you are living your calling?

What values and principles are not negotiable?

What does "not negotiable" mean?

What does "creating home" mean for you?

What does it feel like to really listen, and serve?

What would you do if you knew you couldn't "fail?"

What are you willing to let go of to move forward without cumber?

There would be a lifetime to consider those questions. What a gift.

CHAPTER 42
UNPACKING LOVE

Ben and Frank left *Just Living* after the evening's festivities, and headed for the pub. Ben had been trying to ignore the disquiet in his bones, to deny the moral ambiguity that had been guiding him for the past two months.

He loved Beth. At least, he thought he might.

He couldn't get his heart around what she'd done as a teenager.

He had done horrible things when he was a teenager. And he swore he'd forgiven himself.

Except had he? Really?

They sat in the booth and took the menus the waiter gave them.

"What should I know about the beer?" Ben asked Frank, deferring to him on all things "wordly."

"It's good. You'll like the Scotch Ale," Frank said, not wanting to spend time on niceties. He ordered a couple of sleeves, and a plate of fries, and the waiter left.

"So, why are we here?" Frank asked. "Not that I mind hanging out with you, but, well, you don't really hang out, do you?" he asked. Ben looked at him, glad the question was rhetorical. He thought.

"Well, I think I've messed up. At least, I don't really know if I have, but I want to figure out my one next step. A good one," Ben shared. Frank smiled.

"You think? What's going on?" Frank didn't let Ben, or anyone else, duck. Ben was glad when the beer arrived, and he could look at it. Swirl it. He took a sip and smiled.

"Yeah. It's good." He took a breath. "So, you know Beth and I were seeing each other," he began, and then really didn't know where to go next.

"I knew. Until about Easter, I think. Nora says you've been around less and less," Frank continued for him. "Figured something happened. What was it?" Frank asked, grinning a little. He was going to make Ben tell him everything, even though he'd figured out most of it.

"Well, we had a great time together at Easter, when her brother had his baby. Got to spend lots of time with each other, if you know what I mean." Ben squirmed.

"I don't need details on your relations, if that's what you're asking." Frank smiled.

"Well, then I found out something, and it threw me for a loop and I think I reacted...well...bad...and I can't get past it. Or maybe don't want to. I can't figure it out." The words flew out of Ben's mouth. Frank chuckled in response.

"Okay...maybe you better tell it to me a bit at a time. And I'm wondering -- am I your coach, your counsellor, or your friend right now?" Frank was used to juggling roles, but he'd learned the hard way that he'd better be clear about how he was supposed to show up. More than once he'd had the wrong hat on when with friends, and mistakes had been made.

"I think right now I need a coach," Ben answered, "but a coach who knows my past," he clarified. "And Beth knows all about me, what I did." He took a sip of his beer, looking up for the waiter, hoping for the snacks.

"So, I told her about me, and how messed up I'd been as a child, and why. She took it really good, and listened, and I couldn't have asked for more. She's been patient, and clear with me. That's not the problem." Ben just kept going.

"Then, at Easter, she told me 'her secret.' That's how she described it. And I can't get over it; I never thought I'd know anyone who'd done what she did, and for so many years I've preached against it. I should have known when she questioned my guys inside raising money for the Pro-Lifers," he finished, looking in his beer.

"It's okay, Ben. She told me she'd had an abortion when she was in high school. Her dad influenced her, right?" Frank asked.

"Well, he did, but she was really clear that she consented. She's taking responsibility for making that decision," he said, his voice trailing off. "And I just keep seeing a chubby baby being sucked down...." Ben looked up. "It's awful, Frank. Too many images from the Church. Why can't I get over this? I forgive guys inside all the time what they've done."

"So, what do you want to unpack about this tonight?" Frank asked, as the food arrived. Ben tucked in to the fries, staring out the window.

"I guess I want to figure out why I'm so frozen."

"So, when you say frozen, what do you mean?"

"Well, I can't call her. But I really want to. I don't know what to say. I acted pretty harshly, but I don't know if I've really changed my mind. My reaction today would probably be the same," Ben clarified.

"And so, what *do* you want to change?" More thinking. More fries.

"I think I get now how sheltered my life is. And I'm starting to see how crazy it is that I was so judgmental about things people did. Divorce. Birth control. Affairs. And abortions. It was just all so clear when I was in the monastery, even before that, at school." Frank let the silence grow. Ben looked up.

"I think I'm starting to see how naive I was before. Bunch of old -- and young --self-righteous men making judgment on people over actions they'd never even consider. So much harshness towards regular people!" Ben took another mouthful of beer. "Not that they -- we -- were perfect. No one preached about pedophilia, though. Lots of self-righteousness about homosexuality, even though I knew Brothers who struggled with that.

"I just…I'm ashamed I acted with so much judgment. Dished out so much shame," he finished.

"Okay…let me take a minute. Since you've left the monastery — and I do remember why — you're realizing your church can be pretty harsh on women and people who struggle because they're different. I can't believe you're just thinking about this now," Frank said. "Why is it different with Beth?" Frank caught the waiter's eye and ordered more beer.

"Well, it's not like I'm ashamed to admit I'm wrong. I do that all the time. It's just…I think I'm afraid I'll keep showing what an idiot I am. And besides, I…well, I still think abortion is wrong." Ben sighed. Took a sip, and looked at Frank.

"But I really miss her. I can't stop thinking about her. I think I've forgotten and then one of the inmates will ask about her, or I'll see her across the fields, and my heart does this thing. It's weird. I didn't even put it together why at first. It freaks me out." They sat for a bit, Frank gently asking if there was more.

"Take your time. That's clearly some of it, but…."

"I think I'm afraid of caring that much. It's too powerful," Ben finished. "It would just be simpler to stay single."

"Ah. Penance. Simplicity. Chastity. Poverty. The comfort zone," Frank finished, smiling. "What would it take for you to step beyond it? Really lust after something? Or someone?" Ben felt electricity in his veins.

"Lust? I care about her!" he denied.

"Yes, and I've seen you look at her. She's young. Vibrant. Funny, even. Why not lust?"

"It's not proper for a priest!" Ben's voice squeezed out of his throat, his pitch rising.

"So…you want to be her priest? Because I don't think that's what she's looking for," Frank finished. "I think she likes you. Lusts after you, even." Ben looked shocked. "Have you ever seen how Nora looks at Kate when

Kate isn't looking back? That's how Beth looks at you. What do you want to do about it?" Ben looked genuinely confused.

"I don't know. I really don't. I don't think I want to do anything -- I just want to figure out how to be less stupid in the world. For now. What if I keep making mistakes, judging people? Besides, she's had other relationships, been married, who knows what else she's done!"

"And you're afraid of…?" Frank let his voice trail off.

"What if I'm boring? I think I'm worried that I won't keep up," Ben said. "I don't know how to do 'relationships.' I keep messing up. I think I want to live a little, get some experience before I go there again," Ben finished.

"Oh. That sounds like fun. Go mess up with other people so you don't feel stupid." It was Ben's turn to grin.

"Well, when you put it that way."

"No, YOU put it that way. A relationship is where you might make a mistake, or make a judgment and have to talk about it. But not having a relationship is better? Ben. You know how to have hard conversations. What's stopping you from having this one?" Ben thought about it as he took another mouthful of beer. Frank was right; he did like the Scotch Ale.

"Well, I don't know what to say to her. I'm sorry I judged her, but I don't ever want to have to consider an abortion. I don't know if she'll want another one. Or me, for that matter, and I'm just not ready." He looked deflated as he sat back in the booth.

"I don't think that's it. I know I'm not ready to go back to her, but really this is about figuring out what I believe now, without some doctrine telling me," he said. He played with the last fry, then was embarrassed when he saw he was touching the last without offering it to Frank. Frank waved it off.

"Really? You are shying away from figuring it out why? Because it might be hard? Because, really, I have to tell you, it will be hard," he said. "The hardest thing you've ever done. Would it be worth it?" Frank swirled the last of his beer in his glass. "I know you still go to the Abbey. Attend with the Quakers. Work with all the men, of every denomination.

Religion, really. But you still label yourself Catholic." Ben thought about that for a while.

"Oh my God. Literally. I have to give up the teachings of the Catholic Church. Or some of them. But I already have! I don't agree with them!" Ben looked up, his voice racing. "I might believe in a woman's right to choose. I wouldn't make that choice, but I think they have a right to. Contraception isn't evil. Especially in countries where maternal health is risky. Lots of people divorce -- I don't care! As long as they've tried to stay married." Ben was clearly on a roll, and Frank grinned.

"And what about calling yourself 'Catholic?' Is that a problem?"

"Yeah. I think it might be. For me, not CSC. I have to talk to Peggy."

"And what about Beth?" Frank prodded.

"Not yet. One thing at a time. Really. Maybe later."

"If she's still around," Frank said, watching Ben's eyes grow.

"Yeah, I guess that's a risk," he said. And Frank prodded just a little more.

"And then it's not your decision to make, which is easier," Frank teased. As only a coach could.

A few minutes later they hugged at the door, and Ben was deep in thought as they headed to their homes. He had to get home to send a card to Beth. This weekend was the Feast, and he didn't think he could attend.

He stayed up all night figuring out the words he needed to say to make that okay.

CHAPTER 43
HEN PARTY

Dear God,

Thank you for this place, for my life, for the questions. I feel much closer to my "meaningful life" – or maybe I'm already living it.

Either way, I am glad that I fit my life now. I think I get what people are feeling when they say "authenticity." And the possibilities feel so...right.

And I hold YOU accountable for that.

Thank you. Thank you. Thank you.

I am living fully alive, loving wastefully, and being true to all You are in me...please continue to support me as I discern and follow Your will.

If only I could figure out this thing with Ben. He tells me he's not done, but he's barely looked at me all week.

And when he does, I blush and can't look back. I think I want this more than he does, and that makes me just want it to be over, too.

In the end, though, all will be well. Amen

Saturday Martin and I were banished from the kitchen, and Cook fed everyone lunch outside near the labyrinth. He was preparing for the feast the next day; we were expecting 15 visitors, and I figured out somewhat sheepishly that everyone was pulling out all the stops. I had to remind myself it wasn't all about me, and try to find some comfortableness in letting others show appreciation, so I headed into town for a quick trip to buy some small gifts.

The labyrinth was complete so Kenny and I spent some time sitting beside it; we hadn't walked it since the day we'd finished it. We were waiting for it to be "officially opened" at the feast.

"What do you think of it, now that it's done?" I asked him.

"It's better than I imagined," he sighed.

"I bet you said that about sex the first time, too," I teased.

"I say that about sex every time," Kenny quipped back. "Even if it's only sorta true." I smiled. Later I visited the strays and talked to Kate. She asked me some pointed questions.

"How will you know when you've arrived where you want to be?

"How will you recognize good challenges?

"How will you be different at your new work than you were when you came here?" Kate always has really good questions. *More prayers.*

And, of course, I went to the barn to check up on Buttercup (who was out in the pasture, and just fine), and Topaz (my real reason for going to the barn), who ran to me when she heard me coming (how *would* I do without her?). I packed, and sent my final journals. I hung out with Cook, and told him to stuff his banishment; I wanted to help. And mostly be with him. The day was perfect, just like all the previous ones had been. All of them.

Early that evening, I attended a special open sweat with some youth from town, including Anne. It was good to see her! I was grateful to Spirit for my lessons and my new friendships. I felt reborn as I left the sweat lodge, ready to face life shiny-penny new.

After a light dinner I headed to my room, and then remembered that I wanted to touch base with Nora, Kate and Sally; I loved my women-friends, and hadn't really told them how much I appreciated them. On my bed was a note from Nora inviting me to a "Midnight Hen Party" in the Great Room. We were to rendezvous at 11:30, and the men had been warned off. I grinned.

Under her note was a card from Ben; Nora must have delivered it with her note. Excited, I opened it and devoured his words.

"Dear Beth,

Tomorrow, you get to celebrate! Finishing your time at *Just Living* and your practicum is certainly a great reason to get all festive, and I am honoured to be invited. I am glad that Aaron asked me to help welcome and support you.

We haven't talked about "us" for a while, and I want you to know that isn't because I haven't been thinking about it. I'm still thinking. Because of this, I want you know I'll be at the prison tomorrow instead of at *Just Living*. It's because I still have to figure some stuff out.

I know I was thrown for a loop after Easter. I admit now I thought I'd never known anyone who'd done what you did, made the hard choices. Abortion was something I'd warned and preached against for so long that I couldn't imagine it's a real thing that touches people I know.

I know you'd be better off with someone more like you, someone who hasn't lived closeted away in a monastery. And I don't know what I want yet, so I get it if you have moved on.

Anyways, I want you to know I have been touched by our time together. If you follow through with ordination, Aaron will let me know, I am sure, and I will hold you in the Light during that time.

Whatever you choose to do next, Beth, I have no doubt it will be with honour, and integrity and compassion. Those who get to work with you will be very very lucky.

Deep peace, your Friend,
Ben"

Well, that wasn't what I had hoped for, but at least it was something. Not that I'd figured out what.

I reminded myself that no matter how much I'd hoped for something different, I wasn't going to wait for Ben. Really. I had a life to figure out.

I decided I needed a nap, in anticipation of a late night with "the Hens." As I drifted toward sleep, I was glad I'd decided to stay at Mom and Dad's for a bit until things were settled with the mediation training. I resolved to contact the organization soon, and see if I could move up my start date. I had a tentative agreement to shadow Jag and get on-site training; maybe I'd impressed him at the Victims Awareness thing. Or maybe Nora had given me a glowing reference. Anyhow, now that I was ready to face the world, I was anxious to begin! Veronica said I could stay with her while I was there.

At 11:00 o'clock I woke with a start. Still lots of time! I got up and splashed water on my face, grabbed my fleece poncho and pillow and headed for the back stairs. As my foot hit the top stair, I heard Cook.

"I know what you guys are up to. If any of my food for tomorrow goes missing, I will be disappointed." I turned and saw him grinning from ear to ear, sitting in "his" chair. He stood, and I turned into his embrace. We hugged for a long time, with his chin resting on my head.

"You know I've always got your back, eh Mugwump? Always. And you know where to find me if you need ANYTHING. EVER." I nodded. After a few moments of being together, he declared, "Okay, off with you. And remember what I said about the food for tomorrow. No nibbling!" I promised, and headed for the stairs.

The Great Room had been transformed. The windows were covered with blankets, and the doors were all closed. Candlelight from the bookshelves enveloped the room. A fire was burning, and a whole bunch of blankets and pillows were strewn about the floor. Topaz was sleeping in the middle of all of it, and I could hear laughter coming from the kitchen.

As I tiptoed in, I saw the four women giggling at the fridge – Veronica had come too! I quickly realized why they were laughing; Cook had padlocked the door, but Sally was in the process of using bolt cutters on it. She had a shiny lock, exactly the same, on the counter beside her.

"We should be careful not to take stuff Cook has prepared for the feast...." I said, thinking of my promise.

"Humph...he always makes too much. And he knows we're doing this so I'm sure he made extra. Live a little, will you?" Sally said. I grinned and joined them, quickly getting into the spirit of the night.

When she opened the fridge, there was a tray prepared for us with a note. He might not know how, but he didn't doubt our ability for a second. In a few minutes we had added to the tray, and it was packed with "food with no redeeming features": hot chocolate, some Nanaimo bars, date squares, chips, and fruit and cheese – our one concession to nutrition. "But only because it tastes good," Nora added. Sally re-locked the fridge to confuse Cook in the morning.

"None of them would dream we know how to pick a lock, so let's keep them guessing...don't tell 'em what we did. They'll all be wondering which one of us they have to watch!" Nora laughed as she stashed the ruined lock and bolt cutters under the shelves in her office.

We spent the evening watching videos of Johnny Depp, gushing over him (*Chocolat,* how appropriate), and feasting. We played this truth-telling game and I learned way more about those women my last night than I could have imagined. They had led such interesting, amazing lives! I was beginning to get that "everyone has a story" is a cliché for a reason. At about 2:00 o'clock we all went swimming in the pond, off the dock... and it was FREEZING! We didn't skinny dip in deference to the men on site, but agreed we would put that on our bucket list – somewhere else, of course.

By 3:00 o'clock we were back in the kitchen, designing artwork with our leftovers to greet Cook in the morning...kind of a tribute to his work. It was a giant heart, complete with an arrow constructed out of crumbs, chips, dip, marshmallows and some leftover spaghetti Sally found. We coloured it red by sprinkling paprika all over it, and giggling, we headed for bed. We all slept flaked out in the Common Room, and as I drifted to sleep, I couldn't imagine a better way to spend my last night here. Tomorrow night it was back to Mom and Dad's, after all....

I woke up the next morning early, and crept from the room for my last sunrise at *Just Living*. I picked up a warm toasty kitten and we headed outside to greet the day with my equine buddies. I was feeling two-hearted, totally blissed and heart-wrenchingly bereft in the same moment.

The day passed quickly; meals shared, last minute chores for the feast, and last minute packing. I did take time after lunch to walk the labyrinth with Kenny; he had asked me to do that with him, before I left. It would be blessed and opened officially that evening, but he wanted us to be alone the first time it was walked today. It was amazing, a practice that could be very important.

It was Sunday morning, so I snuck into town and went to service at the little white Anglican Church. It was nice being mostly anonymous; I had met the Rector a couple of times at functions around town, but not many of the parishioners knew me. I worshiped, and darted out before coffee hour. Such freedom!

I wanted to get somewhere quiet to call Glenn. He'd sent me an email overnight that I'd picked up on my phone asking me to call. I knew he'd had a week with the boys over Spring Break. The UBC students had gone up. Maybe that was the news.

I took myself for pie and tea after service, and pulled out my cell phone. I knew I only had a window of about fifteen minutes between his services to talk. And boy, did we dump a ton of info on each other in that 15 minutes.

Seems the UBC students' visit was EXACTLY what he wanted to talk about. A team of two law students (with one grad student along, who was an actual lawyer AND Aboriginal), Julie and three other poli-sci students had stayed for five days. They'd met with Band leaders, travelled with a group of young adults into the back country for some fishing, and collected some herbs with Elders.

They were stoked, and so was Glenn. He was so excited to be making a difference, being the person to bring people together.

"It's the least we Anglicans can do, Beth, after all the harm caused in this area," he'd said. Yes, it was true, we could mostly blame the Catholics, but the Anglicans had had residential schools, too.

"The poli-sci students are going to connect with a couple of social media groups to try to raise money to fund the legal challenge, and the law students are working basically as lackey researchers for the legal team arguing the case." Glenn was happy. And excited.

"Beth, it's hard to explain. Really. I feel like I'm doing things that matter. What's happening might actually make a difference. It's so cool. Anyway, they are planning a protest for the summer, after exams are done. The students are going to come for a sit-in on the land, and they're hoping to ignite the media. It's exciting. And Julie's coming back in two weeks to meet with the Elders again, and she's going to bring the boys up. They had such fun the last time they were here."

Hmmm. I wasn't sure about this. Did Julie have designs on my friend? Donna'd been drunk the last time she'd shown up at Glenn's, and he'd turned her away. He told me he'd told her to come back when she was sober, that he'd wait.

Maybe he was done waiting. Something else in common. Anyhow, we talked for a bit about what I was planning to do next (Victim-Offender training, and then…who knows?), and that I'm talking to the Bishop next week. I told him I was really keen to learn more about trauma and resiliency, maybe do some chaplaincy training. We shall see.

We said a quick goodbye and I promised to call once I'd talked to the Bishop. He wants me to come up in June and visit. I hope I can. He's glad I'm tentatively planning a fall ordination; he promised to come down for it, even if he had to leave his churches in lay readers' hands.

I felt lucky. Maybe I can get him into AVP when he's down. Maybe I could drive the boys up some time this summer. In no time, I was heading back up to *Just Living*, maybe for the last time. At least, the last time for a while.

CHAPTER 44
GOODBYES

Dear God,

Cruising the interwebs last week, I came upon this quote, and it resonated with me.

> *"There's a trick to the 'graceful exit.' It begins with the vision to recognize when a job, a life stage, or a relationship is over -- and let it go. It means leaving what's over without denying its validity or its past importance to our lives. It involves a sense of future, a belief that every exit line is an entry, that we are moving up, rather than out."*
>
> *– Ellen Goodman*

Help me be graceful today, okay? And not too teary....

Your very humble servant, who prays a lot now,

Beth

Around 3:00 o'clock that afternoon, car doors started to slam and I knew our last feast together had begun. I had spent the time after lunch packing my last boxes, and submitting my final documents to Aaron. I really felt "done," and taking stock of everything I'd learned during this practicum left me breathless with gratitude. But alas, no time for sitting around! There was work to be done!

The dining hall was a-bustle with activity, and Martin and Tom were preparing the Sacred Grounds. Frank and Nora were arranging the Sanctuary for a closing circle, and Kenny was fussing over the labyrinth. I swear it's the truth; he was on his hands and knees with nail scissors, trimming the plants! Even the stables had been cleaned, and the horses groomed.

Paul and Kate were cleaning and sweeping the small animal quarters. We were going to do a "travelling road show" with the guests as a sort of "dry run" for the open house planned for next month. (I can't believe I won't be here. Maybe I can come back. Hmmm. SO not letting go gracefully.) Then, after a closing circle, we would eat, and then head to the Sacred Grounds for a campfire together. It would be a rich time! And it all went off without a hitch.

Dad and Peggy acknowledged the blessing of the labyrinth; it was to be called Pipe Dream, Hugh had decided, in honour of hope, and the melding of the Aboriginal teachings of the Medicine Wheel and the labyrinth. Kenny was tickled...and those who chose to walk it together shared a pipe ceremony in the middle as a kind of inauguration. Hugh is a pipe carrier, and suggested it so gently that many felt welcomed to participate. I never would have imagined my Mom sitting cross-legged on the grass passing a pipe around, but there she was, along with me and about a dozen others, gathered on blankets. I'm amazed at her willingness to try anything!

Then we headed to the stables, and Paul surprised us all by leading Buttercup out completely tacked up. Tom rode her around the pasture for a while, and none of us could believe it. She was so feisty, but so happy when she was with Tom. He was content in a way I hadn't seen before, either. Frank talked about healing, and we had a moment to remember Ricky; I explained to everyone there what had happened between us when we painted the fence, and why I had chosen a ladybug to commemorate him. Everyone had tears well up. I hope it wasn't because of how unrecognizable the painting was.

We headed to the Sanctuary and did have a closing circle, but it was a bit of a denouement. It was like a public observance of what we had all been doing all week -- acknowledging that there were changes happening. Martin spoke eloquently of what this place meant to him, and a little about his trepidation that lingered as he headed home. He gifted Nora and Hugh with blankets. (Nora laughed. "Does this mean I'm getting old?" she asked. I could tell she was honoured, though.)

And then, he and Paul and Hugh rose and gifted me with a medicine bundle and name – Little Sister. In the medicine bundle each one put some of their hair, and a tail hair from Buttercup, and a hair they pulled from my head (ouch!)…Paul then braided them together. They added a piece of rock from the Grandfathers and Grandmothers, and some cedar. When I asked the reason for each, Martin simply said, "You figure it out!" I'm still thinking about it. Hugh blessed it. Martin then took off the leather cord from his medicine pouch, and strung it on mine, and laid it around my neck while I wept. I still haven't removed it.

Tom gave me a wooden lap desk that he had made "for all that writing you do – now you don't have to go hide in your room," and a small sandstone circle he'd carved. I'll wear it around my neck, the medicine bundle inside my clothes, and the circle on the outside. It's beautiful. Cook had whittled a wooden spoon from birch, and exclaimed "I'll smack you with it if you get out of line!" The women had handstitched a vest for me, quilted with a symbolic rendering of *Just Living* on the back. Even a ladybug. Glenn sent a note wishing me well, and promising we would spend time together once I was done my commitments. I will travel north soon.

I was overwhelmed with it all, and sat in awe as everyone gifted Martin with his tools for the journey: a beautiful carving knife, some sweet grass, and some things for his bundle. We had our last round of thanksgiving, and there wasn't a dry eye in the house although there was lots of laughter, too. At the end, they asked us to stay seated, and Frank disappeared for a moment. He quickly returned with Topaz, sleepy, in his arms.

"We took a poll, and decided you had ruined her as a barn cat. She's yours, Beth." He put the sleeping cat in my arms, and I knew that as she had grown independent of her Mother, I too was ready to be independent of this place, this experience. I would always welcome visits, but it was time to go off in the world. I snuggled her under my chin, and as people streamed towards the doors, Steve came and gave me a big-brother hug.

"I am so proud of you, Little Sister," he said. "Good work, hard work. But how are we going to get Sarita to accept the cat?" He was grinning, but I could see concern in his eyes.

"Don't worry," I said. "I'm moving in with Mom and Dad for a bit; I hope to be starting training in a couple of weeks maybe in Langley, and Veronica said I can come back then. You guys keep the apartment, and the three of you can have your space. Of course, I'm going to be visiting Daya all the time – you won't be able to get rid of me...." Mom was ecstatic I was coming home even for a short time. Whether she would be once she figured out Topaz and I came as a package deal, I wasn't sure.

"Are you sure that'll give you enough privacy?" My big brother was worried about my sex life!

"Oh yeah...for the time being," I answered.

"I'm sorry to hear that. I thought you and Ben were good together?" I laughed out loud.

"It's all good. Even without Ben, my life is coming together quite beautifully. Not sure what the fall will bring, but onward! I trust I'll figure it out. Training in Langley over the summer. Ordination in October is the next step, and I hope Bishop Tom is supportive. I'm looking at some chaplaincy training in trauma. Kinda bring all my education together, I hope." Steve's eyes gleamed as he looked at me. He gave me a hug.

"I'm proud of you, Mugwump," he said.

We headed to the dining room where we feasted on salmon, "roast beast" and more vegetables than even our crew could consume. Cook was still wondering how we had busted into the fridge; his guess was we had removed the hinges on the door. Ha! There was joy and silliness in the air, as we sat around the backyard on chairs filling our bellies and our hearts.

About 7:00 o'clock, Paul went to start the fire in the Sacred Grounds, and Frank went to fetch his guitar. We ended the evening singing folk songs as the moon rose over the kennels and the dogs began to howl. It was a fitting ending to a perfect time.

About 8:30, the folks from Vancouver started to take their leave, and soon I was saying goodbye. Martin and Kenny and I packed my stuff in Dad's car, and we loaded ourselves and Topaz.

Everyone was grinning, and wishing us well for the journey. Another dénouement, and completely graceless. I wept, but just quietly.

"You okay, Beth?" Dad asked.

"Yeah. I'm really, really good." Mom sighed and put her head back. I cuddled Topaz in the back seat, and she purred.

One more meeting, and I was clear. Finally. Bishop Tom was amazing. It was WILD being treated as a colleague by a man I really respect.

His office was clean and proper. I don't really know how else to describe it. The furniture was fine. Well used, in need of new upholstery. The colour was more than a decade off. And he kind of reminded me of his office, in a kind, gentle way. This was a man who said what mattered, but didn't ruffle many feathers; his predecessor had done enough of that for everyone for some time.

We talked sensibly and clearly about the journey I'd been on. It felt good to talk theologically about what I'd learned at school, and how to articulate my past four months within that context. I told him about my four-month discipline and research on prayer, and how I felt closer to the Creator, more alive with listening than I had been when I started, how it had served me.

I talked a little bit about some of the First Nations teachings I'd received, how they felt Divine, and not in conflict with the Canons of the church. We wondered out loud how things might have been different if, more than a hundred years ago, the Anglicans who helped colonize the West had been open to the Teachings of the Elders.

We sipped a cup of tea together, and shared a few stale cookies from a box in his desk. He was endearing in his grey cardigan with the elbows almost worn through, and I felt lucky. Then, before I knew it, he steered the conversation towards the future. I shared ideas about where I wanted to go, the paths I wanted to explore.

He offered to find some small summer contracts for me, to help pay for the trainings I wanted to pursue (preaching for vacationing priests, when most parishioners took holidays too).

I shared my reticence (still) for parish work, but said I would welcome the opportunity. And I wondered why I hadn't felt free to do that before. Clearly I had changed, because, well, Bishop Tom was not exactly Mr. Dynamic. I was glad that he said he was intrigued by the idea of a specialized chaplaincy. He encouraged my planning. And prayer.

"I'm going to call the National office, Beth, and find out what is being done in other places. I know of some work in Nova Scotia at a prison there. The folks in Quebec are doing amazing stuff, too, mostly Catholics, of course." I told him I didn't know what an end-point might be, but working in a prison hospital maybe.

"Wait a minute. Look at me," he said. I glanced at his face and looked away. "What aren't you saying?" he prompted.

"Well, if I'm really honest, what I'd really like to do is work with crime victims. But I have no idea what that'd look like. There isn't a place to do that kind of work that I know of. Yet. And I think that might be a longer-term leading. I have to learn more first, to really be of service," I continued. Bishop Tom was beaming.

An hour later, he was shaking my hand, and telling me he was proud to serve with me. He knew I was going to be an important person in the church, and that I was a part of the "new face" of the work of being an ordained Anglican priest. And as I blushed, and headed out, he called out to me as I walked down the hallway.

"Beth, I really don't say that to everyone. A few, but not everyone." I was stunned, and didn't really believe it. And really hoped he didn't say anything like that to my Dad. We were getting along better, but I'm not sure I was ready for him to hear that! "Not yours to control, Mugwump," I heard Cook's voice in my head say. And he was right. As usual.

Two weeks later, I was back at Veronica's during the week (with my car this time -- Steve and Sari bought their own FINALLY), and home at Mom and Dad's on the weekends. I shadowed Teresa, who is a restorative justice facilitator. Boy, did I work hard to contribute because I was learning so much and gotta give when you take, right? Teresa was amazeballs. She lived and breathed restorative principles, and had a seamless way of swerving with the clients so that they got what they needed out of the experience.

"We get to work mostly with younger people, but sometimes with adults," she told me. "Usually, they are in conflict with the law for the first time, but I try to remind the folks who refer cases that if it works for first-timers, it is even more powerful for the folks when the courts *didn't* work the first time." Hmmm. Interesting argument.

She worked with Jag, and volunteers (like me), and some administrative support. And she was masterful. She didn't just talk about communication skills like reframing and reflective listening and non-violent communication. Her gentleness exuded out of her pores; she cared and she *was* those skills. I knew, when I talked with her or watched her with other people, that people mattered to her, and we were seen, heard and understood.

We interviewed people, and taught them about what restorative processes looked like. Some people decided to go ahead with this approach; others decided it wasn't for them. In every case she was understanding and supportive.

Then, after about four weeks, she let me come to an actual case meeting between the people affected by an assault. Wow. Such courage everyone showed. It really brought out their best selves. Yes, I think this work makes a difference. It wasn't a murder case, like with Veronica's husband, but this mattered to the people who were involved. Really mattered. And the restorative justice program helped them move forward.

That weekend, talking to Mom and Dad, I told them I was getting clearer and clearer about studying trauma, and how chaplains can help. And how the church, as it is right now, sometimes doesn't do a very good job at that. Dad didn't even disagree.

It's true, I was worried leaving *Just Living* that I would be missing my time there so much that life would seem pale, uninteresting. But actually, I'm finding people to connect with everywhere. And besides, Veronica kept me in the loop...blessedly. Everyone was doing fine without me.

Dear God,

I am finding my kin! I wonder where they were before, when I was looking for something meaningful to connect with. Maybe I just wasn't ready to see them.

Or maybe, I wasn't ready to be seen.

Thank you again....

Beth

CHAPTER 45
HEARING A CALL

Lamentation: To lament; to feel, or express grief, sorrow or regret. To mourn deeply.

Dear God,

I could have lived without the realisation that once I experienced it, I'd know these words don't really capture it. At all.

Why does life have to be so damned hard? Right now, I think I hate you.

And life.

Beth

Two months later, I was still bouncing back and forth between Veronica's house and my old bedroom, and had just finished eight weeks of training and apprenticing in restorative mediation. I'd already preached once or twice (and got paid!), but Veronica told me to stay as long as I wanted. I even got to drop by and see Cook from time to time.

It was June, about a week after convocation, and Bishop Tom and I were still planning a fall ordination. The morning of the call, I was sitting drinking coffee, and cuddling Topaz when the phone rang and I saw it was "*Just Living.*" I didn't expect my world to be turned upside down when I answered. But then, I don't get to be the boss of me.

"Beth, it's Nora. I'm glad I caught you in." We shared mundane social greetings and check-ins; we were both "fine" but I could tell Nora wasn't really. That came through in her voice. Then I realized I wasn't either, because I could tell she wasn't.

"I'm glad I'm reaching you before you started your day. Have you had the radio on this morning?" she asked. "No," I stuttered. Who listens to radio, except in the car?

"Beth, sit down. I've got some bad news. The RCMP just called. Have you heard from Al lately?" I admitted that I hadn't, which, once I said it, seemed a bit weird. I'd talked to him about once a week for the first three weeks or so that he was up the canyon, then, a call or two weeks apart, then, nothing. And I hadn't noticed before just now. I was also knocked a bit sideways when Nora referred to him as Al instead of Martin.

"He's been picked up again, up around Pemberton. They're arraigning him on murder charges," she said. My heart stopped. "Murder, first degree, and sexual assault." I couldn't breathe. This man I thought I knew, I thought I loved…he was capable of killing someone? Well, I knew he *had* killed someone. I just didn't think he would ever do it again.

For just a nanosecond my mind did calisthenics; they "had the wrong guy," I "misheard" Nora, but I immediately let go. I knew he was capable. And then I knew that he is capable, just like the rest of us; with enough pain and hurt visited on us, especially at an early age, we are all potential murderers.

"Oh my God." I repeated the invocation a few times. It didn't add any clarity, and I didn't feel any better. This beautiful man, who I had hugged, who I had learned from and in some ways (but not many) envied…this man who was capable of nursing a sick coyote pup and looking after Ricky, connecting with him in ways none of us could…who had taught me so much about the sacredness in all things, the man whose hair I wore braided with mine in my medicine pouch. He had seemed so grounded and good and genuine, so determined to follow a healing path...I couldn't comprehend it and in the same moment I understood. I started to breathe, just little breaths, promising myself it would help with the hurting. Until the next jolt.

"Tell me what happened, Nora."

"I don't really know, you can guess with the investigation and legal proceedings and all they aren't telling us much. You remember he wanted to stay with us, and we wanted to have him. We'd applied for status as a Healing Centre, and he was going to coordinate that work for us, but the contract hadn't come through from the Feds. The damn Parole Board decided he should leave for six months, to 'prove himself.' Whatever the hell that means. Do we ever really 'prove' ourselves? This. Did. Not. Have. To. Happen. I am SOOO mad I could spit."

And then, I gasped when I heard her do exactly that. I hoped she was in a field, and not sitting at her desk, not that that would have stopped her. I had never heard Nora so angry. The phone stayed quiet for a minute or two, and then I heard her again.

"This totally could have been prevented. You know he won't be 'warrant expired' until the day after he dies, so they could have let him stay." I heard her sniff, imagined her wiping her nose.

I was in shock, but knew when her anger turned to tears. I had never experienced her anger before, but now her humanity was showing, and I felt a little better. It's like it gave me permission to feel everything: doubts, anger, fear, disbelief, despair.

"Well, he stayed with 'friends' back on the reserve near Pemberton. I'd never met these friends, never knew them, which made me uneasy. We tried to keep in touch, but cell phones don't work well up there, and his 'friends' (I could hear the disdain in her voice; I had never known Nora to harshly judge anyone before) don't have a phone. From what Tom and Paul could piece together, he started doing coke again to pass the time or maybe deal with the uncomfortableness shortly after he got up there. There aren't any Parole Officers up there, so he was calling in regularly from a pay phone to his PO's office. The PO never even visited,

I bet. Seems she thought all was well, that Al was 'bringing good things to the reserve.'"

"What happened?" I was scared to hear, but I couldn't wrap my imagination around the big guy on coke. It would be scary, for sure. I did imagine his bad dreams revisiting, the pain resurfacing. Shit.

"He got hopped up and walked to town one night. I only know what the RCMP shared 'off the record.' There were a bunch of 'do-gooders' visiting from Vancouver. Something about the pipeline, and the Elders. I don't really know. Anyhow, it upset Al. Seems he took a knife, broke into the local Anglican priest's place and killed him. They think he believed he was killing a Roman Catholic priest. I guess you can put together what happened as well as I can."

I didn't think it was possible to be more upset, more shocked, less grounded.

"What about the sexual assault?" I asked.

"I don't really know, and you don't want to. Lots of things are sexual assault. Maybe they just found the victim naked, maybe Al did something to him."

"Do you know the victim's name?" I whispered.

"I think the Inspector said Glenn something...Oh my God...Beth, is that Glenn that you know? The one who slept in the tipi?"

"I think so," I whispered, and started to quietly weep for Glenn, for Al, for Bruce and Adam, his boys. Even Donna. "I've got to go, Nora," I whispered.

"Call me soon, Mugwump, okay?" she whispered, and hung up.

I crawled into my bed, and wanted to sleep, to shut out the world. I couldn't begin to think, and certainly didn't want to feel. A part of me wanted to deny it all. A part of me was overloaded, and shut down. I couldn't even see the consequences of all of this, and my mind was rushing to question everything I had believed to be true. I shivered, and shook, and wailed into a pillow. I wanted to hate Al, and was frustrated to find only pity for him.

After an hour or so of numbness I peeled off my clothes and sank into the bottom of the shower stall, wishing the pounding cold water would dissolve me and carry me away. The shivering increased, but at least I was feeling. It was too hard to be human, to physically *be* in that moment, to co-exist beside and inside so much pain and suffering, so much damage. I began to doubt myself, my ability to judge and love wisely, my discernment of God's path for me, and Spirit as I had come to know It in the sweat lodge and the tipi, in the Sacred Circle and the Cathedral. And then I remembered that it wasn't "my" shower stall, and I should get out.

That day, believe it or not, Ben rescued me; I found out later Nora had tracked him down and told him he should. She'd confirmed with the RCMP that it was Glenn who'd been killed, and wanted him to confirm it for me.

I had pruned up, left the cold water. I was sitting on the couch, profoundly ugly and cold in my old robe and stringy hair, Veronica feeding me hot tea, when he arrived. My eyes were red and sore. He talked gently to me, and fed me, but mostly he listened. It felt right, and I didn't question his companionship.

In some moments during the following days, I was convinced I could never do the work again. That I didn't deserve to go on. Over that day, and days that followed, Spirit reminded me of things I needed to see as I struggled with all of it. Ben was a constant in my life; I couldn't stay at Veronica's. I didn't know where my allegiance lay, and I couldn't figure it out so close to *Just Living*. I sure didn't want to go home to Mom and Dad's, or even Stephen and Sarita's, so Ben created a private sanctuary for me at his condo. And let everyone know he was looking after me. People kept calling to check on me, so he took my phone.

The first few days, I bumbled through life like a drunk. Or maybe a zombie. Present, but not really, literally bouncing off the doorways I was trying to navigate through. Clearly my world had tilted. Ben encouraged me to eat delicious soup he concocted (okay, later I found out he reheated -- people were dropping off lots of food, apparently.) Sometimes I ate ravenously. Sometimes I snubbed the lure of the aromas. Who could eat great food when I knew everyone in my life who mattered were struggling? Or dead? Except, of course, that wasn't true. Only a few were struggling.

A few days later, I was still in a deep, dark hole, and Ben had to head into work. He'd taken a couple of days to be with me, but the world was still living, people still picked up their puddle-jumping toddlers at day care, and teenagers still reacted explosively when the police stopped them for jay-walking. So Ben drove half an hour into Vancouver, and tucked me into my mother's kitchen, and then drove an hour and a half out to work, and did the opposite at the other end of the day. Because Ben.

Mom fed me tea, bundled me in a blanket, and made me sit outside in the fresh air for part of each day. She made Ben pack my dirty laundry so she could wash it, and sometimes she sent me back to his place with baking. Over time, I started to bake with her. It was liberating, distracting me for actual minutes at a time.

On the best days, Stephen, Sarita and Daya came to visit. Who can lose themselves in grief when there is a demanding three-month-old niece smiling and gurgling? Waving hands and feet delightfully? Smiling at her daddy? Creating the most incredibly smelly explosive baby poop? And I would laugh at her, and then when I realized I was laughing, I would burst into tears because Glenn would never laugh at his boys ever again. Or his nieces. Or grandchildren. The depth and breadth of the realizing was literally breath-taking. As in, I couldn't breathe.

I had about five showers a day, because that was a place I could wail, weep, lament the losses of friends, of trust, of justice I believed in. And sometimes I showered at night, too. And then it was four showers a day. Or three. And I had to decide if that was good, or bad, or if it just was. And people said the darndest things. Things I learned I would never say to anyone after a sudden loss.

A take on a bad ballad, "God needed Glenn in heaven, that's how good a man he was." I'm sorry, God didn't kill Glenn, Al did. My friend Al. Fuck.

"At least he didn't know what was happening." You know this how? The police haven't even released his body, let alone how he died. And I can only imagine, because I know how Al's friend died at the hand of a priest in residential school. And the horror of the possibilities is terrifying. And I can't even give voice to them. Except sometimes when it's really dark, and the tea is especially hot, I can talk to Ben because, well, Ben. (No, we haven't had "the conversation" yet. Because I don't even know if I want to live, let alone love.)

"Glenn loved it in Mount Currie. At least he was happy when he died, doing what he loved." (Or he's in a better place. Or "It will get better." WTF? It sucks right now, which is where I am.) Really, so if we are happy we should be terrified that a deranged, mentally ill crazy man WHO WE KNOW may come for us? WFT?

"This is awful, Beth. I know just how you feel." Really? Because your friend killed your other friend? Like brutalized, and sexually assaulted and then blood-all-over murdered him? With a knife? Maybe one you'd helped pay for? Someone you'd hugged did that to someone you loved? A guy you thought of as a big brother? I don't FUCKING THINK SO. And besides, really? That's the best you could come up with? People are stupid. And I'm really intolerant when I'm hurting. Grief, they call it. Hell, I call it.

Bishop Tom visited me. *He* was actually lovely. That lump of a "he has no ideas" guy? Well, he's been replaced by a caring and gentle soul. I really like him. We sat in the garden at Ben's and drank tea and ate scones, the three of us. And all he mumbled was "I'm sorry." A perfectly lovely thing to say. And I tried really hard not to say "It's okay," back, because really. It so isn't. And I am not really sure it ever will be again. Okay, that is.

About two weeks after Glenn's murder Nora called me. She'd been keeping in touch, which was really good; I needed her to know I REALLY didn't blame anyone there for what happened. And I said Donna didn't either, but that was probably a lie. Nora said she'd found out that Al is going to plead guilty, and I'm grateful for that. Glenn's family won't have to go through the pain and heartache of a trial. Sentencing will take place in the fall, I guess.

I visited Donna, but didn't really stay long. She was intensely angry at me; she seemed to think I was somehow responsible for Glenn going up North. I knew grief does weird things, but really? I was as shocked as her when he told me in the pub what he was going to do. Anyhow, she did say I could go to the funeral "if the damned police ever release the body." Yup. Glenn was evidence in a murder case. She hadn't even seen him, and hadn't been able to go up to Mount Currie and get the boys' stuff out of the house, because, well, murder scene? I didn't see Bruce or Adam that day; they were out with their grandparents. Donna was quite sauced, but who could blame her?

Glenn's body was finally released, and the family planned the funeral. It was astonishing. And amazing. And it touched my soul. And left me cold. At least no one said "God doesn't give you more than you can handle." The Dean of the Cathedral "presided" at the service, which was attended by a large group of mourners from the quite eclectic groups that streamed through Glenn's life. The Mount Currie band sent two Elders, and one spoke eloquently of lamentation and the humble work Glenn had engaged in during his short time living amongst them.

"We ask the Church to carefully consider who is called to take up Glenn's work, and be a bridge between our hurt and God's healing. Who amongst you can hear our stories and help other settlers understand our journey?" she asked.

And I heard in her words that she was asking who amongst us is important enough to compel change in OUR community. Bishop, you listening? SO not me – I am not influential, but perhaps there is an older priest with compassion who can listen.

Students who had worked with Glenn were there, and were so respectful, resisting the urge to turn the service into an opportunity for more activism. Julie was a mess, and I knew she believed she and Glenn were in the first blushes of romance, and yet, Donna was clear that their family was far from divorcing. Family surrounded her and the boys, providing enough of a cushion between those closest to Glenn and those who wanted to express sadness, and appreciation for his life. It was another dance we didn't know the choreography for.

Luckily, with the crime solved already, there was no police presence – no fear that the perpetrator would sneak into the service. Journalists wanted to cover the crime story, and so I kept my head VERY low to the ground, not wanting anyone to comment that I knew the offender. This meant that Ben and I hung out for a while with Bruce and Adam, which was lovely. My heart broke a little more when I saw they were wearing the "good clothes" they'd received for Glenn's ordination, just a few months ago.

Shielding them from the strength of the emotions that were swirling in that space gave me a chance to hang out under a table, creating a fort with the tablecloths. They were worried about their clothes, but I told them it didn't matter. I hoped they wouldn't get in trouble later.

We chatted a little, while Ben kept surreptitiously feeding us plates of food. Which were disappearing. Who knew kids at funerals needed so much cut up fruit and cubes of cheese? Fancy crackers and apple juice? That little pinwheel cream cheese sandwiches would end up half-chewed, back on the plate? Good taste, those boys.

"Beff, did you love Daddy?" Adam asked.

"Yes, Adam, I did. He was a special man, and he taught me a lot about how I should live. I miss him," I said, aware that I felt really inadequate. Just this side of flawed.

"Me too," Adam said, burrowing onto my lap, and wiping his less-than-clean fingers on my pants. I smiled. Perfect evidence of Glenn's perfect existence, I thought. Both boys were tugging at their ties, and I helped them remove them and open their top buttons. They sighed, and Adam pulled off his leather shoes, too.

"He bought me a bike," Bruce said, looking at the floor beside us.

"I heard about that! He told me you loved it, and he had a lot of fun with you on it. He said you both were really good at riding in the woods. Better than he'd thought you'd be," I embellished. I was really glad I'd talked to Glenn only a few days before he'd died. Been killed, I mean. Was murdered. Bruce sniffed. His voice got really quiet.

"I wish I had it still," he said. Adam squirmed some more, trying to get comfortable in his new stiff clothes. In his new life.

"And my blanket. And Freddy," Adam said, sniffing again. Was he going to start sobbing again?

"Freddy is his stuffed dog at Daddy's house," Bruce said. "And our *Mario Kart*. All our stuff that's there." Wow, I thought. Has anyone thought about how this is impacting these boys? I was sure Donna had.

"Did you talk to your mommy?" I asked.

"Yeah. She said the police have our stuff, and we should just be glad we weren't there when Daddy was hurt," he said. And I could understand Donna's hurt, and fear, and Bruce and Adam wanting something from their Dad's. To remember him by, and, well, *Mario Kart* and bicycles!

"I'm gonna make you guys a promise, okay?" I tried to sound really solemn. They both looked at me with enormous eyes. I smiled, working really hard at not laughing at the ridiculousness of it all.

"I'm going to drive up to your house in Mount Currie, where you stayed with your dad, and I'm going to talk to the police, and your mom, and everybody I need to, and I'm going to do everything I can to get your stuff back, okay?" And while I couldn't promise the moon, maybe I could promise a space program.

"REALLY?" Bruce said, moving from sad to excited in one moment. Luckily I grabbed Adam on my lap, because he was about to start bouncing up and down, and he definitely would have banged his head on the table. And maybe knocked over the coffee above us.

"Shhhh!" I said. "I promise I will do what I can. I can't promise I will get everything, but this is going to be my quest!" I could imagine all the barriers that might get in my way, but at the same time I was thinking about all the ways I could use my contacts to make this happen. Starting with the Elder who was here at the funeral, and Mark Derksen, the RCMP Inspector in Mission.

"I need you guys to use your superpowers to help me though," I said quickly. I could hear Donna and her mother beyond our tent, and they were approaching fast. Clearly they'd heard Bruce's excitement.

"You are going to have to use the Cone of Silence, and not tell anyone about this mission," I said, hoping I was buying time to have another difficult conversation with Donna.

First step, make sure the stuff was safe. The second step, bring it home. I held up my thumb, and it was met by two sticky thumbs. We sealed our pact as the side of our tent was lifted.

"It's okay, they're here with me," I said. "I asked them to come in here for a bit. We were just sharing a few stories, and a piece of cauliflower," I said, holding up a half-chewed piece as evidence.

"Bruce! Adam! What's gotten into you?" Donna said as she pulled them away. Bruce looked over his shoulder at me and winked. Adam giggled at that from his mom's arms. I handed Ben the shoes and ties, and he gave them to Grandma.

And I hoped all would be well in their world, as different as it was today from a few weeks ago. I vowed to stay connected to these boys. Now I had a mission, which shifted something inside me. Someone really important needed me to show up, and to do Important Stuff only I could do. I crawled out from under that table, brushed off my butt (don't they sweep under the furniture in church halls?) and headed over to see Agnes, the Elder, to explain my quest.

It was about three weeks after Glenn died, more or less, that the grey fog started to lift. Not all at once, but from time to time. I wasn't exactly bowled over by sunshine, but I did see a glimpse of the blue sky now and then, as my adventure to Mount Currie started to take shape. Mark had reassured me that the house was locked, and he had pressed the local police to do frequent drive-bys to make sure the boys' things were secure. When Al pled guilty, the officers had taken photos and any evidence they needed for the courts in case of appeal, and had released the scene.

Agnes was working on making sure the Band remembered Glenn with presents for the boys, and I even spoke to Donna and the Bishop and insisted I would go to Mount Currie, and clean the house, empty it and bring back what we thought the family might want. Ben offered to come. I made sure Donna understood that she would be in charge of everything, I was just willing to be the arms to make it happen. And she seemed relieved when I offered. So did the Bishop. After all, who offers to go clean up a bloody crime scene, anyhow?

Ben and I started to make plans for that trip. And sometimes he held my hand, and I squeezed back. And I continued to heal, but some days were better than others. We went for walks in the park, ate fish and chips by the ocean. I trained Topaz to walk on a leash, something she thought was exceedingly weird after being literally raised in a barn, but she was happy to get outside and walk in the neighbourhood with me. That helped me rally. And I talked to Kenny, and Cook, and Nora, and Kate on the phone. And Frank, bless him, brought Hugh over to visit me, and I knew the connection to *Just Living* was real. And strong. And mattered.

Even in the moments I just wished I'd never...

Thank God.

I read this the other day. Somehow it seemed connected, but I'm not really sure yet.

THE SUN NEVER SAYS

Even
After
All this time
The sun never says to the earth,
"You owe
Me."
Look
What happens
With a love like that,
It lights the
Whole
Sky.
– Hafez, 14th century Persian poet

CHAPTER 46

BIG BROTHER IS WATCHING

It is weird bein' allowed to do whatever I want. Like, all the time. I even got mad at Adam and hit him yesterday, and nobody even noticed but him. He cried, and I had to hug him and tell him I wouldn't do it again. And now I have to look after him 'cause no one else is. Even when he gets hurt. An' someone hits him. Even when it's me. It's weird.

Yesterday I even had to sneak up into Grandma's cupboard and get him a snack, 'cause Mom went out and there wasn't dinner, and I didn't want Grandma to make a fuss 'cause I'm big enough. So I got some crackers and juice boxes and two apples, and we had a picnic. But we didn't eat the apples 'cause they were kinda wrinkly. And prolly not 'ganic. Mom says that's important and I forgot until I almost fed Adam it. I'm glad I remembered.

Mom is all sad all the time that Daddy isn't coming back. Like he would ever. He liked it in Currie. He was happy. And we could eat beans and wear no shirts, and put our feet up and stuff. It was funnest that one time Mom came out, but then she left. But Daddy said he liked it there, that's where his "life is now." Which is weird 'cause now he has no life.

Mom's drinking more. And it makes her cry. Or maybe she is drinking because she cries so much. Grandma tries to pretend it doesn't happen, but I know. I hear Grandma telling Grandpa to be nice to Mom. That it's just hard. But I know. Adam doesn't. But I do. And Grandpa does too.

And no one makes us go to school yet. Which is good, 'cause people look at me funny, sad like, and I don't like it when they do that. It better not be like that at school. Anyway, Mom said we didn't need to go back until after the fun'ral. Grandpa said we should, but Mom said no. I hope Adam doesn't miss daycare too much because he'll be sad when he has to go back, but I can't stay there with him this time. I have big school. Grade Four next year. If I get to go to Grade Four. I'm missin' a lot of Grade Three. An' nobody seems to care. 'Cept Grandpa.

Adam's upposed to go to Kindergarten. I hope that happens, 'cause he's real excited about Grade One, an' Kindergarten's important. I liked it. He'll be good at it, too. He's a good kid, when he isn't being a baby.

Last night when Mom went out, and we had our picnic, I put Adam to bed and then it was a little scary in here, so I stayed with him in case he was scared. We left a light on in the hallway, and I could hear Grandpa upstairs, and he was yelling a bit at Grandma, but in a good way. Not scary. Maybe he knew we were alone, or something.

Mom made us try on our "fun'ral clothes" for tomorrow. I wonder why she's makin' us wear ties for the fun'ral. Daddy hated ties. Said they were made by the Devil. I don't get why we need stuff maded by the Devil at the fun'ral. He said they were nooses. He din't even have one, I don't think. I miss him. Lots.

An' I wonder if I'll ever get my bike back. Really. It was the coolest bike. It even had a light on it, and Dad said it was okay to get it muddy. It had big thick tires for mud. And I was good at it. And my Superman pyjamas. It's hard to be Superman for Adam when he cries in the night when I don't have my pyjamas to help me.

Uncle Tim came by last night and took us to McDonald's. I think Grandma called him. Mom yelled at him a little, and said he should get off her back. And then she said McDonald's was garbage food an' he was a bad Uncle, an' he said she wasn't any better. Whatever that means. Anyhow, I made sure Adam an' me ordered apples with our burgers.

It tasted good, not like garbage. And then we played like crazy in the big play thing. And I let Adam win at tag. Even Uncle Tim got in the ball pit an' played until they kicked us out. And Adam cried because we hadn't had our ice cream yet, but then, Uncle Tim said we'd get some and we went through the drive-thru in his truck and it was cool 'cause Mom never lets us eat ice cream in the car. But maybe things have changed now that Daddy isn't coming home. Uncle Tim yelled at mom again when he dropped us off and told her she has to let us be kids. And go to school.

I like Uncle Tim. I bet he wouldn't make me wear a Devil tie. Maybe I'll ask him. He said he'd see me tomorrow, and I'm real glad. I hope he takes us to McDonald's 'gain. It's better than crackers an' juice boxes. Adam is gonna sleep real good though 'cause he's not hungry.

Me too.

CHAPTER 47
LAMENTATIONS

Out beyond ideas of wrongdoing and rightdoing
there is a field. I'll meet you there.

When the soul lies down in that grass,
the world is too full to talk about.
Ideas, language, even the phrase "each other" doesn't make any sense.
mevlana jelaluddin rumi - 13th century

Dear God,

I get it. In a head place. But that long journey Hugh talked about? From the head to the heart?

I don't know if I'll ever understand in my heart. Which still aches, and leaks, and squeezes so much my chest hurts.

I have moments of not hating you. But I still don't understand.

Yes, bad things happen to good people. In my head I get that too.

But really? Fuck you.

Prayerful,

Beth

The next week was busier, which had its advantages. I got my certificate from the agency for doing my training in victim-offender mediation, and visited Mom and Dad. I took Bruce and Adam to the park a couple of times and surreptitiously caught them up on the master plan for the quest and we visited a local market to eat. I worry about them. I filled their pockets with granola bars. Healthy ones.

As I got out in the world more, sometimes I sensed it was blaming me. Even when no one could even know the connection between Al and Glenn, or that I knew them, if people started talking about the crime, my face burned, and I ducked my head. I felt so ashamed that Al had betrayed my trust, his teachings. Even when no one else knew, I did, and I wished I had done something different.

And then I realized that if I had, I never would have known what I prevented. How can you tell when a crime is averted? Is this kind of the reverse of *Minority Report*, or something?

I thought about that a lot, because I had to fill my days with something and it was hard to be with people. So I prayed. And I philosophized. I cuddled Topaz. And sometimes, I snuck out and visited with Kenny because, well, Kenny. It was so easy being with him because he got it without me having to say anything. *Thank fucking God for friendships.* Prayer.

So, what am I struggling with? And what am I remembering?

Sure, there's no "us" and "them," but lots of my friends and colleagues (and Glenn's family) have asked me implicitly and explicitly to choose. I can't. I am torn apart with sadness when I think of Glenn's brutal death. But I am also convinced that he would not, does not, want me to hate Al because of his murder.

I don't know if I'll ever be able to face Al again, or that I'll even be asked. I've learned a few things. Al called 911 and turned himself in. In fact, before he did, they didn't even know Glenn was murdered. He's already been shipped back to Kent, a hellhole of epic proportions where he will be vilified by lifers and other solid cons who want a chance at parole.

The "collective wisdom" (ironic, that) will be that he has blown it for all of them, that's how broken he is. How will the system ever trust anyone again? Al will probably die in prison, and, unfortunately, maybe that's as it should be. I hope the "prison" they put him in is more humane that the one that was constructed for him through his childhood. And that it keeps everyone safe. Including Al.

No prisoner who's in on a violent bit will get parole for quite some time, I know. I don't blame the Parole Board, but I feel sick for those people trying, and understand this is another way that we're all connected. And I feel for the people on the Parole Board who sent Al back to his reserve, and their connection to Glenn's murder. There will be, no doubt, an inquiry. And some sleeplessness. I hope there is learning, too.

Why do I care if parole isn't offered? Because without parole, warrants expire and people are released with no supervision, no way to influence their "reintegration" process, and the likelihood they will reoffend is even higher. Sigh. Parole keeps us safer. Really. Except Glenn.

Al's Parole Officer is going to have to live with a million "What ifs?" What if she'd visited on-site? What if she'd required he travel into town for regular secure urinalysis to check for drug use? What if she'd followed directives to the "T" rather than believing what she wanted to believe was true? Would Glenn still be alive? The Parole Board will probably be playing this game for a while, too. I wonder if Nora plays the "what if" game, too?

Donna is struggling with her own demons, and I don't need to add to them, so I sneak in and out to get the boys. Donna's mother seems grateful when I do it.

I'm going to need to go over this again and again with my heart and mind. The questions are roiling around inside me. Is my heart changed by this? Are my beliefs different? When am I angry? Humble?

Compassionate? Wary? What do I really wish I'd known? What role can prayer play? Could it have made a difference?

Do we, all of us from the "colonizing European culture" share some degree of the blame? Do the churches who (in the name of "civilizing" and "proselytizing") did our best to destroy the culture of the Peoples through Residential Schools, do we really understand yet what we did? Will we ever understand how that process destroyed and continues to destroy so many lives? Where is *our* meaningful accountability?

As Nora says, this path of *Just Living*, this place of *Just Living*, "really ups the ante on everything." I can't "un-know" how futile it is to disconnect the end and the means, that using punishment just adds to the unending spiral of hurt with more pain, harm with more harm.

Will *Just Living* survive the inevitable scrutiny? Will they be able to do the incredibly hard work of loving these men back into community?

Will everyone struggle with when to let go and let the next fellow fly solo? Should anyone ever fly solo?

Can we shine Light on this, and in time, find beauty? Awe? Wonder?

And I think about what could have really changed things. I can't think of anything, which raises the possibility of "the fates." Which I don't believe in. Well, maybe prayer. And I'm not sure I believe in that either. Well, I sort of do. Not because it makes magic happen, except that it has brought me closer to the Creator, which is magical.

Al's reintegration was as perfectly planned as I could imagine. *Just Living* does an amazing job, and he was lucky. It didn't seem like he'd had much time, but really, it had been months; every release possibility had been considered, planned for. But in the end, he didn't seem to care, or it didn't seem to matter. He had all the offers of support anyone moving back into community could hope for, but for some reason, he couldn't ask for it. In his "dark night," he didn't see our Light shining, reaching out to him. And that sucks so hard.

I know we have to let people to make their own decisions, and we can't make that damned horse drink, but I struggle sometimes at night, wondering if there was something I could have done differently, in some way made myself more "accessible." I know we were close, him and I. And Glenn and I, too. And I can't help but know that in some small human way, I dropped a tenuous piece of the web that connects us all, and Glenn died because of it. Brutally. Or maybe, as Tom lovingly says, I'm just "full of my own self-importance." And I'm rambling.

Then my phone rang, and it was Frank, on schedule. He called twice a week as the weeks piled up, and he won't let me disappear. Thank God. I kind of wanted to — to turn back the time machine to November when I started this odyssey. But really? If I took myself out of the equation, would anything else have changed? Well, yes, girlfriend, one big thing would have changed. I'd be mourning Glenn and cursing Al, who I would have known only from the media. Hmmm. Would that help me? Was I willing to unlearn everything just to avoid this "knowing?"

Frank and I talked about what I was going through, "my trauma," and what I could do about it. I started to talk about it as a companion, like a stuffed bear or something, and it helped me with perspective. It was silly, sometimes, taking the handouts I'd received in training, and going through "what's it looks like" in my own life.

Yes, I could take walks in nature. Eat well. Swim more often, walk by the tidal beaches, rock in a rocking chair. And when I did it, I felt better, miraculously. It was weird. Learning about resiliency – an experiential trip I wouldn't will on anyone. *But God, I was grateful for Frank's companionship.* A gratitude prayer.

I think Nora probably bugged him to stay on me, and I love the idea that she is still looking out for me. This time, though, I decided to answer the ringing phone the first time. Maybe I was getting better.

"How you doing, Mugwump?" he started. I laughed. Full belly laugh. Frank chuckled back.

"So, Master of Divinity Beth Hill, I'm calling today to ask for some help." This time I squeaked, trying to keep from taking the laughter into something more maniacal. Help wasn't something I *really* felt qualified for, even with the convocation.

"Everyone at *Just Living* really wants to do a Memorial Circle for Glenn. Well, for us, really. But no one wants to organize it without you. I think they don't want to mess it up, and I'm not sure I've ever heard of the family of a murderer holding a memorial circle for a victim before."

It was like the top of my brain opened up and dark flew out, just for a moment. And there was room for light. I could think of a thousand ways to make it meaningful and at least 950 of them I discarded as either morbid, weird, or just a really bad idea.

"Wow. Are they just doing this for me?" I asked. Now Frank was chuckling.

"Because, it's all…"

"About me," I chimed in, and we finished in unison.

"Kenny said you'd say that, and Cook agreed. That's why I was sent to ask. I think they had a pool going. Sally thought you'd just agree. Nora wasn't sure." As he rattled off their names, their glowing faces appeared in my mind, and I smiled.

"Of course, I will." I said. "Do they really want to see me, though? Do you think it's a good idea? Sometimes I think I have a little neon streak following me around with 'remember you failed' trailing behind me…." My heart grew heavy. Silence.

"Oh Mugwump. I think that you're the only one who sees that neon streak. Maybe you have to ask them about it. And spending some time there might help build some new memories. Based on the new real you, and the new them, too."

We talked a bit more about what might be possible, like visiting the tipi, and walking the labyrinth, which Kenny wanted to rename the Memorial Path. Nice, but I still liked Pipe Dream. Maybe there's a third way. I wondered about adding something to the barn painting of the ladybug, and Frank told me I'd have to come see what the men had already done.

That piqued my curiosity, and I made plans to visit the next Tuesday, on Ben's day off. We'd head out together, and have lunch, and then do some planning with whoever wanted to help. It seemed like a gentle idea for re-entry into what was a tender place.

Frank reassured me that no one had been sent back, and the group is talking about ways to move forward. They aren't getting too much heat because they actually *didn't* want Al to go north, so the inquiry will be focusing on the parole officers. I'm looking forward to seeing everyone, and talking with all of them about what a memorial circle could look like.

I was so grateful for Ben. Am so grateful. He's so calm, so present, so…Ben. We talked about "us," and I really want an "us," but he's all honourable and stuff and thinks I can't make decisions. We do hold hands when we're out, and sometimes he holds me when I cry. Once, we just cuddled a bit on the couch while we watched a movie. I don't have to be any particular way with him, or hide anything either.

And he's Ben. Sometimes I rail against the injustice. Sometimes I weep for Bruce and Adam. He holds me, and isn't asking the world for anything. He was there when I just needed to affirm love and life and all that was good. Even if I didn't deserve it.

And I started to tumble headlong into love, a kind of love that makes it okay to not shower for days, and have stringy hair, and puffy eyes, and see him in his sweatpants after a run and just think, "God, you are glorious." Even as his body bends, and creaks and shows his age. And beauty. I wanted to kiss him. Hard.

Aaron called me, and we struggled with the theology of things. He suggested I reach out to Peggy, which I did. She reminded me how to breathe as my soul laments. Aaron got me to think about our shared belief that love and compassion are always an appropriate response to just about anything, especially when it's hard to do. I'm trying to be loving and compassionate towards Al. And myself. And sometimes, he reminded me, if we were lucky, we experienced overwhelming joy because of it. I'm still looking for that. Skeptical, I admitted.

When Ben and I drove up the driveway at *Just Living* the next Tuesday, I burst into tears. Cook met me at the car, and enfolded me once more into his meaty arms. And I started to laugh out loud with the tears, trying to explain it was as much joy as sadness. I was a mess, and it felt so damned right. Kenny rounded the corner from the labyrinth and tore towards me. And then, we were. The three of us, so close it was hard to tell where one of us stopped and the other began. I felt so raw. And alive.

Cook had prepared all my favourites, and the potato chowder and tuna melts were the best kind of comfort food. Nora, Paul, Frank, Tom, Sally, Kate, even Veronica and Claire joined us and there were so many conversations bubbling up that at one point I just burst into tears at the glory. Which, I admit, kind of threw a damper on that. And was embarrassing. But I waved my hands at them to continue, and Frank handed me his hanky, and I burbled something to Ben about it just being so much goodness, it was a bit much all at once. And Frank told me (just a little infuriatingly) that this, too, is normal.

We talked over coffee and amazing cinnamon cookies about what we want to do at the circle, and I decided that I wanted to understand one thing afterwards. It was hard to really clearly get my head around what it is but I think this is it:

How am I changed because I knew Glenn and know Al? Or is that I know Glenn and knew Al?

And when I said it, we started telling stories. The best kind. Little snippets from Glenn's life, and Al's. Ben told them about me being under the table at the funeral, with Adam and Bruce. I cried a little for the boys, quiet sniffs, and Paul said something about making something for them. Anyways, then I remembered a story about Al I wanted to share, so I did.

I knew one thing for certain. Al said it best when he said it, weeks (lifetimes?) ago. We had been sharing a barbecue at *Just Living* over spring break, giving Cook the night off; some of the youth from the Friendship Centre were there. Veronica was there; she nodded as I told the story, remembering. I had been chatting with Tom, and facetiously asked him, "Hey Tom, what do you think, does punishment work?" Al uncharacteristically jumped in and answered for Tom, joining our conversation and our laughs.

"Bethy, if punishment worked, we'd be surrounded by angels, and I'd be the whitest one," he'd said.

At the time, we'd all chuckled at his cleverness, his dry humour. Now it felt prophetic. As we all knew, Glenn's children most intimately, an angel he ain't. And I ain't St. Beth, either, being so damned mad at him for not reaching out to me or someone else, no matter how much it hurt. For letting the monster out to murder my friend.

Anyhow, a little while later, we'd clarified some plans, left some stuff to the others to figure out, and agreed to get together on Sunday afternoon for the circle. I washed my face, trying to wipe away the puffiness around my eyes, the tracks of my tears, and Ben and I got ready to head out. Hugs were shared all around, over and over again. I promised not to be a stranger, and I really meant it. I wasn't done with this place. Oh, and Cook snuck me some cookies. Of course.

That night, Ben and I finally really kissed.

And more.

And it was just as glorious. Maybe even more glorious.

Thank you God.

For almost everything.

CHAPTER 48
RITUALS

Sunday morning, I rose early and watched the sunrise from the balcony on Ben's roof. As it sent light to world, I had a little conversation with Glenn. I wept as I apologized, said that if our roles were reversed (something that struck me as much more likely than our actual situation, in a quirky, weird way), I would only want Glenn to work on moving towards reconciliation, to building understanding and compassion. I felt his love surround my heart, through our lamentations. I promised him I would always look out for his boys.

Ben and I went to Quaker Meeting. I always felt covert when I attended there, like I didn't want anyone to report me to the Anglican police. We joked about it with the Friends during coffee. I loved the quiet, the connection between us all as we sat, discerning the Will of God. That morning, I shared some spoken ministry about Glenn, and my struggle to explain that I actually did understand how it happened, and I wish it hadn't happened, and I also still loved Al.

After some silence, a Friend stood and began a beautiful lamentation of *Amazing Grace*, which Friends picked up and sang in tender four-part harmony. I wept some more. Would I ever run out of tears?

That afternoon, it was weird to enter the Sanctuary with Tom at the door, and Hugh offering the sage to smudge. And I missed Al – healthy Al – just a little bit more. There were some men from the local minimum security prison who came out and were drumming on the big drum just outside the Sanctuary. Their voices rose and fell and the strength of the drums, of the voices, spoke for the generations of pain and honour that were held in their bones. I heard the sacredness of their welcome, felt the heartbeat of the drums in sync with all the hearts that would never beat again. And remembered my first experience of drums in the Sanctuary.

And then we were in circle. And we shared and laughed and lamented. Told new stories, dreamed new dreams. And the drummers started a big fire in the Sacred Grounds, and then we went there, and sat in the long summer evening, and burned logs and drank coffee.

Hugh handed me an axe at one point; he'd done something for me that I will always remember. That week, after I told him I wanted to wale on Al, he'd had Tom and Paul remove one of the long poles from the tipi. They set it up between two huge rounds that they had chopped a groove into. The pole laid across the logs, with about two or three feet between them, and about twenty sticking out one end. And I waled on the log, until it broke. And the men moved the log so I could break it again. And I chopped, and I sweated, and I grunted with each blow, and I dreamed it was Al's chest I was pounding on.

I think I broke that long pole about eight times before my arms felt like rubber, and my voice was gone. The men had been drumming along with me, not cheering, but accompanying. I felt their strength as I worked on living out my need to rage.

And then they burned the wood, all except Tom who took some of it, and pocketed it. Perhaps to carve later; perhaps there were spirits in the wood. Cook brought hot chocolate, and donuts out, and it was like communion.

The drummers had taken off their shirts, and truly looked like warriors, most playing large hand-drums now, the big drum loaded in a van. Some wore their hair down, streaming over their shoulders to their jeans, others wore braids. Some were shorn. There were coloured handkerchiefs tied around some of their brows, and a part of me wondered if I was looking at gang colours. They didn't try to wipe away the tears, dripping from their faces. And they played on, closing out the night for us, as we stood in a circle holding hands and remembering.

Hugh says he is going to leave the tipi unbalanced, with one pole missing, for a year, through all the seasons as they change, so that we can remember Glenn, and Al, and pay attention to what the Creator still has to teach us about our pain, and our opportunity to live on, past the hurt. The sagging cover looks like it might take up and fly away in the right wind. Hugh reassures me that won't happen, but I do see a gleam in his eye when he flaps it in and out, scaring away the birds. All except one Steller's Jay that keeps returning, looking for something.

One thing that happened with Bob at the circle was amazing. He's decided that since Glenn's death, one thing he can't risk is everyone not being aware of what is going on for him, so he told us to share. I think it's kind of a legacy to how things might have been different if Al had been honest, stayed connected to us.

Anyways, he ended up telling us all that he's a pedophile. Just like that. He explained that he hasn't had any problems or breaches since he's been out, but he says that's because of his Circle of Support and Accountability. Wow. The other men seemed mostly okay with the news. Kenny even alluded to knowing before, and a couple of the others nodded. I hope he doesn't get treated differently since he came clean. Or maybe I hope he is treated differently, just not badly. Maybe his 'coming clean' will help keep people safe. Anyhow, I thought he was brave.

The men had painted a beautiful Celtic cross with a labyrinth in the middle on the barn to honour Glenn. I cried when I saw it; it's perfect. And a Medicine Wheel on the ground outside a tipi. With one pole missing. Of course, that's perfect, too.

While we were bringing stuff into the kitchen, Bob pulled me into the Great Room to talk to me.

"I want to tell you what happened to me a while ago," he began. I invited him to sit on the old couch, and I hoped no one would come in.

"I was going to see Mom, and had to check in at Social Services. I was taking the bus because Paul couldn't get away to drive me, and so I had let myself have an extra hour or two. Bus connections went really well, and I was headed back up the valley and was going to call Kenny to come get me. And for some reason, I didn't." Didn't? I wondered what he meant.

"Instead, I got off by the big park downtown. You know the one. With the dog park and the tennis courts." I nodded. Glenn and I had run Tiger there one day.

"Well, I decided just to take a few minutes to walk around in the trees. At least, that's what I told myself. That I deserved a break, and I do, but not there. Anyhow, a few minutes later I found myself leaning on a garbage can at the kids' park, watching a couple of little boys playing. At first it just seemed so joyful, watching them ham it up with each other on the slide. Their mom was sitting watching them. They were so alive.

"And then it started. I realized about the same time that I was breaching my conditions, and feelings were being stirred up that I didn't like. Well, they were pleasurable, but I REALLY knew right away I needed to get away. I kept thinking of my circle, and you guys up here, and how I was getting my life together and didn't want to blow it.

"But more, Beth, I didn't want to wreck those boys' lives. Really. I got out of there so fast I couldn't believe it." I admit I was trying to make sense of what I had to do with this information, even as Bob was telling me that nothing bad had happened. I looked down at my hands. "Don't worry, Beth. You don't need to report me, I already did. I tore out of there and marched down to the coffee shop and asked to use the phone. I called Kenny, and he came and got me. I told him. He lent me his phone and I called Gerry, and Nora. I know better now.

"But I wanted you to know because I want you to get that *what you did here matters*. I can't say for sure exactly what made me get out of there, but something did, and you're a part of that. Really. Nothing happened that day because of my circle, and everyone at *Just Living* and that's why I wanted everyone to know what I'm dealing with.

"I've gone back on some meds for a bit, and I'm having some extra circles, but that's not your worry. I just wanted to thank you for coming out today, and for everything you've done here. You helped me believe I'm a person. That I have value. And *that* helped me wake up and realize I don't ever want to hurt anyone again, no matter how much I'm hurting or how stressed I am." Bob looked down at his hands, and squirmed just a little.

"Wow. Thank you Bob. That helps. Really." I was stumbling, realizing how much of a difference it did make. Maybe my judgment wasn't so warped.

"And I think you did the heavy lifting, and I want you to know that even if I played a small role, you played a leading one, and that's amazing," I said, taking the big galumph's hand and giving it a squeeze. And then Ben was there, and I wasn't sure how much he'd heard, but clearly Bob had known he was standing behind me, so I didn't freak out.

As we headed for the car, Hugh followed us. He told me he'd seen Al, and he reminded me that Al was being as responsible as he was able to be. The sentencing report was being prepared and would be presented in court closer to Christmas. I was glad Donna and her family wouldn't have to live through a trial, but of course, I also knew it meant there aren't any answers for them, no process to hear about what happened. I doubt the police will answer their questions, or let them pore over the "evidence."

Later, in the car, Ben and I talked about how glad we were to be a part of the ceremonies, the worship in the morning, the drumming and circle that afternoon, the fire that night. How much better I felt for reconnecting with everyone at *Just Living*. It felt so right.

I know I can't change anything, but life…well, it just sucks sometimes. And I'm trying to figure out why it is that even when it sucks I still can't hate Al. God I wish I could hate him. It would be so much simpler.

I've wondered a little if I still believe in compassion and forgiveness after all this, and now that I think about hurt and pain and relieving suffering first. I just can't hate Al. Or even the priest who first caused him suffering. It's just a long litany of pain and hurting others, back as far as I can imagine, and I just want so badly for it to stop.

And if not now, then when, God?

Aaron sent me this quote he'd "happened upon." I get it, but I'm not living it yet.

Well, maybe a little.

> "Although the world is filled with suffering, it is filled also with the overcoming of it."
>
> – Helen Keller.

Truth that.

But I'm still mad at you, God.

And sometimes, I feel You near me, and I'm almost glad that You're there. Like in the voices of the singers….

CHAPTER 49
ACKNOWLEDGEMENTS

A few days later, Bishop Tom called. We met, and talked, and he wanted me to be ordained. Like soon. Not because he's worried I'll leave but because he wants "an outward acknowledgement" of all I've been through.

"You've learned more than most priests do in a lifetime, Beth, and you should be acknowledged for that. I'd ordain you tomorrow if I could, but arrangements do need to be made. Do you mind a summer ordination? I'm not going on holidays. I think your family would be happy. And Ben, too," he said, smiling. I smiled back.

And that's how, just two weeks later, two full months before our first plans, I found myself in Ben's condo praying.

Dear God,

I can't believe the day is here already, I'm doing this…it feels so right and oh, so dangerous, too.

How do I live up to this call? How do I encourage this "club" to live faithfully, to be alive in Your Spirit? How do I encourage them to "see, then, what Love can do?"

I feel so inadequate to wear the cloth, to belong to this exclusive club. How do I make my life welcoming, and be a beacon for Your path?

Am I doing the Right Thing? And what if it feels right now, but I don't trust myself to really know, because...well...I've made that mistake before?

What do I do with this Promise I'm making you? To "solemnly declare that I do believe the holy scriptures of the Old and New Testaments to be the word of God, and to contain all things necessary to salvation; and I do solemnly promise to conform to the doctrine, discipline, and worship of the Anglican Church of Canada." I have to declare that my life will be a precept to your teachings, that I will offer penitence, love, forgiveness, will study the Bible, and truth and yada yada yada...and I'm really unsure of my integrity in this.

Except that right now, this feels so right.

Once again – I'm trusting You that we'll figure this out together, okay?

Maybe this is the precipice I've been dreaming about.

Or maybe nightmaring....

Beth

"Oh my God, you look beautiful." Ben came up behind me and put his hands on my shoulders, kissing my neck. I was standing in front of the mirror, trying on my white alb – the long, boring "dress" that becoming-priests get to wear to be ordained. It had a simple rope belt, and a big fold-over collar. I thought it looked mildly like a curtain. I knew the swish dress I was wearing underneath was *way* nicer, but I smiled back at him in the mirror. I'd never thought about the benefits of being with an ex-monk. He thought my work clothes were...dare I say, sexy?

"I just thought I'd make sure it all works – I panicked that my dress would show through. It doesn't though, right?" I said.

He smiled over my shoulder into our reflection in the mirror.

I'd told him last week that I'd talked to the Bishop about my adventure with Glenn at the Remand Centre last year. It'd been important to come clean to everyone, both in the Church and at *Just Living*. I was surprised when they treated the story like they had the ones of the guys brewing inside; I was so confused that they weren't angry at me, and talked to Aaron about it.

"No harm, no foul," he'd said. "But I'm glad you're telling us. That takes the powerful potential to hurt you away from the story." A few minutes later he clarified.

"Beth, if you reframe 'crime' as harm against people or relationships, what you did doesn't qualify. Really. Like smoking weed, or sex working. It's all in perspective."

Looking in the mirror, I wondered if I'd ever "get it." Sigh. Ben's nuzzle at my collar brought me back.

"Wait a minute," he said, ducking into the bedroom. Our bedroom. At some point, we'd stopped pretending one of us was sleeping on the couch, and I'd really taken over his space. He came back in with a long box. "Roses?" I thought. That would be...kinda weird, I decided. No one would give a man being ordained roses. He gave it to me.

"I was going to wait for the church, but this is better," he said. "Open it now!" I carefully lifted the lid.

Inside was a beautiful stole – the colourful scarf thing priests wear around their necks. Only I'd wear it on one shoulder for the first year, kind of a sentinel warning to people that I was only a becoming-priest.

It literally took my breath away. It was embroidered – by hand, I guessed – and had images of a dove, a cross, a floating flame, all intermingled with a campfire, a tipi, a horse, a cat...it was *Just Living* in a picture. And it somehow reflected West Coast Aboriginal art – echoes of the Medicine Wheel. My breath caught when I saw the ladybug, perched on a tree branch. And the whole stole was beaded. It was quite a fancy thing, even for the Anglicans.

"The guys helped design it a few months ago, even before you left. I think they knew you'd be ordained before you did, and they wanted to let you know they're okay with it. Claire, Sally and Veronica got everybody to do a few stitches. It was Claire who really drove the project," he said. I noticed a spatula, a picture of thyme. Throughout it was a path, winding, turning, like the labyrinth. Every man had something depicted, and I smiled.

"It was almost done when it happened," Ben said. "They were worried about giving it to you. But then Hugh had an idea." Ben's finger moved to the top of the tipi. There was a pole missing. My breath caught.

"I noticed," I said. "How could I not?"

"Kenny insisted on picking it out with tweezers and a razor blade. He used a magnifying glass so he didn't cut the fabric. And he made sure his tears didn't stain the stole," Ben finished, whispering.

"He also embroidered this." Ben's finger traced a Celtic cross, just like the one on the barn for Glenn. Tears were dripping from my chin. *God, I'm a sight!* I'd prayed. I hoped I didn't do this *too* much during the service.

"Oh my God. It is so beautiful. Fancy for a Quaker," I joked. I couldn't take my eyes off of it.

"Well, it is fancy, but the Bishop agreed to let you wear it during the sacrament today if you want," Ben said. "The guys would love it. A few were a bit miffed to do lady's work. But some were so into it. Paul and Tom and Al were adding beads…." Ben's voice trailed off. "I wasn't supposed to tell you yet," he said sheepishly. So Al had helped.

"I wondered." I took a breath. "It's okay, really," I said, tracing the threads that rose from the fire into the dove. The stole was white fabric, but hardly a square centimetre was without colour. The right side was stitched in red, orange and yellow. The other side, the one that would hang over my left shoulder (or my back, for now) was embroidered in greens, and blues, and brown. The labyrinth was depicted in beads, couched throughout the pictures shown. My finger couldn't help but follow them as the colours shifted one into another. I could see this would become a habit, something I would do during long sermons someone else was preaching.

Ben kissed the top of my head, and reminded me that we had to get on the road or I'd miss my own ordination.

"And it was quite a road to get here," he said. "I'd hate to miss the final act." He was smiling, the smile of a lover who knows you well.

The service was amazing. The men from *Just Living* drummed everyone into the Cathedral, lined up in ribbon shirts on either side of the stairs, their song literally stopping traffic. At least the Weather Gods cooperated, and it was warm, and dry. Sometimes, a Vancouver summer is a beautiful thing.

First the friends and family trickled in, then the priests (including Dad, and a couple of chaplains who weren't even Anglican, but had been invited), followed by myself, Stephen, who was supporting me, and Bishop Tom, in his full regalia, complete with mitre and funny hat. We were resplendent.

As we processed up the centre aisle (I had NEVER figured out how LONG it was before), the drummers followed us into the church, drumming from the rear. Their voices amplified even stronger in the amazing acoustics, and it was then I started to weep. As I walked up the aisle, I couldn't help but reach out and hug my friends as I saw them in the church. *They* were a bit embarrassed, I admit, but I hugged each one.

The men from *Just Living*. My mentors. Julia, and a couple of other students from the chaplain's office. Rev. Tom, the UBC Chaplain. Trish. Some of Dad's parishioners. Carol, her son Scott. Veronica, and the other women from *Just Living*. Yes, even Claire. Something had shifted.

Some AVP volunteers, and folks from the Friendship Centre in Mission. I was so humbled, seeing everyone coming to my party! In the front row, Mom, Sarita, Daya and Ben sat, and just behind Ben, Hugh sat with Aaron. As Ben watched us process, stopping to hug everyone, he reached across the pew and put a hand on Aaron's shoulder. I was reminded that this was an outward recognition of God's ordination, Her Call to Service I felt in my bones, and these people, every one of them, had helped me discern. Kate and Nora were holding hands and looked like newlyweds with a secret.

The drums stopped as we reached the steps to the sanctuary (that place that holds the altar), and the silence was deafening. I felt a bit sheepish that I'd taken so long getting up the aisle; later, Paul teased me that he wouldn't be able to sing for a week, he'd had to keep going so long with the honour song. He was pleased, though, I could tell. I sighed as Bishop Tom invoked the greeting, answered enthusiastically with the rest of the people there.

"Blessed be God, Father, Son and Holy Spirit," he said, his voice lifting from the silence that had followed the last beat of the drums.

"Blessed be His Kingdom, now and forever," the congregation gathered responded. And we were off.

And an hour later we were done. I'd accepted, with God's help, the responsibilities of the priesthood. I'd publicly stated my beliefs, and I'd agreed to abide by church canon. My friends had agreed to support me. I was a Deacon! And I didn't feel any different than I had entering the church. Well, not entirely true. I wasn't as nervous. And I hadn't stumbled, or fallen into an altar rail, or torn my alb.

There was a reception in the hall, but I took about 20 minutes getting there. I hung out on the front steps of the Cathedral thanking every person who came. I knew the guys would never go into the church hall; for too many years they hadn't been welcomed, and it wasn't a very comfortable space for them. I was amazed so many had come into the church. It had taken courage and I was grateful.

Before Ben and I went into the hall to shake hands with the Anglicans, I promised to come out to *Just Living* next week. Nora and Kate wanted us to come to dinner, so we made plans. Before that, starting Monday, Ben and I had a quest to complete for a couple of boys.

Until then, a couple of days rest at the cabin. I left my swimsuit at home, and the swimming was glorious.

Thank you God.
For all of it.
All. Of. It.

CHAPTER 50
THE QUEST

Dear God,

There's a Psalm we pray that I like. "May these words of my mouth and this meditation of my heart be pleasing to you." Psalm 19:14

I need that today, but with more...movement. So how about:

May the steps of my feet and the words of my mouth be good with you to guide me. Or something. Or maybe just...help?

Monday morning broke bright and early. Well, early-ish. Ben and I woke in the cabin and packed up; we weren't sure when we'd be back, so we did the few things needed to prepare it for winter. We were on the road, heading for Mount Currie by 9:00, and only stopped once for coffee on the way, at a café in Hope. Yum. Ben had borrowed a friend's truck, so we were set to bring as much back as we could fit. We'd send anything left by Greyhound, I hoped.

Three and a half hours later, we were driving on the land of the Lil'wat Band. A little while later, we pulled up to the RCMP station in Pemberton. We'd taken the long road around, through Lytton, enjoying the mountain views without the hassle of travelling through Vancouver. Pemberton was the closest detachment, and Insp. Derksen had told them we were coming, thanks to Nora. We were greeted with coffee and an invitation into the back room. It may have helped that I sported my new collar; uniforms look like a variety of things, I'm learning.

"We've been keeping an eye on the place. The church gave us keys to hand on to you, and they dropped off some boxes from the church office in the garage. I think some of the women from the church did some cleanup after we released the site," Cst. Burrows said. She looked uncomfortable, and I imagined dealing with families of murder victims who had to clean up crime sites was an uncomfortable part of her job. "Our office administrator called them to let them know you'd be by, so they might drop in," she finished.

Ben and I followed the GPS to the house; the plan was to sort and pack up quickly. We hoped to be on the road back to Ben's that evening. And I knew I might be rushing it just so I could be done the hard job.

I pushed the key into the lock and turned it really tentatively as we headed into the house where Glenn had died. Stepping over the threshold, I called out "Hello?" but no one answered. I was scared to walk into the house, not really sure what would greet me. Ben's hands were on my shoulders, and I felt the weight of his support, the security. I was glad I had waited for him to be available; at first I'd insisted I could do this quest alone, but Ben didn't let me. *Thank God.*

Behind me, a voice called back from behind, on the front porch. "Reverend Hill?" Would I ever get used to that? Didn't help that it was Dad's name first. Ben and I turned, and I stuck out my hand to greet a grey-haired, plump woman bustling up the walkway, being dragged by a much-larger Tiger on a leash. Right. Arrangements for the dog had been made; Donna would take him. I'm not sure she really knew what to expect, though. I promised myself we'd make it work.

"I'm so glad to catch you," she said. "We've done a little work for you, I hope you don't mind," she said. I saw she was embarrassed. "Let me show you what we've done," she finished, sweeping us into the kitchen. Tiger raced off to charge around the house.

Which wasn't pristine, but wasn't a disaster either. Smudges of black fingerprint powder were on doors and windowsills in the living room, and there was a stack of boxes, taped shut and numbered, in the corner. The curtains were closed, and the furniture sparse.

"I'm Clara, the Rector's Warden. Clara Moore." God. She knew Glenn. "I hope we haven't taken liberties, but it was good for us to keep busy," she said, and I felt the ripples that cascaded outwards from this crime. These people were devastated, and as we chatted while she took us through the house, I realized they were struggling too. She grabbed a sheaf of papers from the counter.

"We had to keep busy, so we cleaned up a bit. It was quite a mess," she continued. "We packed up Glenn's things. And the boys'. How are Adam and Bruce?" she asked, and I knew these people loved Glenn, and his boys. I shared a little about them, how I thought they were doing, told her a little about our picnic under the tablecloth at the funeral.

"I guessed you'd be good people," she said, patting my hand. "Glenn talked about you, and you too," she said, turning to Ben. She was tut tutting, and tugging at the corner of her sweater pocket.

"Anyhow, a few women and I washed and sorted stuff. It's amazing how much of that black powder the police got on everything."

I admit, I hadn't been ready for that. Didn't Nora say Al had turned himself in? Why all the mess, then?

"We've put stuff we think the boys will want in some boxes. These things can probably go right back to the thrift store where they came from," she said, pointing to the small stack of boxes in the corner. "But we didn't think it was our job to do that until we got your okay," she finished. I was so grateful. Now I could admit, in the face of just how much work there was, that I had been terrified of what this quest would involve.

We walked through the house, and I noticed shadows of Glenn and the boys everywhere. And evidence of police work.

"I think in case of appeal," Ben said, answering my question before I asked it. He really did know me.

Here was the living room they gamed in. I could see it, almost hear them. Except for the enormity of what *wasn't* in the room.

"I know we didn't ask, but we did some things here. I hope it helps." I looked at Clara and smiled.

"I really appreciate all you've done, Mrs. Moore." She smiled, her shoulders dropped.

"The couch," I said. There was a space in the room where I imagined it had been.

"Yes, and the rug. We took them to the dump. There were some toys that were broken and…well…a mess. I made a list so you'd know what they were, and we took them to the dump, too. The guys in Search and Rescue helped me move stuff, and the police officers and some folks from the church got some things to replace what was lost." She pointed to a pile of boxes in the corner, the ones with a TV on top.

"Those are the boys' things. The box with NEW written on it, well, that's the stuff for Adam and Bruce that the folks here put together."

I brushed a tear from my eye, and Ben handed me his clean hankie. I inhaled the line-dried freshness, my body working hard to not imagine the metallic scent of death I'd anticipated. Tiger nudged his head under my hand, and I scratched behind his ears, working to keep my nausea at bay.

Clara held open her arms, and then I was in them, and I felt like I was being held by the arms of God. Her softness, the proverbial shoulder for my tears, it was all frighteningly alive. She steered me towards the back of the house, where the two bedrooms and the bathroom lay. Tiger followed.

"The boys' room we packed up. Everything in there was fine except for the dirty laundry on the floor from, well, the boys. That made me cry a bit. I took it all home and washed it, and their sheets and towels and stuff. I didn't know if they'd want the furniture, but it's here," she said.

I stood back, amazed at these people who had loved the boys so well. Fallen in love so quickly.

"Thank you," was all I could say. "You've done so much to help, it's amazing," I kept on.

"I'm feeling a little embarrassed, actually. Until I started to tell you, I didn't know quite how much we'd done. It seems...well...maybe presumptuous. But, Rev. Hill, it was awful here, and I didn't want you to see that," she said, again tut tutting.

"Call me Beth, please. This is amazing. I hadn't thought about how much I didn't want to face this, but I'd promised the boys."

"Tiger and I are going to go see if we can scare up some tea after a short walk," Ben offered, "and then we can fortify ourselves to make a plan. Why don't you two finish the tour?" he said, disappearing into the kitchen with Tiger.

We headed for Glenn's room, where Clara had again tidied, cleaned and packed most of Glenn's things.

"I left these things out. I thought you'd want to see them," she said, and I headed for the dresser where some of Glenn's religious jewellery was laid out, with a few small sculptures and paintings of Aboriginal art. "The band members had given these to him. I didn't know if his ex-wife would want them, but I thought you might. Either for yourself or to save for the boys, when they grow up."

Again, I was moved by her kindness. She had placed a small box beside the dresser for those things, and I placed them carefully on the tissue.

"Donna told me she doesn't want any of the furniture, but I think I'll take the kneeler, if that's okay," I said, noticing Glenn's prayer desk in the corner. He'd made it one summer when he was studying Anabaptist traditions.

"Prie-dieu," he'd called it, in a cultural clash of Shaker carpentry and Catholic sensibilities. It folded, and the kneeler had a cushion he'd pieced together horribly. I smiled, remembering him saying, "Well, the Guild isn't going to ask me to help with their stitching, at least," as he'd finished it. Working with the elderly women in the Altar Guild had been the bane of Glenn's existence, but I bet he'd welcome the chore now, given the chance.

"She did say she'd take his clothes and stuff, but I think she really didn't know what she meant. We'll take it all to her, though. We'll put them in her parents' garage and she can decide what to do later," I said, and we strolled to the kitchen when Ben called us.

He'd pulled three chairs off the table, and unpacked one box that had held the "tea fixings," as he put it. "I couldn't find any biscuits in the boxes," he said, "so Tiger and I grabbed the scones you had in the car."

"Lovely," was all Clara said, but I heard, "He's a keeper," in her voice. The stern look that accompanied her comment was clearly directed at me. I thanked him with a hug, wanting her to know I appreciated him.

We settled in, and I thought to bow my head before we began. A quick prayer of thanks, and a blessing on the town, and we were making a list of "to dos." I pulled out the "Quest Action Plan" Bruce and Adam and I had put together, and we checked off to make sure I wasn't missing anything.

Clara was able to reassure us that most of the things on the list were there. The boys' gaming console was in the dump, but the church had passed the plate and replaced it, along with the *Mario Kart* game. The men at the Search and Rescue had even checked the old game to see the "accounts" and had played the new version with new "Rev. Daddy," "Bruce" and "Adam" tags, and achieved miraculous results so the boys would feel that connection with their dad. High scores for each of them had been saved. They had thought of everything, I realized, tearing up again.

"The Elders would like you to come to a dinner tonight. It's not a big feast or anything, because they didn't really want to assume you'd come, but there is some salmon and bannock and a few other things they'd like to feed you. And they'd like to talk to you, if that's okay," she said.

I choked up again. Luckily, Ben's voice was working.

"We'd be honoured. What time should we be there? And where is there?" he asked.

A few minutes later, we had a plan. We were going to move the bikes from the garage onto the top of the truck, and then folks from the church were going to come and help pack the boxes into the truck.

"Keith has been looking forward to it," Clara said. "He made some reference to enjoying *Tetris*," she smiled.

By four o'clock, we were done and had gotten everything we needed to take back packed in. We washed up and heading towards the Lil'wat Band office. I asked Clara if I could visit Glenn's church on the way.

"Glenn had an amazing way of getting us Anglicans together, but we didn't have a church here, Beth. He travelled to Ashcroft sometimes to worship there, and Lytton, and Whistler. But mostly, he gathered us here and in Pemberton. There are no churches though. They were sold a while back. We met in community halls and sometimes in the United Church."

I was surprised; Glenn hadn't really made that clear to me. I wondered what else he'd struggled with.

"The last month or so he was talking to the Catholic Church in town, and we'd shared worship space with St. Christopher's. Do you want to go there?" she asked. "I'm sure I can get a key," she said.

"Was that the last place he worshiped? Officiated?" I asked, and she nodded.

A few minutes later she had dropped us at the Band Office, and was off to look for the key. Blessedly, she took Tiger with her. Ben and I had decided to drop by the church on our way back to Vancouver that night. *Good Lord willing,* I thought. Prayer.

The Band Office was beautiful. Small, welcoming and gorgeous. Soon, we were introduced around, and I admit, other than the Chief, who was named Lillian, I was so overwhelmed with the day that I don't remember much.

The gymnasium where we ate was decorated, but I got the impression from the dust that the decorations weren't just for us. Tables were set up, and we ate, about twenty of us, sharing salmon, salad, bannock, juice, and corn. It tasted like a feast, even if they didn't call it that.

There were traditional dishes prepared by some real culinary artists. Blessedly, there were no formal speeches or anything, but after dinner the Chief said some words about how sorry she was for what had happened, and how her people were determined to help others like Al who continued to "hurt people."

She talked a little about how Glenn had built relationships within her community, and built bridges between them and the students and activists at UBC. Her Nation was determined to continue to oppose any pipelines from coming through these mountains to a port on the West Coast. And after listening to her wisdom and passion for a few minutes, I asked if I could serve in any way as a continuing "conduit."

She smiled, and everything seemed to make more sense. Why I felt compelled to come here. Why these people genuinely cared about Glenn, and Bruce and Adam. And why they were grieving letting him go. Ben spoke a bit.

"I don't know if it makes sense for us to make promises about what we can do, until we know what the next few months are going to look like," he said.

"I do promise you that we'll make sure the connections stay real. I'll make sure Julia, and the Legal Students' Society stay in touch, and that this work doesn't stop," he said, and I nodded along. Emphatically.

"Glenn would have wanted that to happen," I said. "Al, too," I realized. "We have to build on the good connections that were happening. Make some good come from this sadness," I ended. And suddenly, I was tired. Exhausted. Ben had disappeared with Lillian, and were whispering in a corner. I imagined they were sharing contact information, or something.

By seven o'clock we'd collected Tiger, spent a half hour in the Catholic Church where Glenn had worshipped, and were on the road. Ben had a surprise for me.

"We're stopping in Whistler," he said, without inviting a discussion. I was so grateful.

"How will we keep Bruce's stuff safe?" I said, thinking about the bikes and wagon strapped to the top of the truck.

"Lillian called ahead. She's booked us room in a place that has underground parking, near the Cultural Centre. People are going to watch the truck for us, and take Tiger overnight. It'll be fine," he said, and I was glad I'd packed stuff from the cabin.

An hour later, I was curled up in the hot tub on our deck, looking out at the mountains and trying to imagine where all of this was going for me. Ben joined me with a glass of the wine he'd stopped and bought, and some snacks on a plate, and fed my body and my soul. In no time, I was fast asleep, and Ben was doing some work in the kitchen. I slept long, and hard, and didn't wake up until after noon the next day.

It was delicious to be able to spend the energy I needed to grieve, and I wondered how single mothers, and the lonely aged, and poor people coped. Or didn't. I felt so loved, cared for, and rose the next day with a prayer.

Thank you, God, for Your Grace expressed in my life through Ben. And Glenn. And Lillian, and Clara.

And even Tiger.

Weird, I know. Prayer, though.

CHAPTER 51
PROMISES

Dear God,

I continue to read. To work. To pray. Maybe I did learn something with all that study. Today I noticed this in my reading, and it reminded me how hard I'm finding it to do grief and joy, work and waiting, study and mundane chores, sometimes in the same breath.

> *The spiritual life is not a life before, after, or beyond our everyday existence. No, the spiritual life can only be real when it is lived in the midst of the pains and joys of the here and now.*
>
> *— Henry Nouwen*

I don't even know if I need it to get easier, God. Maybe I just need to be easier with it...to take it as it comes. And I'm starting to feel the value in all of it.

I just wish I didn't have to miss Glenn so much to know this.

Amen

Ben and I were enjoying a break after all the things, and were spending time readying the condo for fall. I'd really "moved in," and we'd decided that we "lived together." That morning, we'd raked the walnut leaves in the common garden, helping to clean up in preparation for the winter rains when rotting leaves became as slippery as ice.

It was mid-September, and while the rest of the neighbours headed into work, it was the first day of our weekend. Well, really, it was the first day of *Ben's* weekend; I wasn't working too much yet, but I was starting to think I should be. I couldn't really keep on doing so little for too much longer. I wanted to feel like I was contributing to say...the groceries or, well...the world. Meaningful work meant...well...I should actually be working. I'd figured that much out, and was sorting through the rest. Like answering "Doing what?"

Anyhow, it was late Monday morning, and I was puttering in the kitchen, baking some healthy bread for Stephen and Sarita, and laying some loaves into the freezer for us. Because, well, maybe the six loaves I'd already frozen wouldn't quite see us through the apocalypse? A zombie attack? I loved baking, but I did need to find something else to occupy me.

As I kneaded the hearty dough, I remembered that Bishop Tom had wanted me to touch base. I carefully held a pen in my floury fingers and scribbled, "Call Tom tomorrow" on a Post-it, and stuck it to the cupboard over the oven. I put the loaves in their pans, with a warm cloth draped over them to prevent drafts. To cuddle the yeast, I told myself, hearing Nana Beth's voice in my head.

Ben came up behind me and wrapped his arms around me, kissing my neck. "Laughing at yourself now? Any jokes you want to share?" he whispered.

"Nope. Just hearing voices," I said, turning in his arms to return his embrace. "Nana's talking to me again."

"Wisdom, I bet," he said.

"Must cuddle the yeast?" I admitted. He smiled.

"When you have a minute, do you want to come into the office? I have something to show you," he said, and I took his hand and he led us down the hall into the small spare bedroom-office. His ancient computer was turned on under the antique table, and his monitor was dark. Hmmm. He sat on the bed and patted the mattress. I sat beside him, and wondered what the heck was going on.

"I got an email from Eric this morning. I don't know what to do with it," he said.

"Read it?" I still joke when I'm uncomfortable.

"Wise you are. Wise I did," he said. "He's decided he wants to stay in India for the next...well, he didn't really say. He's entering a monastery there."

"Wow. Maybe I won't get to meet him after all," I said, acknowledging it wasn't all about me even as I said it. Ben laughed.

"No, actually, I think you will. He's coming for a visit and wants us to do something together."

"Camping at the cabin!" Now I was excited, except...camping, small cabin, man I've never met from Ben's past...well, I was still sure we could make it happen. Even have a great time.

"Sort of. He wants to sign title over to us. He says if he enters the monastery it would just make things less complicated because of his upcoming vows, and he trusts us to use it for good." Ben's voice belied how uncomfortable he was with this extravagant gift.

"And?" I asked. It was such a lovely gesture; I couldn't imagine a friend of Ben's NOT giving him a cabin. But I might be biased. Just a little.

"I don't know. It's a lot to accept. And I love the idea of stewarding the cabin, taking care of it. Sharing it with people who need a time to be refreshed. But he owns about forty acres. It seems a lot to accept."

"What would help you decide?" I asked, hoping for one more trip to the cabin before the cold really set in.

"Yes, I think going up there would help," he said, knowing me well. "If we leave now, we can stay until Wednesday." With a smile, he stood up, opening the cupboard and pulling out our packs and other equipment. "Can you get some food together for a couple of days? I'll wrap up the bedding, and sort the clean clothes so we can pack. If you want, you could drop me right at work on Wednesday and head to *Just Living* for the day. We're supposed to have dinner with Nora and Kate that night anyways, right?"

I smiled and hugged him, putting my hand on his chest.

"You are brilliant, my love," I said. "I will even take some work up with me. I have to finish the prospectus for the resiliency training I want to do," I said. My mind was working quickly, making lists and planning.

An hour and a half later, we were packed, the bread was cooling, and Stephen had been called and told to pick it up later, along with Topaz. Ben was running things down to the car, and I was on the phone with the Bishop.

"Bishop Tom," I started, stumbling now that I had him on the phone. "Thanks for the locums. It's been great to feel useful, at least a couple of times this past month." I'd preached at two churches when their rectors had been away. No one had run out of the church when I'd shown up. "If there's any other way I can help out, just ask." Now I was rambling.

"I expect I'll have that prospectus for you mid-week. I've talked to the CSC Psychologist and he's agreed to work with me. The folks at St. Paul's Hospital who did my pastoral training have connected me with a person at Rape Relief to do some trauma training. I think that work will occupy me about two days a week, and I'm still helping out at *Just Living* from time to time," I finished. "If there's anything else you need to approve my plan, I'm happy to work on it," I said.

"Have you talked to Nora recently?" he asked. I raised my eyebrows, ever so slightly.

"No, she talked to Ben over the weekend. We're going to have dinner with her and Kate on Wednesday." I said.

"Great. Why don't we meet for lunch on Friday," he finished. He was clearly on his way somewhere. It was, after all, his day off too. "Call on Thursday and set it up with the office," he said, and rang off. Hanging up the phone I got the impression that HE'D talked to Nora, and I wondered what was up.

By nightfall, we'd hiked into the cabin, and I was serving a delicious hearty stew with thick slices of my fresh bread. The tea was steeping, and I'd even snuck some leftover berry crumble into the pack. And cream.

One perk of hiking up this late in the season was that the foodbox-in-the-tree thing was cool enough that we could bring perishables.

After dinner and clean up, Ben and I sat on our rocking chairs by the fire, reading. We'd talked a little about my plans, and he'd convinced me he had no idea what Nora wanted with the Bishop. He was so lacking in guile that I believed him.

One thing he'd insisted on bringing up to the cabin this time was a large collapsible aluminum box. Heavy, but animal-proof. He started to talk about all the stuff he intended to store in it, away from the mice and rats.

"We can leave our bedding, and some linens," he said. "A few things that I carry in and out all the time." He was talking about his second Bible, and a couple of other books. "Some toiletries, so that we don't have to be bringing things in and out. Spices, staples that won't attract bears."

"You do understand," I said, smiling, pulling the blanket up over my knees. Ben rose to stoke the fire. He went to the kitchen and brought back glasses of wine for us to share.

"Understand what?" he said as he handed me the delicious red.

"That perhaps it is meant to be yours," I said. "That you can steward this space, and make it something meaningful." I wondered if he had other ideas about how to use this place well.

"Come here," he said, lifting me up into his arms. "Let's dance," he offered, putting his phone in a bowl to amplify the music.

We danced by the firelight, and made plans to bathe in the hot springs the next day. And then we made love by the moonlight, streaming in the glass of the cathedral windows over the front porch. For once, I didn't awaken with nightmares, and neither did Ben.

The next morning we made our way to the springs. I had again left my swimsuit at home, but packed big, soft (and so not heavy to carry) towels. Ben carried some food and a blanket and tarp for the wet ground. It was dark, and moist, and cool in the air around the pool, and we sunk in to our necks quickly. It was such a relief to soak, to feel the tension leave my body.

Ben stood behind me and started to rub my shoulders. Oh. My. God. That was a whole new kind of ecstasy. I groaned. It felt so delicious.

I remembered what Frank had encouraged me to do, and tried it. It worked. I was able (for a few moments) to think about Bruce, and Adam, and Glenn, and Al, and all the pain. And I even stayed in it for a bit, without becoming overcome with it all.

"What do you think it would be like to be coming here when we're sixty?" Ben dreamed.

"Amazing," I said. "I think I'd wrinkle a little more quickly, though." I smiled, thinking about it.

"Would we have kids?" he asked. I laughed.

"I hope I have kids. I've never really dreamed about 'our kids' though. Seems presumptive. Do you want kids?" I asked, looking back at him. My heart started fluttering.

"I didn't think I did until I met you. Now I can't imagine not having a family with you," he said.

"Awww...that's sweet," I said. "But isn't that getting ahead of ourselves? Perhaps I should find a job, do something meaningful for a bit...." my voice trailed off, not mentioning the obvious.

"Get married?" Ben suggested.

"Well, talk about it at least." This was awkward.

"How much do you need to think about it?" Ben asked. He was rummaging in his pack. He reached around in front of me and held something in front of my face.

"Beth, would you marry me?" he asked.

OMG! It was a ring! And then I was hyperventilating, and Ben was hugging me above the steaming water. It only took a moment to catch my breath, and then I cascaded right to weeping.

"Well?" he asked, and I felt wonder and joy bubbling up inside, and in another breath I was wrapping my arms around his neck, and laughing out loud, and crying, and shouting a resounding and definitive "YES!" to the trees, to the rain, to the universe!

"I can't believe it! Are you sure?" I asked. I had always assumed we'd talk about it, like we had before I'd moved all my stuff into his house, like when I decided what training to take, and how to support him in the prison. When to let the inmates know we were a "couple." But this was HUGE! And it felt so SO right. This was joy, and it was delightful to feel it so fully. Ben laughed.

"Am I sure? Do you think I would ask if I wasn't sure? Have I ever asked when I wasn't sure?" He smiled at me. "I thought about talking about it with you, and every time I thought about our conversation, I decided I just wanted to propose. I am so sure that I just want you to say yes. I'm more sure than I was when I took my vows," he said, his voice becoming like a whisper. And I knew he meant it. And when I sat in that knowing for just a minute, I knew there was not one thing that made me wonder, "Do I?"

"Yes! Yes!" I said. "I want this!" We sat for a bit, grinning.

"If it's any consolation, I mean 'Yes!' more than I did the first time I said it." I was thinking about my divorce, and the failed "yeses" I'd made in my life. This felt so different. I was giddy. And then we toasted "Yes!" and made love, and dried one another before hiking in the dark back to the cabin for a meal. It was a magical time, and reflecting back now, there is not one thing I would change about us. About this. About my life.

Even, maybe especially, all the difficult bits.

Unless I could have Al and Glenn back. That's the only thing. And I know that's just wishful...whatever.

That night, drinking tea, Ben told me he'd mentioned to Stephen that he might ask me, and Stephen had talked to Mom, who slipped him Nana Beth's ring. Seems my parents had been saving it for me, but because Nana had still been alive (and wearing it) when I got married the first time, this was the first time I'd seen it since Nana had been buried.

"Is it okay?" Ben asked. "I'm happy to buy you something. Us something. Really."

It was darling how discombobulated he was. I was tearing up, imagining how happy Nana would be for me.

"She'd love you," I said. "I'm so happy. This ring is perfect," I said. "I'm a little miffed, though, that you talked to Stephen and Mom before me." Let's face it, I was.

"Well, I did and I didn't. I mentioned to Stephen I was thinking about it, but I told him I wouldn't ask until Christmas. He got excited and talked to your mom. They don't know I wanted to ask you now. Honest. Really." His voice was getting a little high-pitched, and I just couldn't pull it off, pretending to be mad.

"As long as you didn't ask for permission to take me over as property, I actually think its sweet," I said. And I meant that, too. Later, I had to read this bit from my book out loud to Ben. It's perfect.

Let there be spaces in your togetherness,

And let the winds of the heavens dance between you.

Love one another but make not a bond of love:

Let it rather be a moving sea between the shores of your souls.

– Kahlil Gibran

CHAPTER 52
POSSIBILITIES

Dear God,

I think I've used this prayer before, but it keeps popping up in my life.

If the only prayer you say in your entire life is "Thank You," it will be enough.

I think Meister Eckhart said it first. Or maybe recorded it first.

Thank you.

That's enough.

May I remember my privilege well...and wear it with humility.

 The next day we winterized the cabin, packing the aluminum box to leave behind. Bedding, some water bottles, spices, even our wine glasses made it in, and there was more room. I was already thinking about some of the staples I could bring that would let me get all creative in the kitchen in spring. Ben boarded up the windows, and drained the pump, and we locked the door and headed down the hill. I left Ben at the Principle Entrance of the prison before 10:00, and he headed into work. I agreed to pick him up at 5:00 to head to Nora and Kate's for dinner.

The day flew by. I visited a yarn store, and had tea at The Tea Shoppe on First Avenue. I did a little grocery shopping, and even remembered to finish my prospectus and send it to the pastoral care people and Bishop Tom. I had to remember that I was done school, and give myself permission to base the plans on whatever I wanted to learn, not what I thought they'd want to see. I was actually interested in hearing from crime victims about all the ways the churches preferentially serve inmates/ "the fallen sheep," and don't meet the victims' needs after they've been hurt. I was sure I'd learn a lot, that hopefully I could share with ministers later. Maybe some of it would even make a difference.

On the way to Nora and Kate's I asked Ben if he'd be disappointed if I took my ring off until later. He looked a little disappointed, but when I told him I wanted it to be our secret for just a bit, maybe until I had a chance to tell my family and he'd decided what to do about his family, he understood. I put it on the chain with my cross. It nestled nicely under my shirt near my medicine bundle.

We parked at the barn so we didn't get waylaid chatting because we were already late. As I knocked on their screen door, I heard laughing inside, and realized we weren't the only ones invited for dinner. Opening the door, Kate was flushed, chuckling.

"Come on in! You're the last to get here, but you had the furthest to come, I think!" she said, and waved us inside. Frank, Cook, Sally and Gerry were sitting in the living room, with a small bowl of peanuts was in front of them on the table. Gerry, from Bob's Circle of Support, had apparently become a fixture around the place, building in a business model for *Just Living*.

"They were teasing us about our appetizers," Kate said, and I chuckled. Neither of them were known for their cooking, and Ben and I had joked about getting takeout on the way home if the food wasn't edible.

"I love peanuts!" I said, and Nora appeared from the kitchen.

"Don't worry. Cook brought dinner, it gets better," she said, inviting us to gather around the dining room table. "I'm just going to serve.

Lasagna, garlic bread and a great salad," she said. "I bought the wine myself," she added. "I'm quite proud of that."

God, I love Nora. And miss her. I promise not to spend so many weeks away from here ever again.

"Nora was just telling us that they're making wedding plans!" Frank said, and off we went. Turns out Kate and Nora had gotten engaged, which had started a whole cascade of plans. Or maybe the plans had started a cascade of marriage. Not sure. Anyhow, they were excited to tell us of everything that had transpired.

"The Possibilities," Nora called them.

"First," Kate started, "and maybe most exciting, Nora and I put in an offer on a condo last week, and it's been accepted!" Kate was really happy to tell us all the plans about all the rooms of their new place. They'd be moving in next month. "It's just been built, so they're waiting for people to live in it. It's exciting."

Really, I thought? Ya think? They were bursting.

"But who's going to live here, take care of the place?" I asked. Gerry looked up.

"Well, that's part of the news. We've offered Nora a new position at *Just Living*, developing business ventures that will make it self-sustaining," he shared. "She's going to stay in charge of the place overall as the Executive Director, but the focus of her work is going to change."

Now I was really confused.

"We're going to move into the trailer," Sally said, putting her hand on Cook's arm. He was beaming, and they were radiating love between them. "I DID teach the old dog new tricks!" Sally finished.

"That's super!" I said. "But who's going to look after the Lodge?" It was like a game of Jenga, and the pieces kept getting taken out and put on top. What was going to keep the place going? I wondered.

"Claire and another volunteer are going to do shifts," Nora said. "And, well, that leads to what we wanted to talk to you two about," Nora said.

We were eating, passing plates of delicious food. I was itching to know what was going on.

"Okay, enough. What are you talking about?" I asked. Gerry laughed.

"Well, we are going to need an Operations Manager here, kind of like the equivalent of a Keeper in the prisons. Someone to be responsible for the day-to-day running of the place. And we thought you might be interested in the position." I was gobsmacked. Like, really. "Do you have any idea how little real life experience I actually have?" I thought.

"I don't believe it. I'm not qualified," I said. At least four people laughed.

"Um...yes you are. And I'd still be around," Nora clarified. "And everyone else would be too, to help out. Really."

Ideas were churning around in my head, and we tossed a few of them around for a bit before we were all done, and clearing the table. "Operations Manager" really didn't feel right. Residence Coordinator fit my psyche better, so I suggested a change in title.

"How would it work? You don't really do nine-to-five," I said. Gerry spoke up.

"I know, and it's time we create some flexibility into the work to accommodate the needs of the house, but with some realistic boundaries, too. I don't think it's healthy to have everyone working full out all the time. I know you all think that's because mistakes happen – and they do – but mostly it's because it's really bad business. All of the vibrant, successful startups, for example, have flexible schedules and insist on *more* time off for staff, not less. People bring the best of their work to work when that happens. So Nora *is* going to start working 35 to 40 hours a week – whenever she wants to – and the new Residence Coordinator can choose a schedule that works for her. We were thinking between 24 and 32 hours a week, and that doesn't need to be 'set in stone' week to week, because that's the nature of the business.

"We're going to devolve much of the responsibility to the team," he continued. "You would be more like a conductor than a Jill-of-all-trades. What do you think? We believe you have the skills for the job, and you understand the importance of doing it well, *and* asking for help when you need it."

"Is this a job interview?" I asked, smiling. I couldn't think of one reason to say no – I'd be able to do my pastoral studies, too.

"More like a job offer," Gerry said. "We want you to keep a room here, and not feel obliged to stay in it. Maybe one or two nights a week to begin, just so the guys see you around. Ben can stay, too – we'll move a double bed into the room. In fact, nights when things are rough at the prison, he can stay here even if you *aren't* here." I was gobsmacked, and Ben was grinning.

"Did you know about this?" I asked, not accusing him *too* harshly.

"No! Nora asked what you were doing now, and I told her preaching a little, baking too much, and looking for something meaningful. That's all! Honest!"

"As Nora's projects expand, there will be opportunities to change up what you do. You could host victims' retreats at the other centre we are going to build, for example. Or open a bake stand in the market. Help Kenny build a pond to raise salad greens...whatever you decide to get involved in." Gerry was clearly used to selling people job opportunities.

"Of course, there is grunt work," Nora interjected, making sure it wasn't all rainbows and unicorns. "Reports need to be filed, budgets managed, and, well, you know shit happens between residents, and their families, and passes, and well...all the usual stuff. One reason I wanted them to hire you is that the learning curve won't be as steep. I'm actually being selfish," she said.

Cook stood up and started carrying dishes into the kitchen, putting his hands in the warm water. A couple of minutes later, he summoned me.

"Mugwump! I need you!" And I had to go.

"Excuse me," I said, pushing in my chair and oh, so grateful to head to the kitchen. We washed a few dishes, dried a few more, and just got into the rhythm of being side by side.

"You know, Darlin', you don't have to say tonight," he said. I nodded.

"But you know it's what's meant to be, right?" He was looking at me, wiping his hands on the tea towel he'd tucked in his belt.

"Yeah," I said. "You have to PROMISE not to leave, though, okay? I COULD NOT do this without you," I said, hugging his big, inked body.

"I know. I know you totally could. And you don' have to. Takes a village, and luckily you're part of this one. It could be just what the guys need...new stuff goin' on, keepin' their minds busy. You barkin' out orders, keepin' 'em on their toes...." Now I was laughing. Ben joined us, a smile on his face.

He put his fingers to his lips, the age old sign for Shhh...and reached into my collar. He pulled on my chain, bringing Nana's ring to his lips. Cook's eyes were bulging.

"Oh blessed Jehosephat!" he shouted, and I started to laugh.

"So much for secrets!" I said. Ben was apologizing.

"I didn't say anything!" he said. "But I just couldn't help myself!"

And the next thing I knew, Kenny and the other guys were at the door for pie, and everyone was crowding around congratulating us. It was EXACTLY how I wanted them to find out, AND I knew when I swore them to secrecy, I could trust them. Nora's place was overcrowded, but filled with love. And change. And even sadness. But overwhelmingly, people were well fed, well loved, and feeling joyful.

Nora handed me her magical, always-has-reception cell phone and told me to go call Stephen and Mom and Dad. And I did. And they were happy, too. We planned for a family dinner on Sunday, and I smiled. One of many more, I hoped, thinking how blessed I felt.

Life was good. And rich. And hard.

And I laughed. And I cried, too.

And we headed for home.

Blessed home.

Blessed us.

CHAPTER 53

SUPERHEROES

Dear God,

Here I am. Just Living. Just Living, Just Living.

I've had lots of experiences this year, this lifetime, but I know more than ever, I'm still figuring it out.

And I know that competency is an illusion, so I'm glad You're in my life.

I never thought I'd say that. Look at me, growing up.

Love, Beth

I tugged at my clerical collar, and wondered when I would get the time to go online and investigate those fair-trade clergy shirts that were supposed to be so fabulous. And cut for women. Expensive. British. And, best of all, comfortable. Anyhow, at least I was wearing my own clergy shirt this time I thought, remembering a year ago when I had "borrowed" Dad's. Today I actually felt blessed to wear this collar on this rare occasion because it was a command performance.

And I was just a little sad remembering that my co-conspirator, the witness to my badass-ness in my Dad's shirt, was gone. No more laughing together at *that* story over a pint. Sigh.

"Will you wear Daddy's shirt?" Bruce had asked, and it took me a minute to figure out what he'd meant. I thought of Glenn's funky activist T-shirts but of course, he meant the black shirt with the white collar.

"People were so nice to us. He said it was his special shirt, and when you wear it I remember him better." Wow. Last year, I had wondered how anyone could wear such pompous garments; this year I felt like a superhero in it. Maybe because it fit better than Dad's. Except around the neck. Grin.

I was heading into Vancouver to pick up Bruce, and Adam and Tiger. We were going to spend the day together in Mission, hanging out in the park while the men helped Donna move into a new space nearby. They had collected money for the family, and made furniture for the boys, had cruised second-hand shops and done everything they thought would help Donna create "home" for Adam and Bruce. Today was "The Big Reveal," so to speak.

Theirs was an unholy alliance, a dance card inscribed that day in Mount Currie, and everyone was still tentatively figuring out the choreography. Lots of people don't understand the men's desire to contribute ("creepy," they said), and others were certainly critical of Donna's willingness to accept their help. ("It doesn't mean I forgive anyone," she said, "and certainly the boys aren't able to make that decision yet." Except I saw that they did.)

Of course, the boys didn't understand the depth of it all yet, but I suspected they'd LOVE their carefully constructed new bunk beds, with the slide from the top bunk. It had taken shape in the barn, and I'd been impressed with the research into safety that had accompanied the crafting. Of course, the boys would swoon over their side-by-side desks. Because every five-year-old needs a desk, right? Eye roll.

"They'll grow into 'em. School's important," Tom had gruffly insisted. *No one mentioned the irony, thank God.* Prayer.

Tom had also carved some beautiful wooden animals, stored in a toy box Paul had painted with black and red killer whales and eagles. It was a piece of art, but the men wanted it loved and used. A toy box the men had never owned had been dreamed into being, belying the illusion of privilege for these little white boys — tangible evidence of shared pain.

Donna accepted the help, even though she squirmed. It had started at first with her spending more and more time with the boys, and now she wanted her own place. Their own space, as a family. She was (mostly) sober, and the men understood that, too. And Claire had helped her, and that friendship had stuck. Gradually, a plan had taken shape, and Donna had decided to move out to the valley where she could afford to be a full-time mother. And today was moving day.

I'd dropped by *Just Living* that morning to grab the picnic lunch Cook had packed for our adventure, and was happy to give him a huge hug as he loaded it into my car. It felt like he'd been making my life better forever, and the hug lasted a second or two longer when I thought about how much he'd come to mean to me.

"Take care of yourself, Darlin'," he'd said. "We ain't done with you yet." I smiled, and knew I belonged in this sacred place.

"I'll see you Tuesday," I called back over my shoulder. "I'll bring you back the dishes, and if you're lucky I'll even wash 'em first." He smiled, heading in the kitchen door, waving his meaty, tattooed arm at me.

An hour later, I was on the highway with Bruce and Adam in the back; Tiger had joined me in the front seat. He just didn't fit comfortably between the car seats anymore.

"Mom says tonight we're sleeping in our new beds," Bruce chattered.

"Well, it looks like today Adam is sleeping in my car," I bounced back, glancing at Bruce in the rear-view mirror. How did parents do this?

"She says if we're good, we can keep Tiger. I'll be good, right?" he said, sounding tentative.

"Good is overrated, Bruce. Don't you worry about Tiger. He will always be in your life, even if he needs to live with Ben and me sometimes. He is enthusiastic!"

I was grateful that Donna had agreed to sharing "custody" of the big galumph. I remembered his mom was a yellow lab; I think his father must have been Sasquatch. He's huge. And delightful. I bet he tops 100 pounds when he's full grown. Anyhow, Ben and I take him when he is too much for Donna, and I love having him to run with me. He gets me outdoors with his monumental exercise needs, and the fresh air is so good for us. Hard to be mad with a breeze on your face! And he was a gentle reminder of just how much I loved and missed Glenn's friendship.

An hour later, we were in the big park, and I was ready for fun! Ben would be joining us for lunch, after he'd finished at the prison, and he'd let us know when it was safe to bring the boys "home" to their new townhouse. It had all the makings of being a great day, something I relished. I'd had enough crappy days to fill a calendar.

We ran Tiger off-leash in the fenced dog park, playing fetch about a million times until Adam was whiny and Tiger was panting. Then we headed through the park and played Frisbee for a bit, making up our own rules so that fun was the order of the play. A few minutes later, I talked them into heading to the playground. We'd move towards opening that picnic basket, and gathering around the outdoor table to break bread together.

But of course, in the way of little boys, we got sidetracked under the bridge. The brook was pretty "high" thanks to last night's rain, and I smiled. A few minutes later, I'd pulled out a couple of primitive boats Kenny'd made out of scrap lumber, and the boys were racing them in the water. Tiger, of course, was chasing the boys, making sure they didn't fall in, and I smiled. He'd gone from "hopeless drowning puppy" to "protector of the pack" in the past few months. I wouldn't say he'd mastered it, but it was cute to watch. I think he might have "accidentally" pushed Bruce into the water at one point. Luckily, Bruce had great balance, and the water didn't even reach the tops of his boots.

That led to more chasing boats, this time from inside the stream, and before I knew it I was laughing my head off at the increasingly wet threesome. I collapsed onto the grass, and felt something crack in my chest, happiness spilling out. Sunlight dappled through the pine trees surrounding us, and the boys' laughter blended into the harmony that was Creation, and I felt a lump in my throat threaten to become a tear. Or perhaps a torrent.

I threw Tiger's ball into the stream as a diversion, and a new game began. He wanted to get the ball, but didn't want to put his face in the water, so he chased it downstream, barking along the way. The boys were now laughing so hard they were rolling on the grassy banks beside the little stream, and I joined in the hullabaloo even as my heart broke again, differently, when I started missing their Dad. He'd never see them grow up, play, hug their very big, very wet dog. But that didn't diminish the boys' glee. I pulled my sweater around my shoulders, and called Tiger back.

Let's just say the dog didn't want to stop tracking his ball, and I couldn't leave the boys so we raced downstream, chasing Tiger chasing his ball. A few moments later, Adam fell into the brook, and Tiger picked a crying Adam over a lousy ball. He transformed into guardian, and was licking Adam's tears as I hefted him onto my hip and we headed for the clean, dry clothes at the bottom of the hill.

"Don't worry about the ball, Bruce. I have more. Maybe another lucky dog will find it!" I was trying to figure out how to get Bruce to scale down his worrying, and I took his smile as a good sign. I'd take the small victories, for now.

A few minutes later, I was really glad I'd filled the trunk with the boys' things, packed around the picnic basket. I dug out some dry clothes, and Adam's blanket, and soon he was "resting" in the car seat, sucking his thumb. Tiger had wedged himself between the seats, his wet head on Adam's lap. I tucked a towel between them, and closed the door.

"Let's set up the picnic, Bruce," I heard Ben's voice as I turned. I smiled. "If we can find it in this mess," he said, putting things back in the boxes I'd hastily unpacked in the trunk. A minute later, Bruce was showing him the basket, and I was happily grabbing a thermos of coffee from Ben so that he could carry our lunch to the picnic table. He took my hand at the table and kissed Nana's ring. My heart swelled.

Peanut butter and jam sandwiches on homemade bread. Cheese cubes cut into little train cars. Veggies all cut into little fist-friendly sizes. Ritz crackers, because, well, what little boy doesn't love those? A thermos of chicken soup – the kind with alligators -- and plastic cups and spoons to serve it. Homemade cookies – three sorts so that we all had our favourites. There were even apples, pre-sliced and cored with an elastic around them so they didn't go brown. I wondered who'd done the online research to figure out this amazing kid-friendly lunch. Kenny, maybe. That would be like him, helping Cook without picking up a knife.

Ben took Bruce to the Porta Potty, and then we all washed our hands, and dug in. Adam woke a few minutes later, when Tiger decided the lure of food was too great to stay on sentinel duty, and nearly tossed Adam out of the car seat as he liberated himself. Maybe I should have strapped Adam in. How do parents do this again?

Sitting under the now-bare birch trees, wrapped in sweaters and blankets and noshing on Cook's love, I smiled, just a little uncomfortable with my happiness. Ben reached under the blanket and squeezed my hand, and my smile grew, and I said another prayer of thanks.

I'd learned so much this past year, including how a broken heart can mend in all the right ways, and still leak all over the place. And hold so much love it overflows with grace and joy and the Blessings of Creation. And ache something fierce in the darkness of the night. I felt ever so lucky. And ever so alive. And wondered if I'd ever feel whole again.

If someone shows you a Teaching, and you sense its Truth, and then they do something so against the Teaching that it steals your breath and stops your heart, does that diminish the Truth of the Teaching? Does it make the foundation of my belief any less solid? Does all my trust in Glenn's friendship, and wisdom about the Divine, diminish when his Light is ripped from me?

Does all that Al taught me about Justice and Spirituality cease to matter or to be True, because of what he did?

Why can't we always be faithful to what we believe?

And just how big *is* the hurt and the pain?

What must we change, as a people, to make healing and compassion our compelling force? And can it propel us towards "On earth, as it is in heaven?"

And does it ever get any easier, or any more (or less) real?

Thank you God, for this life, this food, these people.

Even when it hurts so much I can't imagine surviving, somehow the intensity of the love holds a balance that makes living possible. Another mystery, still more to explore.

Oh look! A rainbow!

Kidding.

A prayer.

CHAPTER 54

SEGREGATION
KENT INSTITUTION, BC

The prisoner kept his head down and hood up as he paced the concrete yard. He squinted as the sodium yard lights reflected back from the wet pavement; their constant humming drilled into his brain. He knew there was no point in looking up; there was a grill between him and the sky, and the walls that surrounded him were high, dripping with razor wire and electric alarms. The towers with shotgun-wielding guards were always in sight, and the constant banging of gates, bars, and doors helped him avoid the quiet that haunted.

Besides, raise his head and he'd just get soaked. He knew he wouldn't see any of the breathtaking stars that were just beyond this hellhole. And he knew that somehow he would live out the rest of his days doing just this. He had 30 minutes in the yard a day, lock-up the rest of the time. And he was okay with that; it made tracking time just a little easier. Getting sane was another matter.

Dark thoughts coursed through his soul constantly, and he quickly grasped at any chance to escape them. He had nightmares, daytime horrors, and terror-filled flashbacks that played over and over again in his head, and they made him sick and angry and terrified all at the same time. And in his flashbacks, he played the starring role, complete with splattering blood and never-ending screaming.

He filled his days, every possible moment, with a tight regimen. Drawing. Weights made from garbage bags and water. Push-ups. Chin-ups when he could grab the door frame. Rarely bitching with the other men through the bars to aggravate the uniforms. Sleep, when it came. Growling at everyone around him. More push-ups. Counting steps, then rounds, in the yard. Counting minutes until the next meal, the next med line, the next stand-to count.

He knew he acted out constantly, as if everyone else was to blame for his being in this place. He couldn't afford to stop long enough to think about what had happened up north, how he'd ended up cranked again, and hurting. He shook his head to erase the thoughts as he turned the corner to walk the perimeter again. And again. 84. 85. 86. He liked to do 146 circuits or more during his time, which meant focusing on walking fast and not dark thoughts.

He knew his fate. 91. He would never get to a paradise like *Just Living* again, and he knew why. He had gone so far beyond stumbling he didn't even want to think about where he could have redeemed himself, where he could have made a different choice, where the fates could have been shifted. He shook his head, thinking of Nora, Hugh, and Beth, and that man who had stayed one night in "his" tipi a long time ago. 101. 105. He stopped thinking and threw a few shadow boxes as he made another circuit.

The prisoner glanced around. No Steller's Jay today. Where the fuck was she? Maybe he was imagining that she'd started to visit him here. He was sure he'd seen her on the razor wire yesterday. Or was it last week?

Or in a nightmare?

His mind careened back to that June night that led him into the woods, and then here. If he was truthful (and that didn't matter at this point, did it?) he didn't remember what led him towards the path to the house that night. In his messed up head, the path led to the priest, and the priest was evil. That's it.

He remembered that when he first arrived back in his home town after the halfway house he was almost immediately flooded with flashbacks. He figured out from his CSC "programs" that his PTSD had surged, and controlled his waking and sleeping moments, but he also knew that if he told anyone they'd ship him back here, so he tried to "manage" it. Chasing dragons, brothers, and hard women.

And then, before he realized it, the dragons and demons were chasing him back.

Focus. 126. 127. He was running now, determined to outrun them all. Fuck. Them. All. 132. And then the uniform was there, to take him back to his cell. He knew it wasn't right, time wasn't up. Fuck. FUCK! And then he lost it.

"What the fuck! It isn't time! Leave me the fuck alone! I'm not done. Don't fuck with me. LEAVE ME THE FUCK ALONE. Time isn't up!" And then he was spitting on the uniform, who was trying to calm him down. He didn't even hate this guy, but WHAT THE FUCK!

The prisoner wished there was a good-sized rock he could grab and throw. At anyone. Damn them! Damn the memories! His eyes jumped around the yard looking for anything he could grab. Was that his Jaybird up there?

Every time he thought of the people at *Just Living* this happened, and he ended up buried deeper in the dark hole in his mind, which wasn't a lot different from reality but FUCK!

The noise in his head was so loud that he couldn't even hear the uniform's voice talking to him. Then he heard radio static, and voices, and before he knew it he was on the ground in cuffs, and the fucking guards were putting leg irons on him and locking his hands to a belly chain. Fuck.

They tossed him, shuffling, into his house, and he started tossing stuff as best he could with his arms chained. Mostly he wanted to hurt stuff. Make noise. If he was lucky, injure himself. Because hurting your body meant you didn't notice quite so much that your heart and your mind and your spirit were screaming in pain.

He was glad he'd learned that trick early on.

And that he remembered it now.

About an hour later, he'd calmed down, and heard guards outside his cell.

"Fred, can you go in and get his chains off? There's an Elder to see him. I don't think he'll bug out on you," one guy said, and Fred, being the calm guard with a good reputation asked permission to come in.

"There's a visiting Elder here to see you, do you want your chains on or will you cooperate?" Fred asked him. He stayed silent, and Fred entered the cell and started to uncuff him.

"Sorry, man, for before," Al whispered. Fred grunted, an unspoken acknowledgement that he'd heard.

"Who's here?" Al asked.

"A guy says he knows you. Been in before. I think his name is Hugh. He's just coming down onto the range," Fred answered.

Al looked up, panicked. He shuffled farther into the corner on his bunk.

"You okay? You want me to send him away?" Fred asked. No sense in inviting the crazies twice in one shift, he thought.

"No, it's okay. I'm just surprised," Al answered.

"Well, I'm at the console if you want to call me," Fred answered. He knew about Al. Everyone was freaked out about what he'd done, but Fred kinda got him. Except when he was acting crazy, which he wasn't right now. As he left the cell, Fred closed the door and nodded at Hugh as he approached. Fred brought him a chair to sit on in the hallway.

"Al. Sorry it took so long to get back up here," Hugh said as he held his hand through the bars for Al to shake. Hugh knew he'd visited Al early on, but wasn't sure how much Al would remember. Al was still rubbing his wrists, trying to erase the feel of the metal shackles. His head was bowed, and he didn't look up.

"No problem, man," he answered. He felt his face burning with shame.

"How you been?" Hugh asked as he pulled Al in and touched his shoulder. Al's heart was pounding, and he felt bile rise in his throat.

"Been better," Al mumbled.

"Everyone sends good wishes," Hugh said, and Al snorted. He knew how much grief and pain he'd caused. He imagined there were a few people who literally wanted him dead, and a few more who just wanted him to disappear, but he hoped there wasn't anyone at *Just Living* felt that way. Angry, though, no doubt.

"No, really. We've had a couple of circles, and talked about things. Anyhow, I talked to the Elders here and they said you haven't been to ceremony. Do you want to smudge?" Hugh asked.

Al looked up, startled. Hugh wasn't treating him bad. He knew if the moccasins were reversed, he'd want to…well, he couldn't even imagine it.

"Sure," he said, again shrugging. Hugh pulled out some medicine from his bundle, and separated some to light, and some to leave with Al.

After smudging through the bars, Hugh asked if Al still had his bundle, and Al was vague, but looked around and located it in a box under the bed. Hugh gave him the sage he'd brought, wrapping it in a cloth. They sat for a while, and Hugh tried to make conversation without luck. Soon, he started to make moves to leave.

"Look, I'll come one more time and then after that it's up to you. You'll have to ask me to come visit, understand?" Hugh wasn't going to press himself on Al, but he didn't want him to think he was forgotten, either.

"Everyone knew I was coming this morning, and Nora and Cook especially wanted me to let you know they are praying for you. Frank asked me to send his regards too, and to tell you he'll try to get up here again. Everyone wishes they'd been better at staying in touch. We kinda feel like we failed you. And Glenn, too. Not that that's an excuse." Hugh's eyes were piercing and unrelenting.

"Fuck." Al took a deep breath. "It's not on anyone but me, okay, let them know? I think I'm just really fucked up. Broken. And tell them I'm really really really sorry." Al started to tremble just a little, and Hugh thought he heard a quiet sob. He pulled Al into his arms again , awkward with the bars between them.

"One last thing, I just thought of it. Beth is up in Pemberton now, working on cleaning up some of the mess. If she wants to come see you, or ask questions, would that be okay?"

Al jumped, startled.

"What?" he asked, his eyes darting around the cell.

"Just think about it." They stood in silence for a bit.

"And do us all a favour, okay?"

"What's that?" Al asked.

"Start caring for yourself again, okay? It's really important. Everyone will rest a little easier, and your life will be better. Remember the story about the wolves," Hugh said, grinning. Al had always hated that story, the one about an Elder who talked with a young man who said he had two wolves fighting inside him – a good wolf and a bad wolf.

"Which wolf will win, Grandfather?" the young man had asked in the story.

As he left the cell, Hugh looked back and for a moment thought he saw Al smile.

"The one I feed," Al whispered.

"Later," Hugh said, and thought about how life was just like that.

AFTERWARD
CHRISTMAS-TIME

Beth writes...

As a part of my ongoing Resiliency Training, my mentor suggested I take my journals and make them into a written accounting of my past year. I agreed it'd be a good idea.

Here it is. I have edited, re-edited, asked for feedback and advice and then looked again at this, and I feel done. I've sent every piece of it to each of the people mentioned and they've (almost) all read it and given input, ideas, and critiques, and eventually their blessing (some grudgingly). Cook, of course, couldn't read it, though. When I offered to read it with him he said, "Don't bother. Sally says it's good, and I trust you, Mugwump. You'll get it right." A heavy trust, for sure. And Hugh offered to take it to Al, but Al didn't want to see it.

I dedicate this book to Glenn, and the men and women at Just Living, who loved me and have taught me so much. And Al, too.

Somehow, I'm convincing myself that I'm a capable Residence Coordinator. Nora is taking a draft plan for the planned Renewal and

Resiliency Centre to the Board of Directors tonight, so I'm staying on for the meeting. Blessedly. I think we're going to call it Tide's End.

There's a bit of chaos at home; Ben and I want a quiet Quakerly wedding, and Mom, seemingly, wants everything frilly pink hearts and white lace. And she's happy, and it's lovely to have tension we can laugh about. Ben just smiles indulgently; he's talking to his Mom again, and his family may even come for the celebration. Anyhow, nothing needs to be decided before the spring…right?

Topaz purrs when I walk in the door at night. When Ben and I have Tiger I take him for walks beside the river, and am reminded of Glenn and our time together. Ben and I take Adam and Bruce on adventures about every two weeks, and I see Glenn in Bruce's seriousness, and in Adam's sparkling eyes. They are settling into their new home, and Claire and Donna are fast friends.

Nora and Kate have moved, and Kate is working less on site so she can unpack, and "unwind from there" (her words, a prayer). She confessed to me they are hoping for a baby soon…I pray for their family. She and Nora will be perfect parents. And she is growing her coaching practice.

Cook and Sally have moved into Nora and Kate's trailer and made it "home." Doilies everywhere, even fancy toilet roll covers on the back of the toilet tank. Cook is delirious. Sally does all the cooking.

"Din't know it was even possible, bein' this happy, Mugwump," he said last week. He's exploring a partnership with a restaurant in town; he wants to start a culinary arts program for ex-cons. Perhaps some catering as a first step.

"I heard Gordon Ramsay did it, I'll do it too," he said. He's healthier than I've ever seen him.

Frank is still helping with our wellbeing, but playing more, too. His face sparkles when he talks about sailing, and connecting with old friends. It's good to see him so happy.

I think I even saw Tom smile last week. Bob's new title of Accountant fits him well. His circle continues to meet with him, sometimes in the house, and I've been welcomed onto the panel of "Resource People" that the volunteers can turn to.

Just Living is still undergoing scrutiny for what peripheral role they may have had in "all of it." As Nora says, "I guess we better just get used to scrutiny; that's the nature of the beast." I'm learning how to manage that, too.

I can't wait to get started next spring on the plans for diverting some water to build a watercress garden. I've even learned how to jump through hoops with Fisheries to get a permit. Kenny is so excited, bouncing into my office asking me to join him to "turn the compost" when ideas spill out of him. He wants to work with the Agriculture folks at the local university to bring students around to help with some of the development, and to share some of his knowledge. And I think he's actually dating someone, but he's pretty shy about it.

Dan moved on again; this time I'm actually keeping in touch with him. We've started a new program where we send guys out with cell phones with GPSs and a schedule to reach out to them. And they can always reach back. It's working, feels good, and I think Glenn would be happy.

Paul left *Just Living* a little while after Al killed Glenn. He checked himself back into a Healing Lodge on the island, and Hugh supported that. He's back now, and really stepping up as Barn Manager. *Hallelujah*. A prayer. Maybe the best one.

Julia and the other students are still supporting the People of the Lilwat Nation, and I think that court case will be going on long after Daya is a grandmother; I hope we all learn from this. And I'm glad so many have taken up this cause.

There are more volunteers at *Just Living*. Veronica has taken on coordinating them, and Claire and Peggy are a huge help, creating stability. Hallelujah to that, too.

Al is living at Kent Institution. I can't imagine what it is like there, but I met a guard named Fred at a CSC training, and we have conversations sometimes that let me know a little. I'm glad I don't work as a guard, and pray for those who do. Hugh visits Al sometimes, and has told me that if I ever want to talk to him, he can arrange it. I don't want to do that yet, but I've told Hugh maybe someday. I don't know; I'm still wrestling with some questions.

I'm still trying to live my life fully alive, loving wastefully and being faithful to the call. Some days I'm better at it than others.

I remain grateful, overwhelmingly so, for this life I am living. Even when tears find their way onto my cheeks. Maybe especially then.

Changing the world, one person at a time. Is there any other way?

Thank you Goddess,

Beth

ACKNOWLEDGEMENTS

Where to begin? When you've worked on a novel for as long as I have on this one, I have to begin by hoping I remember. I am lucky to be so well supported.

To my family, who patiently made their own meals when I was busy writing, who kindly raised themselves, and are amazing humans. Nat, Jonah, Grace and Brigid -- you are my world. And, of course, our world got even better when Maggie and Jessica joined us. Thank you. For all of it.

To my early readers and coaches, especially Christina Baldwin of PeerSpirit (www.PeerSpirit.com) who helped me first, and kept helping me beyond Draft 8. Thank you for igniting my passion for words. You stuck by me when the telling of this amazing story was truly horrid.

To my recent writing coach and mentor, Wilma Derksen, and her husband Cliff, who offered sanctuary, wisdom, and shared their knowledge, hearts and hospitality so richly. Your publishing house, Amity Publishers, has been a gift, from Sue Simpson's expert copyediting to Odia Reimer's design. Your guidance and support have helped to make this book real. Thank you. Thank you for all you do, for me, and for many.

To amazing editors, Jennifer Glossop, and Kate Unrau. You took an unruly manuscript and helped me realize how much more I had to learn. Your wisdom and teaching made my writing so much more.

Thanks to Rabbi Joseph Meszler for *Prayer at the Funeral of Someone who Committed Suicide* published in *Huffpost Religion*, to Dr. Martin Brokenleg of Reclaiming Youth International, and their work with the Circle of Courage, and finally the Alternatives to Violence Project Canada. Thank you for permission to use your important works in this piece of fiction.

To my later readers, especially Pam Pederson, Gianne Broughton, and Callie Wilson, who kept on giving feedback, and questioning when characters magically appeared from nowhere. That's what happens with rewrites.

Finally, and most importantly, to the men and women in the creative writing groups inside Mission and Mountain Institutions, who have met bi-weekly for years and encouraged me, been brutally honest, and oh, so patient. This book would not be without you.

To answer the question you often asked: When will you be done?
Now. Now is when I will finally finish this.
We knew we were teaching each other to write by listening carefully to one another, and offering feedback. I hope I listened well enough; your gifts were simply immeasurable. All the best bits are because of you. The truly horrid bits are all mine. And while you must remain unnamed, you know that I know who you are. I am so grateful. And I'll be in next week. Or the one after that.

RESOURCES FOR READERS OF JUST LIVING

A variety of resources are available for book clubs, faith communities and other groups. These include questions for discussion, and a resource list for those who would like to explore some of the issues raised in Just Living. Find them via www.justlivingnovel.ca

ABOUT THE AUTHOR...

Meredith Egan is an author and executive coach who has worked with crime victims and prisoners for more than twenty-five years. She has been trained in mediation and peacemaking circles, and has been honoured to learn from many Aboriginal people. Meredith has taught and spoken in schools, universities, prisons and communities throughout Canada and internationally, and served on the Executive of The Church Council for Justice and Corrections.

Meredith is the principal at Wild Goat Executive Coaching (wildgoatcoaching.ca) and lives at the Groundswell Ecovillage in Yarrow, BC. with her dog Mollie, and rambunctious feline sisters Firefly and Filigree. For fun she dabbles in cooking soup for her neighbours, and sampling expensive scotch.

Meredith's four adult children visit often - maybe not only because of the hot tub, board games and amazing view.

Meredith enjoys engaging with book clubs, community groups, students and faith communities.

Contact her at via her website at www.wildgoatcoaching.ca.

To sign up for announcements about Just Living, and other work by Meredith Egan, sign up at www.justlivingnovel.ca.

Countryside RVs.com